AIMEE NICOLE WALKER

ZERO DIVERGENCE

ZERO HOUR
AIMEE NICOLE WALKER

ZERO HOUR

AIMEE NICOLE WALKER

Zero Divergence, noun: no deviation from a course or standard.

After a key piece of evidence goes missing, a suspected serial rapist and killer evades prosecution. More than Royce Locke's reputation is on the line when his investigation into the failed chain of custody suggests Franco Humphries might've had inside help. There's no one Royce trusts more than Sawyer Key to help him right a wrong and uncover the traitor in their midst, but can they do it before the Savannah Strangler strikes again?

Relentless plus fearless equals flawless. Sawyer and Royce have come full circle—from hostile strangers to best friends and lovers. Neither a sniper's bullet nor an arsonist's fire could keep them apart, but what about a psychopath hell bent on revenge? The stakes are high, and there's no turning back now because the zero hour is upon them. Tick tock.

Zero Divergence is the conclusion to the best-selling Zero Hour series, which follows Locke and Key's investigations and evolving relationship. This is a series you MUST read in order. It contains mature language and sexual content intended for adults 18 and older.

Trigger warning: Part of the storyline involves coming to terms with a friend's suicide, which may be difficult for some people to read.

Zero Divergence (Zero Hour Book 3)
Copyright © 2020 Aimee Nicole Walker

ISBN: 978-1-948273-17-6

aimeenicolewalker@blogspot.com

This is a work of fiction. Names, characters, places, and incidents either are the product of the author's imagination or are used fictitiously, and any resemblance to the actual person, living or dead, business establishments, events, or locales is entirely coincidental.

Photographer © Wander Aguiar—www.wanderaguiar.com
Cover art © Jay Aheer of Simply Defined Art—www.simplydefinedart.com

Editing provided by Miranda Vescio of V8 Editing and Proofreading—www.facebook.com/V8Editing

Proofreading provided by Judy Zweifel of Judy's Proofreading—www.judysproofreading.com
Also Jill Wexler and Michael Beckett

Interior Design and Formatting provided by Stacey Blake of Champagne Book Design—www.champagnebookdesign.com

This book contains sexually explicit material and is only intended for adult readers.

Copyright and Trademark Acknowledgments
The author acknowledges the copyrights and trademarked status and trademark owners of the trademarks and copyrights mentioned in this work of fiction.

ZERO DIVERGENCE

CHAPTER 1

"**O**N THE TENTH DAY OF TORTURE, MY TRUE LOVE GAVE TO ME..."
Sawyer debated how to end the borrowed and altered line from the classic Christmas song. He had intended to keep it tame and thank Royce for the ride home from the hospital, but meek didn't fit their dynamic. A welcome-home blow job sounded delicious and matched their personalities better. Glancing over at Royce, Sawyer expected to see a playful smile tugging at the corner of his boyfriend's mouth as he prepared to fill in the blanks, but Royce's gorgeous lips were pressed into a flat line, and his eyes remained fixed on the traffic in front of them. Sawyer had been too excited about leaving the hospital to fully absorb Royce's demeanor when he entered his hospital room that morning. Sawyer raked his eyes over the man who had snatched his heart from the very beginning. Royce's tense posture and white-knuckle grip on the steering wheel clued Sawyer in that Royce was worried about something, but what?

Deciding to test if Royce was paying attention to him, Sawyer said, "Double penetration."

Royce stopped at the red light and turned those stormy gray eyes on him. "One dick suddenly isn't enough for you?"

"It was a test," Sawyer said with a casual shrug, which sent pain shooting down his arm. He bit the inside of his cheeks to keep from crying out, something he'd been doing a lot of since waking up at the hospital after his rescue. Nothing in Sawyer's life had prepared him for the kind of pain that came with having his dead skin removed daily from his third-degree burns and deep-tissue wounds. "To see if you're paying attention," he added.

"Did you mean noticing how your stubborn refusal to ride in a wheelchair caused exhaustion your healing body doesn't need?" Sawyer started to speak, but Royce shook his head. "Or did you mean the pain in your voice just now?" Royce inhaled deeply, a move Sawyer taught him, and released a shaky breath. He shifted his foot from the brake to the gas pedal and accelerated when the light changed. "I notice everything about you, GB. Stop trying to hide your pain from me. Stop trying to put on a brave face. You're in pain, you're worried about your pretty face under those bandages, and maybe you're also a little worried about your dick too." He threw the last bit out to lighten the mood.

Sawyer snorted. "I'm not at all worried about my dick." He'd achieved maximum wood plenty of times during his stay, all thanks to his sadistic boyfriend who liked to play audiobooks to rev him up only to leave him hard and aching because Sawyer's bandaged hands didn't allow him to take his own dick in hand...until now. He glanced down and admired the rebandaged appendages and digits, which allowed for a lot more freedom. "It's my balls I'm worried about, dickhead. You couldn't have jerked me off even once?"

"Couldn't risk your spunk seeping through the bandages on your chest and causing your wounds to get infected."

"You could've swallowed it." Sawyer would've cringed at his whiny voice if not for the smile on Royce's face. "You can make it up to me when we get home." Sawyer's dick started lengthening as he imagined Royce dropping to his knees right there in the garage. His boyfriend made a strangled sound, snapping Sawyer out of his fantasy. "What did you do?" Sawyer asked when he saw Royce's grimace.

"*I* didn't do anything," Royce replied hesitantly. "For the record, I said it probably wasn't a good idea."

"You said this to whom and about what?" Sawyer didn't need to wait for an answer. There was only one person who was notorious for planning parties for all occasions at the spur of the moment. She also happened to have Royce wrapped around her perfectly manicured pinky finger too. *Fuck.* "My mother planned a welcome-home party, didn't she?" Royce's wince was answer enough. "At our house?" *Our house.* It had slipped out easily and automatically like it was a foregone conclusion, even though they hadn't talked about the next step in their relationship. It sounded right and felt amazing, so Sawyer refused to walk it back.

"Yes, but she promised they wouldn't stay long."

Sawyer groaned. "*They?* Who all is coming?"

"Your family and a few of our closest friends who've been worried about you." Royce reached over to hold his hand, then suddenly stopped when he recalled Sawyer's injuries. Sawyer hated Royce's hesitation to touch him more than he hated how vain he'd become, worrying about scarring when he should just be grateful he was still alive to feel Royce's touch on his bare skin—scarred or not—someday.

Sawyer held up his hand, wiggling his newly bandaged digits with the added protection of fingerless gloves. "I have more freedom now. I can do a hell of a lot with these fingertips."

Sawyer thought it was a miracle the burns on his hands weren't more severe, because he'd raised his arms to protect his head when the church altar burst into a wall of flames. His worst injuries were caused by synthetic materials in his clothes melting against his skin and continuing to burn even after the flames were extinguished when he dropped and rolled on the ground. Luckily, his worst wounds didn't require skin grafting, and clothes would hide his scars. He was the only one who'd have to see the marred flesh. *And Royce.* Sawyer was more nervous about that than he cared to admit.

"There's a hell of a lot I want you to do with your fingertips too," Royce said. "It'll just have to wait until everyone clears out. I can't be selfish."

"Yes, you can," Sawyer countered eagerly.

Royce laughed for the first time since walking into Sawyer's hospital room that morning. "About that double penetration stuff…"

"I was seriously just testing to see if you were paying attention. Your dick is more than enough for me."

"Good thing." Royce's matter-of-fact voice made Sawyer grin. "The sky is blue. The grass is green. My dick is enough for you. It's just the way things are." In case Sawyer needed a clearer picture, Royce expanded by laying down some rules. A finger went up. "No other dude's dick will ever be invited to our party." Two fingers. "You need a new dildosaurus."

"Why? Did you break mine while I was laid up?"

"Um, no," Royce replied dryly. "I can't allow you to use the same dildo as our former mayor, or I'll never stop seeing the montage of videos and pics she sent to her boy toy."

"Ugh," Sawyer said. "We'll throw it out as soon as we get home." He knew it would take a long time before Lynette Goodwin's scandalous affair with Ryan Tedrick died down. Not only was the young man someone she had known since he was five years old, Ryan also happened to be her sister-in-law's stepson. It would take even longer for him and Royce to move forward after solving the case of the crazed priest who'd plotted and carried out his plans to expose the sinful people in power and purify the city by fire. The flames had nearly cost Sawyer and Royce their lives.

"Maybe we should wait until everyone leaves before disposing of the retired sex toys," Royce said, gently linking their fingers together.

"Yeah, you're right."

Royce nodded. "I usually am."

Sawyer snorted but didn't argue. He was just content to feel Royce's fingers between his, even if he wished the bandages and gloves didn't prevent him from feeling the heat from Royce's flesh. His happiness dissipated when he saw the volume of familiar cars in his driveway and parked along the street. "A few of our closest friends, huh?"

Royce smiled wryly. "You're loved by all."

Sawyer touched the bandages on his head with his free hand, a habit he'd formed since finding out about the burns. Insecurity was a familiar foe, and he wasn't happy with its reappearance in his life.

Royce clicked the small remote attached to his visor, then drove his Camaro into the empty spot in the garage once the door opened. The motion was effortless, as if he'd been doing it for years instead of only a few weeks. Sawyer recalled the note he'd left on the kitchen counter with the spare garage door opener and a bear claw. They'd been working surveillance on different shifts at the time and had only managed to steal an hour of kissing, talking, and sex each morning.

Dickhead,

You didn't freak out when I gave you a house key, so I hope you'll accept this garage door opener as easily. I have the extra space, and it's stupid for you not to use it. Don't overthink things. No pressure. No ulterior motives.

xoxo

Your Favorite Asshole

He'd thought "your favorite" was a special touch, and Royce had returned to the bedroom to thank him in dirty, dirty ways, even sharing his beloved bear claw with him. At that moment, Sawyer had known Royce was in love with him, even if the actual declaration hadn't come until a few days later when he gave Sawyer a key to his house also.

Royce killed the engine and clicked the button to close the garage door. "Ready for this?"

"Ready for them to go home," Sawyer said, offering the sexiest smile he could muster. Judging by Royce's failed attempt to squelch a chuckle, Sawyer hadn't pulled off the look. At least the blisters and chapped lips had healed enough for him to do that much without his eyes tearing up. "It was a villainous grin, wasn't it?"

"A very sexy one," Royce countered. "I get the impression you want to do very wicked things."

"To you, yes." Sawyer was dying to return to some sense of normalcy, a world that included Royce's dick inside him. He wasn't injured there after all.

"You'll get your chance, GB. I can imagine how frustrated you are, but the setbacks are only temporary." Royce gestured his finger back and forth between them. "We're forever." *Whoa.*

"You're so good at this," Sawyer whispered, leaning toward Royce. Pitiful lips be damned; Sawyer wanted a kiss. His mother opened the door leading to the kitchen before he could meet his objective. "We're busted."

Royce lifted their joined hands and kissed Sawyer's fingertips before releasing him. Then he removed his seat belt and opened his car door. "Need help getting out?"

"Yeah," Sawyer admitted. Walking out of the hospital had taken a lot out of him, and lying mostly flat on his back for ten days straight had taken its toll on his strength and stamina. He'd only managed to release his seat belt by the time Royce walked around the car to open his door.

Royce picked up the picture frame from Sawyer's lap and smiled at the photo Felix had taken of them. The burn unit had strict rules regarding visitors, food, flowers, and personal items since the patients were at high risk for infection. The nurses made an exception for the photograph and even looked the other way when Royce lingered well past visiting hours. Sawyer knew they would've wheeled a cot in for the charmer to sleep on if they could've gotten away with it.

"He sure takes a good photo for a fleabag reporter," Royce quipped.

Sawyer accepted the hand Royce extended to him and eased out of the car. The image of Royce caressing Sawyer's face had helped him retain his sanity when the worst pain or loneliness hit him. Sawyer had kept his eyes fixed on it when the nurses came in each day to remove the dead skin and rebandage his wounds. Sometimes the tears streaming from his eyes had made it difficult to see the adoring look on Royce's face in the picture, but it helped him stay calm and kept him from crying out and upsetting Royce, who'd waited in the hallway per the nurses' instructions.

Royce leaned forward and pressed a soft kiss against Sawyer's mouth. "I fucking love you. Welcome home, asshole," he whispered.

"Aww," his mother said from the doorway, crossing her hands over her heart. She practically vibrated with happiness. His mother had loved Vic, but there was no doubt her bond with Royce was stronger. Maybe she sensed how much Royce needed her maternal TLC after missing his mother for so many years, or perhaps their personalities just clicked better. Regardless, it made Sawyer's heart happy to see the genuine affection between them.

"A party, Mom? Really?"

"I told Royce it was a bad idea," she replied. "He wouldn't listen to me. You know how much he loves a party."

Sawyer chuckled as he slowly made his way toward the door. His mom's eyes were filled with tears by the time he climbed the few steps into his house. "I'm glad you're here." He looped one arm loosely around his mother's waist and hugged her. "I'm just not sure I'll be great company. My energy seems to have abandoned me."

"We won't stay long. I just fixed you a little something to eat since you've existed on hospital food for the last ten days."

"To be honest, I haven't felt well enough to care." Sawyer caught a whiff of his mother's fried chicken and cornbread and felt his spirits lift. His stomach growled, calling him a liar. "Yeah, I could stand to eat."

When they entered the kitchen, Sawyer's sister Grace and his sister-in-law Brianna were setting out the food buffet-style on the kitchen island and counters. Evangeline O'Neal's idea of fixing a little something to eat was actually enough chow to feed a battalion.

"Look who I found," his mom said, getting their attention.

The relieved look on Grace's face was touching. Both she and Sawyer's brother Killian had been mad as hornets when they returned from a family vacation with their spouses and children to find out he was in the hospital. Their parents had decided upsetting them wouldn't be wise, and it turned out to be a smart decision. Children weren't permitted to visit patients in the burn unit since they were little germ magnets, and according to the nurses, they preferred the parents of the bacteria breeders to avoid visiting too. His siblings had to settle for passing messages to Sawyer through their parents or Royce.

Grace started crying as she rushed toward Sawyer. "Easy now," he cautioned before she could plow into him. "Everything still hurts."

"I'll be gentle," she said, easing her arms around his waist and hugging him loosely. "We got sitters for the kids because we didn't want to take chances. Your nieces and nephews can't wait to see you."

"I miss them too."

"Me next," Brianna said, slipping into his arms. "You scared us to death."

"I'm sorry," Sawyer replied, patting her back.

Brianna stood back and looked up at him. "Don't do it again." She turned and pointed at Royce. "You either."

"Yes, ma'am," Royce said. Sawyer regretted not witnessing the waiting room introductions between Royce and the rest of his family.

"Everyone else is in the living room or on the back patio," Mom said. "Go make yourself comfortable, and I'll make a plate of your favorite foods for you."

"Extra macaroni and cheese," Sawyer said over his shoulder.

"There he is," Dad said, rising to his feet. "How's my favorite son?"

"Dad, I'm sitting right here," Killian said dryly.

Baron Key squinted at his son. "What's your name again?"

"Ha ha ha," Killian retorted, ducking when their dad moved to scrub his knuckles over his brother's head.

His mom's heart was in the right place, but Sawyer felt awkward as hell. More than a few of their friends had shown up. All the

8

detectives in their unit plus their spouses had stopped by to welcome Sawyer home and offer their support while he continued to recuperate, including Commissioner Rigby and Sherry. It meant the world to Sawyer that he worked with people who cared so much, but he was exhausted and incapable of making small talk by the time their guests started to leave.

Sawyer noticed Rigby lingering at the door having a private word with Royce before following her wife outside. Sawyer's family, Holly, and Jace were the last to leave. Holly leaned down, kissing Sawyer gently on top of his head.

"You call me if you need anything, okay? That includes straightening this one out." She pointed at Royce in case Sawyer needed clarification about who "this one" was.

"Sure thing, Holls," Sawyer said, smiling up at her.

His father practically had to drag Sawyer's mother and sister out of the house. "We're just a call away, Son. Get some rest," he called over his shoulder.

"Thanks, Dad."

Then the front door shut, and silence descended on the house. Royce sat beside him on the couch, resting his head back against the cushion.

"How long before our boy comes out of hiding?" he asked.

"It could be five minutes, or it could be five hours, depending on his—"

Meow.

"Where's my boy?" Sawyer cooed, which Bones hated more than strangers in his house. Sawyer couldn't help it, though. He'd never been away from his cat for so long and had missed him like crazy.

Bones leaped onto the back of the couch and stalked across it to reach Sawyer, pausing to sniff his bandaged head. As if he sensed how badly Sawyer still hurt, the enormous feline didn't climb onto his human servant's chest like he usually would. As much as Sawyer would love to have the weight of Bones in his arms, feeling his purrs vibrating against his chest, he couldn't risk a claw in his healing wounds. Bones rubbed his head against the uninjured side of Sawyer's face, letting his human know he forgave his absence.

Beside Sawyer, Royce kept dodging Bones's swishing, bushy tail. "Why is he sticking his ass in my face and pummeling my head with his tail?"

"He's blaming you for the extra people in his space. The tail action is code for gird your loins, dickhead."

"Great," Royce said dramatically.

"What did Rigby want?" Sawyer asked, lacing his fingers through Royce's.

"Franco Humphries is walking out of jail a free man on Monday morning at eleven o'clock."

"Fuck," Sawyer moaned. Royce had repeated the conversation he'd had with Rigby about Humphries's pending release, Marcus and the confession tape Royce hadn't yet listened to, and even the status of their partnership on the force going forward. "What did you tell her about us?"

Royce's brow went up. "I didn't confess the many ways I plan to defile you after you take a nap."

"I don't need a nap." God, it sounded like heaven though. "You also know that isn't what I meant. I told you it's okay if you want a different partner. Maybe it's healthier for our relationship if we—"

Royce silenced him by pressing his lips gently against Sawyer's. "You're the only partner for me." He pointed toward the door. "Out there," Royce said, turning his finger around and pointing toward his heart, "and in here. That's why I made you something special."

"You did?"

Royce nodded and grinned shyly. "I can't decorate for crap, but I made it with love." He pressed a quick kiss against Sawyer's lips, then stood up. "Stay here. I'll be right back."

He returned a minute later with a cake carrier in one hand and two plates holding a cake knife and two forks in the other. Royce took off the lid and revealed a tall chocolate cake with chopped pecans sprinkled on top. Sawyer's mouth immediately began watering. "Is that your mom's cake recipe?"

"The one and only. Are you prepared to be wowed?"

"I just really want to shove my face in the cake," Sawyer replied.

Royce laughed heartily. "Would you settle for a slice? I'd hate for you to wear chocolate in your gauze until your home health care nurse comes tomorrow to teach me the proper way to rebandage you in case of an emergency."

"Shut up and feed me cake."

Royce took his command literally, slicing a huge piece, then forking a large bite and holding it to Sawyer's lips.

"Oh my god," he said as the chocolate cake melted in his mouth. "I need this for every occasion."

"I'll bake it once a week if you promise to listen to orders from now on," Royce said, taking a bite for himself.

Sawyer met Royce's stormy eyes. "I'll agree to that if you promise not to give stupid orders." He opened his mouth like a baby bird, and Royce gave him another bite. It was somehow more delicious than the first.

"No more burning buildings," Royce groused.

"It wasn't burning when I ran into it," Sawyer countered. "*You* ran into the burning building." He couldn't be mad at Royce, because chances were, he'd be dead if Royce hadn't risked his own life to pull Sawyer out of the inferno.

"So insubordinate."

They stared at one another in a silent battle of wills for a few seconds before a big yawn ruined Sawyer's fierce expression. "We'll resume this after I take a power nap." Smiling, Royce leaned forward to set the plate on the coffee table, but Sawyer stopped him. "But not until after I eat more cake."

Royce aimed a cocky grin at him. "Got you hooked now."

"You have no idea."

Royce touched Sawyer's face just like he had in the photo, and the adoration in his gray eyes sent warmth spreading throughout Sawyer's body. "Keep it that way."

They polished off the piece of cake, then Royce helped Sawyer get ready for a nap. He was too exhausted to be self-conscious about the bandages covering the worst injuries or the pink wounds that had almost healed.

"I'm going to kiss every single one of them as soon as it's safe," Royce murmured huskily against his neck.

"Lie down with me?"

"Nothing could keep me away."

Once Sawyer was comfortable, Royce gently nestled in behind him, his body heat pouring into Sawyer. "I have missed this so much."

"Me too," Royce said gently. "Welcome home, baby."

CHAPTER 2

"THERE'S MY BOO," DETECTIVE JACKSON BLUE SAID WHEN ROYCE stepped inside the bullpen on Monday morning.

"Sergeant Boo," Royce corrected.

Blue's booming laughter cheered Royce up a little. He'd felt guilty for leaving Sawyer at home, even though Evangeline was spending the day with him, and his home care nurse would be by to change the dressings on his wounds. Misery had been etched on Sawyer's handsome face, or at least the parts Royce saw.

"Are you in a lot of pain? I can get your pain pills," Royce had said.

"It's not too terrible," Sawyer had replied, lying through his perfect teeth. "I'm just jealous you get to go back to work while I lie on my back and stare at the ceiling. You know how badly this sucks."

"I do," Royce replied, nodding. "You'll be back to work in no time as long as you do what Connie tells you."

Sawyer shivered dramatically. "She's scary."

Chuckling, Royce leaned over and kissed Sawyer goodbye. "Just do what she says."

"Yes, dear."

He fucking hated coming to work without Sawyer.

"Your partner will be back in no time," Blue said, correctly reading Royce's mood.

"Thanks, Blue."

"Good morning," Commissioner Rigby said, stepping into the bullpen with a tall, distinguished-looking Hispanic man at her side. Royce recognized Deputy Chief Emilio Mendoza right away and had a feeling he knew what was coming next. "Many of you've had the privilege of working with Deputy Chief Mendoza over the years, and I'm proud to announce I've chosen him as our next chief of police. I am making his promotion official today at noon during a press conference but wanted to show him around so he can get settled quickly afterward. I have every confidence Chief Mendoza will be an amazing fit for the entire Savannah Police Department, but especially the Major Crimes Unit."

"Thank you, Commissioner Rigby," Mendoza said in a baritone voice. "I'm honored by the confidence you've bestowed on me, and I look forward to working with the men and women who make up the MCU. I believe we're going to do excellent work together."

Rigby snorted. "They're going to give you gray hair."

"More gray hair, you mean?" he asked, gesturing to his temples where his coal-black hair had just begun to turn gray. Royce could tell he was a man who would age well, earning titles like distinguished gentleman and silver fox along the way.

Rigby laughed. "Yes. More gray and faster."

"Good to know."

Each of the detectives took turns introducing themselves. Mendoza's handshake was firm, and he gave each one of them his undivided attention, never moving his shrewd gaze away during their brief conversations. He was sizing them up and didn't bother trying to hide it. Royce liked direct people, and he'd always had positive dealings with the man. Mendoza wasn't Rigby, but he would do in a pinch.

"MCU will also be gaining two new detectives. With so much going on, I neglected to give you all advance notice so you could attend their pinning ceremonies this morning and welcome them to the unit. I am counting—" Rigby's words ended abruptly, and she turned to Chief Mendoza. "Sorry. Old habits and all that." Mendoza chuckled and gestured for her to continue. "*We* hope you'll do your best to counter *my* oversight and make them feel welcome." Rigby made eye contact with everyone as she spoke but lingered on Royce during the last bit.

"You can both count on us," Royce said, speaking for the team. They'd never been into hazing or playing practical jokes on the rookies entering their unit. "May I ask where our newest recruits are?"

"And who?" Ashcroft added.

Royce thought he knew the identity of one but didn't speak up.

"The newest members of your team are Christopher Carnegie and Diego Fuentes. They are currently meeting with HR." She directed her attention to Royce. "Once they finish, I want you to give them a tour of the facility."

"Yes, ma'am."

Rigby raised a brow, remembering the conversation they'd had on the morning not long ago when she told Royce he was getting a new partner. He'd disobeyed her request, doing his damnedest to pretend Sawyer didn't exist. Royce had to bite back a laugh because they both knew how that had turned out. The corner of her mouth twitched, letting him know she was thinking the same thing.

"The last time we had a promotion ceremony, Mrs. Rigby brought us pastries," Detective Kyomo Chen said, starting to sound like Royce.

"Did someone say my name?" Sherry Rigby asked, entering the bullpen with a large pink box in her arms. Two tall men strode in behind her. Fuentes aimed a cocky grin at Royce before glancing around the room.

"Team," Chief Mendoza and Commissioner Rigby said at once, then turned to look at one another in amusement.

"I warned you it would be hard for me to let go," Rigby teased.

Mendoza chuckled, "Yes, you did."

"I'll try harder," Rigby said wryly. "Starting now."

Good humor sparkled in Mendoza's dark eyes. "Team, I'd like to introduce you to the newest members of your unit—Christopher Carnegie and Diego Fuentes." Mendoza rattled off a brief bio for the two men before gesturing for them to say a few words.

"My friends call me Topher," Carnegie said. "It's been my goal to join the MCU since graduating from the academy, so it's an honor to work with all of you."

Fuentes stepped forward when Carnegie finished. "Like Topher, making detective was my primary career objective, and working in this unit is the cherry on top of the hot fudge sundae. I am humbled and eager to learn."

"Sergeant Locke, would you like to say something?" Mendoza asked.

Telling Fuentes to keep his hands and eyes off Sawyer came to mind, but it wasn't what the new chief meant. "Welcome to the team, guys. I think SPD has several excellent teams, but I doubt you'll find a greater bunch than the men and women of the MCU. We're more like family than colleagues here. All of us want you to feel welcome, and we want you to succeed because it means we all do. I'm here to assist you in any way I can, and I feel comfortable saying that goes for the other detectives also."

"Thanks, Locke," Mendoza said. "Why don't we allow Carnegie and Fuentes to chat with the commissioner and the other detectives while the two of us meet in my office."

Royce glanced at the pink box Sherry had placed on one of the empty desks and repressed a sigh. He hoped there were bear claws in there, but no matter what she'd baked, it would be delicious and devoured long before Royce returned and had a chance to grab one.

Catching Royce's longing gaze, Sherry Rigby spoke up. "You better grab your pastries first, or else there won't be any left by the time you finish. I have it on good authority that our new chief is fond of cannoli."

Mendoza made an appreciative hum in the back of his throat,

and Royce figured they were going to get along smashingly well. "Yes, I'm the Hispanic man with a passion for Italian pastries. You shouldn't have gone to so much trouble," he said, stepping over to the box. Sherry lifted the lid to reveal dozens of cannoli stacked neatly in the box. "Oh, wow," Mendoza said in awe, taking two pastries. "Better grab yours, Locke."

He'd never had cannoli before, but he'd also never met a pastry he didn't like. Wanting to make a good impression, Royce only placed one pastry on his napkin, then followed Mendoza to the sparse office. He'd heard Rigby had relocated to her new space at city hall while he was on leave, but the starkness bothered him. He'd become so used to seeing her awards and certificates hanging on the walls and family photos and various decorations sitting on the bookcases, credenza, and desk. The room was bare and naked, stripped of personality and warmth.

Mendoza sat down in the leather chair behind the large desk. Royce hadn't expected it to bother him as much as it did, but he knew he'd adjust to the changes eventually. He set his napkin-wrapped pastries on the gleaming mahogany surface, so Royce did the same. "I'm aware I have large shoes to fill."

"Yes, sir."

"You have quite the reputation, Sergeant Locke."

"It's mostly exaggerated, Chief," Royce replied.

Mendoza chuckled. "I wasn't insulting you, Sergeant. Your reputation is for getting things done. You have the best closing rate in the department."

"Nah, that would be my partner, Detective Key. He's batting a thousand."

"Detective Key hasn't been with us long enough for his closing rate to register, but I know of his reputation, and I expect great things from both of you."

"We won't disappoint you, sir."

"See that you don't."

They spent the next fifteen minutes going over Mendoza's goals for their unit, and the department as a whole. He wanted to improve relations between the police department and the citizens; he was dedicated to making sure the correct arrests were made and not just easy ones, and he expected the MCU detectives to lead the way. "Communication and leadership are critical components to achieving my goals, so I want to be very clear and set expectations on day one. This is no longer Commissioner Rigby's unit. All issues that exceed your authority should come directly to me. Going over my head is insubordination and is something I will never overlook or accept. I will never question or embarrass you in front of the officers under your command, and I expect the same in return. I will have an open-door policy, but I will not micromanage the team."

"I approve wholeheartedly of your approach, Chief."

"Glad to know we're in agreement." Mendoza briefly stroked a well-manicured finger over his lips. "Now, about your reputation for breaking the rules…"

"Mostly bullshit stories, sir."

"Let's keep it that way."

Royce nodded firmly. "Yes, sir."

"I'll leave you to show the new detectives around and get started on their training."

"Training, sir?"

"Yes. I'm leaving it up to you to show the rookies what I expect in my department."

"I consider it an honor, Chief." He really thought it was a royal pain in his ass. Royce rose from his seat and picked up his cannoli. "Congratulations again on your promotion, sir. Welcome to the team."

"Thank you."

Royce pivoted and left the room so the man could enjoy his pastries in peace. He found Fuentes and Carnegie getting to know the detectives in their unit. He ate half his cannoli in one giant bite and fought back a moan as rapture spread throughout his body.

Blue didn't miss his reaction. "Better than a bear claw?" Royce held up his thumb and forefinger an inch apart, signaling it was close. "How'd it go in there?" Blue quietly asked once Royce swallowed his bite.

"Good. Mendoza is a straight shooter and doesn't believe in bullshit. Rigby made a great call."

Blue released a sigh. No one liked interdepartmental changes because it was a fifty-fifty crapshoot between things working out great or going tits up. "Glad to hear it," the big man said, clapping Royce on the back.

The phones started to come alive as soon as the citizens of Savannah woke up, so Royce gave Fuentes and Carnegie the grand tour he should've given Sawyer on his first day instead of glaring at him.

When they reached the break room, Royce crossed his arms over his chest and struck his most imposing stance. "This is the most important thing I'm going to say, so listen up," he told them, gesturing to the mug caddy. "None of these cups belong to you. Bring in your own freaking cup and wash it each time rather than take someone else's. Don't bring in bullshit plastic or paper cups either. That's just lazy, and it's bad for the environment. See this coffee pot?" He waited for the rookie detectives to nod. "No one, and I mean no one, takes the last of the coffee without making a fresh pot." Royce approached the sink and opened the cabinets on either side of it. "We keep a variety of dishes on hand for us to use. Most of it's been donated over the years when someone gets a nicer set at home." He pulled open a drawer showing a plethora of mismatched silverware. "If you use dishes or eating utensils, then you wash up after yourself. Our janitorial staff is not your personal cleaning service. Am I clear?"

"Yes, sir," both men replied solemnly.

"Get caught breaking the rules, and you'll get stuck washing everyone's dishes for a month as punishment." He just made that rule up, but they didn't need to know it.

19

"Yes, sir," they repeated.

After the tour, Royce allowed the guys time to set up their desks, computers, and department-issued cell phones. Those were things Sawyer had to do on the fly in between interviewing suspects since he landed his first case before he'd even picked a desk. While the rookies were busy, Royce texted Sawyer.

Hi.

The three little bubbles came up immediately. *Hi?*

Royce snorted. *Sometimes one word can say so much.*

And what exactly is your "Hi" really saying?

He could feel Sawyer's skepticism as strongly as if they were in the same room. Royce typed out a response. *It says I love you and miss you.*

Oh.

Chuckling, Royce asked, *Oh?*

Sometimes one word can say so much, Sawyer replied.

Feels like I've heard that somewhere. What's your "Oh" really saying?

Sawyer's reply was immediate. *I love you and miss you too. It also says you owe me a blow job or handy or something. The chocolate cake was scrumptious, but it can't compare to how good it feels when my dick is in your mouth.*

Royce's body immediately reacted to Sawyer's words. Fuck, he missed having Sawyer's dick in his mouth. He missed everything about the intimacy they shared. His hesitancy to be intimate had nothing to do with a lack of desire; he was terrified of hurting Sawyer. He'd seen the pain etched all over his boyfriend's features when he returned to Sawyer's hospital room after the nurses removed his dead skin and changed his bandages each day. He'd wanted to stay and hold Sawyer's hand, but the nurses refused to permit it. Instead, he stood out in the hallway, knowing Sawyer was in excruciating pain but finding ways not to call out and alert him to it. Selfless. Sawyer always put others first.

Royce could see where his reluctance to be physical with Sawyer might be mistaken as disinterest or disgust, which couldn't be further from the truth. He started to send a response, but the three bubbles popped up, and he waited to see what else Sawyer had to say.

I'm trusting you'll still want me when you see what's beneath my clothes and bandages. Trust me to know my mind and my physical limitations. I. Want. To. Come. On you, in you, or even just near you.

Royce smiled at the message, then replied. *I will take care of you tonight. Just you try and stop me. I fucking love you, asshole.*

Love you more, dickhead.

Royce glanced at the time on his phone, already starting to count down the hours. It was ten thirty already. The morning had gone by surprisingly fast, and he was grateful he hadn't been called out to the scene of a homicide yet. *Ten thirty!* Grabbing his keys off the desk, he started to head out of the bullpen before he remembered he was in charge of two rookies. When he turned around, Fuentes and Carnegie were watching him expectantly.

"Well, come on. What are you waiting for?" Royce asked.

Both men pushed back from their desks in a hurry, then rose to their feet.

"Where are we going?" Carnegie asked.

"We're heading over to the county jail. Franco Humphries is about to walk in thirty minutes. I need the fucker to know I will never give up on nailing him for what he did to those women."

"I call shotgun," Fuentes shouted.

"Damn it," Carnegie muttered, sounding so dejected it made Royce chuckle.

"You kids can take turns riding shotgun," he said in his best dad voice as he led them out of the bullpen.

"Holy fuck," Carnegie said from the back seat. "There's a lot of people here."

He wasn't wrong. Royce had expected a sizable showing, but there were at least two hundred people lined up outside the perimeter of the jail. Some of them looked angry or anxious, but they were greatly outnumbered by the smiling, happy women singing songs and carrying signs touting Humphries's innocence.

"What the hell does her sign say?" Fuentes asked, pointing to a college coed holding a large poster over her head.

Nausea rose up Royce's throat when he glanced over and read it. "Some girls like it rough," he said, his voice barely above a whisper as he remembered the strangled bodies of the four women in their late teens and early twenties. Their lives snuffed out before they'd had a chance to live. "How fucking sick is that?"

"Does this sick son of a bitch have a fan club?" Fuentes asked incredulously.

"Most serial killers do," Royce replied.

He had to honk the horn to part the throng of people so he could drive up to the gates. Four deputies in riot gear moved in to herd the crowd back so Royce could drive into the prison once they opened wide enough.

"It's a damn good thing the gathering is peaceful," Carnegie said. "Those deputies are outnumbered."

Royce thought the tensions might exponentially increase once Humphries cleared the gates. County had jurisdiction here, but Royce would step in and offer aid if they wanted it.

He stopped his car near the entrance to the jail, noting the navy blue BMW, silver Mercedes, and an old green Jeep Wagoner with wooden side panels also parked there. Royce recognized the small woman sitting in the driver's seat of the Beemer as Humphries's wife Tiffany. The statuesque woman piloting the Mercedes was Humphries's lead council, Vivian Gross. Royce found her last name to be extremely fitting in this case. While he believed everyone deserved representation and a fair trial, he could never understand how a woman could defend a man who'd committed such heinous acts against other women. Maybe she believed he was innocent, or perhaps she just wanted the money and notoriety that comes with a high-profile case. The Woody Wagon belonged to Felix Franklin, *Savannah Good Morning's* crime reporter, and a royal pain in Royce's ass.

"All the key players are in place," Royce said, unable to ignore the feeling that they were all pieces—*pawns*—on a chessboard being moved around by an invisible hand. "Feel free to wait in the car to avoid getting in trouble and staying off the serial killer's radar."

"Fuck, no," Fuentes said.

"That goes for me too," Carnegie added.

A few minutes before eleven, they all got out of their vehicles. Vivian Gross slowly lowered her sunglasses so Royce could see her scathing expression, Tiffany ignored everyone and kept her eyes trained on the front entrance, and Felix wiggled his fingers in a playful wave, which Royce ignored. Vivian started to cross the expanse between them but halted when the doors suddenly opened, revealing Humphries, who wore a crisp, dove gray linen suit and a pale pink shirt. A fedora matching his suit sat atop his head, shielding his bald head from the bright sun.

Royce observed his reactions, which were every bit as theatrical as he expected. He held his arms open toward the sky as if he were hugging it. Then he lowered them and said, "Vivian, Vivian, Vivian." Unlike Jan Brady's whiny tone, Humphries's voice sounded like a smooth and silky caress. Humphries opened his arms and his attorney stepped into them for a hug that lasted much longer than was appropriate. Humphries closed his eyes and inhaled deeply, making Royce's skin crawl.

Felix stepped forward, capturing the encounter for the paper with his camera. Royce wondered how the headline would read while he turned his head to study Tiffany Humphries's reaction to her husband and his attorney. She'd taken great care with her appearance for their reunion, wearing a floral sundress and white wedge sandals. Not a hair was out of place, and her makeup looked flawless. Rather than look at her husband, Tiffany Humphries stared down at her clasped hands. Sensing his scrutiny, she slowly lifted her head and briefly met Royce's gaze before turning her attention to her husband.

On the occasions Royce had interviewed her, Tiffany Humphries had exhibited several signs that she was a victim of domestic violence. She'd been skittish and had spoken softly and only when asked a direct question. She'd avoided eye contact, had only expressed concern about upsetting her husband, and always had an excuse at the ready to explain Franco's behavior. Her body language now wasn't happy or welcoming, and Royce worried about her safety.

When Royce returned his attention to Humphries, he had pulled away from his attorney and was walking toward him. Royce crossed his arms over his chest and hoped his expression and body language projected his determination to pursue Humphries to hell and back if that's what it took. Speaking his intentions out loud would only lead to trouble.

"Detective," Humphries said in his cultured, smooth voice. "Oh, it's Sergeant now, isn't it?" Royce said nothing. "Congratulations." Humphries's lips tipped up into a wry smile. "I was sorry to read about your partner Marcus. He seemed so confident and full of life. Who would've guessed he'd kill himself? Why did he do it? Guilt over framing an innocent man of multiple murders, perhaps?" Royce bit the inside of his cheek to keep from responding. He wouldn't allow Humphries to goad him into punching the killer's smug mouth. "What's the matter? Cat got your tongue?"

Royce just stood there staring into his cold, blue eyes.

"Well, this is just boring," Humphries said. "It's been a long dry spell, so I think I'll go home and fuck my wife now." The contrast between Humphries's polished appearance and his crude language was startling and intentional. He loved keeping people guessing about him.

Royce had the overwhelming urge to shout at Tiffany Humphries to get in her car and drive as fast and as far as she could and never look back. He remained silent, knowing from personal experience that domestic violence victims wouldn't leave until they were ready.

"You can go fuck yourself, Sergeant Locke," Humphries said, turning and walking toward his wife. He jogged the final steps to reach Tiffany, swooped her up, and spun his wife around. Once he set her down, Humphries pulled the woman into a hard kiss and lewdly cupped her ass with both hands before pinning her body between him and the car.

"Gross. I hope they're not going to do it right now," Fuentes said, sounding like he was barely suppressing a shudder.

"What a disrespectful prick. Makes me want to apologize to my girlfriend for every time I acted like a jerk," Carnegie said.

Royce chuckled. "You can text her on the way back to the station."

Humphries suddenly pulled back from his wife, smiling broadly. "Oops. I got carried away. I sure don't want to get arrested for public indecency on my first day of freedom in months." Gripping Tiffany's bicep, he guided her around to the passenger side of the car, opening the door and patiently waiting for his wife to get settled before closing it. "Vivian, dear, I'll be in touch soon." Humphries struck a pose for Felix before walking around and climbing behind the wheel of the BMW.

Humphries put the car in reverse, hitting the gas and cutting the wheel sharp to the left, kicking up gravel as he rocketed backward. Then he shifted into drive and sped down the long driveway toward the gate, flipping Royce off as he passed.

"That went well," Royce said dryly, making Carnegie and Fuentes laugh. "Let's head back and watch Commissioner Rigby's press conference."

Unfortunately, they got called out to a vehicular homicide where one seventeen-year-old male ran over another for talking to his girlfriend. The two rookies learned the toughest part of being a detective—notifying families that their loved one had died.

"That fucking sucked," Carnegie said afterward.

"It doesn't get easier," Royce replied. "And it never should. I have several hard and fast rules I will never break. First, you treat all victims the same. Sometimes they have a list of convictions as long as their arm, but you have to shove the knowledge aside. Right then, the only thing that matters is a family has lost a person they loved. I treat the victims' families how I would want to be treated if I were in their shoes. Dignity tops the list. I'd expect the detective to recognize my loss as deeply personal. I wouldn't want false promises or platitudes. I would want them to speak plainly and not use confusing language. You never tell the next of kin their loved one has passed. Passed where? They didn't pass. I didn't tell the grieving mother her son died today. Died how? I told her that her seventeen-year-old son was killed and left no ambiguity. I would want to know as much as they could tell me. My approach may sound simple in theory, but it's much harder when you're facing a grieving family member in the field."

"That's good advice, Sergeant Locke. Thank you," Carnegie said.

Thinking of Sawyer's selflessness, he added, "Never allow this job to steal your humanity, fellas." Royce recalled the second rule to survival on the force. "Never lose your sense of humor either." Then he made one last stop to pick up a gift to their new chief from the unit.

"I'm not so sure it's a good idea," Fuentes said when Royce returned to the Charger and showed them his purchase. Carnegie just laughed.

"Oh, should I have purchased a gift bag too? This reusable shopping bag is probably tacky." Carnegie laughed even harder. "He thinks it's a great idea," Royce said, hooking his thumb over his shoulder toward the back seat where Carnegie was wiping his eyes.

"Fuck no," Carnegie said. "I want no part of this."

Chief Mendoza stepped out of his office the minute the trio entered the bullpen. He glowered and crooked a finger at Royce, silently demanding Royce's presence in his office.

"I'll hold on to that for you," Fuentes offered, reaching for the shopping bag.

"No," Royce said. "I got this."

Carnegie made some strangled sound in the back of his throat. Such rookies.

"Do you recall anything we spoke about this morning, Sergeant Locke?" Mendoza asked once they were in his office. His voice was clipped and brisk.

"You're big on leadership and communication, sir," Royce replied.

"Was dragging the rookie detectives to the county jail to harass Humphries your idea of leadership?"

"Chief, I didn't say one word to Franco Humphries. Not even when he got in my face and gloated about my partner's suicide." That seemed to take a little starch out of the man, so Royce pressed on. "I did not harass him."

"Just your presence could be viewed as harassment," Mendoza countered angrily. "The mayor was just informed that Humphries is filing a civil lawsuit against the police department, the DA's office, and the city of Savannah. Hear what I'm about to tell you, Sergeant Locke, because I will not repeat myself. If we are forced to have a similar discussion about Humphries again, it will be at a suspension hearing. Am I clear?"

"Yes, Chief."

Mendoza took a deep, steadying breath, reminding him of Sawyer in their early days. "I will not allow the sick fucker to kill again, so we need to find other ways to tie him to those homicides. I'm putting you in charge of finding out what the fuck happened to our evidence and who took it. I need your skills in solving those problems, but—and this is the most important detail—do not get caught. Stay away from Humphries. We are going to keep eyes on the man, but they won't be yours."

"Who, then?" Royce asked.

"Leave that to me," Chief replied gruffly. "Find Babineaux solid evidence to take him to trial."

"Again, you mean? I found the evidence to put the bastard away once, but someone stole it before he made it to trial."

"Yes, again. I know Rigby talked to you about finding the traitor amongst us. Can you do that?"

"And train the rookies?"

Mendoza's dark brow shot up. "Too much?"

"I love a challenge, sir. I will get it done." Knowing they would have surveillance on Humphries helped relieve the pressure in his chest, which had started building the moment the sadistic bastard stepped out of jail as a free man.

He knew just the person to help him sort through the files. If there was a needle in the haystack, Sawyer would find it.

"Good to hear." Mendoza looked down at the bag in his hands. "What's that?"

"Oh, um..." Royce thought about Fuentes's warning. Maybe it was a horrible idea at the moment. He debated discussing it with the rest of the unit first, then nixed the idea. Mendoza expected leadership from him, so Royce would give it to him. He held out the bag toward his new chief. "I got you a little gift to welcome you to the team. It's from all of us, sir."

"Oh," Mendoza said, sounding surprised and a little pleased. He took the bag but didn't look inside it right away. "That's very thoughtful of you, Locke."

"I try, sir."

Mendoza reached in the bag and pulled out the box of Just for Men shampoo that gradually replaced gray hair with each use. He stared down at it for a few minutes before meeting Royce's gaze with glittering, dark eyes filled with mirth.

"Get the fuck out of my office, Locke."

"Yes, sir."

He heard Mendoza burst into laughter as soon as he closed the door behind him. He caught the rookies' nervous gazes. "It was a big hit. Now get out of here."

Royce wanted to follow his own advice but had one last thing to do before he could go home to his beautiful man.

CHAPTER 3

SAWYER WASN'T SURE WHAT WOKE HIM, BUT HE WAS GRATEFUL FOR IT when he caught a whiff of the aromas emanating from the kitchen. *Mmm. Bacon, onion, and garlic. Oh my.* He'd taken a pain pill after his mom served lunch and must've crashed hard enough to sleep until dinnertime.

He gingerly got out of bed, relieved himself in the bathroom, and washed his hands without looking in the mirror above the sink. Sawyer knew his vanity was ridiculous, but he couldn't stave off the worry that the damage to his face was more severe than anyone was telling him. It was stupid because neither his mother nor Royce would lie to him about something so serious. Connie had remarked he was healing nicely and even reduced the number of bandages on his head. *Breathe in. Hold. Release.* Forcing himself to lift his head, Sawyer studied his reflection for the first time since waking up in the hospital.

He'd anticipated disfigurement and blistered red skin, but most of his face had healed. The patches of new, healthy skin growing back were pinker than the rest of his pigmentation, but Connie had told him it was normal and temporary. He breathed easier, chiding himself once more for his vanity until he saw the damage to his hair.

"Christ," he said, looking at the singed parts of his scalp where his hair was trying to grow back. The bristles hadn't even achieved buzz-cut height yet, but it was progressing at least. "I look like I have mange." He briefly debated calling his stylist to fix this uneven mess but decided to take care of business himself. Reaching into the bottom drawer, Sawyer pulled out an electric hair trimmer.

Fifteen minutes later, he walked into the kitchen with his shorn hair, expecting to see his mother. Royce was many magnificent things, but he wasn't known for his prowess in the kitchen. Sawyer should've realized he had underestimated him when he'd tasted Royce's double chocolate cake. Once Sawyer got over his surprise at finding Royce manning the stove, he noticed the way his boyfriend swayed to the Elvis song playing quietly from the Bose speaker sitting on the counter. He also observed his ill-mannered feline sitting on the kitchen island where he wasn't permitted. Sawyer might've been pissed if Bones's tail wasn't swishing in time with "Suspicious Minds" and Royce's slow dancing.

And just when Sawyer didn't think his heart could expand any more, Royce started singing along with the song—seriously at first, then with an added Elvis snarl mixed in. Sawyer clapped, and even though his fingerless gloves and bandages muffled the sound, it was loud enough to get Royce's attention.

He spun around, brandishing the spatula as if he might use it as a weapon. "You snuck up on me, GB," Royce said, sounding a little breathless.

"Thank goodness for small favors. Who knows how long I might've lived without knowing you can sing and dance."

Royce turned back to the stove long enough to turn the burner off, then he set the spatula down and crossed the room. His eyes raked in the newly revealed skin and buzzed hair. Sawyer felt self-conscious about it until Royce smiled and ran his hands over the soft bristles. "I think you're giving me too much credit. I'm not sure the noise I was making could ever be classified as singing, or my swaying from left to right as dancing. I've seen junior high kids pull off smoother moves."

"I loved hearing you sing, and I think I need a demonstration of your dance moves."

"You want me to take you for a spin?" Royce asked.

"God, yes," Sawyer replied dramatically. "Did you forget about my texts already?"

"No, baby." *Baby*. It wasn't something either of them used often, but it rolled off Royce's tongue as naturally as when he called Sawyer an asshole. "I have every intention of taking care of you tonight. I thought we'd start with dinner first. I also have a big surprise for you in your office."

"Yeah?" Sawyer looped his arms around Royce's neck and moved closer. "Dance with me first. Just for a minute."

Royce carefully slid his arms around Sawyer's lower back, resting his hands on the upper swells of Sawyer's ass. Pressing his forehead to Sawyer's, Royce began to sing along with the music. Sawyer closed his eyes to keep from crying because it was the first time he'd felt somewhat normal since his injuries. He could feel Royce's body humming with the need to be with him too.

"I love you so much," Royce whispered. "I will always want you."

Sawyer swallowed hard, trying to dislodge the lump of emotion blocking his airway. There was so much he wanted—needed—to say, but he couldn't speak, so he pressed his lips against Royce's instead, hoping his man could feel how much his words meant to him.

Royce slid his hands down to cup Sawyer's ass, pulling him tighter into his embrace, slowly circling them around in the kitchen. The Elvis song ended, and a song with a faster tempo started playing, but they continued slow dancing and kissing until a timer went off.

Royce pulled back and smiled wickedly. "Grits are ready." One last quick peck against his lips, and he released Sawyer to return to the stove.

Sawyer bit back a needy moan and followed him. "Grits?"

"Shrimp and grits. I inherited Aunt Tipsy's recipes with the house. This meal has always been my favorite."

"You've been holding out on me," Sawyer replied.

"Just because I'm willing to exist on bologna sandwiches, instant ramen, and squirty cheese from a can doesn't mean it's all I'm capable of, asshole. I have many tricks in my bag."

"Yeah, well, I'm mostly interested in the ones that make me come tonight."

"Oh, baby," Royce said huskily, "my shrimp and grits are an orgasmic experience."

Sawyer watched as Royce worked confidently in his kitchen. He removed the lid off a smaller pot, then added a few pats of butter and an ungodly amount of shredded cheese. Sawyer thought back to the night when Royce made him try the horrid processed cheese in a can and had a hard time reconciling the vastly different versions as the same man. Royce stirred the pot of grits vigorously until the cheese and butter melted. He dipped his middle finger inside the pot, scooping up a glob and holding it up for Sawyer to sample.

Keeping their gazes locked, Sawyer leaned forward a scant inch and wrapped his mouth around Royce's finger. The grits were delicious, but the way Royce's gray eyes darkened with lust was even better. Sawyer playfully twirled his tongue around the tip of Royce's digit like he planned to do with the crown of his dick as soon as dinner was over. Royce's lips parted, and a staccato breath hissed out. Then he cleared his throat. "Let me sauté the shrimp quickly, and we'll be ready to eat.

Sawyer slowly released Royce's finger, then licked his lips like he couldn't wait for more of everything.

Royce took the slotted metal spatula and scooped out the bacon he'd been frying when Sawyer entered the kitchen, placing it on a plate with a paper towel to drain. He put the skillet back on the burner, turned it back on, and added the shrimp to the rendered bacon fat. Suddenly, Sawyer's growling stomach was more demanding than the erection tenting his basketball shorts.

"Dinner smells heavenly," Sawyer said.

"Orgasmic," Royce corrected.

"Is there anything I can do to help?"

"I stopped at a bakery on the way home and got a loaf of French bread. I was going to spread the garlic butter on top of the slices and pop it under the broiler for a few."

"I can handle that," Sawyer said, moving to the other side of the stove to spread the butter on top of the thick slices Royce had already cut. Partway through, his right forearm spasmed, and he dropped the knife on the floor. Rather than bemoan his nerve issues resulting from his deep-tissue burns, he put the knife in the sink and got a clean one out of the drawer and kept working.

While the bread was toasting in the oven, Royce scooped a generous heaping of cheesy grits in each bowl, then topped them with sautéed shrimp, onions, bacon, and scallions. "Do you want more cheese on yours?"

"There's already enough cheese for six people in the grits," Sawyer replied.

"I barely put enough in for me," he countered.

"I'm fine."

Sawyer chuckled when Royce sprinkled additional cheese over the top of his grits. When the bread was a perfect golden-brown, they carried their food to the table. Sawyer didn't miss the chunk of French bread Royce dropped for Bones en route.

"You spoil him rotten."

Royce shrugged. "He is the best boy."

Sawyer couldn't object to such an honest statement. "Tell me about your day, dear," he said, lowering himself down into a chair. He spooned a large bite and blew on it before sliding the spoon between his mouth. He immediately started moaning when the flavors burst on his tongue. "Oh. Oh yeah. So good."

"I know," Royce boasted. "Do you want to go change out of your sticky underwear, or are you good to go?"

Sawyer laughed, feeling truly happy for the first time in weeks. "I'm good."

"I'll be the judge of that," Royce said, smiling wickedly before sliding a mouthful of shrimp and grits into his mouth.

Over dinner, Royce brought him up to speed on the new chief, new detectives in their unit, and the situation with Humphries.

"He's a creepy fucker," Sawyer said, barely managing to suppress a shudder.

"Mendoza or Humphries?" Royce teased.

"Humphries. I don't know Mendoza."

It wasn't long before Sawyer's metal spoon clanked against the bottom of the empty bowl. Then he ripped off a piece of garlic bread and scooped out the rest of the cheese and grits sticking to the sides of the dish.

"I cannot wait to sample the rest of Aunt Tipsy's recipes, dickhead. These are the best grits I've ever had."

"We better not tell Evangeline," Royce replied.

"Are you kidding? Give me your phone so I can call her. Be prepared because she's going to badger you for the recipe."

Royce laughed. "Better yet, why don't you share the leftovers with your mom tomorrow. I'll copy the recipe for her if you think she'll want it."

"Bank on it."

Sawyer insisted on helping Royce clean the kitchen. Once they finished, Royce took Sawyer back in his arms and spun him around to another slow song on his playlist.

"I guess I wouldn't have taken you as a Motown guy either," Sawyer whispered against his lips. "I love how I'm still learning all these little things about you."

"Layers, right?" Royce asked, remembering how Sawyer had recently described him. "It was my mom's favorite music, so it reminds me of her."

"Is 'Suspicious Minds' one of your favorites or hers?"

"It was her favorite song. How'd you guess?"

Sawyer tapped his temple with his index finger. "Detective,

remember? You just seemed to relax into it and become part of the music, making it obvious the song is special to you."

Then, as if a higher power had taken over DJ duties, the playlist shuffled back around to the song. Royce added extra sway to his hips, singing to Sawyer as they danced in the kitchen. Sawyer couldn't remember a time in his life when he was happier than right now.

"It's hard to imagine the surprise you brought home could top this," Sawyer whispered in between kisses on Royce's neck.

"You'll ditch me and my body if I tell you what's waiting in your office."

Sawyer snorted, cupping Royce's dick through his jeans. "There's nothing I want more in the world than to feel your cock inside me."

"Not even devising a plan to outsmart a serial killer?" Royce asked with his bedroom voice.

Sawyer pulled back and looked at Royce while they continued dancing. "Are you talking about Humphries?"

Royce waggled his brows. "I brought home the case files because you need something to occupy your big, beautiful brain while you're at home recovering, and I need to catch the sick fucker before he kills again. With his pending lawsuit, our hands are tied a bit, or so the bastard thinks. I have an ace in the hole."

"I really, really want your ace in my hole," Sawyer moaned. "Sex first, then we'll solve the case."

Chuckling, Royce dropped his arms from around Sawyer's waist, then took his hand and led Sawyer from the kitchen. Once inside their bedroom, Royce turned and pulled Sawyer into another slow dance. "I've never danced with another dude before," he whispered against Sawyer's lips. "I like it."

"As long as I'm the one you're dancing with."

Royce leaned in and kissed his lips lightly. "I will always choose you."

The slow dance turned into seductive stripping as one piece of clothing at a time hit the floor in between hot, hungry kisses.

Sawyer slid his hand in Royce's hair, fisting the silky blond strands. "I'm going to miss you tugging my hair when you fuck me."

Royce pressed kisses along Sawyer's jawbone. "It's only temporary." He pulled back and looked into Sawyer's eyes. "I have to say the buzzed hair only accentuates your gorgeous bone structure."

Insecurity tried to rear its ugly head, but Sawyer smothered the errant thoughts before they could ruin their evening. "I've thought of nothing else except this moment all day."

"I don't want to hurt you," Royce whispered against Sawyer's lips when the last piece of clothing hit the floor.

Sawyer's head-to-toe injuries were going to make finding a comfortable position difficult, but he had every confidence they'd find a way. "You're fearless, and I'm relentless, remember?"

Rather than lead Sawyer over to their bed, Royce turned him to face the dresser with the large mirror hanging above it. Sawyer's first instinct was to look away from the sight of his patchy pink skin and bandages until he met Royce's gaze in the mirror.

Royce softly trailed his fingers over Sawyer's skin, humming happily in his ear. Every nerve ending in Sawyer's body came alive and danced beneath his touch. Sawyer swayed back into Royce's arms. "Together, we're flawless, baby. No amount of pink skin and scar tissue will change my opinion. Keep your eyes on me. Watch my face so you can see how good you make me feel and how badly I want you."

Sawyer tried to speak, but the only thing escaping his lips was a trembling breath as he turned himself entirely over to Royce, believing he was wanted and knowing he could trust him.

Royce only left him long enough to retrieve the lube from the bedside table. When he returned, he captured Sawyer's mouth in a devastating kiss that threatened to reduce him to a puddle of goo on the carpet. "Touch me, asshole," Royce whispered once they broke apart to catch their breath. "I need you too."

Sawyer started at his collarbone, ghosting his fingertips over defined pecs, bumping them over the planes of his abdomen and stroking over his happy trail until he reached the base of Royce's cock. "I have never resented anything more than I do the bandages and gloves on my hands."

Royce nipped the unmarred skin on Sawyer's neck. "You're only saying that because your asshole and cock aren't bandaged and off-limits."

Sawyer snorted. "True."

Royce turned him around to face the mirror. Sawyer disobeyed Royce's earlier wishes and allowed his eyes to roam away from Royce's face. How could he resist watching Royce's hand stroking his cock or teasing his exposed nipple? He couldn't. Royce's erection was pressed insistently against his ass, making Sawyer throb and ache to be filled.

"Any day now, dickhead," Sawyer moaned.

Royce chuckled as he reached around him to grab the lube off the dresser. "So impatient."

Royce seemed particularly cautious while stretching and prepping Sawyer's ass. "As we've already discussed, my ass isn't broken. Fuck me already."

"I'm only giving in because my balls are ready to burst," Royce replied. *Yeah, sure. That's why.* Royce gently cupped Sawyer's face with one hand while guiding his dick inside Sawyer's tight ass with the other. "Eyes on me, baby."

Sawyer couldn't have looked away from those stormy eyes if his life had depended on it. Royce's mercurial irises darkened to reflect the passion building inside him as he slowly reclaimed Sawyer, working his dick in and out of his tight clench. Royce's stiff posture, clamped jaw, and the fine sheen of sweat covering his body revealed the energy he was expending to hold himself back. Sawyer couldn't accept that. He arched his spine, pushing his ass against Royce and meeting his every thrust.

"My little control freak. You play dirty," Royce growled.

"I play for keeps. Show me you want that too."

Royce's grip on Sawyer's chin and hip turned bruising, but Sawyer hadn't felt more alive in weeks. "Always mine," Royce growled, increasing the tempo. Their bodies slapped together hard enough to vibrate the dresser and knock a bottle of cologne onto the floor. Sawyer still couldn't look away from Royce's eyes as his climax built inside him, the pleasure bordering on pain.

"Always," Sawyer said as he came, pulling Royce over the edge with him. Sawyer was too blissed out to worry about the fall.

"I got you," Royce said softly, wrapping his arms around Sawyer's torso and supporting his weight.

"God, we needed that."

"I hope you didn't mess up Connie's handiwork, or you'll be in trouble tomorrow."

Sawyer snorted. "She's not so scary."

"If you say so. I have the insane desire to salute her every time she walks into the room."

Sawyer turned in Royce's hold and kissed him. "Well, she was an army nurse."

"That explains it."

"I have a great idea," Sawyer said. Royce waggled his brows, making him laugh. "How about you help me clean up so I can get started analyzing the files you brought home. Some boyfriends bring home flowers and wine. Not my guy. He brings home murder files."

"Nothing but the best for baby," Royce teased. "I have a better idea. Why don't I help you get cleaned up so we can lounge around in bed or on the couch and eat cake or ice cream? There has to be a show on about a sunken ship with untold fortunes buried in the sea."

"Too typical. What about a forgotten, buried city in a South American jungle? A bountiful treasure is buried at the heart of the ruins, but you have to outsmart and survive the werepanthers protecting it."

"Bountiful treasures and werepanthers. Somebody got lost in an audiobook today."

Sawyer shrugged. "Guilty. What kind of ice cream did you buy?"

"Rocky road and mint chip." His favorite flavors and both would go great with the leftover cake. It was a miracle he hadn't eaten the entire thing while Royce was at work. Sawyer hummed happily, and Royce kissed his lips. "You can start digging through the files once the television show puts me to sleep. Shouldn't take long."

Sawyer laughed. "Deal."

CHAPTER 4

H

E DREAMED SAWYER WAS TICKLING HIS FACE WITH A FEATHER. NO MATTER how he turned his head or how many times he batted it away, Royce couldn't evade it. The dream was so annoying it woke him from a deep sleep only to discover the tip of Bones's tail brushing against his face. The colossal cat sat on the bedside table as he was prone to do, staring down at Royce like he was the village idiot.

"Knock it off," Royce grumbled. When he rolled over to see if Sawyer was witnessing his cat's behavior, Royce saw the pillow beside his was empty. The bathroom light wasn't on, which meant Sawyer wasn't in the master suite. Checking the time, he saw it was nearly four in the morning. A stupid person would've chalked up Bones's action as coincidence, but Royce knew the truth. The beast was worried about his favorite human. "Good call, buddy," Royce said, scratching the cat behind his ears, earning a *mrrt* sound in return.

Royce didn't bother putting clothes on since the chance of shocking Sawyer's mother at such an early hour was slim. He hooked a right and headed farther down the hallway where soft light spilled onto the hardwood floor through the door Sawyer had left open a crack. Bones ran ahead of him like he usually did when it was time to eat, confirming Royce's suspicions. The cat checked to make sure Royce was still following, then pushed open the door and darted inside Sawyer's home office.

"It's not time to eat, Bonesington," Sawyer said, which was followed by, "Oh," when Royce entered a few steps behind the cat.

"Hi."

"Um, hi." Sawyer sounded nervous, but why?

Royce looked around the typically immaculate space. Sawyer had spread open files across the gleaming mahogany desk in one corner of the spacious room and on the glass coffee table in the sitting area on the opposite side of the office. Along the built-in bookcases lining one wall, Sawyer had taped up copies of each victim's driver's license photo.

"You're going to damage the finish on the wood," Royce said, nodding to the bookshelves.

"I found an old roll of painter's tape," Sawyer countered. Bones jumped on the desk and strutted across the stacks of files. "Traitor," Sawyer said when the big feline plopped his furry ass between Sawyer and the paperwork in his hand.

"He was worried about you. Do you know what time it is, asshole?"

Sawyer glanced over at the antique clock on the bookcase, and his eyes widened when he saw the time. "Oh, wow. It feels like I just sat down."

"What time did you start?"

Sawyer worried his bottom lip between his teeth. "A little after eleven."

Royce's brows shot up. "You've been at this for nearly five hours already?"

"It doesn't seem like it, but the clock doesn't lie."

"Well, you should almost be ready to solve the case, then."

Sawyer snorted. Then he rose to his feet and crossed the room. "I know you don't *need* me to say this, but I will anyway. You and Marcus conducted an extensive investigation into all four deaths of those young women. The reason Humphries is free on the streets has nothing to do with your dedication or competency."

Royce hooked an arm around Sawyer's waist and pulled him closer. Sawyer was correct. He didn't *need* his praise, but he liked hearing it. "Maybe you're not that much of an asshole."

"You're still a ginormous dickhead," Sawyer countered, kissing him thoroughly before pulling back and walking over to the row of photos. Royce noticed Sawyer's range of motion and ease of movement were improving each day. "The things these women have in common are staggering. At first glance, it might not seem that way since they all have different height, weight, hair, and eye color, as well as race. Some serial rapists and killers prey on women who meet specific criteria. They choose slender brunettes with blue eyes and long, straight hair worn parted down the middle who remind them of their mothers or something.

"These victims' similarities are in their socioeconomic statuses. All of them were poor, attending South University on scholarships, and working jobs at the school to help offset their tuition. None of them were enrolled in Humphries's classes or were part of his mentor programs though. Still, he would've crossed paths with a library aid, janitorial worker, a server in the cafeteria, and the dean's assistant numerous times. Each of them lived off-campus in low-income-housing apartments where there were no security cameras."

Royce looked at the faces of the women Franco Humphries had raped and killed, and it felt like they were staring back at him, urging him to get justice for them. Four women who had their lives ripped away from them at the hands of a fucking monster. What made Humphries scarier was he didn't resemble the evil predator their mothers had warned them about when they were little girls. These were mothers whose hearts Royce had shattered when he delivered the news that their daughters were murdered. He would carry their broken sobs in his heart for the rest of his life.

Humphries was the exact opposite of the sadistic killers portrayed in movies and on television. He was handsome, highly educated, well-spoken, and used his charisma to disarm people. As a licensed psychologist, he knew how to manipulate people in a way they couldn't see coming until it was too late. As a professor, his access to young, impressionable minds was limitless.

"He keeps a Venus flytrap in his office," Royce said softly. "How fitting."

"Who? Humphries?" Sawyer asked.

"Yeah. I noticed it when we interviewed Humphries after Harper Thompson's murder." Royce tapped the photo of the fresh-faced African American woman who died a week before her twenty-first birthday. Even in her state-issued ID, you could see the dreamer in her dark eyes. "Harper was an inspiring writer with big plans for her future. Her mother Emma gave me a poem Harper had written. It was titled *Metamorphosis* and compared going off to college to a caterpillar's transformation into a butterfly. I keep it in my locker at the precinct to remind myself why I do this job." He would cherish the poem for the rest of his life.

"Harper was his second victim, right? You didn't interview him after the first college coed died?" Sawyer asked.

"All the ladies lived off-campus, so when we discovered Abigail, we focused on the men she came in direct contact with at the school," Royce said after a brief pause.

Royce shifted his focus to Abigail Madison's smiling face. She was Humphries's first victim, and at eighteen years old, she was also his youngest. Abby was blonde-haired, blue-eyed, and barely weighed a hundred pounds. She would've been no match for the tall, fit man who was more than twice her size.

"She loved children and wanted to become an elementary school teacher. From everything I learned about Abby, it would've been a perfect fit for her."

"We're going to nail him, Ro," Sawyer vowed. "Tell me about the other two women."

"Christina Delmar was his third and oldest victim. She'd led a pretty hard life and hadn't started college until she turned twenty-two."

The redhead with the amber eyes stared back at him from the picture taped to the bookshelf. "Her father died when she was twelve, and her mother struggled financially, working two or three jobs to pay the bills. Christi fell in with the wrong crowd in her early teens, got into drugs, and dropped out of school. She took off for the West Coast when she was seventeen to pursue a music career. She eventually got tired of living out of a VW bus and called her mother for bus fare home. She got clean, obtained her GED, and enrolled in college classes. She died a week before graduation." Royce paused for a minute. "After interviewing Christi's friends and family, I realized we were dealing with someone more skilled than the average serial killer. She was cynical, cautious, and harbored a great mistrust of men, yet she opened her front door for him to walk right in. I know most serial killers are highly intelligent, but smarts alone wouldn't have been enough to lower Christi's guard."

"Is that when you started to suspect Humphries?"

Royce nodded, staring at Christi's picture until it started to blur. "I remembered the Venus flytrap in his office and the psychology degree on the wall along with framed published articles he'd written. Humphries had the demeanor of a psychologist—soft-spoken, patient, and comforting. He said the right things, and he acted the way a concerned professor would about students being raped and murdered in their beds, but there was just something about him I couldn't ignore. He was too...perfect."

"Tell me about Tara Riker," Sawyer said. "The crime scenes from the first three murders were identical except for the victims. There were no signs of a struggle and no bruising or abrasions around their wrists or ankles. According to the ME reports, the only bruising was from the ligature marks around their necks when he strangled them with their bras. The women had either consented to have their wrists and ankles bound, or they were drugged with something that had already faded by the time their bodies were discovered. GHB only stays in the systems for twelve hours. Tara's crime scene was very different. Why?"

Royce ran a hand over his face, mentally recalling every minute detail about her scene. Tara's right foot had been severely bruised, and she'd broken two toes when she repeatedly kicked and tried to fight off her attacker. The ligature marks cut deeply into her wrists and the one ankle still attached to the bed from her attempts to get loose. Her face was covered in contusions, and she had a bloody lip.

"Tara was more of a fighter than a dreamer, I think. She was a former standout athlete at her high school, playing field hockey and basketball, and was a criminal justice major. She had grit. With the first three murders, maybe Humphries convinced them he'd let them go if they were good. They might've been too traumatized to react. Everyone acts differently when faced with a dangerous situation. Honestly, the biggest difference between her assault and the other three was Tara's footboard breaking, which freed her right ankle and allowed her to fight back. The first three didn't get the chance."

"Is that how you think Humphries's semen got on Tara's bed-sheets but not the others?"

"I think he dropped the condom onto the bed when she started kicking him. He just wasn't aware any semen had spilled." From his periphery, Royce saw Sawyer turn and look at him. Meeting his gaze, Royce said, "I promised their mothers I'd get justice for their girls. I know it was wrong of me to promise something I wasn't sure I could deliver, but I did it, and I can't take it back."

"We'll make this right. Together."

"Starting tomorrow. Um, later this morning," Royce amended when he remembered the time. "You need sleep to heal so you can get back to work. I miss my partner."

"Not more than I miss you," Sawyer said.

"Prove it by coming back to bed with me and getting some sleep. We're no good to these ladies otherwise."

"Deal."

Sawyer turned off the light and closed the door, and they all re-turned to the bedroom with Bones leading the way. The only time the feline wasn't permitted in their bed was during sexy times. Bones curled up at the foot of the bed in the left corner, so the humans could spoon in the middle. Royce aligned his front to Sawyer's back and willed his brain to shut down so he could sleep but reliving those crime scenes and talking about the women made it impossible. He'd kept his promise to their mothers, but some son of a bitch interfered, sending him—*them*—back to square one.

Tara, Christi, Abby, and Harper deserved to have justice so they could rest in peace.

"Go talk to their mothers tomorrow," Sawyer said sleepily, startling Royce. He shouldn't have been surprised his boyfriend knew his brain was too worked up to permit sleep. "Tell them you're still fighting for their daughters. You'll feel better, and they will too."

"You're so damned smart."

Sawyer yawned big enough to make his jaws pop. "You would've thought about it once you had your first cup of coffee. Now get some sleep."

Forming a game plan was the trick to settling Royce's mind, and he drifted off for a few peaceful hours.

Sawyer was still sleeping when Royce left, and he hoped he remained in bed a few more hours. Sawyer was usually the one who stuck notes to various surfaces, but Royce was capable of considerate gestures, even if the tone in their communications were vastly different. Royce went around and placed Post-it notes in nearly every room, reminding Sawyer of a few things: eat well, listen to Connie and Evangeline, and get lots of rest. Even though he addressed each one to asshole, Royce's love was evident in each missive.

He left early so he could visit the mothers of Humphries's victims, but none of them were at home or work. He understood the reason why when the desk sergeant, Dunn, informed him he had visitors in the conference room. With his heart in his throat, Royce opened the door, expecting to see anger in each of the women's eyes. The emotion was present, but it wasn't aimed at him, and their determination and conviction shone brighter.

"I tried to find each of you this morning, and now I know why I wasn't successful." Royce sat down across from them. "First, I want to apologize that you didn't hear about Humphries's release directly from me. I know an officer with victim services contacted you, but it should've been me."

"We're not here because of that," Emma said. It was eerie how much she looked like her daughter.

"You're not?" he asked.

All four women shook their heads.

"Officer Andrews was wonderful when she reached out to us," Tara's mom Dinah said.

"That's good to hear," Royce said. He knew Keeley would be an excellent fit for the department. "It still should've been me. Each of you deserved an in-person visit instead of a phone call from a stranger."

"You are an honorable man," Abby's mom Jennifer said. "You looked us in the eye and promised to get justice for our girls."

"It hasn't happened yet," Royce replied.

"Not from lack of trying on your part," Christi's mom Sarah said.

"Do you believe in your heart that Humphries is your man?" Emma asked.

"I do. Nothing has changed my conviction. Marcus and I arrested the right man," he said firmly.

"Then what are we going to do about it?" Dinah asked.

Their faith in him made his heart swell, but Royce managed to keep his voice calm when he said, "*We* are not going to do anything. *I* am going to nail this bastard before he can hurt anyone else. What I'm going to say next needs to stay between us, okay?" he asked, meeting their gazes one at a time. Each of them nodded, so he told them about the pending lawsuit. "Humphries thinks he's tying our hands, but he's not. We just have to be more cautious about tracking his movements."

"I'm so tired of people like him winning," Jennifer said warily.

Royce reached across the table and covered her clasped hands. "He's won this round, but the fight isn't over. We will deliver the knockout blow. I have to believe that, or I couldn't come to work each day."

"I have to believe it too, or I won't get out of bed each morning," Sarah said softly. "I need my baby to have justice, and I trust you to give it to us." She placed her hand over Royce's, sandwiching it between hers and Jennifer's.

"That goes for me too," Emma said, covering Sarah's hand.

"Me too," Dinah said, placing her hand on top. "Let's nail this bastard's balls to the wall."

Royce swallowed hard. "You humble me, ladies."

"What can we do?"

"Stay away from Humphries and his wife and avoid the media. They will take your words and twist them around, adding fuel to the fire. The last thing you want is to be named in a defamation lawsuit."

All four women nodded.

After they left, Royce headed to the evidence locker room, where he found Tobias at his station. "Good morning, Sergeant Locke."

"Good morning, Tobias."

"I suspect I know why you're here. Both Commissioner Rigby and Chief Mendoza informed me you'd be looking into the chain of custody breach for the Humphries evidence. I assured them of my full cooperation." Of course, he did. The man had a cushy job and didn't want to be reassigned to something less savory.

"That's right."

"What do you hope to discover that IA didn't?" Tobias asked.

"The truth, Tobias. I haven't read any of the reports. I am coming into this completely blind. Start at the very beginning, and don't leave anything out. No detail is too insignificant or small."

Thirty minutes later, Royce knew the date and time all the evidence was signed out by the lab courier, and he knew the date and time it was returned to them. All except the bedsheet, of course. It went missing between the lab and the police evidence locker room. Tobias was so thorough Royce was surprised he hadn't learned what the older man had eaten for lunch on those days.

"Can I see the paperwork?"

"Of course."

There were ten pieces of evidence sent to the lab for testing. Each one was labeled and assigned a tracking number, which was the case number plus an alphabetical letter starting with A and advancing until there were no new pieces. Items presented at trial would have an exhibit letter matching the letter in the tracking number. Royce ran his finger over their list of outgoing evidence, noting the tracking number range was S10946-A through S10946-J. The paperwork included a description for each item, and the sheet was listed as S10946-D. Next, he reviewed the forensic science service provider's intake form. The data on the Richmond Laboratories' FSSP receipt was an identical match. The bedsheet made it to the lab, was tested, and produced results that matched Humphries's DNA to their killer.

"And our intake form when the items came back from the lab?"

Tobias handed the form to him. There were only nine items listed, and S10946-D wasn't among them.

"Can I have the outgoing paperwork from the Richmond Laboratories?"

"Which one? The original one showing the sheet on the list of evidence coming back to us, or the one that arrived with the courier that we now know is altered?"

"Both," Royce said.

He reviewed both forms. The only two discrepancies were the bedsheet missing from the forged document and different couriers were listed on both. The fake report looked authentic, so Tobias wouldn't have known the bedsheet was removed. Evidence in a case didn't always come back at the same time. Some tests took longer, and sometimes evidence was sent to another FSSP for further analysis. Tobias knew this better than anyone, so there'd been no reason for him to be suspicious.

How did someone know to take the sheet though? Who had tipped off Humphries? Royce could access visitor logs and request security camera tape from the county jail, but he had to know who he was looking for. He didn't think it would do him any good, either. Humphries was too smart to get caught red-handed. He wouldn't have met with his guy in person; he would've used someone as a go-between. Who? His attorney? It wouldn't have been the first time a lawyer acted in an unethical way to get their client out of trouble. His wife? How would he have explained his desire to make evidence disappear if he was as innocent as he claimed? He started to discount that option, then stopped. Humphries could've convinced her they had framed him to cover up their incompetence.

Looking at all avenues meant Royce would need to request copies of the visitor log and check out every single person who met with Humphries behind bars. From there, he could request security camera footage for any names he couldn't match to a face. But first, he needed to know more about B. Parker, the courier who delivered their evidence on the day in question.

"How familiar are you with the couriers?" Royce asked.

"Very," Tobias said. "These laboratories are very careful who they hire for that position, and turnover isn't common. It's usually the same three fellas who pick up and return evidence."

"And this B. Parker? Had you seen him before that day?"

"Her," Tobias corrected. "It was the first time I'd ever laid eyes on *her*. Pretty little thing, but it was odd, and I even remarked on it. I told her it wasn't often I meet a new driver. She just chuckled and said it was her first time driving that route. She claimed one of their drivers was out on vacation and another was sick, so they were stretched thin with extra pickups. There was nothing out of the ordinary about her demeanor, uniform, badge, or paperwork. The transaction was smooth and effortless like she'd been doing it a long time."

"Did IA have you work with a sketch artist?" Royce asked.

"No." A big grin spread across his face. "You are going to get to the truth, aren't you?"

"Yes, sir."

"Good man," Tobias said proudly. "I don't have much longer before I retire, and I want to see the monster behind bars for good."

"We all do. I'll send one of our sketch artists down to talk to you so you don't have to leave your post."

Royce sought out Cami Everhart and asked her to meet with Tobias when she was free. She eyed him curiously for a second before she smiled widely. Cami was a sweet woman with big brown eyes and a brilliant smile. He'd briefly debated asking her out when she joined the force, but she'd had relationship and kids written all over her. Funny how those two things didn't scare him any longer.

"What?" he asked when the silence grew awkward.

"There's something different about you."

"No," Royce countered.

"Oh, yeah. I'd heard rumors you're off the market now, but I didn't believe them until now. You look settled and content."

"I don't think either of those words are compliments, Cami." They came nowhere close to describing how Sawyer made him feel. "Yes, I am in a relationship."

"Lucky girl."

"Guy," he corrected, then blushed when her smile grew even wider. "Can you work with Tobias today?" he asked, pulling them back to the reason he'd sought her out.

"Of course. I'll visit him in just a few minutes. I just need to send out a mass text to all my friends who were hoping for introductions to you."

Royce just shook his head and walked away. He rounded up his rookies and headed out the door, laughing as they fought over the shotgun seat.

"Where are we going?" Carnegie asked as he buckled into the front passenger seat.

"Back to the prison."

"Is this a daily thing?" Fuentes asked.

"Nope," Royce replied. "We're working a few angles and hoping to see what we can shake loose about our missing evidence. First, we're going to the jail to request visitor logs for Humphries. Then we're going to Richmond Laboratories to interview every single fucking person there until I'm confident none of their employees were involved in taking the sheet. Watch and learn, fellas. Watch and learn."

CHAPTER 5

SAWYER LOOKED AT THE PLATTERS OF FOOD SPREAD ACROSS THE KITCHEN island. "Do you think we have enough snacks for our guests?"

Royce stepped up behind him, placing his hand at the small of Sawyer's back. "Remind me how many people we invited over for poker night?"

"Six plus us."

Royce snorted. "There's enough food here for eighty people."

"It's my first poker night with the unit, and our first time hosting it together. I got a little carried away."

"You're a food snob," Royce countered. "Our poker pals are expecting simple things like little smokies in barbecue sauce and a variety of chips."

Sawyer gestured to the small crockpot with smokies smothered in barbecue sauce and the bowls of chips. "We have those things."

Royce laughed so hard his body shook. "First of all, we don't usually put the chips in fancy bowls," he said when he could finally speak.

"What the hell do you do with them?"

Royce's gray eyes sparkled with humor and joy. "God, I love you. So damn much."

Sawyer narrowed his eyes. "The declaration feels like you're patronizing me."

"Nope," Royce said, shaking his head. "I love the effort you put into everything, although it must be exhausting." Royce leaned in for a long, toe-curling kiss. "We usually just set the bags of chips on the counter and everyone helps themselves. None of us have attended the Evangeline O'Neal school of etiquette like you did." Royce looked at the plethora of food options. "We certainly don't serve each other skewers with fancy cheese, melon, and... What's the meat called again?"

Sawyer chuckled. "Skewers are used for grilling kebobs. Those are cocktail sticks. The meat is called prosciutto. It's thinly sliced Italian ham. Nothing fancy about it." He picked up a cocktail stick and held it to Royce's lips. "Try it. That way, you know I'm not trying to serve weird things to your friends."

"*Our* friends. I already know they taste fabulous because I stole some while you were plating them. I cannot fault your taste in food, even if I think the company you keep is questionable." Royce's devilish grin left no doubt as to whom he meant.

"I'm an excellent judge of character," Sawyer countered.

Royce parted his lips and pulled the melon, meat, and cheese into his mouth with his teeth.

"You make eating look erotic somehow," Sawyer said, watching Royce's mouth move as he chewed.

"It's not too late for me to call people and tell them poker night is canceled. We can eat these in bed." Royce looked at the platters of sandwiches and cookies, the bowls of salad—pasta, macaroni, and potato—and the second crockpot containing sweet and sour meatballs. "Crumbs and sauce be damned."

"We wouldn't need to buy groceries for at least another week," Sawyer countered, sounding like he was giving it serious consideration when they both knew the high stakes riding on a successful poker night. "I'd like to lick the sweet and sour sauce off your—" The doorbell rang, cutting off his brilliant suggestion. "Our guests have arrived."

"Probably not all of them," Royce countered, following close behind Sawyer. "Let them stand out there until you finish what you were going to say. What was the part about licking some sweet and sour sauce off my body?"

"I don't recall what I was going to say," Sawyer said over his shoulder.

Royce made a whiny, needy sound. "I have some suggestions, but only after we let the sauce cool down a bit. Ouch."

Sawyer opened the door and was surprised to find all their invited guests plus one extra had arrived at the same time. They stood in two different groups, both suspicious of the others' presence, reminding Sawyer of high school cliques.

"Three of these things aren't like the other," Kyomo Chen said, tilting his head toward the other group.

"Technically four," said Royce's brother Jace. "I'm neither a cop nor a…" His words trailed off as he tried to figure out who the other three men were. "One of them," he finally said. "I'm Royce's brother and Holly's guy. I just came for the food."

"I am a cop," Jonah St. John said, his soft voice a sharp contrast to the severe scar slashing diagonally across his face from his right eyebrow to the left corner of his mouth. "I work for the Georgia Bureau of Investigation."

Ky, Blue, and Holly scowled at Sawyer and Royce.

"I smell a trap," Holly said.

"What gives?" Ky asked.

"Did you invite the feds too?" Blue questioned.

Sawyer and Royce stepped aside, gesturing for everyone to come in.

"I can explain everything," Sawyer said. "First, let's eat."

"Smells really good," Blue said, sniffing the air.

"Not sure I trust anything coming out of your kitchen if these are the kinds of people you're going to invite to poker night," Holly said as she breezed by, rubbing her hand over Sawyer's bristles as she went. "That cut actually looks good on you. It shows off your bone structure."

Royce lifted a brow as if to say "See. I told you."

"Funny," Rocky Jacobs said. "I was thinking the same about the lot of you." The good-natured smile slid from his face when Jace glared at him. "It was a joke, pal."

"I'm not your pal," Jace retorted.

"I'm sure my boo has a perfectly good explanation why he invited a reporter, a private investigator, and a GBI agent to a night usually reserved for MCU detectives," Blue calmly said on the way to the kitchen. "I'm more than willing to test out all the food to make sure it isn't tainted."

"Taking one for the team, huh?" Felix asked. He sounded shy and uncertain, which were two words Sawyer never associated with the man. He was the last to enter the house, and instead of heading to the kitchen like the others, he stopped in front of Royce and Sawyer. "Should I have reviewed my will to make sure everything was in order before I came over?"

"Are those lobster rolls?" Blue asked excitedly.

"Yes, Blue," Royce replied to him before returning his full attention to Felix. "We didn't invite you here to rough you up, jackass."

"Then why?" Felix was wise to be skeptical after the stunts he'd pulled in the past—both distant and recent.

"We need your help," Royce replied grudgingly, sounding as if the words were ripped out of him instead of offered freely.

"On?" Felix asked, crossing his arms over his chest. Sawyer recognized the stance and resolution in his eyes. He wasn't budging from the spot until he knew what he was facing. His dogged determination made Felix a stellar reporter and had kept him alive when facing off against criminals who didn't want their activities exposed. He'd made a lot of enemies.

"Catching Humphries before he can kill again," Royce said. "I've heard you're good at getting people to talk to you and uncovering truths killers don't want dragged into daylight."

Felix looked from Royce to Sawyer, his amber eyes searching and assessing. "I can't stand injustice."

"We need that passion," Sawyer said, then nearly swallowed his tongue at his poor word choice, considering he was standing with his former one-night stand and his boyfriend. "Christi, Tara, Abby, and Harper could really use your skills."

"I'm in," Felix said, nodding firmly. He stepped around Sawyer and Royce to head into the kitchen until Sawyer called out his name. Felix stopped abruptly, then turned to face him.

Sawyer kissed Royce quickly and winked. They'd discussed the conversation Sawyer was about to have with Felix. Royce didn't agree it was necessary, but he respected that Sawyer did.

Royce leaned closer, pressing his mouth against Sawyer's ear. "Mine."

"Always," Sawyer replied.

Felix watched the exchange with a quirked brow and smartass snarl. "You wanted me to watch you too play kissy-face?" he asked once he and Sawyer were alone.

"No. I wanted to apologize to you," Sawyer said. "I should've done it a long time ago."

It took a few blinks for Felix to clear the astonishment from his eyes. "For what?" he asked, sounding befuddled.

"For using you," Sawyer replied simply. "And for ignoring you during all the times you reached out after that night. I felt guilty for betraying Vic and ashamed I used a friend to ease my loneliness."

"Horniness," Felix corrected, rubbing the back of his neck as awkwardness bloomed between them. "Did you know how I felt about you?"

Sawyer shook his head. "I would've acted differently had I known, or at least I think I would have, but I wasn't making good decisions then. I was so fucking depressed and lonely."

"Don't forget human," Felix said, then chuckled. "I just thought I was horrible in bed."

Sawyer shook his head. The shared laughter that followed eased the tight ball of tension in his gut. "I'm sorry I let you think that by ignoring you."

"You have nothing to apologize for, Sawyer," Felix said softly. "I knew you weren't emotionally ready for sex, even if your body was. I couldn't stand the thought of you with someone else. I had convinced myself we would be great together, but I got over my disappointment quickly enough. And contrary to what some of my stupid stunts would leave you to believe, I haven't been pining for you. I was just being a petty bastard. Maybe we both forgive each other and put it behind us."

"Deal," Sawyer said.

Felix's gaze wandered to the kitchen. Sawyer shifted his attention there, too, and his eyes locked on Royce chatting with Jonah while filling two plates. "Vic would really like Royce, and he'd love seeing you this happy again."

"He would," Sawyer agreed, nodding. He still felt Vic's presence in his life, but it was different now. The memories were no longer steeped in pain. They were a warm, shimmering part of his past. After his death, Sawyer hadn't been sure loving Vic was worth the misery of losing him, but he knew better now. He wouldn't change a single moment they shared, not even the last ones before Vic died. Sensing their eyes on him, Royce looked over and winked at Sawyer. That dickhead was his future.

"What's the deal with the PI guy and GBI agent? What's their role?" Felix asked, pulling Sawyer's attention back to him. The reporter narrowed his eyes suspiciously.

"So, you already know Rocky Jacobs?" Sawyer asked.

"I know *of* him," Felix clarified. "I've never introduced myself to him."

Sawyer tipped his head toward the kitchen. "There's no time like the present. Besides, you don't want to miss out on the lobster rolls."

"I sure as fuck don't," Felix replied, heading toward the kitchen.

He paused after a few steps. "Don't think I didn't notice how you avoided my question about Jacobs and St. John."

"You'll know soon enough, Felix."

"Tell your boyfriend to stop calling me Fleabag," he groused. "I prefer something like Felix the Fabulous."

Sawyer snorted. "It would take a miracle for you to earn that title from him, but I'm going to enjoy watching you try."

"What's the deal with St. John?"

"The deal? What do you mean?" Sawyer asked. Was Felix approaching his question from a different angle, hoping to trick him into answering him?

Felix chuckled. "Is he single?"

"Oh." Sawyer hadn't seen that coming. "I honestly don't know anything about his personal life." That wasn't entirely true. Sawyer knew something very interesting and decided to have a little fun at Felix's expense because he deserved a little payback. "Other than Commissioner Rigby is his favorite aunt." Sawyer didn't know about the favorite part, but Felix was no stranger to embellishing a tale.

The look of dismay on Felix's face was so comical Sawyer couldn't stifle his laughter. The reporter would get no encouragement from Rigby's direction if he pursued her nephew.

"You're an asshole," Felix said, shaking his head.

"Only Royce is allowed to call me that," Sawyer said seriously.

"You two are so fucking weird."

"If by weird you mean amazing, then I agree," Royce said when they joined him. He handed Sawyer a plate piled high with enough food to feed four men. "I might've gotten a little carried away. I'm just happy to see your appetite returning."

It was amazing what returning to daily orgasms could do for a man's outlook on life, as well as his appetite. Still, until Sawyer could return to the gym full time, he needed to keep an eye on what he ate and the size of his portions. Then he noticed that nearly half the food on his plate was fresh vegetables, and the simple gesture made him lean forward and kiss Royce without considering their audience. Then again, everyone knew they were a couple. Rocky and Jonah probably hadn't known it until they visited Sawyer in the hospital and had witnessed Royce's dragon-like protectiveness firsthand.

"God, how times have changed," Holly said from the opposite side of the island. "A few months ago, we would've been eating processed cheese from a can on crackers, and Royce would be dodging texts and calls from lady friends all night instead of smooching his boyfriend." She bit into a meatball, happily humming while she chewed. "Who said change was bad?"

"Not me," Royce said, waggling his brows at Sawyer, earning catcalls from Blue and Ky. When Royce's smile faltered, Sawyer knew he was thinking about Marcus. A few months ago, they wouldn't have been in Sawyer's house for poker night, and Marcus would've been alive. He suspected Royce's mind had traveled to the cassette tape he kept tucked away in his bedside table drawer next to Marcus's lucky hat and cell phone.

He'd seen Royce pick up the cassette tape several times since returning home from the hospital, but instead of listening to it, Royce released a long sigh and placed it back in the drawer for safekeeping. He'd listen to it when he was ready to hear Marcus's confessions to his priest and not a moment before. This was their first poker night since Marcus's death, and Sawyer had known it would be hard on everyone in the unit.

"The players are sure as hell different," Ky groused, glaring daggers at Felix.

"He's on our side this time," Royce told Ky.

"What side? Poker isn't a team sport," Blue said. "Are we playing Pictionary instead of poker?"

"Eat, then I'll explain," Royce said. "I promise."

"This won't go well," Holly mumbled under her breath.

"What are these?" Jace asked suspiciously, gesturing to the cocktail sticks.

"Meat, cheese, and melon. Don't act like a jerk," Royce said. "Just eat it."

"Who's acting?" Jace asked. "I've never seen this kind of meat."

"It's called prosciutto, and it's a thinly sliced Italian ham," Royce said. "It's the best thing you'll ever eat. So, shut up and stick it in your mouth."

"Save your dirty talk for *after* we leave," Holly told Royce. Then she held up a cocktail stick so Jace would take a bite instead of glare at his brother. Just like Royce, Jace made a big show of slowly pulling the food off the stick with his teeth. Holly seemed to be as equally affected as Sawyer had been earlier.

Shut up and stick it in your mouth. Sawyer laughed because Royce had used similar words during foreplay when he was eager for Sawyer to suck his cock. Jace turned a questioning gaze his way, and Sawyer wasn't sure if it was because the man-on-man talk made him uncomfortable or what.

"Please tell me you don't let him talk to you like that," Jace said to Sawyer after swallowing his food.

"Mind your own business," Royce said. "Eat your food."

Jace rolled his eyes and walked away with a giggling Holly by his side.

"Did you know Holly giggled?" Sawyer asked.

"Only when things are going well with Jace. They're going to make it this time, GB. I can feel it in my gut."

Sawyer leaned closer. "Maybe what you're *feeling* is lingering arousal from our unfinished business?"

Royce winked, then shifted the conversation back to something more appropriate. "I'm glad Jace came with Holly, but I'm not sure what to do with him when it's time to discuss our plan."

"Put him in the corner? Explain to him that he's entered the cone of silence?"

Shaking his head, Royce said, "Smartass. We can ask him to step out to the back patio."

"I'm not going to ask your brother to step outside while the adults have a conversation," Sawyer whisper-shouted.

"I can hear you," Jace said dryly. "If you guys had been honest about your intentions, I would've let you law dogs have your secret meeting."

"Reporter," Felix said, pointing to his chest.

"You say that like it's a good thing," Rocky said jovially.

"Better than a PI," Felix retorted. "At least I'm held to *some* standards."

Rocky released a dry bark of laughter. "Standards? Loose ones, maybe. Reporters say whatever the fuck they want to without anyone holding them accountable. When backed into a corner, you refuse to name sources."

"Uh-oh," Sawyer said. "If Rocky starts screaming about fake news, I'm going to throw him out."

Royce nodded. "Maybe this wasn't such a good idea."

"It's called the Shield Law, moron," Felix fired back. "I do not make shit up, so don't take your beef with another reporter out on me."

A shrill whistle split the air, causing everyone to turn their heads toward the person who made the noise. Jonah returned their stares. Everything about the man was large except his voice, which was quiet and a little raspy. He was living proof that a person didn't need to yell to be a leader.

"I don't know Royce and Sawyer well, but I do know they're straight shooters. If they want us all here tonight, then they have a good reason. Why don't we eat the delicious food they've provided and give them a chance to talk without us jumping to conclusions and starting fights with one another."

"There's always one in every crowd," Ky said, shaking his head. One what? Instigator? Heckler? Ky laughed when he realized everyone was looking at him. "A voice of reason," he clarified. "Listen to the big man and shove food in your faces before we piss the bruiser off. Or keep puffing out your chests like idiots so I can eat all the good snacks and leave the carrots and celery for you." The last part motivated everyone to make their plates and stop bickering.

Rather than talk shop like they usually would, the MCU detectives discussed the weather, sports, and local politics because of the mixed crowd.

"This is as bad as some of the ladies' luncheons my mother attends," Ky said.

"There's nothing ladylike about your mama, Ky," Royce said, earning a snicker from everyone except Sawyer, who elbowed him. "What the hell?" Royce asked, rubbing his rib cage. "Get your mind out of the gutter, GB. Wait until you meet Min-Anh, then we'll talk."

"My ma could outdrink a sailor," Ky said, grinning from ear to ear.

"She cusses like one too," Blue added.

"Interesting," Sawyer said. "I can't wait to meet her."

"Be careful what you wish for," Ky returned.

Some went back for a second round of food, but Sawyer barely finished half his plate. Holly and Jace started cleaning up the kitchen until Royce shooed them out.

"Ro, I don't mind stepping outside if you need privacy. It's a nice evening, and hanging out by Sawyer's pool isn't a hardship," Jace said.

"Nonsense," Royce quipped. "You just need to acknowledge you've entered the cone of..." He turned and looked at Sawyer. "What's the rest?"

"Cone of silence. It was just a joke."

"You can trust me to keep my mouth shut," Jace assured them.

"I have to admit. I'm beyond curious about this gathering. Will we actually play poker tonight?" Felix asked.

"Are you any good?" Jonah asked him.

Felix raked his gaze over the big man from head to toe, then smiled wolfishly. "Damn good."

"We can play poker after we discuss the real reason we invited you over," Royce said.

"This better not be one of those fucking multi-level marketing schemes," Holly said. "I do not have startup money to give you. I will not hock your vitamins or anything else you want to sell. I won't be your damned guinea pig either."

Sawyer laughed until tears spilled down his face. "Oh, god, Holls. Tell us how you really feel."

"I need your help to put Franco Humphries back behind bars where he belongs," Royce said solemnly. "That's why I called you all here. I need people I can trust because I can't run this investigation on the books since the fuckface is suing the police department, the DA's office, and the city of Savannah."

"I'm in. Tell me what you need," Blue said unwaveringly.

"Me too, Ro," Holly said. "I'll always have your back."

"Me three," Ky said.

Sawyer and Royce looked at the three men who weren't part of the MCU. Jonah nodded, Felix gave them a thumbs-up, and Rocky released a deep sigh.

"It's going to cost you," he said solemnly.

"You want me to *pay* you to help catch a serial killer?" Royce asked incredulously.

"No, jackass. I want you to apologize for hurting my feelings during the Wembley investigation."

"I hurt your feelings?" Royce asked.

"You questioned my character and accused me of tipping off David Wembley so he'd have time to get into position to take out the man who killed his daughter and her fiancé."

Sawyer looked at Royce. "You did?"

"Yeah," Royce said sheepishly. "I called him when I was still doped up after surgery. I had to take out my rage on someone." Royce shrugged. "This bastard was as good a target as any."

"See. No respect," Rocky said, shaking his head. "You want me to go out on a limb for you."

"No, I want you to go out on a limb for Christi, Tara, Abby, and

Harper. I want you to help me stop Humphries before he rapes and kills again. I should think that would be enough if your character is as sterling as you're implying."

Rocky knew he'd been had and threw his hands up in surrender. "Fine. I'm in."

Royce nodded. He quickly retreated from the room and returned with the new case file they'd started. "Let me bring you up to speed." He recounted the incidents from earlier in the week, starting with his visit to the county jail when Humphries was released. "Chief Mendoza asked me to look into the chain of custody issues and I dove in the next day, starting with interviewing Tobias. The man has a stellar memory, excellent record-keeping, and worked with the sketch artist to render a drawing of the courier who returned the evidence to him." He handed it to Blue.

"You've been busy, boo," Blue added before passing it to Holly on his right.

"That's nothing," Royce said, waving his hand. "I'm just getting to the good parts." The sketch circulated the seating area. Felix set it on the coffee table when he was finished. Sawyer bit his bottom lip to keep from laughing when everyone leaned a little closer. "I took the sketch to Richmond Laboratories and showed it to every employee. None of them admitted to recognizing her or the B. Parker alias she used."

"As in Bonnie Parker?" Jonah asked.

"We think so," Sawyer told him. "We think it was her way of being funny."

"Who the hell is Bonnie Parker?" Jace asked.

"Bonnie Parker was half of the famous criminal couple, Bonnie and Clyde."

"She did steal the bedsheet," Ky commented.

"Does that make Humphries Clyde, then?" Felix asked.

"That's one of the reasons we asked you to join us. You've investigated Humphries thoroughly for the paper. Can you look through your notes and check with your sources to see if there's a Clyde in his past anywhere? It might seem like a leap, but we can't afford to leave any stones unturned."

Felix removed his phone from his pocket and began typing notes. "Yeah, sure. I've done numerous podcasts on the murders over the years. I probably have a thousand documents."

"You do a great job," Jonah said.

Felix looked over at him and smiled. "Thanks, man."

"I can help you dig through the data. I'm kind of an expert at it," Jonah said.

"Is that what you do for the GBI?" Felix asked.

"In essence. I built a supercomputer with artificial intelligence. She can puzzle through complex things our brains can't."

"Stella," Royce said. "She's a hot number too. Jonah also does behavioral analysis."

"I'd love to have your assistance," Felix told Jonah.

"What can I do?" Rocky asked.

"I need you to help me find Reginald Dozer," Royce said.

"Okay," Rocky agreed, typing notes into his phone too. "Who is he?"

"He's the courier for Richmond Laboratories who was supposed to return the evidence to our precinct. He'd logged ten items of evidence and their tracking numbers, signed off on the transfer of custody, and promptly disappeared off the face of the earth."

"Whoa," Holly said. "Do you think he's dead?"

"He's either dead, or Humphries gave him enough cash so he could disappear without a trace. According to his neighbors, he never returned home from work that day."

"Humphries is a college professor, right?" Jace asked. "How could he afford to offer the amount of cash it would take to disappear for good?"

"He comes from a wealthy family," Royce replied.

"Big oil money from Texas," Felix added. "His grandfather's net worth rivals Gates and Bezos."

Jace whistled in response.

"Does Reginald have a family or anyone we can interview?" Ky asked.

"Nope. He is a childless widower and only child to parents who are both deceased."

"No aunts, uncles, or cousins?" Blue asked.

"Not that I could find, and I've been digging for four days now," Royce said. "I cannot request warrants for bank records, because I'm not supposed to be investigating anything remotely connected to Humphries."

"Leave it to me. I need all the information you have on Dozer," Rocky said. "Birthdate, social security number, driver's license number, last known address, and things like that."

Royce pulled out a sheet of paper containing all of Dozer's details. "Here you go."

"Where do I come in?" Holly asked.

"Do you have a college-age undercover alias with an established social media presence?" Sawyer asked.

"I have several," Holly replied.

"Humphries has a huge fan club and online following. Can you infiltrate them and see if you can win their trust? Our girl Bonnie is most likely a member," Sawyer said.

"She's probably the pushiest member or the one claiming to be in charge," Jonah offered. "She'll claim to know Humphries best and will even act possessively toward him."

"I'm hoping she's stupid enough to brag about what she's done. Then we can track her down and follow the trail back to Humphries or his attorney," Sawyer said.

"And, Jonah," Royce said, pulling out several sheets of paper and a flash drive. "I have the prison visitor's log and video footage. Can you feed them both to Stella? Attorney and client meetings aren't recorded, but personal visits are. Maybe Stella can uncover a secret code he used with visitors to give us an idea of what Humphries was up to behind bars."

"Sure," Jonah said. "You got it."

"One last thing before I whip all your asses at poker," Sawyer said.

"In your dreams," Jace grumbled.

"Serial killers tend to escalate their crimes, but Humphries never did. While his murders weren't committed exactly a year apart, he never upped the timeline. Royce and I think he was getting his jollies elsewhere. Felix, did anyone ever talk to you about his lecture circuit?"

"Holy fuck," Felix said in awe. "I never thought about it. I know he lectured some, but no one ever provided me with an official schedule or even brought it up in conversation. I'll do some digging around to see what I can find." He looked at Jonah. "Then we'll look for unsolved crimes that are similar in nature to our ladies during the times he visited."

"He could've gone with a different MO out of town, so look for unsolved murders involving women. Don't just look for coeds who were found bound, raped, and strangled in their beds," Sawyer advised. "I hate to give this bastard any credit, but he's brilliant. I have a feeling any murder spree away from home would be completely different from those here. They would've been more impulsive and less tediously planned out, I think."

"I agree," Jonah said. "He'd capitalize on an opportunity."

"If he's so brilliant, how'd you guys eventually get his DNA for testing?" Rocky asked. "He wouldn't have given it voluntarily."

"Oh, but he did," Royce said. "Once we realized we had a serial rapist and killer, we asked for male students and professors to voluntarily submit for DNA testing. Anyone who refused became a suspect. Franco Humphries gave a sample. He's that arrogant."

"Foolish," Rocky countered. "I don't know how he avoided getting his prints in their apartments, but one slip and his run was over."

"He might've worn gloves as part of his bondage role playing, and he could've wiped the place down after he killed the ladies," Royce said. "He's either naturally bald or shaves his head. If he keeps the rest of his body hairless, then it diminishes our chances of finding

DNA sources at the crime scene. Some people don't like body hair on themselves or others."

"They say most serial killers want to get caught," Jace said.

"It's true with some of them," Jonah said. "Humphries is a completely different animal. Voluntarily submitting his DNA only added to his fun and excitement."

"Sick fucker," Jace said.

"What about us?" Blue asked, gesturing between himself and Ky.

"This part is the hardest to say out loud," Royce admitted. "What I'm about to say cannot leave the cone of..." He looked over at Sawyer.

"Silence."

"Yeah, that."

"You got it, Ro," Ky said.

"I'm always looking out for my boo," Blue added.

"The only way B. Parker would've known to steal the evidence on that particular day is if she had an insider at the lab or..."

"Our police department," Ky said, finishing for him.

"I need to discreetly screen every crime scene tech, every member in our unit, every person who works at our precinct, and everyone working in the DA's office. Those are the people who collected, stored, shipped, or requested testing on evidence. They'd have a vested interest and might ask for status updates. I have to look at every single person. This order comes straight from Commissioner Rigby, and I'd rather lose a toe than disappoint her."

"You can count on me," Blue said.

"Me too," Ky added.

It wasn't easy to think about a traitor working amongst them, but it couldn't be ignored either.

"What are we calling our secret mission?" Holly said.

Royce glanced at Sawyer and smiled.

"Operation Venus Flytrap," they said together.

CHAPTER 6

ROYCE THRUSTED HIS HIPS FORWARD, BURYING HIS DICK TO THE HILT inside Sawyer's ass, eliciting a long moan from his man. "Is this what you wanted? What you've begged for?" Royce circled his hips, then leaned forward long enough to bite the back of Sawyer's neck.

"Mmmm, I'm not sure," Sawyer said breathlessly. Royce had spent the last twenty minutes working Sawyer into a fevered, panting mess. He liked it a fucking ton too. "Do it again so I can decide."

Royce pulled back and pushed in hard enough to rattle the head-board against the wall, then paused again.

"Yesss," Sawyer moaned. "More. Hurry."

"What's the problem, GB? Are you eager to leave our bed and return to work?" Royce knew Sawyer was beyond ready to get back to the job after three weeks of recovering at home. Royce also knew the job had nothing to do with the way Sawyer's body trembled beneath his. Royce stroked his hand over Sawyer's spine, from his nape to the crack of his ass, watching goose bumps pop up in the wake of his fingers.

"My problem," Sawyer replied, shifting his knees further apart and lowering his upper body to the bed, putting his pert ass on perfect display, "is that you're a damn cock tease. Literally." His golden boy loved to play dirty too.

Royce chuckled but didn't move; he couldn't or else he'd spill inside Sawyer too quickly. "Did I dream your late-night confession? I could've sworn you told me one of your fantasies was being woken from a deep sleep by an eager tongue licking your cock. Did I misread the signals?"

It had been challenging for Royce to fall asleep after Sawyer planted the idea in his head, and he woke up long before their alarm went off. Royce had started his seduction by tracing the outer shell of Sawyer's ear with his tongue, then pressing kisses along his neck. Sawyer had hummed and tried to turn in Royce's arms, but Royce tightened his hold on him, so Sawyer settled for grinding his ass against Royce's groin. Hums turned into moans, and Royce shifted so Sawyer could roll onto his back. Capturing one flat nipple between his teeth, Royce had gently tugged until Sawyer started to writhe. Sawyer's eyelashes fluttered, but he never opened his eyes when Royce kissed a path toward the other nipple, sucking it hard. Royce might've wondered if he was making a mistake if Sawyer hadn't fisted his hands in his hair and held him against his chest, showing how much he loved nipple play. Even half-asleep, Sawyer was calling the shots.

Royce had started kissing a path down his abdomen, even though Sawyer's fingers tightened in his hair, trying to get him to return to his nipples. Sawyer spread his legs, making room for Royce, who'd kept his gaze trained on Sawyer's face while he licked his semi-erect cock until it was as hard as steel. Royce hadn't wanted to miss the moment Sawyer opened his eyes. He'd needed to see awareness dawn on the features he loved so much and witness lust replace sleepiness in Sawyer's expression. The reality of the act was far sexier than he'd imagined the previous night; every sigh and needy moan was indelibly etched in Royce's mind.

Sawyer's full lips had tilted into a satisfied smile before his eyes even opened. "Dickhead," he'd whispered hungrily.

Sawyer's eyes had slowly opened, his gaze zeroing in on Royce, who'd begun circling the head of Sawyer's cock with his tongue. Royce wasn't at all surprised when Sawyer had lifted his hips and tried to push his dick deeper inside Royce's mouth.

Even though his cock had throbbed, Royce tamped down his need to make Sawyer's fantasy come true, drawing out the blow job until Sawyer had begged for relief. Even then, Royce had taken his time stretching Sawyer's ass open with the Dildosaurus II before his restraint had broken, and he'd commanded Sawyer to get on his hands and knees. Then he replaced the toy with his lubed dick bringing them to this moment.

Sawyer whimpered with need and frustration before answering Royce's question. "No, you didn't misread the signals. You gave me exactly what I wanted. Now fuck me."

Royce retreated until only the head of his cock remained inside Sawyer. He ran his thumb over the stretched, puckered hole trembling around his erection. "You never hide how much you want me, and it's so fucking sexy." By fulfilling Sawyer's fantasy, he'd worked himself to the edge of climax before he'd even lubed his cock and slid past the first ring of muscles. "There's nothing I won't do to please you, except share." Royce slammed forward until their bodies slapped together. "Mine," he growled in Sawyer's ear.

"Always," Sawyer whimpered, arching his back and pushing his ass back to meet Royce's thrusts. "I'm going to come."

Thank god. Royce canted his hips, aiming his cock at Sawyer's prostate and making him shake and come apart after a few strokes. Royce followed him over the edge on the next thrust, then collapsed on top of him. "Too heavy?" he asked.

"Shut up, and let me soak this in," Sawyer groused.

While Sawyer hadn't fully recovered, more than ninety percent of his burns had healed enough to not require bandages. Only a wound on his left leg and one on each arm still required daily dressing changes. After weeks of physical therapy, his nerve damage had recovered enough to pass his firearm tests. Royce had noticed a slight tremor in Sawyer's left hand on rare occasions, but nothing so severe that he continued to drop things.

"I'm kind of pissed I won't get welcomed back with a promotion and a box of pastries," Sawyer teased.

Kelsey had texted Royce the previous evening, informing him she was bringing in a few dozen of Sawyer's favorite cupcakes. Royce wasn't going to ruin her surprise though. Instead, he slapped Sawyer's ass and eased his softening dick out of his tight clench.

Flopping onto the bed beside him, Royce said, "You should take your sergeant's exam. You'd ace it."

"The unit isn't big enough for two sergeants," Sawyer said, rolling to his back and looking at him.

Royce hadn't thought about it before, but Sawyer was right. He'd likely have to take a vacant position elsewhere in the department. Cupping Sawyer's face, Royce kissed him soft and slow. "You're capable of great things, and I will never be the person who holds you back from achieving them."

Sawyer smiled drowsily. "I'll know when the time is right, dickhead. Until then, I'm more than happy to be your partner."

"Don't even think about going back to sleep. We need to hit the shower—" Royce's phone rang, cutting him off midsentence. He looked at his phone and groaned when he saw Chief Mendoza's name on the caller ID. "This can't be good." He hit the accept button and said, "Good morning, Chief."

"Locke," the man said grimly. "We have a very big problem. I need you and Key to meet me at River's Crossing Estates on Riddick Lane." Mendoza rattled off the street number and specific unit. *Great.* It was just another Murder Monday.

"Yes, sir. We'll be there in twenty minutes or less." He rolled off the bed and headed to the shower, knowing Sawyer was right behind him. It wasn't common for dispatch to contact the chief of police before homicide detectives, which meant they were dealing with a high-profile victim. "I'm afraid to ask who was murdered, sir. I know I'm not lucky enough for it to be Franco Humphries."

"Humphries is in Puerto Vallarta with his wife," Mendoza said. "Which only complicates our lives further."

"Because?" Royce asked.

"He has an alibi."

He took the chief's implication on the chin like an upper cut from a heavyweight boxer, feeling dizzy and disoriented. "Another coed?" he asked before remembering the location of the homicide. The River's Crossing townhomes were swanky and nothing like the apartments where Humphries's victims had lived.

"Just get here, Locke," Mendoza said before disconnecting the call.

Royce stared at his phone for a second before setting it down to turn on the shower. "Our new chief has a bad habit."

"Uh-oh," Sawyer said. "Did he hang up without saying goodbye?"

"Yep."

"He didn't seem like a rude person when we met Friday afternoon." Sawyer squirted toothpaste on his toothbrush. "This homicide must be a big deal. Who is it?"

"He didn't say."

They rushed through their shower and grooming, only stopping long enough for Sawyer to feed Bones while Royce made two mugs of coffee.

"These single-use coffee machines are convenient, but I don't think the coffee tastes as good," Royce said when they entered the garage.

"That's because you like your coffee twice as strong as the average person. I'm sure we can find coffee pods that would give you the kick in the ass you need. Which car are we taking?"

"You don't want to drive separately?" Royce asked.

"No," Sawyer replied. "It's doubtful Mendoza will take the time to look up our home addresses and calculate the feasibility of us carpooling."

"Yeah, okay," Royce said. "You drive since you're a control freak."

Sawyer grinned instead of denying the accusation since he was guilty as charged. He pulled the key fob from his pocket and unlocked the door. "Where to?"

Royce rattled off the address on Riddick Lane. "Those are luxury townhomes."

"Yeah," Sawyer agreed. "Factor in the location plus dispatch calling Mendoza to the scene before us, and I think we're heading into a cluster fuck of epic proportions. What did Mendoza say beyond giving you the address?"

"He told me to slap you on the ass to wake you up and for both of us to get down to the scene," Royce replied.

Sawyer snorted. "Yeah, right. It's weird Mendoza didn't give you a name, right?"

"Very. He just said we had a big problem, and Humphries having an alibi complicates things even more."

"A copycat killing?" Sawyer asked. "It's the only thing that makes sense. Why else would Humphries factor in the chief's concerns if he's out of town?"

Royce hadn't thought that far ahead, but it made a lot of sense. "Christ."

He'd hoped the early hour would've given them a break from gawkers and gatherers, but he was wrong. Even at six in the morning, it looked like every River's Crossing resident was lined up on the sidewalk in front of their crime scene. They weren't the only ones out in full force. Royce counted three news vans and spotted Felix chatting with a uniformed patrolman near the police barricade.

Felix glanced over but didn't acknowledge them. They'd all agreed not to meet or discuss their mission publicly.

"This feels like déjà vu," Sawyer said. "My first day on the job and my first day after medical leave feel eerily the same. Cryptic directions to report to a crime scene, media frenzy, and a large crowd of spectators."

"Want me to glare daggers at you and act like a dickhead?" Royce shook his head before Sawyer could reply. "Don't answer that."

They showed their shields to the officers acting as crowd control, then strode up the sidewalk to where Officer Bobby Jones stood with his clipboard by the front door of 602B.

"We gotta stop meeting like this, Bobby," Sawyer said.

"This reminds me of your first crime scene with the SPD," the African American man with the easy smile said. "You know the routine. Sign in and suit up."

Royce took the clipboard and entered their names, arrival time, and shield numbers while Sawyer grabbed booties and gloves for them from the boxes Bobby kept by the front door.

"I was just telling Locke how similar the crime scenes felt. And like last time, I bet you can tell me who the deceased is. It must be salacious as hell to garner this amount of attention before the sun is even up."

"Dispatch didn't tell you?" Bobby asked Sawyer.

"Chief Mendoza called and just said for us to get our asses down here," Royce told him.

"Far be it for me to ruin the new chief's surprise," Bobby said.

"More like he didn't want to deal with the questions that were sure to follow once he lowered the boom," Royce corrected.

"Sergeant Lock! Detective Key!" a reporter yelled from the barricade. "Can I have a moment of your time?"

"We have no comments," Royce replied, which would've been true even if he weren't clueless. "Keep your secrets, Bobby. I have a feeling I don't want my reaction to learning the identity of the victim broadcasted on the news." They slipped on the booties and gloves and headed into the house.

The interior of the home was modern chic with a white-on-white monochromatic scheme interrupted only by chrome accent pieces and an occasional pop of color scattered throughout the first floor, making the black powder residue smudges from dusting for prints stand out in stark contrast in the pristine environment. The place, although fully furnished and expensively designed, felt impersonal to Royce. There were no pictures displayed anywhere to give a clue as to whose home they stood in.

"Can you imagine Bones living in a place like this?" Royce asked. "He'd ruin a white couch in five minutes or less by yacking up his cat food all over it."

Beside him, Sawyer chuckled. The sound never failed to warm his soul, and Royce fought off the urge to reach for him, even though they appeared to be the only two people downstairs at the moment. "This place is definitely not intended for kids or pets. It reminds me of the model homes Vic and I looked at when we were trying to decide if building a new house was the right fit for us. Nothing about this townhouse resembles the other crime scenes either. Harper's apartment could probably fit in the powder room we just passed."

Looking around the room, Royce couldn't help but compare the opulence to the places Christi, Tara, Harper, and Abby had called home. He wondered if they'd dreamed of living in places like this one someday. "Maybe our guess was way off."

"Locke, Key, up here," the chief called.

They looked up and saw him standing at the top of the stairs, observing them. But for how long? It was a good thing Royce hadn't reached for Sawyer after all.

"Yes, sir," Sawyer said, heading toward the steps and leaving Royce to follow him.

"Sorry to start your first day back so early, Detective Key," Mendoza said once they reached the landing at the top of the steps.

"I was eager to get back, sir," Sawyer said.

"This case is going to be a PR nightmare for the department, fellas," Mendoza said. "I need you at your very best."

"You can count on us, sir," Royce said.

Mendoza studied them for a second and must've liked what he saw because he nodded curtly, then pivoted and walked toward the master bedroom. Royce and Sawyer exchanged curious glances before following him.

Two things struck Royce like a punch to the gut when he walked into the bedroom, helping him to understand the chief's somber mood and dread: the identity of the victim and how similar her death had been to Humphries's victims.

Someone wanted them to believe Franco Humphries had struck again.

CHAPTER 7

SAWYER LOOKED AWAY FROM THE SPRAWLED WOMAN ON THE BED WHOSE open robe didn't afford her any modesty. It never got easier seeing a person violated so heinously. "Is that Humphries's attorney?" he asked in disbelief.

"Yes. Vivian Gross," Royce said.

Sawyer recalled the story Royce told him about the bizarre encounter between Humphries and Gross outside the jail, which was confirmed by the photographs Felix ran with his article the day after Humphries's release.

The ME, Dr. Fawkes, was leaning over the woman whose wrists and ankles had been secured to the bed by restraints. "She's in the flaccid stage of rigor mortis."

The general rule for rigor mortis is 12:12:12. Twelve hours for her body to have reached full rigor, then twelve hours in the rigid stage before it had started reversing itself. Her contracted muscles would've started relaxing during the flaccid stage, which was the final twelve hours in the equation. "So, Ms. Gross died within the last twenty-four to thirty-six hours?"

"I'd say closer to thirty-six," Fawkes replied. "There's still some rigidity in the larger muscle groups, but not much."

Looking around the room, Sawyer noticed the apparent signs of a struggle. The bedside table next to the right side of the bed was shoved against the wall hard enough for the corner to puncture the drywall. A lamp on top of it had been knocked over, and a cell phone, watch, and a paperback book had fallen to the floor during the collision. While he couldn't see bruises on the front of Ms. Gross's body, he anticipated Fawkes finding contusions on the back of her thighs if she were the one who'd crashed into the table.

"Was she sexually assaulted?" Royce asked quietly.

"There are no external signs of bruising, tearing, or bleeding, but I will check for any signs of internal vaginal or anal trauma during her autopsy." Dr. Fawkes pointed to two round burn marks on Vivian Gross's chest above her left breast. "Those look like a stun gun caused them. I suspect her attacker used it to subdue her so they could tie her to the bed and strangle her." Fawkes straightened and looked at Royce and Sawyer. "Upon entering the room, I saw our victim was strangled with her robe belt and thought the Savannah Strangler had struck again."

Savannah Strangler was the nickname the media had given to Humphries once it became apparent they were dealing with a serial rapist and killer.

"The Strangler didn't use sex restraints purchased from adult stores like the ones utilized to incapacitate Ms. Gross. The college coeds were all restrained with articles of their clothing. Ms. Gross put up a valiant fight, as well." Fawkes lifted a hand and pointed to the dried blood beneath her nails. "So far, I haven't found wounds on her body that would've generated the dried blood we see here, so I don't believe it belongs to Ms. Gross. We were never able to collect foreign DNA from anywhere on the coeds' bodies."

"It appears Ms. Gross was interrupted while taking a bath," Mendoza said, gesturing toward the master bathroom.

Sawyer and Royce walked to the doorway but didn't enter because the techs were busy collecting evidence. From their vantage point, they could see the filled bathtub and gutted candles lining the wall opposite the bath pillow suctioned to the tub. There was a half-empty wineglass tucked in the corner and a tablet lying on the fuzzy bathmat on the floor.

"She either left the bath prematurely with intent to return, or she ran the bath and lit the candles and was killed before she had a chance to enjoy them," Royce said.

"This could be staging, but to what point?" Sawyer asked. Turning to look at Royce, he held up a finger. "No sign the victim cooked dinner for her assailant. Christi, Tara, Abby, and Harper had all prepared a meal for their guest." They'd never had the opportunity to eat the food, but they had gone to the trouble of cooking, which explained why there was no forced entry. They had invited their killer into their homes. Sawyer held up two fingers. "Signs of a struggle and DNA beneath the nails." Three fingers. "Ms. Gross wasn't expecting her killer." Four fingers. "She's still partially dressed where the others were nude." Five fingers. "Different restraints." Sawyer could've voiced a few more points, but it wasn't necessary. They both knew this crime wasn't committed by the same person who'd killed Tara, Christi, Harper, and Abby.

Royce's mouth tipped up slightly at the corners when he saw Sawyer had borrowed his method of ticking off facts. "And Humphries is in Mexico with his wife."

"So, are we dealing with a copycat killer? If so, are they trying to impress Humphries?" Sawyer asked.

"By killing the lawyer who engineered his release from jail? That doesn't make much sense," Royce countered. "What if they only want us to believe it's a tribute killing? Vivian Gross has represented some of the vilest people in the state of Georgia, and as successful as she was in the courtroom, she couldn't win them all. What if someone took advantage of Humphries's release to get revenge against her and frame him?"

Sawyer nodded as he considered it. "Makes a lot of sense. The person was loosely familiar with the Savannah Strangler's MO but didn't know the details you'd deliberately kept from the press, such as the set tables with untouched dishes of food and unopened bottles of wine. They took what they knew and set the scene to frame Humphries. It's believable."

"They just didn't know he was on vacation in Mexico," Mendoza said, joining them. "That will not prevent the media from going crazy, and I see this playing out only one way."

Sawyer's stomach dropped. "It will add more fuel to Humphries's claims that the police set him up."

Mendoza nodded. "That's my biggest concern. For us to dispute his allegations, we'd have to reveal the details we kept out of the press during the initial investigations. I'm not prepared to do that at this time, and I want you both to keep that in mind when the media starts dragging your names through the mud."

"His," Sawyer countered, pointing to Royce. "I'm the golden one."

"Most people would think I'm insane for assigning this case to you, Locke, especially considering the way Gross has been hammering you and Wilkes in her recent interviews. Don't make me regret my decision."

Royce nodded curtly. "You got it, sir."

"Who found Ms. Gross?" Sawyer asked.

"Her personal assistant," the chief replied. "His name is Kendall Blakemore."

Sawyer's brow rose. It was a bit early in the day for a personal assistant to show up at her house. What the hell did they *assist* her with? "Where is Mr. Blakemore?"

"In the spare bedroom waiting for you to interview him," Mendoza said.

With the crime scene techs and Dr. Fawkes doing their thing, the wisest course of action was to interview the assistant, then notify the next of kin and interview coworkers until they found a person of interest to zero-in on.

They exited the bedroom and stopped at the closed door on the opposite side of the hallway. Sawyer lightly rapped his knuckles against the wood, and a female patrol officer opened the door. When she stepped aside for them to enter, Sawyer caught sight of a slender, young man with white-blond hair sitting on the side of the bed. He'd propped up his bare feet on the side rails and hunched forward as if he were trying to curl into a ball. One arm hugged his stomach, and the other lifted a tissue to his mouth, muffling the sobs escaping him as he rocked back and forth. A shock of blond bangs fell forward, acting as a curtain to shield the young man's face.

"I'll just step out into the hallway," the officer said, offering them a grim smile. "Let me know if you need anything."

"Thank you, Officer Calhoun," Royce said.

The man on the bed must not have heard Sawyer knock or them enter the room because he let out a startled gasp, jerking his head up when he heard Royce's voice. He rose swiftly off the bed and crossed the room, giving them a closer look at his face. Maybe it was the puffy eyes or blotchy red face, but Kendall Blakemore barely looked old enough to drive. Though, his troubled, pale blue eyes belonged to someone far older than the man standing in front of him. Sawyer considered himself a good judge of character and wasn't fooled often, not even by the best charlatans. He prided himself on not having a cynical heart, even though he'd seen the very worst humanity was capable of inflicting on one another. Something about this guy with the sad eyes triggered his protective instincts, and he had to work hard to keep his objectivity in place.

"Do you know who killed Vivian? Was it that scumbag she helped walk from jail? Isn't that the kind of thing he did to those girls?" Blakemore's rapid-fire questions came one after the other. He didn't pause to breathe or allow them to answer before moving on to the next. Kendall's shoulders started shaking violently, and he began sobbing again. He turned his back on them and walked a few feet away in what Sawyer assumed was an effort to gather his composure. Royce and Sawyer exchanged a quick glance before stepping farther into the room.

"I'm Detective Key, and this is my partner, Sergeant Locke," Sawyer said. "I know this is a very upsetting time, but we need to ask you some questions."

The man took several calming breaths while keeping his back turned toward Sawyer and Royce. Sawyer used the time to glance around the room, which was drastically different from the rest of the house. Vibrant impressionist paintings in bold hues hung on the wall, a scarlet comforter covered the bed, and the furniture, while still modern, was black instead of white. Clothes were strewn over a chair, an open dresser drawer, and the foot of the bed. This room was lived in, but by whom? Sawyer's eyes locked on a large photo hanging on the wall next to the bed. It was a close-up image of a gorgeous young man with white-blond hair, seductive blue eyes, and pouty, glossy lips. The model wore an intricately designed masquerade mask, but Sawyer had no problem recognizing Kendall Blakemore.

Beside him, Royce cleared his throat. Sawyer turned to meet his gaze and was met with a quirked brow. It seemed like Royce also recognized the man in the photo and mistook Sawyer's interest. Sawyer rolled his eyes and continued looking around the room. He noticed a backpack next to the bedside table and a couple of textbooks, *Practical Contract Law for Paralegals* and *Wills, Trusts, and Administration*, lying on top of the bed, as well as a laptop, notebooks, highlighters, and pens.

"Do you reside here, Mr. Blakemore?" Sawyer asked.

The man sniffled a few more times, then turned to face them. If his grief was an act, he was one of the finest actors Sawyer had ever met. "Vivian let me move in when she found out my parents kicked me out for my queer ways. I was living out of my car at the time. I'd gone into work early one morning to wash up in the sink so no one would know I was homeless, but Vivian caught me as I was exiting the restroom."

"She just let you move in?" Royce asked. It didn't match what he knew about the hardnosed woman.

Blakemore lifted his chin higher. Anger and resentment temporarily eclipsed the sadness in his glacial gaze. "I wasn't her boy toy if that's what you're implying."

"Not at all," Royce said calmly. "I'm sorry if it's the impression I gave you, Mr. Blakemore. How long have you lived here?"

"I rent the room. I couldn't afford to pay Vivian much, but I earn my keep. So what if I work weekends at The Cockpit as a waiter to supplement my income from my law firm to pay for college and expenses? I make more serving drinks to horny men in two nights than I make in two weeks at Elderwood, Johnson, and McClary." Blakemore narrowed his eyes at Sawyer. "What? You don't believe I earn good tips, Detective?"

The Cockpit had been Sawyer's favorite watering hole when he was looking to score. He vividly recalled the barely there uniforms the servers wore. The owner had chosen an aviation theme to match the club name and hired the hottest men to don the pilot's hat, aviator glasses, mesh crop tops, and navy blue booty shorts with gold aviator wings on the crotch and the club's name on the back, making every horny man want to bury his dick inside those cockpits. Sawyer had gone home with a few servers prior to meeting Royce but had never run into Kendall there. He had zero doubts Blakemore raked in the big bucks on the nights he worked.

"I'm not questioning your earnings," Sawyer replied. "I'm just surprised you're old enough to serve drinks in a club."

Blakemore snorted. "I'll be twenty-five next month." Sawyer would need to see proof to believe it but decided to let it drop since it wasn't essential to the case.

"How long have you rented a room from Ms. Gross?" Royce asked, getting them back on topic.

"Almost nine months," he said. He closed his eyes, and fresh tears spilled down his face. "I've worked as her assistant for five years. You couldn't find two more different people than Vivian and me if you tried, but we just clicked from the moment we met. I taught her how to lighten up and laugh, and she taught me how to stand up for myself, even to the people I should've never had to fear. She bought me the biggest bottle of champagne when the Supreme Court ruled gay marriage bans were unconstitutional. She championed me every step of the way when she had nothing to gain in return. I cannot believe she's gone. Did *he* do this?"

"Who?" Royce asked, playing dumb.

"You, of all people, know exactly who I'm talking about, Sergeant Locke," Blakemore said dryly. "Franco Humphries." He said the name slowly and succinctly enunciated each syllable.

"I can't answer those types of questions during an ongoing investigation," Royce countered. "I am curious why you immediately assumed Humphries killed her. The man owes his freedom to her—freedom she felt he deserved, by the way. You think Humphries repaid her faith in him by killing her?"

Blakemore snorted. "Do not mistake her faith in the legal system as faith in her clients."

"Are you saying Ms. Gross believed Franco Humphries was guilty of raping and killing those women?" Royce asked.

Kendall Blakemore shook his head, his lips tipping up in a sardonic smile. "Nice try, Sergeant. Vivian didn't discuss her personal thoughts about her clients' innocence or guilt with me. She did, however, express her commitment to making sure the police follow the letter of the law and not railroad people through a corrupt system."

Sawyer glanced at his partner to judge his reaction. The skin around Royce's eyes tightened, and his eyes turned a flinty, cold gray. When his lips curled into a mocking sneer, Sawyer knew he needed to intervene before Royce said something they'd regret later. They needed this guy to help them.

"You still haven't explained why you jumped to the conclusion that Humphries was our killer," Sawyer prodded.

Blakemore shrugged. "He's always rubbed me the wrong way."

Always led Sawyer to believe Blakemore knew Humphries, or at least knew of him, longer than the few months Gross had represented Humphries. Then again, maybe he'd retained Gross for other legal matters in the past.

"Always?" Royce countered, voicing Sawyer's thoughts.

The blond man pinched the bridge of his nose and sighed. "He just got under my skin since the first day I stepped into his classroom." Royce wondered if Blakemore was familiar with any of the professor's victims.

"I saw your textbooks on the bed. Are you taking paralegal studies at South University?" Sawyer asked.

"I am," Blakemore said, dropping his hand and meeting Sawyer's gaze. "Yeah, I knew Tara Riker from school. I didn't know her well, and we didn't hang out, but she was a nice person. Vivian and I argued a few times about her representing Humphries. She just kept reiterating that everyone deserves legal representation and a fair trial." Blakemore looked at Royce with a conciliatory expression on his face. "I didn't mean to imply you are corrupt, Sergeant Locke."

Royce nodded politely but allowed Sawyer to continue the interview.

"Why don't you tell us how you discovered Ms. Gross," Sawyer said.

A hard shiver rolled its way through Blakemore. "I haven't talked to her since I left the office on Friday evening. I stopped by here to do some homework and shower before going to my gig at TC. I hooked up with a guy that night and didn't come home until this morning. I think I got home around four thirty. I have early classes every Monday, then head to the law office around lunchtime."

"You didn't communicate with her over the weekend to let her know you weren't coming home?" Royce asked, breaking his silence.

"I'm not a child who needs permission, Sergeant."

"Of course not," Royce said, but it sounded patronizing to

Sawyer, and judging by Blakemore's sour expression, he thought so too.

"You said you've been gone since Friday night," Sawyer said. "We're going to need the names of the people who can confirm where you were this weekend."

"People?" Blakemore asked, his voice lowering as his eyebrows rose toward his hairline. "What kind of slut do you think I am?" *Uh-oh.*

"You're not a child who needs permission," Royce reminded him before Sawyer could respond.

"Touché," Blakemore said dryly.

"When I asked for a list of names, I was referring to your coworkers and whoever can account for your time. I'm not judging you," Sawyer told him.

"You guys actually think *I* killed Vivian?" Blakemore asked, a hint of panic creeping into his voice.

"It's standard procedure for us to ask these questions, Mr. Blakemore. No one is accusing you of any wrongdoing," Sawyer replied evenly.

"Fine," Blakemore said. Then he pivoted and walked over to the bed where he picked up a notebook and a pen. He opened the notebook, flipped to a blank page, and started writing. "I'll list my hours and the bartenders working each night, which is a lot easier than remembering the wait staff. As for my hookup, it was the same guy each night. I stayed over at his place."

"You didn't come back here at any point to grab an overnight bag?" Royce asked.

Blakemore snorted but didn't look up from his task. "I keep extra clothes and uniforms in my locker at TC. I didn't need clothes for the rest of the weekend." The blond man let out a sigh as if he were reliving happier moments. "I didn't get his phone number, and I don't know the guy's last name since it's not like we yell them out in bed, but I ordered Chinese food through my Door Dash app and had it delivered to his home." The blond man pulled his phone out of his back pocket and began thumbing through his phone. After finding what he was looking for, Blakemore jotted the address down. "Here you go," he said, crossing the room and handing the sheet of notebook paper to Sawyer who folded it and moved on with the interview.

"Did you notice anything out of place when you arrived this morning?" Sawyer asked. "Were any doors unlocked? Was anything missing?"

Blakemore shook his head emphatically. "Nothing felt off, and the front door was locked like usual. The responding officer told me the laundry room door was unlocked when he walked the property. I guess that's how her killer got in. Vivian must've taken the trash out and forgot to lock the door."

"Did she do that frequently?" Royce asked.

The blond man nodded. "I honestly didn't pay enough attention to my surroundings to realize if anything is missing or disturbed. I knew something was wrong when I saw her bedroom light was on. Her door was closed, but I could see the light spilling onto the tile floor from beneath the door. While Vivian was an early riser, her being awake at four thirty was strange. I thought she was sick. I knocked on her door, but Vivian didn't answer. Her Mercedes was in her parking slot, so I knew she was home. I knocked harder and shouted her name." Blakemore's voice got louder, and his cadence sped up as he relived the anxiety he'd experienced while standing outside her door. "I just fucking knew something was wrong, but—" His words choked off as another sob wracked his body. "I never would've guessed I'd find her dead."

"Do you mind taking a look around with us now to see if anything is missing?" Sawyer asked.

"Sure," he said, nodding. "I'll do my best."

The price tag on the luxury townhouse was probably steep, but it didn't come with a lot of square footage. A living area, small dining room, generously sized kitchen, home office, and powder room made up the first floor, while the second story boasted two bedrooms and two full bathrooms. Like with their bedrooms, Blakemore's bathroom was as cluttered as Gross's was tidy.

The final stop on their tour was the home office located in the rear of the home, adjacent to the kitchen.

"I shouldn't let you in here," Blakemore said, turning and blocking the doorway. "She brings work home often, and attorney-client privilege is still in force."

"Her files are protected, not her entire office," Royce replied calmly, even though Sawyer could sense how much his partner disliked the younger man. "I need you to look around and let me know if you notice anything missing. We'll get one of the partners from the law firm to supervise us collecting evidence from her home office."

"Oh," Blakemore said, sounding disappointed Royce wasn't putting up a bigger fight.

"We need to notify her next of kin," Sawyer said, changing the subject. "Can you tell me who that is?"

"Vivian was an only child. Her parents were in their mid-forties when she was born and are now both deceased. She might have living relatives, but she's never mentioned anyone to me. I'm sure Vivian has her estate in order. Bill Elderwood is the senior partner, and he probably has copies of her paperwork on file at the office. I can call him if you like."

"We'll take care of that," Sawyer replied. "I'll take his phone number if you have it."

"Uh, yeah," Blakemore said, pulling his phone from his back pocket. He rattled off the number so fast Sawyer had to ask him to repeat it twice. "Oh, I just thought of something. Her husband would officially be her next of kin since their divorce wasn't final, right?"

"Husband?" Sawyer had heard the woman's name mentioned hundreds of times but never in conjunction with a husband. He'd seen her at dozens of events but never with a date. He always figured she was married to her career.

"Jack Vincenzo."

"The state senator?" Sawyer asked, recalling the lanky blonde who appeared on the statesman's arm at a fundraiser not long ago.

"The very same," Blakemore said. "I know you're wondering how you've never heard about it, but very few people know. They got married when they were kids; I'm talking barely out of high school. They got a dissolution sometime during college, but their lawyer never filed it with the courts. Jack found out when he applied for a marriage license to wed his latest arm candy. Vivian was stalling, and Jack had grown increasingly impatient."

"Why do they need to sign new paperwork if it was only a matter of filing the documents?" Royce asked.

"The lawyer they'd hired lost the paperwork. He was disbarred a few years back and has disappeared off the face of the earth." Blakemore lowered his voice. "Vivian said he'd crossed some dangerous people and probably had a lot of help disappearing. Anyway, there were no papers to file, so they had to start over from scratch. Handling a dissolution for broke-ass twenty-somethings is a no-brainer, but they're no longer those kids. They both had a lot to lose if their divorce wasn't handled properly."

"Why wouldn't Ms. Gross want to sign the divorce papers?" Royce asked.

Blakemore exhaled deeply and released a shaky breath. "Truthfully, I don't think she ever got over him. I think Vivian saw this as fate intervening. Maybe she hoped he'd have a change of heart. Based on the huge fight I overheard last week when he called her, I would say it was hopeless."

"How huge?" Royce asked.

"I heard him say, 'If you don't sign the papers, I will kill you.'"

Sawyer looked at Royce. "That's pretty huge."

CHAPTER 8

VIVIAN GROSS HAD BEEN MARRIED TO JACK VINCENZO FOR DECADES. ROYCE still couldn't believe it, but he tamped down the urge to tell Blakemore to hurry the fuck up as he walked around Gross's home office. The scheme inside the small room was as sterile as the living room. The white, glass, and chrome were so bright they practically screamed. Royce wondered how Gross could hear herself think in the space. The only spot of color was a bouquet of pink roses on the credenza behind her desk.

What felt like an eternity later, Blakemore said, "Nothing is out of place. Her expensive MacBook is still here, so the motive isn't robbery."

He started to tell the kid to leave discovering the motive to the professionals but caught himself, which was a good thing considering the guy looked like he was on the verge of collapsing at any minute. "You won't be able to stay here as long as the home is a crime scene. Do you have a place you can go?"

Blakemore briefly closed his eyes and nodded. "I can bum around on a friend's couch, I'm sure. Can I pack some clothes and get my school stuff?"

"Of course," Royce told him, pulling out his business card and handing it to him. "Here's my number if you think of anything else we should know."

"Thanks. I wrote my cell phone number on the paper," Blakemore said, nodding toward the forgotten folded paper in Sawyer's hand. Finding out the identity of Blakemore's mystery man took a back seat to the bombshell the guy dropped on them. "Please let me know if I can help in any way. Vivian was a good person. She didn't deserve to die like that."

Neither did Tara, Abby, Christi, or Harper. Royce said, "We'll be in touch if we have more questions."

"I'll just head upstairs and pack a bag, then," Blakemore said. He glanced around the space, looking unsure if he should leave the detectives in her office. He must've decided he didn't have the energy left to argue with them because he nodded and left the room.

Royce gestured for Sawyer to lead the way, then closed the door behind them, securing the room like he'd assured the kid he would. They found Chief Mendoza in the living room. He was talking quietly into his cell phone, so they remained in the dining room, giving him privacy to conclude his call. Glancing up, he raised his forefinger, signaling he needed a minute.

"I bet he wants to give you a different finger already," Sawyer said quietly.

"Most likely," Royce agreed, meeting Sawyer's gaze. "So, are you familiar with The Cockpit?"

Humor shimmered in Sawyer's warm, brown eyes. Royce knew the answer, but Mendoza wrapped up his call and waved them over before Sawyer could confirm his suspicions. That only made the immature hissy fit rising inside him worse. He'd get over his irrational jealousy without making Sawyer feel guilty over choices he'd been free to make. Royce was so busy clapping himself on the back that he missed half of the exchange between Sawyer and their chief.

"Seriously?" Mendoza asked, leading Royce to believe Sawyer had already dropped the bomb. The chief moved closer and lowered his voice. "Senator Jack Vincenzo?"

"According to the kid," Royce said.

"What kid?" the chief asked.

"Blakemore," Sawyer clarified. "Locke calls everyone under the age of thirty a kid," Sawyer told Mendoza. "He acts like he's turning ninety-four in a few weeks instead of thirty-four."

Royce just shrugged. "In many ways, I feel like I've aged sixty years since my last birthday." He refused to let his mind wander to just how different his celebration would be this year. It would be his first one without Marcus since they met as kids, but then again, it would be his first *with* Sawyer. One man would never replace the other because their roles in his life were vastly different, but Sawyer was his key to everything he'd ever wanted, plus the things he'd never allowed himself to wish for when he blew out birthday candles as a kid. Sawyer was his everything.

"I imagine so," Mendoza said sympathetically. Then he shifted the conversation back to the case. "Do you have any reason not to believe Blakemore?"

Royce and Sawyer exchanged a glance before shaking their heads.

"No, sir," Royce said.

"I can't see what he'd gain from lying about Ms. Gross being married, especially to someone as high profile as Senator Vincenzo."

Mendoza nodded. "It's nearly impossible to believe they've kept the truth buried during this hostile political climate."

While Royce didn't follow politics closely, he read the paper every day and knew Savannah's other golden boy, Jack Vincenzo, was engaged in a highly contested re-election bid with both a challenger from the other party and one within his own. With the primary elections only five and a half months away, his campaign could not afford this kind of scandal.

"According to Blakemore, things had turned really nasty between them recently, and he threatened to kill her."

Mendoza narrowed his eyes. "How recently?"

"Last week." The timing was as suspect as the brilliance of Vincenzo's white smile. *Those damn teeth would fit right in around here.*

"Shit," Mendoza said. "Tread lightly, gentlemen. The senator was just in town for the weekend for a fundraiser. I'm not sure if he's still here or if he's returned to Atlanta."

"We'll head out to his residence here first to see if he's home. If not, we'll call his office and find out where he is so we can speak to him in person. There's no way I'm making this notification over the phone and missing his reaction," Sawyer said.

Mendoza nodded sharply. "Keep me informed."

"Yes, sir," they said at the same time.

"What about Carnegie and Fuentes, sir?" Royce asked. "Do you want them to shadow us today?"

Mendoza said, "Not while interviewing high-profile persons of interest. I'll have them assist the uniforms conducting the neighborhood canvass."

"Fair enough," Royce said.

Mendoza's phone rang again, and he stepped aside to answer it. "Good morning, Commissioner Rigby," he said as Royce and Sawyer walked away.

Once inside the car, Sawyer handed Royce the folded piece of paper Blakemore had given him since he was driving. "You can see who the mystery Romeo is while I drive out to Vincenzo's place."

"You know where the man lives?" Royce asked, then realized how silly his question was. Sawyer's family had money and prestige, so, of course, Vincenzo courted them. Sawyer had probably attended functions at the man's home on more than one occasion since he was elected to the state senate to represent their district in 2016.

"My parents are big supporters," Sawyer admitted. "You'll find this part interesting."

"Yeah?" Royce asked. It was too dark outside to read what Blakemore had written on his note, so he flipped on his phone flashlight while Sawyer navigated.

"He lives in the same gated community as Clark Seaver."

Royce jerked his head over to look at Sawyer. "You don't say?

This case is too fucking similar to Putz's." Locals knew Clark Seaver as Jacque, the yoga instructor, but Sawyer, and now Royce, knew the man's other alias was Randy Dagger, former gay porn star. After they'd started dating, Sawyer told him Randy was Vic's favorite porn star, which prompted Royce to confess he'd never watched gay porn. Sawyer remedied the situation immediately, but Royce had wanted to avoid Randy's porn scenes in case they ran into him again. "If this case mirrors Putz's, it will end with you tripping an elderly man while in pursuit."

"The fool tripped over his own two feet," Sawyer groused, making Royce grin. "God, do you want to guess how many times I jerked off while thinking about you on your motorcycle? You added extra swagger to your strut after climbing off the beast."

"Hey, now. I don't strut." Royce's voice was barely more than a croak since his mouth had suddenly gone dry. "We have a homicide to solve, so let's keep our focus there."

Sawyer hummed in the back of his throat. "Yeah, okay."

To distract himself, Royce turned his attention back to the piece of paper Blakemore gave them. He skipped past the names of the club employees to reach the guy Blakemore had spent every non-working hour with since Friday evening.

"Holy shit," Royce said, then started laughing.

"What?" Sawyer strained to get a look at the page.

"Keep your eyes on the road," Royce admonished playfully.

"Is it someone we know?" Sawyer wanted to know.

Royce continued to laugh as he turned off the flashlight and pulled up the contact he was looking for on his phone. He placed the call on speakerphone to appease Sawyer's curiosity.

"This had better be really fucking good." Jonah's voice was heavy with sleep and extra gravelly.

Sawyer's mouth gaped open, and Royce had to stifle a laugh.

"I bet you are exhausted after the weekend you had," Royce replied.

"And how would you know what I did this weekend?" Jonah asked, sounding alert suddenly.

"He's about five-ten, has white-blond hair and really light blue eyes," Royce countered.

"And he bought you Chinese food," Sawyer added.

"What the fuck is going on?" Jonah demanded to know. "Is something wrong with Kendall?"

"He's physically fine, but someone important to him died over the weekend," Royce said, then filled Jonah in the rest of the way.

"Vivian Gross is a victim of a copycat killing, and Kendall is her roommate and was the one who found her body," Jonah slowly repeated like he couldn't believe it.

"And you're his alibi, buddy," Sawyer said. "Blakemore claims the two of you met on Friday, and he spent all his free time with you. He said he arrived home around four thirty this morning."

Jonah cleared his throat. "Yeah, it's true. I mean, I don't know where he lives, so I can't vouch for the time he arrived, but he left my place at just after four." He sighed heavily, and Royce imagined he scrubbed one of those ham-sized hands over his face. Now that he knew Jonah was Kendall's mystery man, it was hard not to picture them together. They were as different as night and day in looks, size, and demeanor. Of course, he'd only seen Blakemore at one of the lowest times in his life, so it was unfair to judge his personality based on the encounter. Jonah had obviously liked what he saw and hadn't wanted to let go of him.

"We're going to interview his coworkers at The Cockpit to verify he clocked in and out when he was supposed to and hadn't disappeared for great lengths of time," Sawyer said.

"Um, he was probably late returning from one or two dinner breaks over the weekend," Jonah said sheepishly. *Damn. How skimpy are the servers' uniforms?*

"Does that mean you hung out at The Cockpit while he was working?" Royce asked.

"Some, but I didn't stick around for the entire duration of his shifts." Jonah cleared his throat. "Just a good chunk of each one."

Sawyer and Royce exchanged grins. *Poor Felix.* Royce hadn't missed the way Felix had nearly come in his pants when he laid eyes on Jonah.

"Where is Kendall now?" Jonah asked.

"He said he was going to pack a bag and go stay with a friend," Royce replied.

"I should've asked for his phone number," Jonah groused.

Royce clicked the flashlight back on and aimed his phone at the sheet of paper. "I'm going to do you a solid, and I want you to remember it someday. Got a pen?"

They heard Jonah opening drawers on his end. "Why can't I ever find a pen when I need one?"

"Don't worry about it," Royce said. "I'll text it to you after I clear it with Blakemore first." He shouldn't assume it would be okay with Blakemore if Jonah had his number just because they spent a lot of time naked together over the weekend. One could argue that Blakemore would've given his phone number to Jonah if he'd wanted the big man to have it.

"Yeah, okay," Jonah said. "That's only fair. Thanks, Royce."

"No problem. Talk soon, big guy." Royce disconnected and called Blakemore's number.

"Hello," Blakemore said. It was apparent he'd been crying again.

"Mr. Blakemore, this is Sergeant Locke calling. We confirmed your alibi with Jonah, and he'd like to speak to you. Is it okay if I share your number with him?"

"You called him this early?" Blakemore asked, sounding astounded.

"Jonah is a friend," Royce told him. "He's worried about you."

"Oh," he said softly. "That's nice. It's okay if you give him my number. Thank you for checking first."

"No problem. Take care," Royce said before ending the call.

"I don't want to start an argument, but 'take care' isn't technically the same as a goodbye."

"Bullshit," Royce groused as he texted Blakemore's number to Jonah. Then he turned his head and looked at Sawyer, who looked ridiculously gorgeous in the glow from the dashboard. "You're too handsome for your own good."

"Shut up." Sawyer absently raised his hand, touching his face where the skin was still pink and healing.

"I bet the waiters at The Cockpit fought over serving you," Royce teased. "I know how you like to leave a big tip."

"How do you even know I've gone there?" Sawyer asked.

Royce laughed. "You made a face when Blakemore said he worked there."

"I made a face?" Sawyer shook his head. "You're just guessing and looking to rile me up or trick me into answering a question before you have to ask it."

Sawyer wasn't entirely wrong, but Royce recognized the effort Sawyer exuded to *not react* to the name of the club. His facial expression was more neutral than usual, which Royce had learned was his way of masking what he was feeling or thinking. Since they'd been talking about Blakemore and The Cockpit at the time, Royce knew damned well what had rattled his composure. Throw in Jonah's smitten reaction to Kendall, and there was only one question on Royce's mind. "How sexy are their uniforms?"

Sawyer squirmed a little in his seat before answering. "Pretty damn hot. It's an aviator theme." Sawyer described the uniforms in minute detail. "Not that I imagined Blakemore in the uniform or anything."

"Have some fond memories from the club, huh?" Royce asked. It took a monumental effort on his part to stifle the jealousy rising inside him.

Sawyer braked at a red light and looked at Royce. "If by fond memories, you're referring to meaningless sex where both parties get off quickly and without emotion, then yes. I didn't make the kind of connection there that Jonah made with Kendall." Sawyer briefly closed his eyes and took a deep breath. "I wouldn't trade what I have with you for an army of waiters dressed in those uniforms or endless nights of meaningless, emotionless sex."

Royce chuckled, making Sawyer frown. "The light is green."

Sawyer shifted his attention back to driving. "You don't believe me. Is that why you laughed?"

"Of course, I believe you," Royce said, reaching over to cup the back of Sawyer's neck. "I'm the second half of this whole, so I know damn well what we have is precious and rare." He chuckled again. "I just can't help thinking The Cockpit's uniform sounds like something a tribute band would wear while paying homage to The Village People."

Sawyer laughed so hard he cried. He was still wiping tears from his eyes when they pulled up to the ridiculous guard shack at the fancy-schmancy gated community where Randy Dagger and State Senator Jack Vincenzo lived. The liveried dude guarding the wrought iron gates looked like he couldn't fight his way out of a wet paper bag. The man's thick mustache weighed more than the rest of him.

Sawyer held up his badge, expecting the guard to unlock the gates immediately. Instead, Mustache Man picked up a clipboard with a pen attached to it by a string. The guy fumbled around with the dangling pen for a good thirty seconds before he outsmarted it—an inanimate object incapable of thought or evasive maneuvers. Royce sent up a prayer of gratitude this man wasn't armed.

"I need to write down who you're here to visit." Mustache Man's nasally voice and attempt at bravado grated on Royce's nerves.

"This badge says you don't," Sawyer countered. "You may write down our badge numbers and the time we enter or leave, but I am not required to state my business to you. You're more than welcome to call the station and confirm our identities. If you're not going to pick up the phone, then open this gate right now, or I'll arrest you for obstructing official police business."

Mustache Man let out a nervous squeak as he released the gates.

"Have a nice day," Royce yelled through Sawyer's open window as they drove off. To Sawyer, he said, "I'm so turned on right now."

"The mustache does it for you, huh?" Sawyer quipped. "You're imagining it tickling sensitive areas, aren't you?"

Royce shuddered hard and not in a good way. "And there goes my arousal." He might like having Sawyer tickle his inner thighs with a mustache, but not the idiot back at the guard shack.

Sawyer laughed. "Probably a good thing." He glanced over at Royce before taking a left at a fork in the road. "Care to tell me what got you so worked up?"

"Your forcefulness back there with Mustache Man. It does for me what those little aviator uniforms do for you."

"Shut up about the uniforms, will ya?"

"You know I love you, right?" Royce asked.

"Um, yeah, but I'm not sure I like where this is going."

Royce reached over and placed his hand on Sawyer's thigh. "Last night, as I drifted to sleep, I told myself there was nothing I wouldn't do to please you. I've had a change of heart."

"Okay, I *definitely* don't like where this is going."

"I discovered the one thing that's off-limits," Royce continued.

"Just one?" Sawyer asked sardonically.

"I will not put on the aviator uniform for you and parade around."

Sawyer burst into another round of laughter. "I get the impression you think I've lived a much more exciting life than I've actually led. I have never once asked anyone to dress up and parade around to please me."

"Not true," Royce emphatically said, waggling his finger. "You asked if I still owned my Marine Corps dress blues."

"I did, and the idea of how you'd look in that uniform makes my eyes roll back in my head."

"Not while you're driving, GB," Royce warned.

Ignoring the last part, Sawyer continued. "But I never mentioned you parading around in it. I only wanted to strip it off you."

Royce's mouth went dry again, or maybe it hadn't fully recovered from Sawyer's show of muscle with Mustache Man. "Is this a good time to mention I dug out the uniform from the closet to see if it fits?"

Sawyer made a noise that was part growl and part hum. "And did it?" he asked hopefully.

"Sadly, no. I was a scrawny kid back then."

"It's the thought that counts," Sawyer said wistfully. "Just so we're absolutely clear, I would wear The Cockpit uniform for you, if it pleased you."

"Are you trying to say you're a better boyfriend than I am?" Royce asked, recalling the tight booty shorts Sawyer had described. They'd make Sawyer's toned legs look two miles long, and the mesh crop top would show off his ripped abdomen and pecs. Royce was two seconds away from taking him up on his offer when he heard Sawyer chuckling low. He'd nearly fallen for it. "Asshole," Royce groused.

"Dickhead," Sawyer returned playfully, as he followed the road deeper into the subdivision. He turned on to a side street, then slowed down as he approached a long driveway that disappeared into the woods. Sawyer sighed, and the mood shifted in the car. Their reprieve from madness was over. They dealt with death every day, and finding healthy ways of coping, such as teasing one another, helped prevent burnout. "My mom thinks Jack Vincenzo is a great man, so he better not prove her wrong."

Flashing red and blue lights appeared in the distance behind them just as Sawyer turned into the driveway.

"What the fuck?" he asked, stopping the car.

"Those aren't the right lights for a police vehicle," Royce said, squinting into the darkness. "Private security?"

Shifting the car into park, Sawyer growled in irritation. "Fucking Mustache Man must've called someone."

It took nearly a minute and a half for the golf cart with emergency lights on top to reach them.

Don't laugh and make the situation worse. Don't laugh and make the situation worse. Don't laugh... Royce caught sight of the glorified mall cop sauntering to their car and couldn't make it through reciting his edict a third time before his body shook with laughter.

"Damn you, dickhead." Sawyer cleared his throat and fought back a laugh. "What seems to be the problem?" he asked when the rent-a-cop approached his window.

"My problem is that the two of you took off before Randy could do his job properly," the man said. His voice held enough twang for four men. He raised his hand to the can of pepper spray on his utility belt.

Sawyer, the voice of calm and reason, pointed at the man and said, "You better have a really sure hand because I will arrest you if you blast me in the face with pepper spray, either accidentally or on purpose. I offered to let Randy call the station to confirm our identities, but he chose to open the gates instead. I don't see how that's our problem."

"You intimidated him," Mall Cop countered. "Now, I find you turning into Senator Vincenzo's driveway?"

"You're out of your mind," Sawyer countered. "He's employed to protect the residents in this community—some of the wealthiest in Savannah, by the way—and he can't remain calm long enough to make a simple phone call to the police station to verify our badges are legit? I call bullshit."

"You cops are all the same. You think your badge excuses—"

"Shut your mouth, get out your cell phone, and call the station, or I'm going to arrest you for obstruction and have your golf cart towed to the impound lot. Your choice."

Two minutes later, Mall Cop stomped back to his golf cart after confirming their identities and sped away at fifteen miles per hour.

"Tell me this is all just a weird dream," Sawyer said, continuing up the driveway.

"I wish."

Sawyer pulled up in front of the massive house and put his car in park. Royce blew out a whistle as he looked up at the stunning three-story brick house. The strategically placed landscape lighting bathed the first floor in soft light, giving the grand home a welcoming glow in the predawn hour.

"Vincenzo is a former federal prosecutor, right?" Royce asked.

Sawyer nodded. "And Vivian was a criminal defense attorney. They both studied the same laws, but their approaches would've been drastically different." He smiled wryly. "It's probably why their relationship failed."

Porchlights suddenly flipped on, the front door opened, and Senator Vincenzo stepped onto the porch wearing sleep pants and a Duke University T-shirt.

"Paul Blart must've called him," Sawyer groused.

Royce was shocked Sawyer even knew that movie since slapstick comedies weren't his style, but he wasn't surprised they'd both thought of the white knight on the golf cart as a mall cop. "Yeah, well, the element of surprise is still on our side if he's not expecting us to notify him about Gross's death. I bet you a blow job he will lawyer up."

"I'll take that bet." Sawyer killed the engine, released his seat belt, and opened the door.

Royce followed his lead and joined him at the bottom of the porch steps.

Always the statesman, Jack Vincenzo greeted them with the patented politician's smile, but there was no disguising the worry in his dark eyes.

"Sawyer," the man said warmly, extending his hand. "I told your parents at the benefit they hosted over the weekend that I was sorry to miss you and hoped to catch up before returning to Atlanta. This wasn't what I had in mind."

Royce stiffened at learning about the benefit, but his steps didn't falter. He hoped his shock didn't register on his face. The likelihood

Evangeline hadn't invited Sawyer to attend was small, but Sawyer had never brought it up. Was it because Royce hadn't been included? No way. That wasn't Evangeline's style, and the woman loved him, which meant she'd invited them both, and Sawyer hadn't even seen fit to mention it to him. Just like Royce's celebration dinner that never happened because of their injuries from the fire. Insecurities Royce thought he'd conquered rose to the surface once again. Was Sawyer embarrassed by him?

"This is my partner, Sergeant Locke," Sawyer said, yanking his mind back to the case. "I don't think the two of you have met."

"I haven't had the honor, yet," Royce said, extending his hand to Vincenzo. Royce hoped his irritation and resentment weren't obvious because it wasn't aimed at either of the men standing on the porch with him. He directed it solely at himself for his inability to bury his feelings of inadequacy. He needed to trust Sawyer had a good reason and set it aside to discuss later when they weren't about to tell a state senator that a person he once loved, a woman he was supposedly still wed to, had been murdered.

"The honor is mine," Vincenzo said, firmly shaking Royce's hand. "Come on in. We can talk in my study."

When they stepped inside the home, Royce noticed a woman wrapped in a pale-yellow terry cloth robe standing on the landing at the top of a grand spiral staircase. He nodded and said, "Ma'am."

Vincenzo looked up to the second story when Royce spoke, and his eyes softened when they landed on his fiancée. "Go back to bed, dear. Everything will be fine."

"The police are here. Something is very wrong," she countered. "Is Jack in some kind of danger?"

Royce thought it said a lot about their relationship that she assumed he was in danger instead of legal trouble. "No, ma'am," he assured her. He returned his gaze to meet the senator's. "This shouldn't take long."

"By all means," Vincenzo said, gesturing his hand down the hall.

"Follow me." The senator headed toward the back of the house without waiting to see if they listened. He was used to people obeying his commands, and it showed in his proud bearing and confident stride.

But they didn't immediately follow him, because Sawyer had turned to look at Royce. Dark eyes searched his gaze. He knew, or at least suspected, where Royce's mind had gone upon learning about the benefit, and he wanted assurances they were okay.

Royce's demons were his to battle, and he knew Sawyer had his own to contend with. He had every intention of discussing it with Sawyer like a grown-ass adult, but it would wait for an appropriate time. He winked at Sawyer and said, "Let's not keep the senator waiting, asshole."

CHAPTER 9

T HE DREAD IN THE PIT OF SAWYER'S STOMACH EASED WHEN ROYCE winked and used his pet name, but his reprieve was short-lived. The politician's plastic veneer cracked when they reached his study, exposing human vulnerability on the statesman's handsome features. The room was designed to give a bold, masculine feel with a dark stain on the desk and built-in bookcases, navy blue leather furniture and red and blue plaid wallpaper covering the walls. The strategically placed windows would allow enough sunlight to keep the space from feeling oppressive, but at the early hour, the dark colors seemed to absorb the light from the fixtures throughout the room.

Rather than make a power move and sit behind a desk fit for a president, Vincenzo opted for the sitting area near a grand fireplace. The senator looked like he'd aged a dozen years since he first greeted them outside. "A million scenarios have run through my mind during the short walk to my study. Lucinda is correct; no good comes out of a visit from the police at this hour of the day. So, let's just rip off the Band-Aid, shall we?"

Before they could notify him of Vivian's death, they had to first confirm he was legally her next of kin. Since Sawyer knew the senator on a more personal level, he decided to take the lead. "Senator, I have to ask questions that are awkward and will feel invasive, but it's unavoidable." Vincenzo flinched but nodded for him to continue. "Are you the legal spouse of Vivian Gross?"

Vincenzo's eyes widened, and the color leached from his face. "Vivian? Oh my god. What's this about?"

"Before I can answer your question, I need you to answer mine," Sawyer said.

Vincenzo rose to his feet and paced to the fireplace, where he propped an elbow on the mantel. Keeping his back to them, he said, "Yes, she is still legally my wife. We got married when we were just eighteen years old. We thought we knew all there was about life and love. No money? We didn't care because we had each other. We both came from humble beginnings, and we believed we could achieve our dreams together and have a fairy-tale love. It was us versus the world. We were such stupid fools," Vincenzo said wistfully. When he turned to face them again, silent tears ran down his cheeks, leaving silvery trails in their wake. "Is she..." Unable to voice the unthinkable, he let his words trail off.

Sawyer swallowed hard. "I'm sorry to inform you that Vivian was a victim of a homicide over the weekend."

"God, no," Vincenzo said, covering his face with his hands to muffle his anguished sobs. Sawyer and Royce allowed him a few minutes to gather his composure before continuing.

"We were informed this morning that you're her next of kin," Royce said.

Vincenzo lowered his hands. "Informed by whom?" Even during grief, Sawyer could see the wheels turning in his shrewd brain. Was he wondering who knew his secret and could expose him?

"We're not at liberty to disclose that information, sir," Sawyer told him. While his mother believed Jack Vincenzo was a decent man, Sawyer wasn't willing to risk Kendall's safety. Politicians had resorted to shady and often deadly tactics to silence people standing in the way of what they wanted. He also wouldn't lie and tell Vincenzo his secret was safe because that wasn't a guarantee he could keep.

The tension faded from Vincenzo's body, and his shoulders slumped forward as he returned to the sitting area and lowered himself to his chair. "It doesn't matter, does it?" he asked, staring into space. "Vivian is gone."

"I'm afraid so, Senator," Royce said.

Vincenzo took a deep breath, then pulled himself together. The vague, distant expression in his dark eyes morphed into sharp awareness, and his slack body returned to a rigid, proud posture. "I'm not only her next of kin, I'm also your primary suspect. Is that right?"

"No, sir," Sawyer said. Of course, he was a person of interest, but they'd get more information out of the man if he believed otherwise. Police work was often like poker, and a detective had to know when to hold his cards and when to show them. Sawyer liked to win—both at poker, as their friends had painfully learned, and solving crimes. Besides, they only had Kendall Blakemore's word that Vincenzo had threatened to kill Vivian over the paperwork. "Can you tell us about your relationship with Ms. Gross and any insight you might have about who would want her dead."

"She was the most vivacious and infuriating person I have ever known, but there was no one you'd want fighting in your corner more than Vivian. She was fierce and tenacious, but Vivian never let her ambition skew her ethics." Vincenzo glanced at Royce and chuckled. Sawyer glanced at his partner, but Royce had fixed his neutral mask back in place by that time. "I know it sounds odd for a former prosecutor to boast about a criminal defense attorney's moral codes, but it's true. She didn't need to cheat or lie to beat opposing counsel in the courtroom. She exposed their flaws and their failures at due diligence. To her, there is nothing more egregious than a society with a corrupt justice system that sends innocent people to prison. Shouldn't all lawyers feel that way? While the world will remember Vivian for her more sensational clients, Vivian would want us to memorialize her work with the Innocence Project."

"She sounds like the kind of person who shows up empty-handed to a brawl and manages to whip everyone's ass," Royce said.

Vincenzo relaxed a bit more and smiled sadly. "Sounds like you know the type, Sergeant."

Royce slightly tilted his head toward Sawyer and did a not-so-subtle double jerk. "Sharp brain and sharper tongue."

The senator nodded. "I hope you're better at making friends than Vivian was, Sawyer." Vincenzo winced. "Should I refer to you as Detective Key under the circumstance?"

"That won't be necessary, Senator," Sawyer replied. "When did you find out your attorney never filed the dissolution paperwork with the courts? And forgive me for asking, but how did two aspiring attorneys fail to notice they'd never received final paperwork?"

Vincenzo quirked a brow. "Come on, Sawyer. Surely, you remember what law school is like. You don't eat, you don't sleep, and you only think about the next class or exam. The grueling schedule prevents most law students from working unless it's clerking for a judge or fetching coffee and making copies at a law firm. That wasn't Vivian's and my reality. We would've starved. She waited tables at a popular diner while I delivered pizzas in addition to clerking. We were lucky our bosses worked around our schedules as best they could, but it left no time for us as a couple. I bet we only carved out a few hours a week for one another. We made the best of our time at first, but then, outside influences interfered, and it wasn't long before we spent all our time fighting instead of... Well, you get the picture."

Sawyer did get the picture and nodded.

"Outside influences? Like an affair or pissed-off families?" Royce asked.

"No affairs," Vincenzo said, shaking his head. "Regardless of how angry she made me, Vivian was the only woman I wanted. I was referring more to our circle of so-called friends. Vivian and I attracted and bonded with different groups of people. My buddies used to claim Vivian carried my balls around in her backpack, and her friends accused me of repressing her. They never understood how much we loved one another and how hard we craved our bond. It was pretty hard to reinforce the connection when we only had an hour or two together each week, and it wasn't long before their ugly words and jeering began to wiggle into our psyches, creating doubt where there'd never been before." Vincenzo hung his head, and his shoulders began to shake with another round of tears. "The day Vivian told me she wanted a dissolution was the worst day of my life...until now."

"I'm sorry we're forcing you to relive painful memories, Senator," Sawyer said kindly.

The man raised his head and met Sawyer's gaze with bloodshot eyes. "But you're not finished, right?"

Sawyer shook his head. "I'm afraid not, sir."

Vincenzo's posture stiffened with resolve once more as he braced himself for another emotional onslaught. "I didn't agree to the dissolution right away, but after six months of living apart, I knew Vivian wasn't coming back to me. I gave in and signed the papers, hoping we'd find our way back to each other again someday if I made it easier for her to leave me then." The senator sighed. "Dissolutions are easier and often don't require the parties to appear in court, so I thought everything was above board when I received final paperwork containing the judge's signature and the county clerk's filing documentation. I was too upset that my dream girl got away to realize they were forged. I just never questioned it."

"Until you recently got engaged?" Royce asked.

Vincenzo paused for a minute, then nodded. "We found out when we filed for a marriage license."

"Did your fiancée know about your marriage to Ms. Gross prior to that?" Sawyer asked. He'd met the woman the previous year but couldn't remember her last name.

"Lucinda knew about my past with Vivian from the very beginning."

"How?" Sawyer asked as a follow-up.

"I told her early on in our courtship when we discussed past relationships," Vincenzo said. "I've never tried to hide the fact that I'd been married. It just wasn't something that came up in conversation. My campaigns focused on how I could serve others and achieve the dreams I had for my district. While I certainly didn't act anti-family, marriage never entered the conversation."

"Never in an interview?" Royce asked.

"Reporters would ask if I was in a relationship, and I would answer honestly. I have dated over the years, but I hadn't found another woman I wanted to share my life with again until meeting Lucinda Fairchild."

"How did Ms. Fairchild take the news that you were still married to Vivian?"

"About as well as you can imagine," Vincenzo replied dryly. "She was disappointed at first, which grew into outrage when Vivian refused to play nice."

"Did you meet with Ms. Gross in person or speak to her over the phone at any time to discuss the situation, or did you handle everything through your attorneys?" Royce asked, getting to the heart of the matter.

Vincenzo hesitated as Sawyer expected a smart attorney would. "I asked my attorney to do all the communicating in the beginning, thinking it would expedite the situation."

"It didn't?" Sawyer asked.

"No," Vincenzo said somberly. "I thought showing up at her office or front doorstep after all these years would make matters worse. Vivian was a cunning lawyer who eschewed emotion in favor of facts, after all." He released a deep sigh and shook his head. Sawyer couldn't tell if he was reliving the moment they'd reunited or chastising himself for his error. "Vivian was still a human, and we can only run from past hurts for so long before it catches up to us."

Sawyer nodded "What happened?"

"About eight weeks ago, I set aside my pride and self-preservation and went to speak to her."

"Where?" Sawyer asked. Vincenzo opened his mouth as if to answer but quickly closed it again. "Senator, it's better to tell us now if we're going to find your fingerprints or DNA inside her home."

He sighed and nodded. "I didn't want to risk anyone overhearing us in a public place or at Vivian's law firm, so I surprised her at home one Saturday evening." When Kendall would've been working. "She opened the door, our eyes met, and I realized my mistake."

"Going to her home?" Royce asked.

He shook his head jerkily. "No. My mistake wasn't that I'd communicated through an attorney or showed up unannounced and uninvited at her door. My error was thinking I'd ever gotten over Vivian in the first place."

Sawyer knew where this was going. "In what parts of her home will we find your DNA, Senator?"

Vincenzo winced and dropped his head, breaking eye contact. "Probably every room except the guest bedroom."

"Including the master bedroom?" Sawyer asked. He would not give the man an easy out.

Vincenzo met his gaze once more. "Yes." Even though he anticipated the answer, it still felt like the man punched Sawyer in the gut. *Never meet your heroes.*

"How frequently did you visit Vivian's home?" Royce asked.

"As often as my schedule permitted. I had a lot of campaigning events in the area and took advantage of the proximity to meet with Vivian, either in her home or at my hotel."

"Including this weekend?" Sawyer asked.

"I spent Friday night at her house instead of staying here since Lucinda wasn't making the drive from Atlanta until a few hours before the benefit at your parents' home on Saturday." His answer surprised Sawyer because it didn't line up with what Kendall told them. It was possible they fought and made up, but it was also probable one of the men was lying, or not telling the whole truth. Vincenzo started to cry again. "When did she...die?"

"We arrived on the scene after five this morning, and the ME gave us a rough estimate of twenty-four to thirty-six hours," Royce replied. "What time did you leave her house?"

Vincenzo's brow furrowed as he contemplated the question. "I left just after nine on Saturday morning because I had a meeting with my campaign manager at ten thirty. Vivian made a big breakfast for me just like she used to do when we were first married. The woman loved to cook and was remarkably good at it."

"Senator," Sawyer said firmly but not unkindly, "we need you to account for your whereabouts from the time you left her home until we arrived at your house this morning."

"You can't possibly think I killed Vivian." Vincenzo shook his head as if the mere thought was ludicrous. "I wouldn't harm a hair on her body."

Sawyer remembered the dried blood beneath Ms. Gross's fingernails. While the senator didn't have visible scratches or scrapes from a recent fight, his skin beneath his clothes could tell an entirely different story. He'd been cooperative up to this point, but he'd make them produce a warrant to search his body or collect a DNA sample.

"Is that why you threatened to kill her last week if she didn't sign the divorce papers?" Royce asked, taking off the kid gloves.

Vincenzo's entire demeanor changed right before their eyes. All traces of the broken man disappeared, and the merciless prosecutor and poised politician took his place. "This conversation is over, gentlemen. I'd like for you to leave. If you wish to speak to me again, I suggest you do it through my attorney. His name is Richard Eckstein."

Sawyer and Royce exchanged a glance, then rose to their feet. Neither of them wanted to leave, but they both knew he was finished cooperating…for now.

"We will be in touch with Mr. Eckstein," Royce said before turning to exit the study.

Sawyer followed Royce but paused at the doorway, looking over his shoulder at the man whose body shook with fresh tears. His gut instinct said Vincenzo wasn't their killer. The man was a liar and a cheater, but that didn't make him a killer. His grief seemed genuine. Sensing Sawyer's perusal, Vincenzo lifted his head and met Sawyer's gaze.

Sawyer turned and faced him. "If you truly loved Vivian as much as you claim, you'd help us find her killer instead of hiding behind your lawyer. You disappoint me, Jack," Sawyer said, stripping the man of his title.

"My constituents won't understand if this gets out," Vincenzo replied, digging himself deeper in a hole as far as Sawyer was concerned. "The truth will crush Lucinda, and I want to spare her from the heartache and humiliation."

"Don't bullshit me. I think it's funny how you didn't give two fucks about Ms. Fairchild until you're at risk of having the truth get out. You're not worried about your fiancée. You're worried about losing your bid for re-election."

"Your mother wouldn't approve of you talking to me like this," he said, lifting his chin arrogantly.

"If my mother knew your true character, she'd never have let you cross her threshold. This is the only warning you're going to get, Jack. Stay away from my family. Do not take calls from my parents or return their texts and emails. Consider our endorsement rescinded."

"You're not going to tell them about the affair," Vincenzo scoffed. "Divulging details of your investigation will get you in hot water with the upper brass, Sawyer."

"It's Detective Key," Sawyer countered, revoking the man's right to use his first name. "You don't know what I'm capable of doing to protect the people I love. Keep that in mind, and do the right fucking thing here."

Sawyer turned around and nearly ran into Royce, who'd stopped and waited for him.

"Threatening a senator, huh?" Royce asked with a quirked brow. "I think your gold is starting to tarnish a bit.

"Write me up, Sarge," Sawyer said, skirting around Royce and heading toward the front door.

Royce followed at a more leisurely pace, so Sawyer had time to get himself under control before Royce joined him in the car. Neither man said anything until they cleared the woods and neared the end of the driveway.

"This is why I didn't accept my mother's invitation to the fundraiser this weekend," Sawyer said when he made a sharp turn onto the road. "It had nothing to do with being ashamed of us. I stopped going to these things a while ago, and I don't know why my mom persists in inviting me. There was no way I was going to spend even a few hours of my final days on leave rubbing elbows with liars and cheats when I could be home naked with you. I've had a lifetime of the political bullshit, and I hate it with a passion."

"I think you hate how disappointed you are that someone you liked and respected turned out to be human," Royce said softly.

"Human? Is that what you call a cheating bastard?"

Too late, Sawyer realized what he said. He wanted to kick himself in the ass. He knew how hard Royce struggled after learning Marcus had cheated on Candi. Royce still couldn't reconcile the man he'd loved with the one who lived a double life for three years. "God, I'm sorry."

Royce placed his hand on Sawyer's thigh, calming him. "I'm not condoning what Vincenzo did, but I can at least understand better now that sometimes people take pieces of our heart with them when they leave us. Vincenzo thought he'd healed and decided he was ready to move on with Lucinda. It just took one brief encounter for him to realize Vivian still owned a large piece of him. He should never have acted on his feelings the way he did, but give him time to step up and do the right thing. I think he'll surprise you."

"Not as much as you just did," Sawyer admitted.

Royce squeezed his thigh once more before retracting his hand when the exit and guard shack came into view.

As they approached, they triggered an automatic sensor to unlock the gates. Mustache Man and Mall Cop stared daggers at them while they waited for the gates to open, then stupidly flipped them off as Sawyer accelerated past the shack once the gates parted wide enough for the car to fit through.

Royce rolled down his window, stuck his head out, and yelled, "Have a nice day."

Sawyer laughed at his partner's antics. "That's a tamer reaction than I was expecting."

"Those dumbasses aren't worth a lecture from the chief."

"True," Sawyer agreed. "Where to now?"

"Bytes and Brew," Royce replied. "I want a breakfast sandwich and good coffee. The partners won't be arriving at the law office for another hour or two."

"Always worried about your stomach," Sawyer teased.

"Second only to my dick, GB."

CHAPTER 10

R OYCE SCRUBBED A HAND OVER HIS FACE. "THIS CASE IS GOING TO BE A fucking nightmare, especially when word gets out about the affair. People love sex scandals."

"Especially with politicians," Sawyer added. "Don't you find it remarkable that neither Blakemore nor Vincenzo knew about one another? Vincenzo referred to Blakemore's room as the guest bedroom instead of her roommate or tenant's room. Blakemore didn't indicate he knew Vivian's pining resulted from a renewed relationship with Vincenzo that had failed."

"Yeah, I agree it's odd, but not impossible," Royce said. "I mean, their arrangement could've easily been adjusted around Blakemore's work schedule with weekday romps at hotels, saving the overnight stays at her place for weekends."

"Why never at his place?" Sawyer asked.

Royce thought about it for a second. "Having sex with her in the bed he shared with Ms. Fairchild is the lowest of the low blows." Like it often did when infidelity came up in a conversation, his mind wandered to Marcus. His friend could've invited his girlfriend Amber over on the weekend he'd died since Candi and the kids were away visiting family, but he'd chosen to stay at Amber's apartment instead. Why? Was it Marcus's way of keeping his lives separate, or had he worried

Amber would've lingered and prevented him from going inside the garage and starting the car with the door closed? Marcus was complex and flawed, and he might never understand his friend's choices.

Bullshit! Stop being a coward and listen to the fucking tape if you want answers.

Royce swallowed hard against the bile rising in his throat. He was afraid of what he would hear on the tape. Plain and simple. He felt like he was barely clinging to the brightness Marcus had brought into his life as it was. Royce could finally remember happier times with Marcus, and he wasn't ready to discover worse things about his best friend that would set him back to reliving the nightmare of discovering his body every time Marcus's name was mentioned. Royce wasn't prepared to let go of the good. Who could blame him?

"Do you know what else I find hard to believe?" Sawyer asked, snapping Royce out of his gloomy thoughts.

Royce turned to look at Sawyer. "Hmm?"

"That Ms. Fairchild didn't know something was going on with Vincenzo." Sawyer glanced over and met Royce's gaze. "Think about it. Vincenzo's campaign staff would've scheduled his events long before he found out his dissolution never went through. Ms. Fairchild would have his speaking engagements and fundraising appearances in her calendar since she likely accompanied Vincenzo to many of them. He'd have to inform her of any new additions or deviations from the original plan. Wouldn't she notice excessive changes?"

"You make a good point," Royce said, letting Sawyer's words mesh with his thoughts. "He claimed Ms. Fairchild knew about the situation with Ms. Gross, so wouldn't she be included in discussions with attorneys, or at the very least ask for updates if Vincenzo excluded her from those meetings?"

Sawyer nodded. "You'd think."

"We need to know more about Ms. Fairchild and figure out what she knew about his reunion with Vivian Gross and when she found out," Royce said. "I think most people know when their significant other has fallen out of love with them or is engaging in an affair. There has to be unmistakable signs, right?" Sawyer nodded and Royce continued. "If you suddenly couldn't get it up for me, or your sex drive tanked out of the blue, my first concern would be your health. Once those worries were laid to rest, my brain would start leaning in other directions."

Sawyer nodded. "Same."

Fuck. Had Candi suspected? Had Marcus grown distant and less affectionate? Did her heart make excuses for the things her brain pointed out to her? It was easier to deny things that were blatantly obvious when facing them held severe consequences and drastic changes, not only for you, but for your children too. Royce had lived in a state of avoidance since finding out the confessional recording existed.

"Do you think I'm a coward?" Royce asked suddenly.

"What? No," Sawyer said, sounding aghast. "Have I given you the impression I think that?"

"No, asshole. It's all the self-reflecting bullshit I've started doing since I met you." Royce held up his hands and inspected them. "I have fewer scratches on my knuckles since I'm not dragging them around as much anymore." They laughed at his silly joke. "I meant the way I keep hiding from Marcus's tape."

"Knock off the enlightened thinking if you're only going to produce self-recriminating thoughts. I'd rather kiss your busted knuckles than see you doubt yourself. I have news for you, Ro. I don't know too many people who would've handled this situation with Marcus better than you have. Look how I reacted back there with the senator when a virtual stranger disappointed me. Marcus was more like a brother than a best friend."

"Sheer terror is preventing me from listening to it," Royce admitted.

Sawyer reached over and gently squeezed Royce's knee. "Fear isn't cowardly, babe. It's a defense mechanism. You're starting to heal and don't want to bust open the wounds."

Royce covered Sawyer's hand. "As much as I want to stop hurting, the idea of causing Candi more pain guts me, Sawyer. How the fuck am I supposed to tell her about Amber?"

"You've decided to tell her, then?"

Royce nodded. He wasn't sure when the answer solidified for him, but it had. "I said I wanted to wait until the IA finished their investigation. They've cleared him of wrongdoing and Candi has started receiving the benefits owed to her. Do you think it would be selfish of me to burden her with the truth now?"

"I think it's unfair for you to carry the burden alone," Sawyer replied.

"I'm not alone. I have you and Holly. I can suck it up and never tell her."

Sawyer was quiet for a while, and Royce knew he was rolling things around in his brilliant brain. "Is that what you would want if the situation were reversed? Or would you want to know the whole truth so you could find a way to heal?"

"I would want to know, but I'm not sure it's fair for me to decide for her," Royce countered.

"So don't."

Royce tipped his head and studied Sawyer while he drove. "What do you mean?"

"Why not listen to the tape and find out what you're dealing with first, then give it to Candi and let her decide if she wants to hear it. If she says no, you can hang on to it in case she changes her mind. If she says yes, you hand it to her and let her listen at a time of her choosing."

"Is that what you would do?" Royce asked.

Sawyer nodded. "Yes, unless there's something on the tape that could cause irrevocable damage."

Royce thought about it for a second. "You don't think finding out about the affair would be considered irrevocable damage?"

"Like we discussed, I think at some level Candi knew something was wrong in their marriage. Either Marcus had a multiple personality disorder that he could channel at whim and lead two completely separate lives for three years, or he gave distinctive clues along the way that she ignored."

"If she'd chosen to bury her head in the sand, isn't it cruel for me to force her to acknowledge the truth now?" Royce countered.

"Back then, she probably thought it was a phase they could work out. Now she knows it will never happen. Royce, you wrestle with doubts every day because you feel like you should've seen his death coming and prevented it. How do you think she feels? As close as you were to Marcus, Candi knew him on a completely different level."

Royce thought about it in terms of his relationship with Sawyer. Holly and Candi were his dearest friends, and he'd do anything for them, but his bond with Sawyer was so much more profound. Not even his friendship with Marcus could come close to touching what he shared with Sawyer. "Yeah, you're right."

"I usually am," Sawyer teased as he found a parking spot near the café. Once he killed the engine, he aimed those warm brown eyes at Royce. "I will support whatever you decide, but knowing you the way I do, guilt will eat away at your soul if you don't give her the opportunity to choose what's best for her."

"You think you know me, huh?" Royce asked, interjecting humor into the conversation. "What am I thinking now?"

"That you need to call Chief Mendoza with a doozy of an update while I get in line for food and beverages."

Royce had a hard time tearing his eyes away from Sawyer's mouth. What he wouldn't give to be back in bed with those lips stretched around his—

Sawyer cleared his throat.

"Yep. You know me. That's exactly what I was thinking."

Sawyer chuckled as he exited the car. Royce dialed the chief and admired Sawyer's long strides and delectable ass while waiting for Mendoza to pick up.

"Locke," the chief said firmly. "What do you have for me?"

Royce spent the next few minutes bringing Mendoza up to speed.

"Christ," the chief growled in frustration. "Could this fuckery get any worse? This is going to be a media shitstorm of epic proportions. No raincoat, umbrella, or rubber boots will prevent us from getting covered in it. Do you know who the senior partner is at her law firm?"

"The kid said Bill Elderwood," Royce replied.

"Get his address and make the notification ASAP."

"You don't want us to wait until office hours?"

"His agency is actively suing us, Locke. The last thing we can afford to happen is Elderwood accusing us of going through Vivian Gross's client files or computer while processing her home. I want you to tell him I am personally on the scene and no one will go in or out of her office until someone from their firm can come and remove the law firm's property."

Royce didn't bother to remind the chief that he and Sawyer were in her office with Blakemore. He decided to alter the message for Elderwood slightly. "I'll take care of it, sir."

"Keep me posted."

"Will do, sir."

Royce blew out a breath and called the station to get an address for Elderwood before going inside the café. Sawyer had already ordered and was waiting at the pickup area, chatting with Levi, who didn't look quite as deliriously happy as he had the last time Royce saw him. Levi and Diego had stopped by to see Sawyer at the hospital a few times before he was released, and Levi practically radiated sunbeams from his soul on each occasion.

"Uh-oh," Royce said as he approached, earning a glare from Levi. "Boy problems?"

"Oh, look. It's Sergeant Obvious," Levi said drolly.

"Wow," Royce said. "I thought we made peace."

"Yeah, I thought so too," Levi replied. "It turns out I still don't like you."

Sawyer looked at him with a quirked brow, and Royce shrugged. He had no idea why Levi was mad at him.

"What did I do?" Royce asked defensively.

Levi heaved a deep sigh, his shoulder slumping in defeat. "It's not your fault. You were only trying to help, even if you did it out of guilt instead of friendship." The thing was Royce could see himself and Levi as friends if the other man would let his guard down just a bit.

Royce leaned forward and lowered his voice. "What did Diego do?"

Levi's cheeks turned bright red, then he looked nervously at Sawyer before meeting Royce's gaze again.

"Can you give us a minute, GB?" Royce asked.

Sawyer looked between him and Levi, then nodded.

"Spill it," Royce said once Sawyer was out of earshot.

"Diego hasn't done *anything*. That's the problem."

Royce shook his head. "I don't get it. You're mad because he hasn't done anything wrong?"

Levi rolled his eyes. "He hasn't done anything right either, dumbass."

The cause for Levi's grouchiness hit him square between the eyes. "You mean the two of you haven't..." Royce let his words drift off as he counted back the weeks since he took the bull by the horns and pushed the two fools together. Time had been a blur lately, but at least a month had passed.

Levi shook his head.

"Are you still going out on dates?"

"We cooled off a bit when he was studying to take his detective's test, but we've gone out a few times since his promotion." Levi smiled gently. "He admires you."

"That's good to know. Diego's going to be a great detective," Royce replied, then pursed his lips as he thought for a few moments. "Is it possible you're both misreading the situation or waiting for the other to make the next move?"

"Nah," Levi said. "I don't do it for the guy. He's probably worried about what you'll think if he stops calling me."

Royce shook his head. "That's not the Diego I've come to know the past few weeks. Let me tell you a secret." Royce leaned closer and lowered his voice. "Even the shrewdest detectives miss clues sometimes, Levi." He nearly laughed as he recalled the many missteps he and Sawyer had taken. "Rather than assume he's not interested and give up, take a leap and make your move."

"You make it sound so easy," Levi mumbled.

Royce glanced over to where Sawyer sat at a table by the big picture window. He was observing patrons coming in and out of the café. Sensing Royce's attention, Sawyer glanced over and smiled at him, making heat bloom in Royce's core, spreading outward until he felt warm all over. Royce winked before facing Levi again.

"Nothing worth having is ever easy. Look at the successful business you've built. Are you going to tell me it was easy?"

"It wasn't," Levi replied softly.

"Relationships aren't easy either," Royce said.

"Their order's up, boss," a lanky college-aged kid said as he approached with a white paper bag and a drink carrier.

"Thanks, Mike," Levi said, taking the items from the employee, who nodded at Royce and walked away.

Royce took the drink carrier and bag, smiling at Levi. "I know how hard it is to trust your heart to someone else. I also know I will be grateful until my dying breath that I found the courage to live my truth."

Levi tilted his head to the side. "Does that mean you weren't out until you met Sawyer?"

Royce nodded. "I'll tell you about it sometime if you're interested."

Levi smiled shyly. "I am. And thank you. Can I please ask you not to repeat this conversation to Diego?"

"You don't have to ask," Royce said.

"Thanks. Be safe today."

"Just today?" Royce asked, walking backward.

Levi chuckled. "Smartass."

"Take care," Royce said, then turned around and walked toward Sawyer, who was watching the interaction with unabashed curiosity. Royce tipped his head toward the front door, indicating they had to go.

Sawyer rose to his feet and followed him outside. "What's the big hurry?"

"Chief Mendoza wants us at Elderwood's house ASAP." He filled Sawyer in on their conversation as they walked to his car.

"The chief has a valid point," Sawyer said as he started the engine. He took the coffee cups from the carrier and placed them in the cupholders between the seats, then he held out his hand for his sandwich. "I can eat and drive."

"Like you can audiobook and drive?" Royce quipped.

"Ha ha ha." Sawyer unwrapped his sandwich halfway, then eased into traffic. "As much as I love a breakfast croissant, it won't move me quite like the books do." Sawyer took a big bite of bacon, egg, and cheese croissant and moaned like a true food slut.

"Pretty sure I heard you make that same sound the other night when you were cooking dinner and listening to one of those books. You nearly chopped off a finger."

"I'd still have nine more to make you happy," Sawyer replied. "Where to, Sarge?"

Royce rattled off the address from memory before taking a bite of his sandwich. His euphoric whimper rivaled Sawyer's slutty moan. "Levi sure knows what he's doing," Royce said after he washed the food down with a sip of coffee.

"That's what Diego says," Sawyer teased, then glanced over when Royce didn't immediately reply. "What's that face mean?"

"What face?" Royce asked.

"You look constipated."

"Fuck you, asshole. I'm thinking hard."

"About what?"

Royce took another sip of coffee before answering. "The conversation I just had with Levi."

"What was that all about, anyway? Since when did the two of you become confidantes?"

"I'm the one who set him up with Diego, and I'm the one he's going to blame if things don't go well," Royce said.

"They broke up?"

"I don't know if they are officially a couple," Royce replied. "I just know things aren't going the way Levi would like them to."

"How?"

Royce chewed his bottom lip while debating what to say. He promised Levi he wouldn't share their conversation with Diego, and he knew Sawyer wouldn't betray his confidence. "I think Levi wants to climb Diego like a tree but is waiting for Diego to make the first move. So far, that hasn't happened."

"You mean they haven't had sex yet?" Sawyer asked in disbelief.

Royce nodded. "Levi thinks Diego isn't interested in him like that but won't call things off out of fear he'll piss me off."

"No way," Sawyer said. "We saw the way Diego looks at Levi."

"Like he was holding the moon and stars in the palm of his hand," Royce absently said while looking out the window.

"I was going to say like a piece of double chocolate cake, but we can go with moon and stars, Romeo."

Royce snickered. "It's all your fault. I was perfectly fine with being a closeted romantic curmudgeon."

"I'll gladly take credit for enticing you out of the closet and revealing all the amazing facets of your personality," Sawyer said. "What did you tell Levi?"

"I told him to take the bull by the horns and make his move," Royce said. "I don't know why Diego is hesitating. Maybe he's misreading the signals Levi is putting out. It's a real shame they're wasting precious time."

"We're not getting involved," Sawyer said resolutely.

Royce snorted. "I never said we were," he said, even as his mind was rolling through fix-it possibilities.

Sawyer shook his head. "You're formulating a plan. I can feel it."

"Am not," Royce lied, deciding a double date soon might be just the thing to prod the knuckleheads in the right direction.

They didn't have to wait long for Bill Elderwood to answer the door wearing a sweaty tank top and damp gym shorts. His white hair was soaked and plastered to his head and sweat ran down his tanned face. The man was probably in his late sixties but had the physique of someone much younger. His brow furrowed into a deep V over shrewd, icy blue eyes when recognition dawned on him.

"I apologize for my appearance, but I wasn't expecting Savannah's finest at my door before seven in the morning," Elderwood said, wiping his face with the towel he'd slung around his neck.

Royce and Sawyer had discussed who would do the majority of the talking before exiting the car. Sawyer hadn't topped the shit list at Elderwood's firm *yet*, so Royce thought it would be best if he made the notification while Royce observed, at least until they saw how the attorney reacted to Royce's presence.

"We're sorry to interrupt your workout, sir, but in light of the circumstances, we needed to contact you now rather than wait until business hours," Sawyer said.

"Circumstances? What happened?" the older man asked. His body went rigid, and it was apparent he was bracing himself for the worst.

Sawyer was as compassionate as the situation allowed when he broke the news to Elderwood about Gross's homicide. A stunned look washed over the man's face, dimming the brilliance in his eyes as if Sawyer had extinguished his spark.

"No, there has to be some mistake," Elderwood finally said emphatically. "Vivian cannot be dead."

"I'm afraid she is, sir," Royce replied.

"How? When?"

"Her tenant found her body early this morning after returning home from a weekend away," Sawyer said. "The ME estimates she died within the last twenty-four to thirty-six hours."

"Kendall found Vivian?" he asked, confirming the senior partner knew about their living arrangements. "Oh, that poor kid. He must be devastated," Elderwood said. "He idolized her."

"He was very shaken," Sawyer confirmed.

"Where is he now? Is he okay? You don't have him at the station, do you? I understand that the person who finds the body is often a suspect, but Kendall isn't capable of killing another person. I will be representing Mr. Blakemore, and I request you don't interview him without my presence."

We're all capable of killing under the right circumstances. Royce wisely kept his thought to himself. "He packed some things and is going to stay with a friend for a while. Kendall's alibi has already been confirmed," Royce said.

Elderwood narrowed his eyes and studied Royce intently. "You're one of the detectives on the case? Isn't that a conflict of interest?"

Royce remained calm and kept his gaze steady on the lawyer. "No, sir. It's not. I am committed to bringing Ms. Gross's killer to justice."

"I want to believe we're on the same side for once," Elderwood said. Royce didn't feel obligated to convince the man of anything. The proof was in the Southern banana pudding. Royce and Sawyer would solve the case, then trust Babineaux to prosecute the killer to the fullest extent of the law.

"We all want to uncover the truth, and we all want justice for Ms. Gross," Sawyer said smoothly. "There is no conflict of interest here." His boyfriend sounded every bit as polished as the politicians he claimed to dislike. "To show our good faith, Chief Mendoza sent us here to inform you he is personally guaranteeing no one will search her home office without a representative from your law firm present.

We will make sure her client files and any agency property are returned to you without interference or inspection."

Elderwood tipped his chin up a higher notch. "How is your chief going to guarantee that?"

"He's at the scene now and will remain there until someone shows up," Sawyer replied.

"I guess that will have to do," Elderwood said. "I'll shower and go over as soon as we complete this interview."

Sawyer nodded and began asking the standard questions they'd ask any employer.

Elderwood hesitated when Sawyer asked about Gross receiving threats. "You don't represent the powerful clients we do without ruffling feathers. People are convicted in the court of opinion long before they make it to trial, Detectives. They want to rule guilty or not guilty by the way a victim or defendant makes them feel instead of facts presented. Don't get me started on the media. Of course she received threats from angry people, especially women who don't understand her motivation. She hasn't told me about any recent threats, but she probably wouldn't have."

"Why?" Royce asked.

"Vivian and two other lawyers were vying for partner. Vivian was the only female candidate, and to be honest, worked harder and acted tougher than her male counterparts. She would've worried we'd view her as too soft if she spoke up." He sighed deeply and frowned. "If anyone knows about recent threats, it would be Kendall. He managed her mail, email, and phone calls, as well as kept her court calendar up to date. If the threats exist, we will cooperate and turn them over to you as long as they don't contain confidential information."

"I appreciate that, sir," Royce said.

Sawyer asked about conflicts in the agency, earning a scoff and harrumph from the older man. "I won't dignify that with an answer."

"What about her social life. Do you know if she was seeing anyone?" Royce asked.

"Vivian was very private. I'm not aware of her dating anyone, but again, Kendall would probably know."

They wrapped up the interview a few minutes later and left the lawyer to shower and get ready.

"What do you think?" Royce asked Sawyer when they jogged down his porch steps.

"I think we need to talk to Kendall again."

Royce looked at Sawyer over the top of the car. "I agree." A second interview with Blakemore was high on his priority list, second only to Senator Vincenzo. One would be much easier to accomplish than the other.

CHAPTER 11

E VEN THOUGH KENDALL HADN'T REQUESTED THE PRESENCE OF AN attorney at any point during their first interview, Sawyer thought the wisest course of action would be to wait and question Kendall, as well as the rest of the law firm staff, once Elderwood left the crime scene. "It's a sign of good faith and shows we're committed to solving her case *and* playing by the rules," Sawyer told Royce, who grumbled but agreed with him. The adorable scowl on Royce's face made it super hard for Sawyer to resist leaning across the console and kissing his lips once they reached the precinct.

The wait gave Royce time to digest the bitter pill he'd nearly choked on. Sawyer searched the internet for any potential suspects by looking up details on cases Vivian Gross lost within the last year, or even older ones if the client had the resources and connections to order a hit and make it look like Humphries did it. Ms. Gross didn't just represent clients in Savannah, so they broadened the scope to Atlanta and other areas as well as South Carolina, since she was licensed there too.

They also used the time to set up another Operation Venus Flytrap meeting. They wouldn't be able to share the particulars of the case with Felix, Jonah, or Rocky present, but they could reassess their next steps for their joint endeavor in light of Ms. Gross's death.

Nearly three hours later, Elderwood made sure all the key players were at the firm and willing to assist them in their investigation. He greeted them with cordial handshakes, then introduced each of the attorneys and their key staff members. The mood was as somber as they expected, and their shock and grief seemed genuine instead of forced.

They decided to start with Kendall because he was closest to Gross and looked like he was barely holding himself together.

"Did you drive?" Sawyer asked the younger man, whose head was bent forward as he silently cried. His curtain of white-blond bangs hid his face from them.

Blakemore slowly lifted his head and met Sawyer's gaze. "No. Jonah drove me here and is waiting in his car." Sawyer couldn't say he was surprised, because there was a gentleness about the big man that most people probably missed because of his size and wicked scar. Blakemore faced Elderwood. "Thank you for giving me a few days off. I know it's not convenient since I'm most familiar with Vivian's caseload."

"You take all the time you need, Kendall. I know how much Vivian meant to you."

Blakemore nodded. "You don't have to stay," he told Elderwood. "I have nothing to hide from the detectives."

The senior partner's left brow shot up toward his hairline. "Are you sure, Kendall?"

"I am, sir. I'll request your presence if things head in a direction I don't like."

Elderwood ping-ponged his gaze between Sawyer, Royce, and Blakemore. "I don't advise it, but I will respect your wishes. You know where to find me."

"Yes, sir. Thank you, sir," he said, offering Elderwood a weak smile.

Sawyer doubted the rest of the interviewees would be as cooperative, so he wasted no time diving into questions. "Can you tell us about angry clients or anyone mad enough at Ms. Gross to send her threats. Mr. Elderwood said you'd be in the best position to know."

Blakemore flinched. "Not to sound crass but dealing with hostile people was an everyday thing."

"I know your head probably isn't fully engaged in the interview, and your heart surely isn't. We're not trying to overwhelm you," Royce said kindly. "We just need a place to start. Can you give us the ones who were the angriest, starting with the most recent threats? You can always call either one of us if something else occurs to you."

"Yeah," he said, nodding jerkily. "I want to help you find who killed Vivian."

"We know you do, Kendall," Sawyer said, using his first name for a softer approach, even though he was eager to compare Blakemore's list to the one he made.

"Mickey Hendrix comes to mind," Blakemore said.

"Without breaking confidentiality, can you tell us why you think he's mad enough to harm Ms. Gross?"

Mickey Hendrix was in prison for life after murdering his long-time business partner, so he couldn't have personally committed the crime. He had plenty of connections and money to hire it done though.

"He recently lost his appeal and blamed her."

"Can you tell us why he formed that opinion?" Royce asked.

Blakemore hesitated for a few seconds. "He claimed she was ill-prepared and no longer cared about him since she'd already made the bulk of her money on his first trial." He closed his eyes and took a calming breath. "He also accused her of having an affair with Humphries and referenced the photographs taken outside the county jail when he was released as proof." The ones Felix took of Humphries embracing Gross had been picked up by The Associated Press.

"Could there be any truth to his allegations?" Sawyer asked.

Stiffening, Blakemore asked, "Which part? The alleged ineffective counsel or the reasons he said were behind it?"

Blakemore's rigid posture and defensive tone meant they'd need to tread lightly. If both Sawyer and Royce were playing nice cop during this interview, one of them would need to be the nicer cop. Sawyer was up to bat.

"Look," he said gently. "Neither of us is looking to victim shame anyone, Kendall. All we want to do is find out who killed Vivian. We can't do our job if you're withholding crucial information to protect your friend's image."

Blakemore closed his eyes and inhaled deeply. After a brief pause, he reopened them and relaxed his posture. His pale blue eyes looked sad instead of wary. "She was my friend."

"Then help us get justice for her," Royce implored. "Don't restrict your answers only to the things you saw or heard. We want to know how you felt about situations too. If someone gave you a bad vibe, then we want to know about it. Leave it to us to sort out the facts from feelings with follow-up questions and investigating, okay?"

"Yeah, okay," the young guy agreed.

"Could there have been truth in *any* of Mr. Hendrix's accusations?" Royce tried again.

"Over the past few weeks, Vivian seemed distracted and maybe a little more distant than usual. She either forgot about appointments or showed up late to them. She nearly missed filing deadlines with the courts in a few cases, which was so out of character for her. I knew something was going on, so when I found out about the marriage..." His eyes took on a dazed expression as he let his words trail off. He blinked after a few seconds, and his eyes zeroed in on Sawyer. "Did you talk to Vincenzo?"

"We did," Royce replied.

"And?"

"We can't share the details of the interview with you," Sawyer said. They knew when the affair between Vincenzo and Gross began, according to the senator at least, but not when Vivian first became aware their marriage was still intact or when Kendall first learned about the situation. Sawyer posed those two questions to him now. He'd have a chance to compare the answers to Vincenzo's later.

Blakemore tilted his head slightly to the right, and he tapped a finger against his lips. "From what I recall, Vincenzo's attorney reached out to Vivian about three months ago."

So, Vivian had only known she was still married to Vincenzo for twelve weeks and allegedly spent eight of them engaging in an affair with the senator. Her association with Humphries went back further than three months, so *maybe* they had been involved before she rekindled her relationship with Vincenzo. If so, prisons had their own rumor mill, so it wasn't improbable that Humphries would've bragged to another inmate about having an affair with his attorney. The inmate could've told a guard at the county jail, and he might have passed the information along to a buddy who worked at a state prison, who then told Hendrix. They couldn't rule out the possibility.

"How did Vincenzo notify her about the marriage? A phone call, letter, or email? Did the attorney come to see her in person?" Sawyer asked.

"Matt Schultz is his name," Blakemore replied. "The coward served Vivian with official papers."

Impatience started to build inside Sawyer. Blakemore was answering their questions with as little information as possible, requiring them to prod him for more details after each response. Vivian had trained him well.

"At the office or home?" Royce asked.

Blakemore scoffed. "Home. Schultz wasn't stupid enough to embarrass Vivian at work."

"Were you there when she received the documents?" Royce countered.

"I was," Blakemore replied. Sawyer was prepared to poke some more, but the dam finally broke, and information flooded out freely. "It was a Wednesday. I know this because it was my late night at school. I was in the kitchen reheating the Chinese food Vivian had ordered for me when the doorbell rang. It had to be at least nine o'clock by then. We were both surprised because neither of us received many visitors, and we sure as hell weren't expecting a process server." A faraway look briefly washed over Blakemore's face before he refocused his thoughts. "I will never forget the way Vivian gasped and placed her hand over her heart. The paperwork fell to the floor, and she bolted up to her room. I wrestled with my conscience over following her upstairs and asking what happened or picking up the documents and reading them for myself."

Sawyer didn't ask which he'd chosen because the answer didn't feel pertinent, and he wanted Blakemore to stay on track. Pragmatism won out over curiosity.

"I followed Vivian upstairs and found her curled up in a ball on her bed, sobbing as if someone had just broken her heart," Blakemore said, assuaging Sawyer's curiosity. "I retreated to the kitchen for a bottle of wine and two glasses. Then she proceeded to tell me everything from how they met to the decision she'd made to end their marriage when they were in law school." Blakemore shook his head. "I was shocked to find out she was married to the state senator but blown away by her confession that she had never stopped loving him and deeply regretted giving up on their marriage when she was younger."

"I don't personally know Ms. Gross, but I imagine getting served instead of receiving a phone call from Vincenzo stung," Royce said.

Blakemore nodded. "It was a blow to both her pride and heart. I watched her shift from a despondent woman to a furious one who wanted Vincenzo and his attorney to know she wasn't rolling over and playing—" A high-pitched squeak escaped him before he slapped his hand over his mouth.

Dead.

Vivian Gross wasn't going to roll over and play dead for the senator. Had she signed the papers and given Jack Vincenzo the dissolution *she'd* asked for years ago, would she still be alive? Or was this all just an eerie coincidence?

Blakemore gathered himself and continued. "She hired a lawyer and filed for a divorce."

"Who is her divorce lawyer?" Sawyer asked.

"Madeline Chesney-Stowe," Blakemore replied.

Sawyer wasn't surprised in the least that Gross had chosen the most successful divorce attorney in the state.

"Ouch. Even I know who Madeline Chesney-Stowe is," Royce said. "I hope Vincenzo girded his loins."

"Exactly," Blakemore said smugly. "Vivian was fighting back."

"They were at a stalemate, then?" Sawyer asked.

"Yes, that was the impression I had until I overheard the conversation between them the previous week where Vincenzo threatened to kill her."

People made stupid idle threats all the time but never with real intention to cause someone harm. Sawyer had even heard his mother threaten to murder his father in his sleep over something silly. He and his siblings didn't stay up all night worrying about their father's safety because they recognized it as one of those things people said. The difference here is that someone *did* kill Vivian Gross. It was up to Royce and Sawyer to find out if Vincenzo had said something stupid out of frustration, anger, and hurt, or had eliminated someone who could cost him his re-election bid.

"Can you repeat verbatim what you overheard?" Royce asked.

Blakemore nodded. "I heard Vincenzo say 'I gave you what you wanted all those years ago, and it's not my fault the lawyer *you* hired turned out to be a fraud. Why won't you show me the same courtesy now and give me what I want?' Vivian told Vincenzo he knew damn well why she wouldn't give in and no amount of finger-pointing, begging, or tugging at her heartstrings would change her mind. Vincenzo replied with 'I could just kill you right now, Vivie.' She laughed and hung up on him."

Sawyer stared at Blakemore for a few seconds, contemplating how to proceed. "What you said now is drastically different than what you told us earlier this morning." He was proud of how calm he sounded.

"I don't think it sounds that different," Blakemore said defensively.

"You told us Jack Vincenzo, a state senator, threatened to kill Ms. Gross if she didn't sign the divorce papers," Royce said.

"That's how it came across to me. You said you wanted my impressions," Blakemore replied.

"We did," Sawyer agreed, moving the conversation along. "Are you aware of Ms. Gross meeting with Vincenzo privately?"

"What? Hell no. The guy is still breathing and moving without a permanent limp, isn't he?" Blakemore countered. "She was planning to make a trophy out of his balls."

"Is that what she said?" Royce asked. "Or is this another of your impressions?"

"That is a direct quote from Vivian after concluding the phone call where he threatened to kill her. A week later, and she's dead. A coincidence? I think not."

Sawyer wanted to know how everything broke down between Vincenzo and Gross, and how they went from a joyous reunion and passionate affair to bitter enemies. He needed the senator to be forthcoming if he was going to get the truth.

"This morning, you were certain Humphries did it," Royce reminded him.

"I wasn't thinking clearly. What reason would Humphries have to kill Vivian? She got his case dismissed." Blakemore's shoulders inched up closer to his ears. The last thing they wanted was for him to clam up or get Elderwood back in the room because they'd put him on the defensive.

"Let's circle back to Mickey Hendrix and his accusations," Sawyer said, steering them back toward a potentially less volatile subject. "You mentioned she was acting out of character and chalked it up to the situation between Ms. Gross and Senator Vincenzo. Could there have been something else going on? Was she seeing someone romantically? Someone she didn't want you to know about, perhaps?"

"Are you actually accusing her of fucking Humphries?" Blakemore asked angrily.

"No. No, I am not," Sawyer said emphatically. "There are many reasons she might keep a new relationship quiet, Mr. Blakemore. Maybe she wasn't convinced it was going anywhere and would rather avoid awkward questions later when the relationship fizzled out. There's also the possibility people might see her love interest as a conflict of interest."

Blakemore narrowed his eyes. "Or maybe he was already engaged to someone else." He sat up straighter in his chair. "That's what you're trying to ask me indirectly, isn't it? You think Vincenzo was seeing Vivian."

"I'm not one to beat around a bush, and I said no such thing," Sawyer replied.

"Did Vincenzo tell you he and Vivian were seeing one another?" Blakemore asked, then shook his head. "No. I don't believe it. Vivian Gross would never be some man's mistress. She'd never accept taking a back seat to another woman or allow herself to become attached to a man who was too much of a coward to admit his feelings for her. And besides, I would've known."

"How?" Royce asked.

"Vivian would've told me. We were close," the younger man said, his voice barely above a whisper.

Sawyer could've pointed out that she didn't share her history with Vincenzo until after she found out they were still married. Had Blakemore not been home at the time to witness her shock, Sawyer doubted Gross would've shared the news with him then either. Some things were too personal to discuss, even with people you loved and who returned your affection. Royce and Marcus came to mind. Royce had never felt comfortable telling Marcus about his attraction to men, and Marcus had never confessed his affair to Royce. Each of them had their reasons for keeping secrets to themselves, yet their bond was undeniable.

"What about angry clients besides Hendrix," Royce said, circling back to their first question.

"There are several others who might've been mad enough to want her dead," Blakemore said after a brief pause.

Several more? Most people would be pressed to name one person who wanted to kill them, but then again, most people weren't Vivian Gross, defender of mafia bosses, killers, and rapists.

Sawyer was glad he'd taken the time to dig up dirt on Vivian's court hearings before coming. Sure, the information he had was one-sided and biased by whichever reporter, mostly Felix, wrote the story. In addition to Hendrix, he'd had Ed Menske down, who the FBI wanted for racketeering, human trafficking, and money laundering but had to settle for a tax evasion conviction instead. The man was incarcerated at Jesup, a low-security facility, rather than doing hard time at Georgia State Prison, a maximum-security prison. While Sawyer thought the thug should be grateful, it was doubtful Menske felt that way. Bart Jesper, son of a billionaire tycoon, also lost his appeal for a new trial six months ago. He was convicted of kidnapping and killing his ex-girlfriend. Then there was Gretchen Wilcox, who worked for a crime family in Atlanta and was probably the most dangerous of them all. From what Sawyer read, Vivian and her colleagues thought her acquittal was a slam dunk, then blamed jury bias when the verdict came back guilty of first-degree murder the following week. Out of all of them, Gretchen was the one with the stiffest sentence. With Jesper, the jury bought the idea that he hadn't gone to his ex-girlfriend's home with the intent to kidnap and kill her, so he was looking at twenty-five years compared to Gretchen, who was facing the death penalty at her sentencing hearing in a few weeks.

The conference room door flew open and slammed against the wall. Blakemore, who had his back to the door, jumped up and pivoted toward the threat while Sawyer and Royce stared at Elderwood's flushed face.

"So much for being on the same team," he snarled. "I consider your egregious act a break in the truce we formed this morning."

"Would you mind telling us what *egregious act* you're referring to?" Royce countered. "We have been completely honest with you, Mr. Elderwood."

Blakemore looked back and forth between them. "What's this about, sir?"

Elderwood jabbed a finger in their direction. "They stole a file."

"No, we didn't," Royce and Sawyer said at the same time.

"I don't think so, sir," Blakemore said uneasily. It took guts for the guy to stand up to the man who signed his paychecks.

"Can I ask which file is missing, Mr. Elderwood?" Sawyer asked. "Its disappearance might be part of the case."

Elderwood ignored him and spoke to Blakemore instead. "Why do you think they're telling the truth?"

"Because they could've searched Vivian's office without me being present, but they asked me to look inside the room to see if anything was missing."

The older man pinned Royce and Sawyer with a glare. "I thought you said no one was going into her office until I got there."

"We said no one would search the office or remove evidence without you being present. We asked Mr. Blakemore to tour the home with us to see if anything was out of place. He claimed nothing was missing in her office or anywhere else in the house."

"It's true, sir," Blakemore said. He could've thrown them under the bus by telling the senior partner that he'd left them in Gross's office alone while he went upstairs to pack a bag, but he remained silent. Self-preservation, perhaps? "Are you sure it's missing?"

"I was there when they searched her home office and vehicle. It wasn't in either place, so I assumed she'd left it at the office. The file is nowhere in this building either," Elderwood said.

"What made you look for it?" Royce asked the attorney.

"I need to divide her caseload amongst the other attorneys, and they need to prioritize their schedules based on depositions, meetings, and court dates. The Humphries file is the only one unaccounted for out of dozens. I know it sounds cold, but some of her clients have trial dates for next week, and these things are scheduled months in advance. Our firm's reputation depends not only on us picking up the fumbled ball and running with it, but also winning." Comparing his slain lawyer to failed football plays was what sounded cold, not the expediency or necessity of rearranging the other attorney's schedules. "That means emergency meetings with each of her clients to assure them they're in capable hands."

"I understand, sir," Royce said.

Blakemore gasped. "I didn't see her briefcase anywhere in the house."

"Describe it," Sawyer said.

"It's a burgundy leather Burberry briefcase. It cost more than two weeks of my salary. Maybe three. She's had it for as long as I've known her," Blakemore said. "I can't believe I didn't notice it wasn't in her office."

"Shock does strange things to a person's comprehension and perception," Royce said sympathetically. "It's why detectives interview witnesses and persons of interest multiple times."

Vivian Gross was dead. The only things reported as missing were her briefcase and Humphries's file. The police didn't have it, which meant Vivian's killer took it. And Humphries, the serial rapist and killer, just happened to be out of the country when Gross was the victim of a copycat or tribute killing. What were the odds?

Sawyer's phone vibrated. He looked at his caller ID and swallowed a groan when he saw the name on the screen. He'd forgotten he had the man's number programmed in his contacts. He glanced up at Royce. "I need to take this."

"Sure," Royce replied, then continued speaking to Elderwood and Blakemore about the missing briefcase and file.

Sawyer stepped out into the hallway, closing the door behind him, and glanced around to make sure he was alone. "Detective Key," he sternly said into the phone.

"Things got out of control in a hurry this morning, and I take full responsibility," Jack Vincenzo said calmly. "I shouldn't have reacted the way I did, and I'm sorry. I was—*and still am*—in shock. I want to speak with you and Sergeant Locke again, Sawyer. Please. You were right. Vivian deserves my cooperation, and I want to help. No matter the cost."

Sawyer heaved a sigh. "Okay, but we're currently at her firm interviewing the lawyers and staff. I can't say how much longer we'll be."

"I understand. Just call me back when you're on the way."

"Will do." Sawyer disconnected without saying a proper goodbye.

The door to the conference room opened just as Sawyer slid his phone inside his pocket. Blakemore poked his head around the door. "Is it okay to come out?"

"Sure," Sawyer said. "I just finished my call. Is Sergeant Locke done with your interview?"

Blakemore nodded. "For now." The blond man looked like he barely had the strength to walk to the car. He took two steps toward him and tripped, stumbling into Sawyer, who raised his arms to catch the guy so he didn't faceplant on the floor. The impact was hard enough to carry them both into the wall.

"Oops," Blakemore said, but he didn't pull out of Sawyer's loose hold or straighten away from him. He looped an arm around Sawyer's waist, rested his head against Sawyer's shoulder, and appeared to melt into him.

"Looks like you've hit the wall," Sawyer said.

"Of muscle," Blakemore replied, his voice muffled by Sawyer's shirt. Then he began to cry. "I can't believe she's gone. My beautiful Vivian."

Someone cleared their throat. Sawyer jerked his head toward the sound and found Royce and Mr. Elderwood watching them with vastly different expressions. Royce's lips quirked up on the left side, and his eyes twinkled with humor. Sawyer was so going to catch hell for this. Elderwood's brow furrowed over narrowed eyes as he studied the scene before him. Suspicious bastard.

"Maybe you should call your friend, Kendall," Elderwood suggested, sounding grandfatherly.

"She's dead, Mr. Elderwood," Blakemore said, then began crying harder.

"I meant the one who drove you here and is waiting for you in his car," the older man said.

"Oh, yeah. I forgot."

Sawyer met Royce's gaze once more, and he hoped his boyfriend could read the silent plea for him to do something. Before he met Royce, and under different circumstances, Sawyer might have liked having Kendall Blakemore in his arms.

"I'll give him a call for you," Royce told Blakemore.

A few minutes later, Jonah escorted Blakemore out of the building. The gentle giant didn't seem to mind supporting the slender guy's weight as they walked.

"I know you have a lot going on right now, Mr. Elderwood. Why don't we continue the staff interviews so we can get out of your hair?" Royce suggested.

Elderwood absently ran his hand over his head. "Yes, that sounds like a good plan." He didn't apologize for his outburst and accusation, but they were better off to let it drop and keep the interviews going. "I'll be back in a few minutes. I need to see who isn't on the phone right now."

Once they were alone, Royce turned his attention to Sawyer. "What was the phone call all about?"

"You're not going to bust my balls about Blakemore?"

"Of course, I am. It can wait until the interviews are over."

Sawyer snorted. "The senator is ready to talk."

"Hell fucking yeah."

CHAPTER 12

"**D**AMN," ROYCE SAID AFTER NOTICING THE CHANGE OF GUARD WHEN they returned to Vincenzo's gated community following the interviews at Elderwood, Johnson, and McClary. After Blakemore left, they had learned didley squat from the lawyers and staff employed at Gross's law firm. The news of the attorney's murder broke during their drive over, leaving Royce in a fighting mood after hearing the radio broadcast.

"Easy there, or you'll rip the steering wheel out of its column," Sawyer chided.

Royce glanced at his hands and noted his white-knuckled grip. Funny how he hadn't noticed the tingling in his fingers from lack of circulation until Sawyer drew his attention to it. "The news had to break eventually," Royce groused, then heaved a sigh.

"Let's be grateful they don't know the truth about Vincenzo's relationship with Gross yet," Sawyer countered.

Royce snorted as he came to a stop next to the gatekeeper's shack. "I'm not sure we know the truth about their relationship." Royce held up his badge when the guard opened the window and leaned toward him. Rather than argue with them as the bonehead had done earlier, the new guy nodded and opened the gates for them to pass through. Accelerating into the community, Royce said, "What a fucking letdown."

Sawyer chuckled. "I love you." Then he gasped dramatically. "Is that declaration prohibited during work hours, Sergeant Dickhead?"

Royce's heart swelled, then galloped like a runaway horse. He would never grow tired of hearing Sawyer say those words—in any form, or at any time. *Play it cool, Locke.* "I guess I can let it slide just this once, but if I'm making exceptions to the rules, I'd prefer to slide my dick into your mouth while you kneel at my feet in one of the shower stalls in the locker room. I have a totally different idea on how our private and professional relationships should mingle...*if* I were making exceptions."

Sawyer cleared his throat and shifted in his seat. "Is that a particular fantasy you've had about me?" His voice suddenly sounded as thick as molasses.

"Only since the day we met," Royce admitted. *Damn! It was getting hot in here.*

"And why haven't you shared the fantasy with me?"

Royce glanced over at his partner, his love, his freaking *everything*. "Because you'd make it come true, and then I would want it all the time."

"That would be a bad thing, huh?" Sawyer asked.

Was it? Yes! Maybe. "Do you really want people in our precinct to overhear us going at it in the shower? Or is it the thought of getting caught that sends your blood racing to your cock?"

"We're not talking about *my* fantasies right now," Sawyer countered.

"We shouldn't be talking about fantasies at all, but since it came up..." Royce cupped the growing bulge in his jeans just in case Sawyer was confused about the *it* he was referring to. His damn dick had a mind of its own.

Sawyer didn't answer right away, so Royce glanced over at him when they stopped at an intersection. His boyfriend's face was flushed pink and little beads of sweat dotted his upper lip. Sawyer hooked his finger in the open collar of his polo shirt and repeatedly pulled the material away from his body, fanning himself. Continuing his perusal down Sawyer's torso, Royce's gaze snagged on his boyfriend's crotch. He would tease him about his reaction if he weren't sporting a semi-erection also. Returning his attention to the road, Royce turned onto the same side street Sawyer had taken earlier.

"The thrill for me would be watching you try your hardest not to let anyone on the other side of the curtain know what was going on," Sawyer said, unwilling to let the subject drop.

Oh god. Resisting this man was nearly impossible. Royce reached forward and cranked the air-conditioning higher, then angled the vent to blow cold air directly on his face.

"Could you do it?" Sawyer asked. "Let me suck you off without giving us away?"

"I don't know," he replied honestly. One of the things he loved most about sex with Sawyer was how vocal they both were. He couldn't deny how much the prospect of Sawyer blowing him in the shower stalls at the precinct turned him on. "I know it's probably not a good idea to put either of us to the test. You do this humming thing when you blow me. That's bound to echo around the shower room and create a stir." Like the one in his pants. *Damn Sawyer.* He couldn't go into Vincenzo's house with a raging boner.

Sawyer chuckled. "We either need to change the subject or find a secluded spot to rub one out really quick." There was no doubt which option they both preferred, just as there was no question which one they'd choose. "What do you think about Blakemore's revised statement concerning Vincenzo?" Sawyer asked.

Recalling the way Kendall Blakemore had plastered himself against Sawyer did a great job of stirring his anger instead of lust, easing the ache in his groin.

"I honestly don't know what to think about the kid," Royce replied. "I don't think he's lied to us, but he's stretched the facts to suit whatever narrative he's pushing at the time. On the one hand, it's hard not to view Vincenzo's words as a threat in light of the situation, but had he been more specific this morning, I probably wouldn't have leaned on the senator so hard during our first interview, which might've prevented us from making a second trip."

"Doubtful," Sawyer replied. "Other than Vincenzo, none of the people closest to Vivian seemed willing to speak freely to us. Getting information from Blakemore was like pulling teeth, and it only got worse with each person we interviewed. The higher up the food chain we climbed at the law firm, the quieter the person on the other side of the table from us became."

"They view us as the enemy," Royce said. "I don't agree with them, but I get it."

Vincenzo didn't greet them on the porch on their second arrival. He wasn't the one who answered the door either. A silver-haired butler in a crisp black suit showed them to Vincenzo's study where the senator sat in the same place they'd left him hours earlier, only this time Vincenzo wore a navy blue suit, crisp white shirt, and striped tie instead of sleep pants and a faded Duke T-shirt. He also wasn't alone. The man sitting beside him looked like a bulldog with sagging jowls, drooping eyes, and puffed-out chest. The blond buzz cut didn't positively accentuate this man's bone structure in the same way it did Sawyer's. The bulldog wore a charcoal suit, pink shirt, and paisley tie that looked as expensive as the senator's and the ones hanging in Sawyer's closet. Must be a lawyer thing.

Vincenzo and Bulldog rose to their feet when Royce and Sawyer entered the study.

"Can I offer refreshments to anyone?" the butler asked the room at-large.

"No, thank you, Jervis," Vincenzo replied.

Speak for yourself. Royce was willing to bet twenty bucks that Vincenzo always had pastries in the kitchen. Not as good as Sherry Rigby's, but he'd offer himself up as a tribute to find out. He debated joking about it to ease the mounting tension but decided against it.

"Detective Key, Sergeant Locke, I'd like you to meet my attorney, Matt Schultz."

"Your divorce attorney, right?" Sawyer asked, extending his hand to Schultz, who raked his dark gaze over Royce's boyfriend.

"So, you've heard of me?" the man asked slyly, his wide grin parting the heavy cheeks to hang like saddlebags on both sides of his face. Vincenzo's scowl matched the fire burning low in Royce's gut.

"Just this morning when I discovered Senator Vincenzo is married to Vivian Gross," Sawyer replied. *Zing!* "You're the idiot who thought it was wise to send a process server to her home rather than offer an honest and open dialogue." *Ouch!* Sawyer was going for the jugular.

The joy dimmed from Bulldog's eyes, and the good-ole-boy smile slid from his face. "Was married," the tactless man corrected. "Death is certainly cheaper and more expedient than a divorce." Schultz started laughing like his comment was funny instead of crass.

Vincenzo wordlessly walked over to a coffee cart and poured himself a cup. Every line of his body was stiff and unyielding. Did he want to punch Schultz out as severely as Royce did?

Schultz sobered when he realized no one else in the room found his remark funny. He blew out a shaky breath. "Am I in the hot seat, fellas? I thought you were coming to put the screws to Jack." More inappropriate guffaws followed.

Sawyer scowled at the attorney, and Royce expected steam to come out of his partner's ears at any minute.

"No one is getting screwed," Royce said tersely. "We only want information that will help us catch Ms. Gross's killer. We learned about the senator's marriage to Vivian Gross earlier this morning and notified him of her passing since he was her next of kin. We asked questions that made him uncomfortable, and he asked us to leave." Royce shifted his gaze to the senator. "You stated we should contact Richard Eckstein if we wished to speak to you again, so we expected him to be present, not your divorce attorney."

Vincenzo had turned to face him during Royce's remark and now stood pinching the bridge of his nose. He lowered his hand and met

Royce's gaze head-on. "To be honest, I would prefer Richard was here with me today, but he had court commitments he couldn't reschedule and wasn't able to make the drive from Atlanta. I thought having *an* attorney present was better than none." Vincenzo looked at Schultz. "I thought wrong. Your presence is no longer required, Matt."

"Wait a minute," the attorney said, holding up his hands. "Let's discuss this. You asked me here to make sure these guys didn't exploit your situation with Ms. Gross to get you to talk. I might not be a bigshot defense attorney, but I am familiar enough with the law to keep you from incriminating yourself."

Vincenzo crossed the room and set his coffee cup on the oval table between the four leather club chairs placed strategically around it. He held out his arms and looked at Royce and Sawyer. "I have nothing to hide from you. There's nothing anyone can say about me or do to me that will hurt more than losing the love of my life." *Whoa.*

"Where's Ms. Fairchild?" Sawyer asked.

Vincenzo sighed heavily. "I told her everything after you left. We ended our engagement, she packed up some things, and has returned to Atlanta." *We, not she. Interesting.*

"That wasn't smart, Jack," Schultz said. "She's the kind of woman you want by your side on the campaign trail and residing with you in the governor's mansion, or even the White House someday."

"You're getting way ahead of yourself," Vincenzo replied, waving a hand to dismiss the idea. "Right now, those aspirations hardly seem important."

"We might need to speak with Ms. Fairchild during this investigation. Will you provide us with a phone number to reach her?" Royce asked.

"Of course. I only ask that you give Lucinda a day or so to process what I've done." *It wasn't a promise Royce could keep, so he chose not to react.*

"Aren't you worried she'll reveal your story to the press out of spite?" Sawyer asked.

"She signed an NDA," Schultz said.

Since when did an NDA stop anyone? An eager reporter would happily protect Ms. Fairchild's identity, and besides, there was at least one other person besides their attorneys who knew the truth, giving Lucinda plausible deniability. She could simply say that whoever tipped off the police about Vincenzo and Gross's marriage was the same person who leaked the story to the press. Royce would do everything in his power to protect Kendall's identity, even if the man annoyed him.

Vincenzo snorted. "She could get around the document a dozen different ways, Schultz. The fact that you don't know it affirms my decision to ask you to leave."

Schultz shrugged and said, "It's your funeral, Jack."

"No," Jack said bitterly. "The only funeral in my foreseeable future is my wife's." His voice broke on the last word, and he slumped down into a chair as if his legs would no longer support his weight.

Schultz started to pick up a file folder on the coffee table.

"Leave it," Vincenzo said tersely. "I've already paid for the information inside it."

Schultz muttered something unintelligible as he tucked his tail and left the room, resembling a scalded mutt instead of a proud bulldog.

Royce and Sawyer exchanged a glance before they sat across from the senator.

"What a putz," Vincenzo said. "I should've fired him the moment he mentioned serving Vivian with the new dissolution papers. He was looking for thrills and fireworks, and I should've been smarter."

"Do you want to pick up where we left off?" Sawyer asked. "Or do you want us to come back when Eckstein is available?"

Royce wanted to glare at Sawyer but kept his gaze on Vincenzo instead, studying his demeanor and looking for any signs that the grief and cooperation was part of an act. Cynical was Royce's middle name, but this stripped-down, defeated version of the senator rang true. Gone were all traces of the polished public servant who glad-handed supporters, assured his constituents, and kissed babies.

"I meant what I said. I have nothing to hide," Vincenzo said gruffly. "Ask me anything."

Ninety minutes later, Royce and Sawyer were sitting across a desk from Mendoza, bringing him up to speed. His office had changed a lot since Royce's first meeting with the man, transforming from a stark, bare space to a warm environment with the addition of family photos, commendation plaques, bowling trophies, various certificates of achievement, and several plants.

The chief steepled his hands together, then rested his pressed fingertips against his chin dimple while Royce and Sawyer started their debriefing with the interviews at the law firm.

Mendoza lowered his hands. "There's a big difference in tone between Blakemore's first statement and his second concerning the conversation he overheard between Gross and Vincenzo. What did Vincenzo have to say about it during the second meeting?"

"While he couldn't confirm it was a direct quote, it sounded like something he would've said to her in a heated moment," Sawyer replied.

"He remembered using the nickname he'd given her years ago and recalled she laughed and hung up on him. Vincenzo was adamant that he hadn't meant what he said and hadn't killed her," Royce added.

Mendoza's gaze volleyed between the detectives. "Do you believe him?"

Royce and Sawyer exchanged a glance. They'd talked about the interview during their drive back to the precinct and were in complete agreement. "We do," they both said at once.

"Why?" Mendoza asked.

Royce had waited for a jarring reminder that a new chief was occupying the office, and it had finally arrived. It wasn't because Rigby had never asked him to clarify an issue or explain his thoughts, but her method and demeanor varied greatly from Mendoza's. Rigby would've approached the conversation by asking probing questions as they occurred to her. The new chief, while not in the least antagonistic, was challenging Royce and Sawyer to convince him. Mendoza wasn't about to make it easy for them by asking questions until they put in the effort. Rigby's manner was more expedient, but Mendoza's tested their acuity and awareness.

Responding with something asinine like "gut instinct" wouldn't work here. "Vincenzo's openness to discuss the affair—how it began, when it began, and how it ended—for starters," Royce said. "Shock might've loosened his tongue this morning, but he was just as forthright the second time around."

"More so, in my opinion," Sawyer added.

Royce nodded. "The senator admitted to arguing with her the following week and confirmed he said 'I could kill you, Vivie' or something similar. Naturally, we asked how they progressed from a blazing affair to a volatile argument ending with the words he'd said and Ms. Gross hanging up on him."

Mendoza quirked a brow as if to say "and..." Maybe the new chief wasn't as patient as Royce had first thought.

"He simply said it was how things were between him and Vivian," Sawyer said. "They didn't know how to do things the way normal people did. Everything was fire and ice with them. Then he dropped some huge bombs on our lap."

Royce snorted. "Atomic bombs. Plural."

Mendoza straightened in his chair and narrowed his eyes. *Aha! Got him.*

"The first surprise was when Vincenzo admitted he had decided to break off his engagement with Lucinda Fairchild," Sawyer told the chief. "They were running out of time to obtain a marriage license before their ceremony, and he had to choose. Vivian or Lucinda? He told us he'd spent too many years without Vivian and wasn't willing to spend another day pretending she wasn't the love of his life. Things got ugly when he informed his attorney, Matt Schultz, that he no longer wished to proceed with a divorce."

"The guy is an idiot," Royce added.

"King of idiots," Sawyer agreed. "Schultz discouraged the move, then confessed he'd hired a private investigator without Vincenzo's prompting to dig up dirt on Vivian. His goal was to pressure her into signing the paperwork, escalating the proceedings so they'd have time to obtain the marriage license without postponing the wedding."

"And that's when Vincenzo really rocked our world," Royce said.

"I can feel more gray hairs coming in as you speak," Mendoza said dryly, folding his arms over his chest.

Royce grinned. "Good thing you have our thoughtful gift to fall back on."

Sawyer leaned forward in his seat, drawing Mendoza's attention. "Let the record show I had no part in the decision. No one consulted me or asked for my opinion, and I did not contribute money."

Mendoza laughed. "Noted." He looked at Royce and circled his fingers in the air, urging him to get on with it.

Royce sighed, hoping the bus Sawyer threw him under was one of the smaller types like the one Daniel rode to preschool instead of the heavy, double-decker kind they used for big-city tours.

Royce aimed a good-natured glare at his partner, then continued. "According to Vincenzo, a guard at the county jail had secretly recorded Vivian and Humphries engaging in sex while he was incarcerated, which Schultz's PI uncovered. Recording devices aren't permitted in the rooms where the attorneys meet with their clients since whatever they talk about is confidential. I don't know who made the recordings or how, and we only have Vincenzo's word that they exist, but I believe him." The anguish and disgust had been real.

"Audio or visual?" Mendoza asked.

"Both," Royce said. "Vincenzo instructed Schultz to destroy them and insisted the PI destroy his copies too. After the meeting, the senator called Ms. Gross, and they argued. He told her he'd use the recording against her if she didn't sign the papers. She was adamant her affair with Humphries had been brief and had ended before she and Vincenzo rekindled their relationship."

"The senator claimed he was too hurt to believe her or even listen. The argument escalated into whatever Blakemore overheard. They hung up, and Vincenzo encouraged Schultz to keep digging."

"Christ," Mendoza said, scrubbing a hand over his head. "Could this get any more complicated?"

"Yes," Royce and Sawyer said at the same time, trading quick smiles.

"Not long after we arrived, Vincenzo kicked Schultz to the curb, but insisted the file he'd brought with him stay," Sawyer informed the chief, nodding at the file he'd placed on Mendoza's desk. "There are photos of Ms. Gross and Franco Humphries kissing in what appears to be the doorway of a motel room. The image has a time stamp from Thursday of last week, but we all know how those things can be manipulated. Vincenzo claims the photos were taken two days after the argument where Gross had told him she was no longer seeing Humphries."

"Interesting," Mendoza said, studying an enlarged photo of Gross and Humphries embracing. "Let's start building a timeline. Tuesday, Vincenzo and Gross argue about the sex tapes. On Thursday, Gross meets Humphries in a room at The Honeyhole Suites."

Royce snorted and Sawyer coughed when they realized the chief recognized the popular motel that rented rooms by the hour and identified it by the nickname it had earned over the years. The establishment was popular among sex workers and high school kids alike because they didn't ask for ID before handing over keys to a room. Royce had attended more than a few parties there back in his wilder days. He wasn't the only one it seemed.

Mendoza grinned wryly. "I was young once too, fellas."

Royce didn't feel brave enough to ask how Sawyer knew about the place, and Sawyer surely didn't want to hear about his adventures with the Mason twins.

"When did Schultz share the photos with Vincenzo?" Mendoza asked, steering them back on topic.

"Schultz had emailed the photos to Vincenzo as soon as he received them from the PI on Thursday night. He brought the print versions with him today," Royce said.

"Did Vincenzo contact Gross about the images?" Mendoza asked.

"Vincenzo told us he hadn't wanted to believe they were true because a part of him had held out hope Ms. Gross had been telling the truth, but the irrefutable proof said otherwise," Royce said.

"So, he just decided to let things go?" the chief asked. "It doesn't sound like Vincenzo to me."

"Rather than confront Ms. Gross about the photos, he decided to let Schultz handle things from there on out," Sawyer said. "Instead of breaking off his engagement with Ms. Fairchild like he'd planned earlier in the week, Vincenzo told her he had the ammunition he needed to expedite the dissolution. He was confident Gross would give in without a fight."

Mendoza tipped his head to the right. "Yet, he ended up spending the night at her house on Friday night."

"We're getting there, Chief," Royce said.

"Get there faster," Mendoza quipped.

"Gross called Vincenzo on Friday morning and said she needed to speak to him urgently," Sawyer said. "He told her all communications needed to go through their attorney, but Gross told him she wasn't calling about their divorce. She needed his professional opinion on how to handle a sticky situation regarding new evidence she uncovered which shed a different light on a client."

Mendoza's entire body tightened, and his nostrils flared. "Which client?" he wanted to know.

"Gross refused to say over the phone and asked if Vincenzo would meet her at her home. He claims she sounded rattled," Royce replied.

"Vincenzo told us he hadn't intended for them to have sex and had only wanted to make sure she was physically safe, so he could end their affair for good," Sawyer said. "He'd brought small copies of the photos taken outside the motel room as an insurance policy."

"Whoa," Mendoza said. "Why do I get the impression there's more?"

"There is," Royce confirmed. "Vincenzo said Gross was in a state of panic he'd never witnessed before, and when he pressed her for specific details, she would only say her conscience demanded she turn the new evidence over to the police, but it would lead to her getting disbarred. She couldn't see any way around it, and even if she miraculously retained her license to practice law, she'd be out of a job and have a tattered reputation. No firm would hire someone who'd betrayed a client and dragged her firm's name through the mud."

"She wasn't wrong," Mendoza agreed.

Sawyer nodded. "Vincenzo said one minute he was consoling her, and the next, they were in her bedroom. Afterward, Gross went to retrieve a smoke from the senator's suit pocket and found the pictures of her and Humphries."

"The senator smokes cigarettes?" Mendoza asked.

"It wasn't tobacco," Sawyer clarified.

"Ah," Mendoza said, absorbing the new information with a wry grin. "I'm guessing Ms. Gross wasn't happy about the photos and woke up the good senator to have a conversation?"

"A fight," Sawyer corrected.

"Fire and ice," Royce reminded Mendoza, using air quotes to emphasize he was quoting Vincenzo verbatim. "She told Vincenzo it was a misunderstanding. She'd claimed to have requested the meeting to inform Humphries about the recordings. She was certain he wouldn't want his wife to find out about their affair. Humphries allegedly claimed he didn't care if Tiffany found out and asked Gross for a chance at a real relationship now that he was out of jail. Gross told Vincenzo she'd said no, had attempted to leave, but Humphries caught her at the open door, spun her around, and kissed her. Gross claimed she only gripped his biceps because she'd lost her balance. It was a kneejerk response and not a passionate embrace like the photo portrayed. She'd pulled back as soon as she gained her equilibrium, clocked him a good one, and fled."

"They must've reached an agreement because he ended up staying the night," Mendoza said.

Sawyer nodded. "Vincenzo believed Gross was telling him the truth."

"Why? He could dismiss the recordings as old, but what about the photos? She must've been very convincing when she explained how the scene with Humphries played out."

"According to Vincenzo," Royce emphasized, looking at his notes. "Vivian told him she regretted the day she met Humphries. She emphatically stated she would never have taken him on as a client if she'd known the truth about him, and she certainly never would've let him put his filthy hands on her. She didn't know what came over her. She likened their interactions to being under his spell. He saw the loneliness she tried to hide beneath a power suit and exploited it. Ms. Gross implored Vincenzo to believe her."

"What did she know at the time of her death about Humphries that she hadn't known sooner?" Mendoza pondered out loud.

"And is this the knowledge she referenced in her conversation with Vincenzo on Friday morning?" Royce asked.

"If so, whatever she discovered compelled her to turn it over to the police, even if it meant she might not practice law again," Sawyer added.

"That's *if* Vincenzo is telling the truth," Royce reiterated. "The man voluntarily submitted to a DNA test, which we dropped off to Fawkes on our way back to the precinct. We'll know if the blood under her nails matches Vincenzo's profile. If so, we'll get a court order to search his body for scratches."

"There's one way to prove part of her story at least," Mendoza said as he picked up his cell phone from his desk. He never revealed the identity of the person who answered on the other end. "This is Mendoza. Did you have Humphries's detail last Thursday?" The chief waited for a response. "What happened outside the motel room?" Mendoza's jaw worked from side to side. "You didn't think to tell me about this incident? First, I want to know when a suspected serial rapist and killer is meeting women in a motel. Second, you tell me when the woman happens to be his attorney who Humphries forcefully grabs and kisses against her will. Did she hit him a good one at least?" Mendoza nodded at whatever the person said. "Good. Some PI shouldn't be doing your job for you, got it? Keep me posted, or I'll find someone else for this detail."

Royce fought off the urge to salute the man, and he wasn't the one getting his ass chewed. It irked him that Mendoza kept the identity of the people tailing Humphries a secret, but he understood it was best for the case. If Humphries spotted Royce following him, all hell would break loose.

Mendoza was still scowling after he disconnected the call. "Vivian's account of what happened outside The Honeyhole Suites is accurate. We have a big problem. Vivian Gross was contemplating turning in a client on Friday, she ends up dead sometime between five p.m. on Saturday evening and five a.m. on Sunday morning, and her briefcase with a client file is missing. Not just any client file, but the one she got into an altercation with, and the same one we think she was getting to roll over on. That's a motive for murder. Humphries was out of town, but it doesn't mean he didn't have help silencing a problem."

"Are you sure, sir?" Sawyer asked. "What if Humphries escorted his wife to the security checkpoint, then left the airport and rented a car without their detail catching on. I don't mean to imply I doubt your judgment, but I do question the person who failed to inform you about the incident between Humphries and Gross."

Mendoza turned his dark, inscrutable expression on Sawyer. "You don't think I've double-checked to make sure Humphries didn't give them the slip? I have a contact in the TSA who obtained video footage of Humphries boarding his plane in Savannah at noon and his connecting flight in Denver six hours later. What I would really like to know is when Humphries had planned his trip? Was this a spur-of-the-moment, romantic getaway, or an alibi?"

"We'll see what we can find out," Royce said.

"Discreetly," Mendoza reminded them.

Royce nodded. "Of course, sir."

"I want to know who Gross talked to between Friday morning when she called Vincenzo up until she died on Saturday night or Sunday morning. I want to know if we can tie this to Humphries in any way."

"I'll request a warrant for her phone records. Knowing she spoke to someone isn't the same as being privy to the conversation," Sawyer said. "Her client list isn't privileged information, so it's worth a shot."

"Fair enough," Mendoza said. "Do we know who this PI is? It's highly unlikely that no other copies of the sex tapes exist. Find the PI and find his source inside the prison. I want to know what else the guard knows."

"On it, Chief," Royce said as he and Sawyer rose to their feet.

Mendoza raised a hand, stopping them before they could leave. "One more thing. You two aren't the only ones with twists to reveal. The neighborhood canvass didn't turn up any witnesses to the crime, but Chen learned that Kendall's absence for the entire weekend was highly unusual. He frequently stayed away on Saturday nights, but rarely on Fridays, and never on Sundays. Several neighbors remarked on his absence."

"Interesting," Royce said, absorbing the information.

"We'll interview as many club coworkers as possible to find out if he acted oddly this weekend, or disappeared for unexplainable stretches in time," Sawyer added.

"Sounds good," Mendoza replied. "Now get out of here and solve this case."

Once outside his office, Sawyer glanced at his watch before grinning broadly. "Hungry?"

"Getting there," Royce replied.

"I know a place that serves excellent wings."

Royce narrowed his eyes. "You don't say?"

Sawyer's ornery smile and glittering dark gaze made him afraid. Very, very afraid.

CHAPTER 13

STOPPING AT HIS DESK, SAWYER TURNED TO FACE ROYCE. "BEFORE WE head out for lunch, I want to make a few calls and get started on the warrant for Gross's landline at home and also her cell phone."

"I'll go talk to Dottie and request the warrant. Do you have a particular judge you wish to send it to?" Royce asked him.

Sawyer had already narrowed it down to two judges in Mendoza's office. "Andrew Reinhardt or Seth Hastings." While he didn't know either man personally, he knew their reputations well. They were tough on attorneys and wouldn't just automatically dismiss the warrant without reviewing it thoroughly. "If we produce a well-written warrant that acknowledges the special circumstances and limitations, I think either man would sign off on it."

Royce nodded. "I trust your instincts." He lifted his hand like he was about to touch Sawyer, then jerked it back when he realized where they were. "Asshole," Royce muttered under his breath when he walked away, leaving Sawyer to chuckle in the bullpen by himself. He loved being irresistible to Royce Locke.

Sawyer glanced over at his desk and noticed the large pastry box from his favorite cupcake bakery sitting on it beside a cluster of mylar balloons that read "welcome back" and "we missed you."

The thoughtful gesture had Kelsey's name written all over it. It was another uncanny parallel to his first day on the force when Kels had surprised him with cupcakes and balloons after his mother revealed it was his birthday when she stopped by to take him to lunch. Sawyer almost expected Evangeline to sweep in at any moment. It was like a bizarre episode of *The Twilight Zone* and *Groundhog Day* all rolled into one. Was this some big universal do-over? He hoped not because he was deliriously happy with how their relationship had evolved, and he could go the rest of his life without seeing Royce get shot again or reliving the panic of getting trapped in a burning building.

Even though he was healing—physically and emotionally—recalling the final moments before Royce found him still had the power to send his pulse soaring and turn his legs to limp noodles. Grateful for a rare private moment in the bullpen, Sawyer pulled his chair away from his desk and flopped down in it. He caught a glimpse of his reflection in the darkened computer monitor and barely resisted the urge to touch his mottled skin. Stop being a vain asshole. *Breathe in. Hold. Release.*

He forced his gaze away; his eyes landed on the cheerful pastry box. It wasn't there when they'd arrived to meet with the chief, which meant Kelsey had stopped by when he was in Mendoza's office. Sawyer removed his cell phone from his pocket and dialed Kels. The call went to voicemail, and he had to settle for hearing her recorded voice in her outgoing message.

"Kels, I'm sorry I missed you. Thanks so much for the cupcakes and balloons. You're the best. Hopefully things settle down and we can hit up our favorite Mexican restaurant for lunch later this week. I'll drop by your office later to share the goodies. Love you."

After he disconnected the call, Sawyer powered up his computer and searched the internet for articles on Humphries that included interviews with neighbors who seemed to support him.

"What are you doing?" Royce asked when he returned a few minutes later.

"Do you remember how media outlets blasted those images of Humphries with his long-haired Dachshunds all over the place?"

Royce's brow furrowed as he sat down at the desk across from his. Sawyer's fingers itched to smooth out his stress lines. "Yeah. Cute little pups."

"I'll be sure to tell Bones you feel that way," Sawyer replied dryly.

Royce snorted. "I'll call you a liar while slipping him a chunk of bread. We'll see who he believes."

"Who?" Ashcroft asked, sauntering up to their desks. "Welcome back, kid."

"Thanks, Ashcroft," Sawyer said, inwardly cringing at the nickname. Ashcroft couldn't have been much older than him. The man was caustic and often rude, but he was a good detective. Rather than answer his question, Sawyer opened the pastry box and extended it to him. "We have cupcakes."

"Don't mind if I do," Ashcroft replied, helping himself to a mint chocolate chip cupcake as he plopped his ass on the corner of Sawyer's desk. "No one tell Mindy about this. She's put me on a diet again." The Andy Sipowicz lookalike rubbed a hand over the round gut protruding over his belt and straining at his shirt buttons. Concerned one might pop loose and put out his eye, Sawyer discreetly scooted his chair over to give himself some more space. He propped his left ankle on his right knee, then leaned back in his chair to strike a conversational pose, hoping his distaste for Ashcroft's inability to respect personal space wasn't too obvious.

Royce raised up and stretched across the expanse of their desks, snagging a strawberry and cream cupcake for himself. "I think Mindy Ashcroft is as real as Santa Claus."

"She *does* exist," Ashcroft dramatically said, sounding like the M&M's in the commercial who faint when they discover Santa is real.

"Then why have none of us ever met her?" Royce countered. "I've met everyone else's spouse or significant other besides yours. Why is that?"

Ashcroft tipped back his head and laughed heartily. "You have looked in the mirror, haven't you?"

Royce looked at Ashcroft like he'd lost his mind, but Sawyer understood. Ashcroft wanted to keep his wife away from the hottest detective in the unit—one who'd had a reputation for being a man-whore. Ashcroft was smarter than he looked, and Sawyer had to bite his lip to keep from laughing.

"You're off the market now and into dudes these days, so I guess there's no harm in bringing her around to meet everyone."

"Wait," Royce said, holding up his hand. "You thought I was going to have an affair with your wife? You think that poorly of me?" Royce's voice pitched lower as his frustration rose.

Sawyer wished he had popcorn to eat while watching the confrontation play out but settled for a German chocolate cupcake instead.

Ashcroft shrugged. "Come on, Locke. You knew damn well what your reputation was, and you both fed into it and played off it at the same time. It shielded you from all of us trying to fix you up with our wives' friends, sisters, or cousins."

"True," Royce said, conceding the point. "I never would've slept with any of your wives or girlfriends."

"Right. Now we know why."

Royce opened his mouth to argue more but must've thought better of it because only a long sigh slid from those gorgeous lips.

"So, what were you two lovebirds arguing about?" Ashcroft asked, then bit off half his cupcake in one bite. Telling the man to keep his voice down would do no good since he only had one tone: loud.

"We're fighting over who our cat likes best," Royce said with a negligent shrug. Our cat. It was the simplest remark, but if Sawyer were a cartoon, he'd be making heart eyes at Royce. Judging by the smug smirk on Royce's lips, Sawyer might actually be shooting hearts at him.

Ashcroft choked on the cupcake, and it took him a few minutes of sputtering to right himself before he could speak again. "Oh, how the mighty have fallen, Locke," he said, shaking his head as he exited the bullpen, leaving them alone again.

"Why the fuck were we even arguing over our cat to begin with?" Royce asked when they were alone again. He snapped his fingers. "Ah. We were talking about Humphries's dogs and how the media kept showing pictures of the man with them as if to prove he can't be a serial killer if he dresses up his wiener dogs for Halloween and poses with them for pictures."

Sawyer knew Royce's wheels were spinning when he tilted his head and stared off into space.

"We are not *ever* buying a Halloween costume for Bones," Sawyer said before the idea could take root. "We're especially not wearing matching costumes with the cat. That's a level of gayness I will never achieve."

"I wasn't thinking that," Royce countered unconvincingly. "Wait, there are levels of gayness? Like an epic video game where you must complete challenges to advance? What's it called?" He leaned forward, bracing his forearms on his desk. "How many tasks have I completed and what have my prizes been so far? Is there a point system? What are the rules? Why am I just now learning about this? I would've expected someone like you to explain things better during orientation?"

Sawyer laughed harder with every question until he couldn't breathe. "Orientation?"

"That time you dry humped me in your home gym," Royce whisper shouted. "After I blew my load, you should've told me how many beginner's points I achieved. I aced that gay porn challenge, yeah? I definitely remember my prize that night." Royce waggled his brows. "Oh, I bet offering up my ass was the mack daddy of all challenges. That was a reward in and of itself."

"Stop," Sawyer said between gasps, wiping the tears from his face. No one could make him laugh and live in the moment like Royce could.

Royce smiled sweetly and ate his cupcake while Sawyer pulled himself together. Sawyer ached to reach across their desks to swipe the dot of icing at the corner of Royce's mouth, then lick it off his thumb. He settled for tapping his own lip. Royce's tongue darted out to capture the icing, and Sawyer couldn't help but track its progress. He finally glanced up and met Royce's stormy gaze.

Giving himself a good mental shake, Sawyer said, "If you weren't coming up with costume ideas for Bones, then what were you thinking about?"

Royce chuckled. "I, uh, don't remember now since you distracted me. Why don't you share the significance of your computer search?"

Sawyer cleared his throat. "If the trip to Mexico was a last-minute decision, he would've scrambled to make arrangements for his dogs. Sure, he might've boarded them on short notice, or he might've trusted a close neighbor to look after them."

Royce straightened in his chair and grinned. "I love the way your brain works, GB. Even if he did board the dogs, he or his wife would've probably asked a trustworthy neighbor to keep an eye on the place."

"Exactly," Sawyer said, grinning at his partner. "Once we find the right neighbor, one of us can call them and impersonate someone who wouldn't raise red flags. You know reporters have made these people's lives a living hell at times."

Royce nodded. "What's a safe choice?"

"You think it over while I find the right person to call."

A few minutes later, Sawyer found what he was looking for. Lucretia Meyers had lived by the Humphrieses since they moved into the neighborhood six years ago. Several media outlets interviewed her on multiple occasions and even included photos with most of the articles. One piece referred to her as Lulu instead of Lucretia, indicating the woman had built a rapport with the reporter.

"Found her," Sawyer said, then read off parts of an interview where she talked about dog sitting for the Humphrieses. "'No one who loves animals the way Franco does Beatrice and Pumpernickel can be bad.'"

"She's the one," Royce agreed. He searched for a contact number, then took a big sip of water before picking up the phone and dialing. "Hello, is this Lucretia Meyers?" Royce had added vibrato and slowed his cadence to disguise his voice. Sawyer averted his gaze so he wouldn't start laughing and blow Royce's cover. He'd been horrible at phone pranks as a kid. "This is Sylvester Goodfellow calling from South University," Royce continued. "I'm sorry to bother you, but—" Mrs. Meyers must've cut him off because he stopped talking suddenly. Sawyer looked up and noticed the delighted gleam in his partner's eyes. "Yes, ma'am. I am calling about Franco. I'm trying to get ahold of him, but he's not answering his phone or returning my messages. Franco listed you as an emergency contact if we couldn't reach Mrs. Humphries, which is also the case. I thought you might be able to help me. It's imperative I speak to him." Royce blinked rapidly and fiddled with the collar of his polo shirt.

Sawyer nodded to encourage him and mouthed, "You're doing good."

"Well, that does make sense," Royce said in response to whatever Lulu said. "A second honeymoon before he starts back at the university is just what they need."

Sawyer's heart sank. Humphries was returning to his favorite hunting ground. Jesus. He didn't know if the university believed in the man's innocence or was afraid Humphries would bring a lawsuit against them too.

"I wouldn't answer my phone either if I were them," Royce told Lulu. "He didn't mention anything to me when we talked last week, or I wouldn't have bothered him. What's that?" Royce asked. "It was a last-minute decision? Uh-huh. Yes, I see. I'll patiently wait for him to return my call. Thank you so much, Mrs. Meyers. Good day to you, ma'am."

Royce returned the desk phone to its cradle. His gray eyes looked a little wild when they met Sawyer's. "They're taking the fucker back."

"They probably don't have a choice," Sawyer countered, knowing it was the last thing Royce wanted to hear. "The DA dropped all charges against him, and there was no credible evidence tying him to the four coeds."

"Everyone has a choice," Royce said. "They could've offered him a severance package. They could've asked him for more time to let things die down first."

"We need to consider that they believe him," Sawyer said, playing devil's advocate. "What did Lulu say about his second honeymoon?"

Royce exhaled deeply and released the breath slowly. Sawyer raked his teeth over his bottom lip to keep from smiling at the evidence of his influence on the man he loved. "Lulu said it was a spur-of-the-moment decision because he hadn't expected to get reinstated so quickly. It was now or never, according to her. They asked her late Friday morning to watch the dogs and dropped them off on Saturday before leaving for the airport. They're due back on Wednesday afternoon."

If they come back.

Sawyer knew they were both thinking it but neither wanted to say the words out loud. The idea that Franco Humphries could live out the rest of his days enjoying the beach life in Mexico after raping and killing at least four women was too sickening to comprehend.

Sawyer sat up straighter in his chair and narrowed his eyes while he rolled the timeline around in his head. "Friday, as in the day Vivian Gross was wrestling with her conscience about new evidence that had suddenly come to light. Evidence she had wanted to turn over to the police. Either she had the goods on Humphries, and he had someone silence her, or this is all a big coincidence."

"I don't believe in coincidence," Royce replied.

"Neither do I, but I'm running out of ideas on how to pursue this further without speaking to Humphries directly."

"I think the first thing we have to do is verify Humphries is telling the truth about the university reinstating him. He could've lied about it to his neighbor, knowing he could come up with a dozen different excuses for why it didn't pan out later."

"I agree," Sawyer said. "What are you thinking?"

Royce heaved a sigh. "As much as I hate to say it, I think we need to ask Felix to poke around his contacts. While you're reaching out to him, I'll call Jacobs and let him know we need help finding the PI on Schultz's payroll. Maybe they can both obtain the information in time for the meeting tonight."

"Deal," Sawyer said, then picked up his phone to dial Felix. His call went to voicemail, so he left the reporter a detailed message. When he hung up, Royce was still verbally sparring with Jacobs.

"I'm not kissing your ass, dipshit," Royce groused into the phone. "Are you going to do this or not?"

Sawyer shook his head and unfolded the list of names Blakemore had given them. They needed to interview the managers, bartenders, waitstaff, and bouncers at the club who worked with Blakemore over the weekend. The likelihood of finding all of them working the same shift was nil, but he hoped to interview as many of them today as possible. Royce's voice got louder, and his tone grew snappier, then he exchanged another round of insults with the PI, so Sawyer decided to call The Cockpit to find out if anyone on the list was on duty now.

A few minutes later, he hung up the phone and noticed Royce watching him intently.

"Know the phone number by heart, do you?" Royce asked. "Is that one of the gayness challenges?"

God, he loved to stir the jealous beast residing beneath Royce's skin, but this wasn't the time or place for it, so he held up the piece of paper and pointed to the phone number Blakemore provided them.

"Oh," Royce said.

"None of the people we need to speak with are working right now," Sawyer informed him.

"Figures since you got me worked up over the idea of eating wings for lunch," Royce said.

"I can treat you to the second-best wing place for lunch and save the best wings for later when we interview the staff at The Cockpit," Sawyer suggested.

"I'm not so big a fan of chicken wings that I want to eat them twice in one day," Royce replied. "I know my eating habits can be as atrocious as a fourteen-year-old boy's at times, but even I'm not that bad."

"Now or later, then?" Sawyer asked. "You pick."

Royce rose from his chair. "You're going to eat chicken wings?"

"I'll order a large salad and a small order of wings," Sawyer said. "It's all about the balance." He pocketed the car keys and led the way out of the bullpen. "I had to leave a message for Felix. What did Jacobs say? Does he have any idea which PI is working for Schultz? How many private investigators can there be in Savannah?"

Royce chuckled bitterly. Sawyer stopped and faced him, searching his boyfriend's face. Then it dawned on him why Royce and Rocky were fighting. "No fucking way."

Royce nodded. "Rocky said there's more to the story than meets the eye. I told him we'd give him one chance to explain why he kept this information from us."

"I think I lost my appetite," Sawyer said. The cupcake suddenly felt like a brick in his stomach. They'd trusted the PI even when common sense dictated they shouldn't. No one liked to be made a fool of, but especially not veteran police officers who should know better.

"You need to keep up your strength," Royce said, nudging Sawyer's arm with his elbow. "I don't want you fainting at the first sight of a pretty boy in an aviator costume."

Sawyer's lips curved into a slow smile. "You're such a dickhead."

Royce's playful wink said, "True, but I'm your dickhead."

CHAPTER 14

STANDING IN THEIR KITCHEN AND SURVEYING THE FOOD CHOICES, Holly said, "This is a letdown."

Sawyer chuckled and shrugged. "Pizza and garlic knots were the best I could do on short notice."

Royce elbowed him playfully. "I told you not to go overboard for our first meeting because they'd come to expect it every time."

"Damn right we do," Blue said, his forlorn tone matching his hangdog expression.

"You couldn't have added a few chicken wings into the mix?" Chen asked.

"We had those for lunch," Royce said. "No one eats wings twice in one day."

"Speak for yourself, little bro," Jace said as he helped himself to the pizza and garlic knots.

"Oh, hey," Holly said, "I wasn't bitching because I expected lobster rolls, but you could've at least bought us bread dicks again, Sawyer."

Jonah had just taken a bite of a garlic knot, and it got lodged in his throat. Felix patted the big man's back during the coughing fit that followed. "Bread *dicks*?" Jonah asked once he could breathe without coughing. "Did I hear her right?" He looked to Sawyer fo

Sawyer shrugged. "We ordered garlic knots once and got bread dicks instead."

Holly and Royce jumped in, embellishing the hell out of the story and making everyone laugh. It was a good stress breaker. By the time their Operation Venus Flytrap meeting commenced at six thirty, everyone had heard about Vivian Gross's murder, and the speculations were all over the place. Sawyer embraced the humor because he didn't know when he'd get another chance to laugh at something simple.

The doorbell rang, and Sawyer set his plate down on the kitchen island. "That must be Rocky." *It better be him.*

"I'll come with you," Royce said, setting his plate down too. He pointed his finger at Jace. "Don't spit on my food."

"What the fuck?" Jace asked. "We're not children. And why does it take both of you to answer the door? Oh, wait. Do I need to pinky-swear that I'll keep my mouth shut before you answer the question?" Jace looked at Holly. "What's the cone thingy called again?"

"Silence," she replied dryly. "You should practice it sometime."

"Ouch," Royce said as he followed Sawyer out of the kitchen. "It better be Jacobs." Their visitor hit the doorbell three more times in rapid succession before they reached the front door. "Yep, it's definitely that fucker."

Sawyer opened the door and glared at the PI. "It's about time you got here. Tardiness only makes me angrier."

"Yeah, yeah, yeah," Rocky said, pushing past Sawyer and coming to a halt when Royce stepped into his path.

The home had an open-floor concept, so the rest of the group could plainly see the confrontation taking place in the foyer. Sawyer glanced over, and sure enough, everyone else had their eyes glued to the interaction, wearing various expressions ranging from amusement to concern. Jace was the concerned party, but Sawyer knew he wouldn't intervene unless Royce was in danger, which was not the case here.

"Look," the PI said, holding up his hands, "I know you have questions. I don't blame you."

"Well, as long as you don't blame *us*, then I guess it's okay." Royce's accompanying eyeroll matched his sarcastic tone of voice.

"You're not the only ones who are obligated to keep parts of your investigations confidential. I wrestled with my conscience on what to do. Uphold my contract to my client, or do the right thing? I had decided to tell you guys about it before I even heard what happened to Vivian Gross."

"I want to believe you," Sawyer said.

Rocky grinned wryly. "Be mad all you want, but I think you'll change your mind when I tell you why I'm late. I assure you it had nothing to do with avoiding a confrontation with you guys. I got a call this afternoon that will possibly break Operation Venus Flytrap wide open. I'm pretty sure I know who our Bonnie Parker is."

"You've just bought yourself a stay of execution," Royce said grimly. "I still don't trust you."

"Well, I still don't like you. We're even," Rocky quipped.

"Come on in and grab a bite to eat," Sawyer said, aiming a *be nice* look at Royce.

The others greeted Rocky with various reactions. The law enforcement officers in the room were wary, the reporter was downright hostile, but Jace was friendly and offered his hand to the newcomer.

Rocky picked up the last clean plate off the island and began opening lids to pizza boxes. "Ah-ha. Hawaiian pizza! Someone in the universe is looking out for me."

Royce shuddered. "Should've known the PI likes ham and pineapple on pizza."

"No pizza shaming," Sawyer countered. Royce had already made his displeasure known when Sawyer placed the order. He'd told Royce that those who eat processed cheese products out of an aerosol can are in no position to criticize others. The teasing led to

174

good-natured name-calling which led to kissing and would've morphed into best-natured hand jobs if the people and pizza hadn't arrived.

The vibe in the room had changed drastically with Rocky's arrival, and it seemed like the group fed off the tension they'd picked up from Sawyer and Royce. On the bright side, it meant they ate and got to the meeting quicker, but on the reverse, it meant a cloud of volatility floated above them like fumes just waiting for a spark to ignite it.

Fumes. Ignite. One minute, Sawyer was standing in his kitchen eating pizza, and the next, he was trapped inside the burning church. Sawyer had never experienced heat like that before in his life. Every breath he took seared his throat and lungs as his airway seemed to shrink smaller and smaller. The acrid smell of his burning clothes and flesh made him sick to his stomach. The pain throughout his body was so severe it was a miracle he hadn't blacked out. Then he heard someone calling his name through the billowing, black smoke. The voice sounded like it was coming from a great distance away, and Sawyer briefly thought it was Vic calling out to him as he transitioned to the afterlife. No. He wasn't ready. He didn't want to leave Royce and the happiness he'd found. Then he heard the voice again, but this time it was closer and more distinct.

Asshole! I'm coming. Where are you?

Royce bumped his hip into Sawyer, jarring him back to reality. "You okay? You're as pale as a ghost."

Sawyer set his plate down on the island. For the second time that day, the food he'd consumed turned heavy in his stomach, killing his appetite. He forced a smile on his face. "Yeah. As good as can be expected, considering the circumstances."

"Speaking of circumstances," Rocky said, seizing the moment to address the group. "I think I found the break we need."

Felix snorted, then said, "Wow. Aren't you a grandiose fucker?"

"Wow. Look who's showing off his five-dollar words," Rocky countered.

"Oh, for fuck's sake," Holly groused. "Both of you shut the hell up. No one wants to see your tiny dicks, so there's no need for you to whip them out and wave them around. Jacobs, tell us what you know."

"That's my girl," Jace said, hooking an arm around her waist and pulling her close so he could kiss her temple. "Badass."

"Which you'll see firsthand if you forget to put the toilet seat down in the middle of the night again. Nothing wakes you up like falling into a toilet."

Sawyer's mind drifted back to the way Royce had woken him that morning. Royce hip-checked him once more, but this time he saw desire in his boyfriend's gaze instead of worry. Royce knew exactly where Sawyer's mind had gone.

"I've been working on getting information about our missing courier for Richmond Laboratories," Rocky said. "When trying to find someone older like Reginald Dozer, it pays to dig through yearbooks because their generation often stays in touch. I know my parents still go on vacation with friends they made in high school. I have yearbooks at my office dating back to 1922, and they've paid off dozens of times in the past. I learned our pal Reginald was a star athlete. He was captain of the baseball and basketball teams his senior year of high school back in 1962. To this day, those teams still hold several school records. I made a list of his closest friends based on various photos in the yearbooks and archived newspaper articles. I compiled a list and began tracking his friends down. Sadly, several of them died in Vietnam, but I was able to locate a few friends who retired in Florida and one who now lives in Arizona. I struck out locally since the only friend still around here lives in a nursing home. His dementia is severe and requires round-the-clock care."

Rocky set his plate on the counter and wiped his hand on a napkin.

"Reggie's best friend in high school was his co-captain, Clyde Brothers, who now lives in Florida with his wife. I decided to pretend to be a reporter writing an article about a sport anniversary. How hard could it be, right?"

"Fuck you," Felix snarled.

"You couldn't get so lucky," Rocky replied.

The two men stared daggers at one another. *Here's the spark that will ignite the charge and scorch us all.*

"Why don't the two of you do us all a favor and just fuck already," Jace said.

The PI and the reporter aimed their disgust at Jace, but neither voiced their opposition to the idea. *Interesting.*

"As I was saying," Rocky said, getting back on track. "I called to talk about sports, and let Brothers ramble as long as he wanted. When he started to tire out, I asked him about Reginald. I told him I hadn't been able to track him down, and no one had seen or heard from him in a while. Clyde admitted it was strange but said they'd drifted apart a bit after Reggie's wife died. Then, Clyde commented on the irony of the situation since his granddaughter had called recently and asked questions about Reggie too. She said she'd met him while on the job. Reggie had seen her last name and asked if she was related to Clyde. She wanted to tell her grandpa about the conversation. Then Clyde branched off to talk about their hunting and fishing adventures together over the years."

"What's her name?" Royce asked.

Rocky waited for a heartbeat, making sure he had everyone's attention. He pulled up a picture on his phone and held it up for them to see. He'd snapped a picture of a black-and-white image in a yearbook, but there was no denying it matched the drawing the sketch artist made while interviewing Tobias. "Meet Bonita Brothers."

"Bonita and Clyde," Sawyer whispered. She was blonde, pale, and had light-colored eyes with features so generic she could blend in anywhere without drawing attention to herself.

"Naturally," Rocky continued, "I prompted Clyde to tell me how his conversation with Bonita went. This woman is good. She got her grandfather to admit Reggie was a childless widower and only son to parents who died a while ago. He didn't think twice about revealing Reggie's personal story."

"What do you want to bet she sized up every courier to see which one would make the best target?" Jonah asked.

Rocky nodded. "Reggie was an easy mark with no family to report him missing right away. The police probably weren't notified until after he missed work for a day or two."

Sawyer recalled the police report he'd dug up on the missing courier. "The evidence swap happened on a Friday, and Reggie's supervisor reported him missing on Tuesday after he failed to show for work on two consecutive days." Bile burned his esophagus. "By that time, Reggie had probably been dead for almost four days."

"We don't know he's dead, GB," Royce said gently, but Sawyer could see the resignation in his eyes.

"I agree with Sawyer on this point," Rocky said. "I accessed his bank records. There were no unexplainable deposits indicating he received a payoff or sizeable withdrawals to show he planned to run. There has been zero activity on any of his accounts since he disappeared."

Further proof Reggie wasn't living out his days on the same beach in Mexico Humphries was visiting. Bonita "Bonnie" Brothers killed him to steal the evidence. But how did she know when to take it, and had Humphries put her up to it?

"What was Bonita's job that brought her into contact with Reggie?" Sawyer asked.

"She worked at Sattler and Sons florists," Rocky replied. "I called and asked to speak to her but was informed she no longer worked there. The person who answered got suspicious when I started probing further, so I don't know when she left her job or why."

"What do you want to bet Miss Bonita Brothers delivered flowers to all the key locations?" Blue asked. "No one thinks twice about delivery people."

"The DA's office, our precinct, and even the lab where Reginald worked," Sawyer said, nodding. "What do you want to bet they all received flowers around that time?"

"I know for a fact people discuss shit they shouldn't with a delivery person close by," Rocky said. "I've used the disguise plenty of times."

"Uh-huh," Holly agreed.

"You're not fully out of the doghouse yet," Royce said, pointing at Rocky, "but this is a damn good start. Sawyer and I will take a trip to Sattler and Sons tomorrow morning and interview the staff there. If nothing else, maybe we can get a list of all her deliveries in the past four months. We can start with current ones and work our way backward, paying special attention to key dates in our timeline."

"Anyone else have updates?" Sawyer asked.

"Stella and I reviewed all the prison footage Royce sent us," Jonah said. Sawyer loved how the agent made his supercomputer sound like a human sidekick. "Bonnie never visited Humphries in prison. We also didn't pick up any secret code used between Humphries and his visitors."

"I've come up empty trying to find a public travel schedule for Humphries. It would seem the universities have removed all traces of his speaking engagements," Felix said. "I know of at least three universities off the top of my head that were mentioned in various articles, but you get a big goose egg if you type in the universities plus Humphries's name in the browser."

"Lucky for us, I know someone with amazing computer skills," Jonah said wryly, a telling blush staining his cheeks. *How interesting.* Sawyer had meant to ask how Avery was doing with his internship. They'd met the young hacker while investigating The Purists, which had turned out to be an insane priest who used the information parishioners confessed to him as ammunition to blackmail or expose them so he could build a new order. The kid could've freaked out and run from trouble when Royce asked for his help but had chosen to stay and direct firefighters to the correct part of the building. Sawyer and Royce were alive because of Avery Bradford. "Nothing is ever fully deleted once it goes on the internet." Jonah started typing notes on his phone.

"Thanks," Felix said appreciatively.

"No problem," Jonah replied. If the big man noticed Felix's attraction, he didn't let on.

Rocky watched the exchange and rolled his eyes.

"What about you, Holls?" Royce asked. "Anything exciting happening in Humphries's fan club?"

"Bizarre is more like it," Holly replied. "There are no Bonitas or Bonnies in the group, but there is this one chick who raises red flags every time she posts or comments."

"Why?" Jonah asked, sounding riveted.

"Her name is Beatrice, and unlike most of the women in the group, she's never expressed a lot of respect or gratitude for Vivian Gross. As you can imagine, when the news of Vivian's death broke in the group, most of the members were horrified. Some of them mentioned having a candlelight vigil in Vivian's honor tonight. Beatrice got snotty in some comments, reminding everyone it was a fan club for Humphries, not Vivian."

"Interesting," Sawyer said. "Why does the name Beatrice sound familiar?" he asked Royce, who shrugged.

"Beatrice Ryen is her name," Holly said.

Sawyer thought the name held significance but couldn't be sure why. It hadn't come up during any interviews. "I wonder if Beatrice Ryen disliked Vivian enough to want her dead? There's no way in hell Humphries personally killed Gross."

"How do you know?" Jacobs asked.

"He's out of the country," Royce said. "This information doesn't leave the room. So far, the media hasn't picked up on it, and we want to keep it that way for as long as we can."

"I should go to the vigil. There's no way Beatrice will be able to resist attending and showing her ass," Holly said.

"No fucking way," Jace said. "I don't want you anywhere near that psycho."

Holly tilted her head to the side and leveled Jace with a glare so hot it could've melted an iceberg. "Weren't you just the one who called me a badass?" she asked.

"I did. It's true," Jace said, nodding. "That doesn't mean I want you sticking your neck out there when you don't need to. Royce and Sawyer are going to interview the florist tomorrow. We think this woman is a killer, Holls."

"I'm a cop, Jace. I put killers away," she countered. There was no anger in her voice, only firm resonance. Jace's mouth opened to argue, but then he must've thought better of it. Instead, he took a deep breath and kissed her temple once more.

"I'm not convinced you showing up there is the best course of action, right now," Royce said.

Holly turned her laser-like gaze on the younger Locke brother. "Why?"

"We're close, Holls. I can feel it," Royce replied. "You know better than any of us that it's all about the timing with undercover work. If we push too hard, we'll scare her off."

Holly heaved a frustrated sigh and conceded with a nod.

"Beatrice Ryen, aside from having a first name starting with the letter B, has a lot in common with Bonita Brothers," Jonah said, scrolling through his phone. He showed the screen to Holly. "Is this the right profile?"

"Yeah, she used to have a Dachshund as her profile pic but changed it to a vase of flowers today."

"Dachshund?" Alarm bells started ringing in Sawyer's head. "Let me see the photo, please."

Jonah turned the phone around so Sawyer and Royce could see the screen.

"That's not just any wiener dog," Royce said. "That's Humphries's dog, Beatrice. The photo was one of the Halloween pictures the media blasted all over the place."

"Ryen," Sawyer said absently. "Pumpernickel is a type of rye bread."

"Holy fuck. It is her," Royce said. "Bonita Brothers is our Bonnie Parker *and* Beatrice Ryen."

CHAPTER 15

ROYCE'S HEART POUNDED IN HIS CHEST. "WE JUST NEED TO TIE ALL these loose strings together."

"What about the profile picture of the flowers?" Sawyer asked.

Jonah nodded and pulled up Beatrice Ryen's current profile picture.

"Fuck me," Sawyer and Royce said at the same time.

"Those look like the pink roses in Vivian Gross's office," Royce said.

"They *are* her flowers," Sawyer said in a voice barely above a whisper. He cleared his throat. "I recognize the ivory vase with cherubs on it. This psychopath took photos of the flowers in her office for whatever reason."

"Trophy?" Royce asked. Why not just take the flowers with her, then?"

"I toggled between the two profiles while you guys were discussing the candlelight vigil. Both women are claiming to major in psychology at South University," Jonah said.

"Her grandfather mentioned she was enrolled at South, but my discreet inquiry revealed she just suddenly stopped attending classes," Rocky informed them.

"It's an avenue we need to explore," Sawyer said.

"They also have the same birthdate," Jonah added.

"Isn't that careless?" Felix asked. "If you're smart enough to create alternate personalities, then why not make it drastically different from your real identity?"

"It's smarter to keep your fake profile as close to your real one as much as possible," Jonah replied. "It's much less likely you'll trip up and give yourself away if you're only changing minor things."

"It's true," Holly agreed. "You don't try to pass yourself off as a brain surgeon if your only work experience is as a fry cook."

"We're back to questioning how Bonita Brothers knew the evidence was moving, and whether she acted alone or on orders from Humphries," Sawyer said.

Royce nodded. "Here's what we're going to do. Ky, I know you and Blue were unable to find a connection between anyone employed at SPD, the DA, or Richmond Laboratories and Humphries or anyone named Parker, so I want you to run Bonita Brothers's aliases against the visitor's log from the county jail. Flag any females, especially ones with names starting with the letter B. This is starting to sound like a weird episode of *Sesame Street*," Royce said, shaking his head while the rest of them laughed. "I don't recall any other women visiting him except his wife and Vivian Gross, and Jonah and his software didn't recognize her, but please triple-check for me."

"You got it, Sarge," Ky said.

"What about me?" Blue asked. "I want a task. I want a task."

"Ass kisser," Ky teased, elbowing Blue.

"If I can get a list of Bonita's deliveries, I'll put you in charge of scrubbing the list to find ones made at key locations," Royce replied. "Maybe one of the individuals who received flowers is our traitor."

"No problem," Blue said.

"Felix, were you able to confirm Humphries is returning to work at South?" Royce asked.

"Yeah, it's true. The board was divided, but not about

Humphries's innocence. According to my source, none of the board members believed he committed the rapes and murders, but many of them didn't want to reinstate him due to the scandal it would invoke. They're trying to keep their decision quiet for as long as they can."

"Can you make sure it doesn't happen?" Sawyer asked.

"Absolutely," he said with a firm nod and wicked grin.

"Well, I hate to throw you all out, but Sawyer and I have witnesses we need to track down tonight," Royce said, pinning Rocky with a look to remind him they had much to discuss. He wasn't the only one Royce wanted to have a private word with though, so Royce shifted his attention to Jonah. The big man nodded. Message received.

"Yeah, sure," Holly said drolly. "Why not just admit that getting close to solving the case is revving up your engines, and you need to blow off steam."

"Get out, Holls," Royce said affectionately.

"Fine," she said, grabbing Jace's hand and pulling him from the kitchen.

"We never even got to sit down," Jace grumbled. "Our ma taught him better manners than to invite people over and make them stand around the kitchen island to eat."

"It's young love," Holly replied.

Ky and Blue laughed, snagged some leftover pizza, and headed out too, leaving Jonah, Felix, and Rocky. Felix sensed a scoop but wasn't dumb enough to ask probing questions or stick around after finishing the slice of pizza on his plate.

"See you around," he tossed over his shoulder on his way to the door.

"Divide and conquer?" Sawyer asked Royce.

Royce nodded. "Which one do you want?"

Sawyer tipped his head to the side and pressed his forefinger to his lips for a few seconds. He wasn't fooling Royce, so it was no surprise when he answered. "I'll talk to Jonah in the study while you and Rocky work out your differences."

"Don't hold your breath, GB."

Once they were alone, Royce opened his mouth to blast Rocky with his opinion about the PI's moral character, or lack thereof, but the man held up his hand to stop the tirade before Royce could start.

"I reported the prison guard to the warden as soon as I became aware of the situation. I followed up this week only to discover the man is still employed and wasn't reprimanded as far as I could tell, so I forwarded the details to the Federal Bureau of Prisons."

"After you shared the information with Chad Schultz, who could've done God knows what with it," Royce countered.

"Schultz hired me to do a job, and I did it. He wanted dirt on Vivian, and I gave it to him."

"How in the world did they get videos?" Royce said. "There are no cameras in the attorney meeting rooms."

"There have to be hidden ones because there's no denying what I saw. I don't feel good about it, and I deeply regret sharing the information with Schultz, especially if it resulted in her murder."

"What about the photographs you took of Vivian and Humphries outside the motel? Why'd you frame them to look like they were sharing a passionate embrace?"

"What photos? I shot a video of the encounter, including when she clocked him upside the head for kissing her. If there are photos, Schultz printed them off to push whatever narrative he was trying to feed to his client."

"You don't know who the client is?" Royce asked.

Rocky shook his head. "Do you?"

"Sure do," Royce replied smugly. "I'm not telling you, so don't bother asking. Why didn't you tell me about Vivian and Humphries? You knew they carried on an affair in prison, and you witnessed him grab her and force a kiss on her last week. You didn't think I should know about it?"

"In hindsight, yeah. I should've told you, but Gross seemed to have it under control."

As much as Royce wanted to continue calling Rocky out on his poor judgment, the surveillance detail Mendoza had put on Humphries made the same dumb decision. He could continue to re-hash everything Rocky did wrong over the past few weeks, or he could acknowledge the sincere regret he saw in Rocky's eyes and heard in his voice.

"Wait," Rocky said suddenly. "Why am I groveling? I found the person who stole your evidence *and* I gave you a suspect in Vivian Gross's murder."

Royce rolled his eyes. "It's the same person."

"Doesn't make it less true," Rocky said. "You should be thanking me."

"Get out of here and take the rest of the bullshit pineapple pizza with you."

"That's all the thanks I need," Rocky said, rubbing his hands together before picking up the box. "Seriously, I want to make things right about the recording."

Royce nodded. "If your report to the FBP goes nowhere, let me know. We have to shut this down. I can't believe I'm going to say this, but we know a certain reporter who'd love to blow the whistle on corruption at the county jail. Sometimes the press can get justice when powerful people try to bury these types of things."

"Agreed." Rocky headed toward the front door, then jerked to a sudden stop. "Whoa! What the fuck is that?" he asked, pointing to Bones who'd come out of hiding to climb up on his cat perch to watch the birds splash around in the birdbath.

"Our cat, moron, and I'll feed you to him if you don't get the fuck out."

Rocky didn't stick around to find out if Royce was joking. A few minutes later, Sawyer and Jonah entered the living room.

"Damn, that's a big cat," Jonah said. "How much food does he go through?"

"Depends on which one of us is feeding him?" Sawyer replied.

Royce could only nod. He tended to spoil Bones too much.

Jonah grinned at Royce. "Have fun at The Cockpit tonight."

"Not as much fun as you had over the weekend," Royce countered.

"Touché," the big man said on his way out the door.

"Well?" Royce asked Sawyer once they were alone."

"Jonah said he and Kendall fooled around in his truck on Friday and Sunday nights, so we should expect him to be late getting back from dinner those nights. He stayed away from the club on Saturday night until it was almost closing time."

"That helps."

"He's also going to do some digging to see if he can find anything connecting Blakemore and Bonita," Sawyer added. "I don't think Blakemore is involved in Vivian's death, but we can't afford to get careless."

"Agreed," Royce said.

"Ready to do this?" Sawyer asked.

Royce smirked. "I'm ready to do *you*."

"Later, dickhead. We have pretty boys to interview."

Even though Sawyer had vividly described the uniforms and décor of the club to him, Royce was still stunned when they walked in. He was expecting a bar like any other he'd entered or maybe even a male version of The Alley Cat, but he was so wrong.

The owner had taken an empty warehouse and converted it to a multi-level club with ceilings so high in the main section that actual planes hung suspended from the metal rafters. The Alley Cat had sported a large stage and gilded cages with dancers inside them, but The Cockpit topped it by a country mile. The stage was constructed to look like a giant airplane wing, and above it, male dancers wearing angel wings and silver G-strings gyrated to the loud music on platforms above the crowd.

Beside him, Sawyer laughed. Royce knew he was gawking like an idiot, but he'd never seen anything quite like it. "The fog machines adds a nice touch, right? It makes them look like they're dancing on clouds."

Royce nodded. "This is like Elton John meets the Air Force museum." Then he began singing lines from "Bennie and the Jets." He turned and looked at his boyfriend. "What level of gayness is this? How many points do I earn?" He tipped his head to the side. "Wait? Do I have to bang a waiter here to earn points?"

One such waiter stopped and smiled at Royce. He wore the uniform Sawyer had perfectly described down to the tiny shorts. "Hell, yes. I'll stamp your scorecard, baby."

"Fuck no," Sawyer growled. "Move along." Sawyer pulled Royce into his arms. "Knock it off with the gayness challenge crap, although you'd win bonus points for the Elton John reference if we were keeping score. There's no wrong or right way to be gay or bi or anything else. I want you to experience all the things you've denied yourself, but I selfishly don't want them to include anyone except me."

Sawyer pressed his lips to Royce's, making him forget they were only there to confirm or disprove Blakemore's alibi. Royce's pulse pounded to the beat of the music, and he tightened his grip on Sawyer, deepening the kiss until catcalls and whistles pierced the air around them. It didn't matter that they both wore their badges and shoulder holsters, or even that they were on duty. Royce recognized this space as a safe zone where they didn't have to worry about who was watching them. Even without the pretty eye candy every-fucking-where, he could see the appeal of places like this. Royce just hoped they could find a place where there wasn't so much techno music.

He reluctantly broke the kiss and smiled at Sawyer. "You're the only person I want, GB." Royce waggled his brow. "And I accept."

Sawyer's brow furrowed, and he blinked repeatedly. "You accept what?"

Royce's face hurt from smiling so broadly. "Your offer to wear this uniform for me. Oh, maybe when you serve me poolside drinks." Royce looked around some more. "This place is so over-the-top. It surely has a souvenir shop. Don't think we're leaving here with only a coffee cup."

Sawyer tilted his head back and laughed. "Maybe a shot glass too if you're a good boy."

"I'm *always* good."

Sawyer took a deep breath, and Royce knew his mind had leaped ahead in time to when they were home alone. Then Sawyer nodded toward the bar where men dressed in flight suits opened to their navels filled drink orders and flirted with patrons. "Let's get started."

The two bartenders they needed to speak to, Drew and Brett, were both working. They approached them individually, so they wouldn't influence one another's answers. Both men were all smiles until they noticed Sawyer's and Royce's badges.

"No way I served an underage person," Dave said defensively. "I always ask for IDs."

"Relax," Sawyer said. "We're not here about that."

"Oh," the guy said, "okay, then. What do you want?"

"Do you know Kendall Blakemore?"

Dave snorted. "Everyone knows Sugar." Sugar, huh? With the kid's white-blond hair, Royce could see it.

"Did you work with him this weekend?" Sawyer asked.

"Yeah, all three nights," Dave said. When Royce and Sawyer drilled down deeper, Dave insisted nothing unusual had occurred. "I don't remember any weird absences," the bartender told them.

"How can you be sure?" Royce countered. "This place is way busier on a Monday evening than I expected, so it must be wall-to-wall thrashing bodies on the weekends."

"Sugar is one of our most popular waiters," Dave replied. "If he disappeared for much longer than his dinner break, then I would remember it."

The other bartender had a much different tale to share. "Yeah, Kendall was gone a lot this weekend," Brett informed them, contradicting Dave's account. This was one of the reasons why eyewitnesses were so unreliable.

"Describe a lot," Sawyer told him.

"Kendall was late getting back from dinner all three nights," Brett replied with a casual shrug.

"How can you be sure?" Royce asked him.

"We took our dinner break the same time each of those nights," the bartender said. "Kendall told me he'd met a hottie here Friday night, and the guy kept returning."

"You think he hooked up with the guy during dinner?" Sawyer asked.

"He didn't brag about it or anything because Kendall is private about most things. It's the impression I had anyway." Brett nodded to the far-right corner of the club. "See that emergency exit sign?" Sawyer and Royce glanced over, then nodded. "Go through the door, and it will lead to some offices, our locker rooms, and storage. The second door on the left is where you'll find Erik. He was the manager on duty most of the weekend. Maybe he can confirm when Kendall swiped in and out."

Sawyer slapped a hand on the metal bar top. "Thanks, man."

Brett smiled prettily and raked his eyes over Sawyer. There was no mistaking the invitation in the bartender's eyes. "Anytime, and I do mean it."

Royce nudged Sawyer in the direction of the offices before he had a chance to acknowledge the flirtatious bartender. A few minutes later, they'd somehow parted the sea of men. He knocked on the manager's closed door and was surprised when a string of yelled curses followed. "For fuck's sake," an angry voice snarled. Royce and Sawyer rested their hands on the butts of their guns when they heard heavy footfalls quickly advancing toward them from inside the room. A short, balding man yanked open the door. "Can't a guy get a—"

Royce would've gestured for him to continue, but his open fly, untucked and rumpled dress shirt, and flushed face told him everything he needed to know. "Are you Erik?"

"I am," he said. His eyes roamed from Sawyer to Royce, taking in the badges around their necks and the way their hands rested on their service weapons. "This isn't what it looks like."

Sawyer snorted. "It never is."

"We'll head back out to the club and give you a few minutes. We can come back and chat," Royce said. He had no desire to overhear the manager finishing up, nor did he want to have an awkward exchange when whoever was in there exited the office.

"Why don't you guys go on up to the VIP lounge and wait for me there. I can see you're on duty but have a Coke and some wings on me? We have the best in town."

"So I've heard." Royce thought about declining his offer but suddenly wanted to see what all the fuss was about. How good could the wings be?

"Our VIP lounge is on the—"

"We'll find our way," Sawyer said.

"Tell Jesse I sent you. He'll get you settled, and I'll be up in a few minutes."

Royce was surprised when Sawyer stopped by the bar to ask Dave where the VIP lounge was located.

"So, you haven't earned enough frequent flyer miles to qualify for the VIP lounge, huh?" Royce teased.

"I told you I didn't visit as often as you imagined."

Royce just laughed and followed Sawyer through the crowd until they reached a metal staircase where a large man stood at the bottom. He wore a brown leather bomber jacket over an impressive bare chest, dark wash jeans, black boots, and aviator glasses.

"Are you Jesse?" Royce asked. He received a grunt and a slight nod in response. "Erik sent us. He said you'd take care of us while we waited for him."

Jesse nodded again and gestured for them to head up the steps.

"A man of few words," Royce remarked when they reached the second floor. Looking around the space, he noted the décor looked like an upscale first-class lounge at an airport. The VIP waitstaff wore tiny gold shorts with the bar's logo printed on the ass and nothing else unless you counted the smiles and the shimmery substance dusted on their bodies. No shirts, no hats, and no glasses up in the VIP lounge.

"I don't think we're in Kansas anymore, Toto," Royce said.

Sawyer laughed, then guided him to an empty booth where a sexy, dark-haired waiter promptly greeted them. "Hello, I'm Maverick. What can I get you, fellas?" Maverick. Really? Was another waiter called Goose? Where was Ice Man?

Royce gestured for Sawyer to order for them since he was the expert on all things wings-related at The Cockpit.

"What do you think?" Sawyer asked when they were alone once more.

"I think I understand why this was a favorite place for you to pick up dudes," Royce countered. "I can also see why Blakemore makes more money in a weekend here than he does a few weeks at the law firm."

"You want to come back here sometime when we're not on duty?" Sawyer asked.

"Depends on how good the wings are," Royce answered. "This club music is shitty, I'm not a good dancer, and I have the only guy I want to bump, grind, and get sweaty with, GB. Why? Do you want to come back?"

Sawyer shook his head. "No. I just don't want you to get bored."

Royce leaned forward and kissed Sawyer. "No fucking way, asshole. I am happy to skip over the things you consider rites of passage to get my big prize." Royce cupped Sawyer's face, brushing his thumb over the stubble on his jaw. "In case you haven't figured it out yet, you're my prize. I fucking love you."

"I fucking—"

"There you are," Erik said, sounding like he sprinted up the stairs to find them. "Have you ordered yet?"

"We have," Sawyer told the man, scooting closer to Royce in the semicircular booth to make room for Erik to join them.

"It won't be long before the food arrives, then," Erik said. "What can I help you with?"

Royce explained why they were there and the information they needed.

"Sugar was here all right," Erik said. "He caught the eye of a patron on Friday night that the divas were practically fighting over. They must've had some insane chemistry because the guy kept coming back and requested to sit in Sugar's section."

"The divas?" Royce asked.

Erik shrugged and said, "You know the type."

"Enlighten me," Sawyer said dryly.

"The extra pretty, high-maintenance ones who view every sexy, rich guy as their potential future husband and will stop at nothing to get their attention, including sabotaging one of their coworkers."

"Sounds entertaining as hell," Royce said, earning a glare from Sawyer.

Maverick returned to the table with the wings and Cokes. Royce's mouth started to water when he got a whiff of the chicken. They sure as hell smelled like the best in the city.

"Can I get you boys anything else?" the waiter asked.

"No, we're good," Sawyer said.

"Okay, then. I'll be back to check on you soon." Maverick winked before sauntering off, his swaying hips garnering Erik's attention.

"We need to know if Blakemore was late getting back to work from dinner or other breaks. Can you get us the times he clocked in and out?"

Erik snapped his head back around to look at them. "Now?" he asked, shifting his gaze toward the pile of wings.

"Yep," Royce said, not wanting to spend any more time with the sleazebag.

Erik heaved a sigh. "I'll be back in a few minutes with a printout."

Royce picked up a wing and waved it at him. "Thanks."

Once they were alone again, Sawyer said, "I'm not letting that guy comp us anything. He gives me the creeps. I regret not sticking around in the hallway to make sure the person in his office was there of their own free will."

"We can ask around before we leave to make sure he's on the up-and-up." Royce didn't like the idea of the manager using his position to gain sexual favors from employees.

"Yeah, that works," Sawyer said.

They exchanged nothing but grins once they started digging into the food. They really were perfect wings. Crispy on the outside and juicy on the inside. They'd demolished the plate, including the side of celery, by the time Erik returned.

"Here you go," he said, setting a document on the table.

Royce wiped his hand with one of the wet towelettes provided. Then he picked up the printout. "How long are their dinner breaks?"

"Forty-five minutes," Erik replied.

Royce noticed Blakemore had taken an extra fifteen minutes on Friday and Sunday but had clocked out for a full ninety minutes on Saturday night. Royce handed the paper to Sawyer once he wiped his hands. Sawyer glanced at the times, then snapped his gaze up to meet Royce's.

Where had Kendall Blakemore gone on Saturday night for ninety minutes?

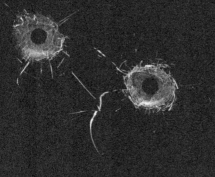

CHAPTER 16

"IS THERE ANYTHING ELSE I CAN HELP YOU WITH?" ERIK ASKED, LOOKING between Sawyer and Royce.

"Yeah," Sawyer said, leaning forward. "I better not find out you use your position as manager to gain sexual favors from employees."

The man's face went as white as a sheet, and he flopped back against the seat as if Sawyer had physically struck him. "I would never—" Erik sputtered.

Royce held up his hand, cutting him off. "Save it, buddy. I am going to ask around, and if I don't like what I hear, I'm going to knock on your door again, and I can promise you won't like it."

Erik narrowed his eyes but wasn't stupid enough to argue with Royce. "If you don't need anything else, I'll just be going."

"Make sure our waiter brings us the bill," Sawyer said. "We don't accept comps."

Erik shrugged. "If you wish."

"He does," Royce said.

Sawyer watched the manager slink away, then turned his attention to Royce. "What's the likelihood Jonah got his evening romps

"Blakemore had to know we were going to ask, so why not be upfront with us?" Sawyer asked.

Royce considered it. "If nothing else, it gave Blakemore time to come up with a plausible story that contradicts Jonah's statement. I doubt Blakemore knows much about Jonah beyond his penis size and favorite position."

Sawyer nearly choked on his sip of Coke.

"Don't be jealous, GB," Royce teased him, reaching over to pat his back like Felix had done for Jonah earlier.

"Don't be a dickhead," Sawyer said once he could breathe without hacking more.

Royce winked. "It comes so naturally."

Sawyer leaned forward and kissed Royce's smiling lips. "We got what we came for, so let's go home."

Royce pressed another kiss to Sawyer's mouth, tracing the curve of his lower lip with the tip of his tongue. "Yeah, let's go home."

Sawyer signaled their waiter over, then handed over his debit card before the guy could set the bill on the table.

"In a hurry, I see," the much younger guy noted. Maverick raked his gaze over Royce and smiled wickedly before looking at Sawyer again. "Honey, I cannot blame you. Good luck getting him out of here in one piece."

Sawyer briefly tensed until Royce's hand found his thigh beneath the table. Just that little touch eased the jealousy burning in his gut. What the hell had come over him? He hadn't liked the first flirty waiter's response to Royce either. He'd been ready to cause a scene, which wasn't like him at all.

"Not my type," Royce whispered against his lips.

"That body glitter would get *everywhere*," Sawyer said.

Royce chuckled. "I could live out the rest of my life without testing the theory. I've battled it enough during crafting projects with Marc and Daniel. Once, I bought them slime with glitter in it for Christmas. Candi packed it in one of their backpacks when I watched

196

the boys while she and Marcus went someplace." The memory made Royce's gray eyes shimmer brighter than Maverick's gold dust. "Of course, I didn't know the boys brought it with them until they dug it out and smeared it into the carpet in the spare bedroom after I made them blanket forts." Royce laughed and shook his head, tightening his grip on Sawyer's leg.

"Did you get the slime out?" he asked.

Royce shook his head. "No, I ended up removing the carpet and replacing it with laminate flooring. Candi was horrified, but Marcus laughed and said I deserved it." Royce smiled and released Sawyer's thigh to cup his face instead. "Marcus said something afterward I quickly laughed off and dismissed."

Leaning into Royce's touch, Sawyer said, "What was that?"

"He told me I'd know better when I had kids of my own. He said it so naturally as if it were a foregone conclusion." Royce smiled broadly. "Keep in mind, I hadn't gone out with the same girl more than two times since high school, so I asked him how much he'd had to drink with dinner. Marcus just laughed and said, 'Just you wait and see. Everything changes when you meet the right person.' And you know what?"

"What?" Sawyer managed to croak out.

"He was right."

"Oh."

Tears burned the back of Sawyer's eyes, and he had to blink a few times when his vision blurred. He recalled the night he'd cried while telling Royce his dreams of having a family had died with Vic. Royce had told him his dreams weren't gone; they were delayed. It had been a bittersweet breakthrough in their early partnership because, in his next breath, Royce made it clear it wouldn't be him fulfilling Sawyer's dreams by acknowledging he'd be jealous of Sawyer's future husband. Was Royce ready to admit how wrong he'd been?

Instead of forcing the tears back, the blinking sent a few spilling down Sawyer's cheeks. He should've been embarrassed for losing his shit in the middle of the VIP lounge, but he wasn't. Royce leaned his forehead against his, brushed the tears away, and swallowed hard. It helped ease Sawyer's nerves to see Royce struggle with his emotions too.

"Everything does change when you meet the person meant for you," Royce said. "I crave things I never realized I wanted before, and I find myself suddenly impatient to have them. Blanket forts and glitter slime were things I had planned to experience only as a favorite, honorary uncle, but never as a father, until I met you, and now I can't wait. Someday, I'm going to make you mine in every possible way, and we're going to raise some hellions."

Sawyer chuckled as tears streamed down his face. "Maybe we skip the slime part, yeah? Play-Doh is a slightly safer choice."

"Agreed," Royce said, pressing his lips to Sawyer's to seal the deal.

When they broke apart, Maverick was standing there with Sawyer's debit card and slip for him to sign. "You two are so adorable."

"Thanks," Royce said while Sawyer pocketed his card.

The waiter sighed. "I hope to find what you have when I'm old too."

Royce fell back against the padded booth, laughing, while Sawyer scowled at the kid with the ink pen poised in the air. "Kid, you're supposed to wait until *after* you've collected your tip before you insult us."

"Oops, my bad," he said before sauntering off.

Sawyer added his standard twenty-five percent tip, then signed the slip with a flourish before tossing the pen down and sliding out of the booth, pulling Royce in his wake.

They headed down the metal steps, nodding at Jesse when they reached the main floor. Sawyer had every intention of heading straight for the exit until he caught sight of a familiar guy with white-blond hair moving lithely between dancing men with a heavy drink tray in his hand.

"I'll be damned," Royce said in his ear. "Guess he's making our job a little easier tonight."

They slowly followed behind Blakemore, which allowed them to observe as he served the drinks. He flirted and teased, but since the blond wasn't wearing the aviator glasses, Sawyer could see the pain in the younger man's eyes. He hadn't been faking his grief, and even though Kendall Blakemore had some explaining to do, Sawyer still didn't believe the man was involved in Gross's death.

Once he placed his last drink, Blakemore turned and started walking toward them. It took him a few steps to notice Sawyer and Royce, and when he did, his steps never faltered, even though mild surprise registered on his face. "Good evening, Detectives. Checking up on me?" he asked when he stopped in front of them.

"How could we be doing that?" Royce asked. "You told us you only work on weekends?"

"I normally do," he replied smoothly. "I think we both know what I really meant, though."

"We do?" Royce asked.

Blakemore heaved a loaded sigh and rolled his eyes. "Fine. We'll play your games. You're here to check on my alibi even after your *friend* confirmed my statement already."

"Our friend told us he made you late returning from your dinner break on Friday and Sunday nights," Sawyer said. "We got curious about how things went on Saturday and imagine how surprised we were to discover you left for ninety minutes instead of forty-five. Care to tell us where you went? We know you didn't meet Jonah."

Blakemore's nostrils flared as he inhaled deeply. "It's a personal problem, and I don't care to discuss it right now."

"You may not have a choice," Royce countered. "Especially if we can prove Vivian died within the window you were gone."

Blakemore sucked in a sharp breath and staggered backward a few steps. Sawyer wasn't surprised Royce used his bad-cop tactics to shock a response out of the younger man. "Leave," Blakemore said sharply. "You don't get to harass me at work. If you want to speak to me again, you can do so by going through Bill Elderwood."

"You don't want to do that, Kendall," Sawyer said, hoping his voice sounded gentle and friendly. For good measure, he turned on Royce. "Must you always be such a dickhead?" Royce just shrugged. Facing Blakemore again, Sawyer held his hands up. "I don't believe you hurt Vivian, and I know you want to help us find her killer." Even if his half-truths and misleading remarks stated otherwise. "Just tell us where you went on Saturday night."

Blakemore broke eye contact as he debated his options. After a few seconds, his gaze collided with Sawyer's once more. "I met my mother. She called me crying earlier in the day. She was convinced my stepfather was having an affair and asked me for advice." He took a deep breath and shook his head.

"The mother who was responsible for you living out of your car?" Royce questioned. Sawyer couldn't blame him for the doubt that had crept into his voice.

"I might've exaggerated a little bit," Blakemore conceded.

"Which part?" Sawyer and Royce asked at the same time. Exchanging a glance, Royce gestured for Sawyer to go ahead.

"Which part did you exaggerate? The homelessness or your parents kicking you out?"

"They didn't kick me out of their house," Blakemore said after a pause. "They made my life so miserable that I thought living in my car was my best option. I refuse to pretend to be something I am not. My stepfather had said it was one thing for me to be queer, but I could at least act like a man and stop embarrassing my family." Blakemore's face flushed with anger or humiliation; Sawyer couldn't be sure which. "Do you know what I did to earn such heinous remarks?" When neither Sawyer nor Royce took the bait, he said, "I wore lip gloss to a dinner party my family hosted." Blakemore laughed bitterly. "Stan was so worried one of his business associates would cancel a contract with him when he should've been concerned about how much his only son and heir liked the way lip gloss aided my mouth when working it up and down his dick. He said my lips tasted like Sugar."

Sugar. Is that how he got his nickname? It wasn't Sawyer's business. "I'm sorry, Kendall," Sawyer said, and he meant it.

"My mom stood by and let Stan say the most hateful things to my face. What mother does that?" He shook his head. "Don't bother answering me. It was a rhetorical question. What you should be asking is why, after what she did, or didn't do in my case, would I give her the time of day?"

"She's your mom," Royce said softly. "I'm pretty sure most kids in your situation would've answered the call and met their moms. My question is, what did she expect you to do about her marital problems though?"

"She suggested we could get a place together, and it would be the two of us like it used to be before she met Stan," Blakemore said. "Mom also hoped I could help her get started on a separation agreement since I am studying to become a paralegal. I told her I didn't have enough schooling under my belt yet, but I knew some basics. I promised to talk to Vivian about it on Monday. I told her we'd find a way." Blakemore took a deep breath. Misery was etched all over the guy's face, and his shoulders slumped like he carried the world on them. "I called my mom today to let her know what happened to Vivian, and she was appropriately sad she had died and moderately concerned I was the one who found my friend's dead body, but mostly Mom wanted to tell me she'd had a change of heart. *Again.* She'd overreacted and decided to work things out with Stan. *Again.* And by work things out, she meant she is going to overlook another affair. It wasn't his first rodeo, and I promise it won't be his last."

"That's tough," Sawyer said sympathetically.

Blakemore shrugged. "It was the wake-up call I needed. I can't stay with Jonah forever, so I picked up an extra shift when a coworker texted me today asking if I could cover for him. Let me give you my mom's number. You can call her and confirm my statement."

Sawyer pulled his phone from his pocket and typed the number into his note app as Blakemore rattled it off. "I only ask that you don't tell her about Jonah."

"She knows you're gay, right?" Royce asked him.

"Of course, and she's never had a problem with it, but I don't want her getting her hopes up that I've met 'the one.'"

"Jonah isn't the one, huh?" Royce asked.

Sawyer looked over at his partner. What was with him and the matchmaking lately? Was he looking to start a side hustle or have a backup plan in case this policing thing didn't pan out?

"Neither of us is looking for a serious relationship right now. And in case I got a different idea, Jonah made a point of letting me know I was staying in his guest room. We had a great weekend, but it was nothing more than a hookup. It just took us a while longer than usual to work each other out of our systems."

Royce shrugged. "If you say so."

Blakemore glared at Royce. "I just did. Any other questions?"

Even though he thought Blakemore wasn't involved in Gross's death, Sawyer wasn't willing to tip his hat and show a picture of Bonita Brothers to him. He decided to go a different route. "I noticed the bouquet of pink roses in Vivian's office. Were they a recent delivery? Do you know who they were from?"

"Vivian had some kind of floral membership at Sattler and Sons and received bi-monthly deliveries," Blakemore replied. "She chose Saturday afternoons to receive them. The flowers usually arrive before I leave for my shift, but they were late this weekend. I left before they showed up." Then Blakemore's eyes widened. "The delivery person might've witnessed something. You gotta talk to them."

"We'll do that first thing in the morning," Sawyer assured him. "Did the same person deliver Vivian's flowers each time?"

Blakemore shook his head. "No, but surely the florist keeps a record of deliveries."

"I'm sure they do," Sawyer agreed.

"Take care, kid. We'll be in touch if we have more questions," Royce told him.

"Forgive me for saying so, but I hope not," Blakemore quipped.

"Sugar! What the hell are you doing here?" a whiny voice asked from behind them.

Sawyer and Royce turned around and found two waiters appraising Blakemore. One guy was blond and had on a uniform like Blakemore's, and the other man was a brunet who wore gold shorts and body glitter like the VIP lounge waiters. Both men sported pissy expressions as they raked their eyes over Blakemore in disbelief.

"Spence, snagging the hottest guy ever to grace this club over the weekend wasn't enough for this slut," the golden guy said.

Blakemore threw his head back and laughed, making the two waiters look at one another before casting their gazes back on Blakemore, who had tears running down his face. "Oh, god, that's rich, Tyson, considering I saw you sucking off Spencer's boyfriend in the parking lot during dinner breaks this weekend."

Blond boy narrowed his eyes at golden guy. "Bitch, he better be lying about you and Brett."

Ah, no wonder the bartender was so sure about Blakemore's dinner breaks.

"Baby," golden guy said, "would I hurt you that way? We're besties."

Blond boy let out an ear-piercing battle cry and launched himself at his former bestie. Unfortunately, two more waiters were walking by with heavily laden trays of drinks and wings. Sawyer got hit in the eye with a chicken wing, and booze and soda rained down over his head. His eye burned like someone had poured acid in it, and through his one good eye, he saw Royce move in to separate the two divas who had started to thrash and roll around. In the process, they knocked over a patron, who toppled into another waiter, who fell into a guy dancing at the edge of the floor, creating a domino effect.

In the uproar, fights broke out all around them, which was why Erik fired the two waiters when the gold dust settled and Royce and Sawyer were forced to haul Spencer and Tyson into the station when a patron wanted to press charges for bodily harm. He had slipped in spilled milk and broken his wrist, so there was no avoiding the arrest. Rather than radio for a patrol unit, Royce took the opportunity to lecture the two bickering men whenever he could get a word in edgewise.

"Have some fucking respect for yourselves," he snarled.

Then he started questioning them about Erik's management style and whether the guy abused his power. The divas told them Erik was a jerk, but they weren't aware of any inappropriate behavior. Royce gave them tips on how to get out of an unwanted position and urged them to report sexual harassment if it ever occurred.

"Yes, daddy," golden guy purred from the back seat.

Sawyer wanted to kick the kid in his gold lamé-covered crotch but couldn't deny this side of Royce was sexy as hell.

When they reached the precinct, Sawyer sent Royce to the locker room to clean up since he'd taken the brunt of the damage. He had ranch dressing matted in his hair and buffalo and barbecue sauces splotched across his neck, face, and shirt. Sawyer had never been so happy to hand anyone over to Officer Doughman for processing.

Every step Sawyer took toward the locker room made him happier and hornier. He knew exactly where to find his man and how he wanted to end their night. Royce wasn't even surprised when Sawyer whisked back the shower curtain in the last stall—their stall. The one where Royce let down his guard and showed Sawyer his vulnerability that first time. The same spot where Sawyer realized his feelings for Royce Locke were much stronger than he'd realized.

"It's about fucking time," Royce said, smiling at him. "Did you hand Frick and Frack off—"

Sawyer pressed his finger to Royce's lips, stopping the flow of words. He started to drop to his knees, wanting to play out Royce's fantasies, but his boyfriend stopped him with a jerky headshake.

Sawyer lowered his hand and started to take a step back. He thought Royce had wanted this, but maybe he'd read the situation wrong.

Royce gripped Sawyer's hips and pulled him close. Pressing his lips to Sawyer's ear, Royce whispered, "I don't want you kneeling on the shower floor. It's gross. There's no telling who used it last or what they did in here." Royce nipped his earlobe sharply. "I only want you covered in my spunk from here on out. See the bottle of lube on the shelf?" Sawyer glanced over, and sure enough, he spotted a travel-size bottle. "I put it in my shaving kit a while back just in case."

Sawyer briefly debated asking what he meant by just in case, but his blood was quickly flowing south and taking his ability to think logically with it. Did it really matter anyway? Hell no.

"So, fuck me, baby," Royce whispered roughly. He turned around, presenting his luscious ass to Sawyer.

Sawyer palmed Royce's firm globes and began massaging them, eliciting an indecent moan from his man. "Shh, someone is going to overhear us," he whispered in Royce's ear. Due to it being mid-shift and a late hour, the risk of getting caught was lower, but wasn't that part of the turn-on? "We'll get called to the chief's office," Sawyer said huskily.

Royce shuddered. "That's so not sexy."

"Oh, sorry. This is new territory for me too."

Reaching behind him, Royce cupped the back of Sawyer's head to pull him closer, then turned his face and melded their mouths together. The position was awkward, and it was impossible to kiss Royce as deeply as he wanted, but it took Sawyer's mind off his bumbling attempt to rock his boyfriend's world. He spread Royce's ass cheeks and rocked his hips forward, rutting his cock along Royce's crack.

Royce broke their kiss with a moan. "Get the lube. Want to feel you inside me."

Sawyer pinched Royce's ass and laughed when he yelped. "Not enjoying this, huh?"

Royce gripped Sawyer's right hand and brought it around to his rock-hard cock. "Seems to me I'm enjoying this just fine. Now fuck me."

Sawyer took a lot of jabs from Royce for being a control freak, but it was true. Royce would thank him later when he was balls deep inside him though. Sawyer ignored Royce's curses and continued stroking his cock while nibbling on his shoulder and neck, only stopping when he was in jeopardy of coming too soon.

The snick of the flip-cap opening seemed loud in the locker room, but even if someone had walked in, they would've thought it was shampoo. That was until Royce moaned and begged for more like the bossiest bottom this side of the Mason-Dixon line when Sawyer took his sweet time stretching Royce open for him.

"You'll pay for this," Royce said, sounding ragged. "As soon as I recharge."

"Uh-huh," Sawyer said, adding a third finger and pegging his prostate.

"Fuck me now, asshole. I mean it."

"Or you'll what?" Sawyer asked thickly. "Walk out of here and leave me hanging?"

"God, no," Royce said. "I'll beg prettily until you take mercy on me."

"That," Sawyer said, removing his fingers and aligning his dick to Royce's ass, "is more like it." He thrust forward, burying himself to the hilt on the first drive.

Luckily, he'd had the forethought to cover Royce's mouth with his palm, which muffled his jubilant cries. Royce rose on his tiptoes and arched his spine, pushing back harder against Sawyer's penetration, urging him to fuck Royce hard. Sawyer had something else in mind though. Sawyer wanted to go slow and feel Royce unravel from the inside out and revel in the beautiful gift that was Royce Locke's body. He started by sliding his hand from Royce's mouth to wrap around his neck, feeling Royce's pulse race beneath his thumb.

"Asshole," Royce whispered when it became apparent Sawyer wasn't going to give in.

"You do have the sweetest one I've ever had the privilege to know," Sawyer replied. "I can never get enough. Feel the way you grip me?"

"I will get even," Royce promised.

Sawyer was on the verge of losing control and putting them both out of their misery when the locker room door opened followed by the unmistakable sound of rubber soles squeaking and smacking against the tile floors. Royce stiffened in Sawyer's hold when the footfalls got louder as the person drew nearer to their shower stall, which only made Royce's pucker tighten harder around Sawyer's cock.

Squeak. Smack. Squeak. Smack. Then silence when the person stopped on the other side of the shower curtain.

"Uh, Detective Key?" the voice asked timidly.

"Yes, Officer Doughman," Sawyer said, retreating until only the head of his dick was inside Royce. "Is there a problem with the intake paperwork?" How the fuck had he managed to sound so calm?

"Um, no, sir. Have you seen Sergeant Locke?"

Have I ever. Sawyer silently slid his dick back inside the tight clench. "I'm sorry, but I haven't. He probably went home already. He was covered in chicken wing gunk, booze, and body glitter."

"Oh, okay."

Sawyer clamped one hand over Royce's mouth and gripped his throbbing cock with the other. Standing on the balls of his feet, Sawyer canted his hips and fucked Royce with slow, silent strokes. "Sorry, Doughman." His voice sounded strained because Royce had nipped his palm and squeezed his ass around Sawyer's cock.

Sawyer was close. So fucking close. The way Royce trembled in his arms said he was too. Fantasy or not, Sawyer didn't want to blow his load inside Royce with Officer Doughman standing on the other side of the curtain. He tightened his grip on the base of Royce's cock. If Sawyer couldn't come, Royce couldn't either. Then he realized the quaking was from suppressed laughter. Sawyer leaned forward, sinking his teeth in the tendon straining in Royce's neck. Royce hissed, pushing his ass back against Sawyer and wanting more. There was no way Doughman hadn't heard him, just like there was no way he hadn't missed their open duffle bags and two pairs of boots on the bench in front of their lockers.

Sawyer released Royce's neck to lick over his teeth marks. "Is there a message or something I need to give him?" he asked, hoping to prod the young officer along.

"Oh, from me? No, sir. One of the guys from the bar had a question for him."

I just bet. "Go back and tell those troublemakers Sergeant Locke is already in a relationship," Sawyer said firmly. "He's crazy in love and isn't accepting phone numbers or friend requests on Facebook."

Royce laughed harder. Unfortunately for Sawyer, it created friction around his shaft that threatened to topple his control. *Don't come. Don't come.* He was hanging on by a thread.

Officer Doughman chuckled. "I'd heard as much, but I thought I'd ask if it settled these hellcats down a little bit."

"Sorry. I can't help you, Doughman," Sawyer said gruffly.

"Um, have a good night, sir," the young cop said.

Squeak. Smack. Squeak. Smack.

Sawyer waited as the retreating footfalls got quieter, and the door opened and closed before he started moving inside Royce once more. It only took a few more strokes before both men were grunting and coming, uncaring who might overhear them by that point.

Sawyer eased out of Royce's ass before turning his boyfriend around and kissing him long and slow. Then he washed the ranch dressing out of his hair.

"So, on a scale of one to ten, how entertaining did you find the divas fighting?" Sawyer asked.

"Not very," Royce admitted.

Smoothing his hands down Royce's corded biceps, Sawyer said, "At least you didn't almost lose an eye to a chicken wing."

Royce laughed. "True."

Shyness suddenly washed over Sawyer. "What about the rest?" Had he fulfilled Royce's fantasy or ruined it?

"Better than I ever imagined, GB."

CHAPTER 17

ROYCE DREAMED OF MARCUS AGAIN. IT HAD STARTED HAPPENING MORE frequently, and he knew it was his subconscious urging him to listen to the damn tape. Unaware of his inner turmoil, Sawyer slept peacefully beside him while Bones was sprawled out between their bodies.

In the dream, he and Marcus had been at the lake again, but this time they were alone. Instead of fishing from the shore like usual, they'd been sitting in a small rowboat Royce hadn't recognized.

Marcus had cast his line, then laid the rod on the bottom of the boat. Looking at Royce with twinkling blue eyes, he said, "You'll feel much better if you listen to the tape."

"What tape?" Royce had asked.

"Stop playing dumb and listen to it. You already know the worst and still love me. Right?" Marcus had asked, sounding uncharacteristically uncertain. One of the things Royce had loved most about Marcus was his confidence. "I know I let you down, Ro."

You let yourself down. That wasn't what Royce said, though. "Of course, I still love you." Royce set his fishing pole down too. The urge to hug Marcus and reassure him had been strong. They'd never been super touchy-feely, and Royce had often wondered if it was because Marcus had known about Royce's crush on him when they were younger. If so, Marcus had never let on that it bothered him. He had also never exploited Royce's feelings to get his way when he could have so easily.

"Will that change if you listen to the tape?" Marcus had asked, his voice a cloudy mix of hesitation and misery.

"Never," Royce had vowed.

Marcus tipped his head to the side and studied Royce. "Promise?"

"Yes," Royce had replied without hesitation. He might get mad, he might wrestle with feelings of betrayal, but he would always love Marcus. He would forgive his best friend because that's what you did when you loved someone.

Marcus had risen to his feet, making the boat pitch from side to side. Royce gripped the aluminum vessel with both hands, trying to steady it.

"What are you doing?" Royce had asked.

"It's time to rock the boat," Marcus had said, using his weight to make it bob from left to right.

"Cut it out, Marcus."

"Just listen to the damn tape, Ro. And by the way, I really like Sawyer."

Marcus dove into the water, leaving Royce floating in the middle of the lake all by himself. That's when he woke up, his stomach swaying just like the boat had.

Son of a bitch. Some dreams were so damn real. Glancing at the time on his phone, Royce nearly snorted out loud when he noticed it was three a.m. The Devil's Hour. Oh, the irony. Marcus had been right. It was past time for him to grab the demon by its horns and cast it back to hell where it belonged, then deal with repercussions from hearing Marcus speak his secrets out loud. There'd be no more plausible deniability going forward. Royce snorted. Who the fuck was he trying to kid? It was much too late for that anyway.

Royce quietly opened the bedside drawer and removed the mini-tape player, the cassette box that felt more like a ticking bomb, and

Marcus's cell phone. Royce hoped seeing Marcus's smiling face would help ease the pain from whatever he discovered about his best friend.

He carried those things to Sawyer's office and started to close the door, but Bones darted through at the last minute. By keeping the beast close, he wouldn't wake up Sawyer and rat him out as Bones had done a few weeks ago when Sawyer stayed up too late looking at case files.

The hint of citrusy furniture polish reminded Royce of Sawyer's aftershave, and he took comfort in the familiar scent. Sawyer wasn't physically in the room with him, but he still managed to calm the rioting emotions brewing inside Royce.

Bones leaped up on the loveseat next to him. "You're not supposed to be on the leather furniture," Royce said, picking the fluffy beast up and setting him on his lap. "And now you no longer are." Bones purred as Royce scratched his ears, rubbed beneath his chin, and stroked his back.

Bones curled into a ball on his lap after a few minutes, and Royce could no longer justify delaying the inevitable. With a trembling hand and racing heart, Royce removed the cassette from its case and popped it into the player. He blew out a shaky breath and hit play.

"Forgive me, Father, for I have sinned. It has been six months since my last confession," Marcus softly said. A broken sob followed his words.

It had been months since Royce had heard Marcus's voice, and he expected him to sound like he had in the dream. That was the Marcus he remembered. He stabbed the button to stop the tape as tears filled his eyes. God, how did he have any tears left? *Just breathe.* After collecting himself, Royce restarted the recording.

Father David spoke in a calm voice as he recited passages by rote, guiding Marcus through a litany of sins, starting with small things like white lies until he reached the big whopper.

"I've been unfaithful to my wife, Father David," Marcus said softly, then began to cry harder. "Candi and I have struggled hard lately, and we fight all the time about everything. I didn't mean for it to happen. I love her and hurting her is the last thing I want to do." Marcus groaned. "This is so embarrassing."

"I can't help you if you're not willing to be honest with yourself and God, son," Father David said.

"I went to a bachelor party two months ago and met a stripper. How cliché, right, Father?"

"I wouldn't know," Father David replied.

Bachelor party? Whose? No one in their unit had ever held one at The Alley Cat nor had they invited strippers to a private gathering that Royce had ever attended. For fuck's sake, Marcus hadn't even told him this much. The reason for his silence was quite apparent, considering it was where he met Amber, or Crystal, as Marcus knew her.

"It was for my cousin Todd," Marcus said. "His best friend hosted the party and hired some strippers from a local club to, um, entertain the groom and his guests. I was uncomfortable and pissed no one had warned me what was going down, or else I wouldn't have attended. Candi and I came to an agreement early on in our relationship that those kinds of activities don't belong in committed relationships. The idea of some guy rubbing his junk on my wife makes me irrationally angry. What a hypocrite."

"Why didn't you just leave, then?" Father David asked sensibly.

Marcus exhaled a deep breath. "I didn't want to draw attention to myself. It's one thing to agree with my wife that I had no business hanging out with strippers, but it didn't mean I wanted the guys to know Candi had me by the short and curlies. Oh, sorry, Father. I didn't mean to be crude."

"It's quite all right, my son."

"I thought I could just fly under the radar and watch the festivities without getting my hands dirty."

"Ah," Father David said. "You didn't count on the paths your mind took."

Marcus sighed. "Now, I understand why you're always telling us that avoiding temptation means not putting ourselves into the path of things that will trip us up. Yeah, this one girl caught my eye. She was the sexiest woman I had ever seen. I wanted to touch her in indecent ways but shield her from the others at the same time."

"How did things evolve from looking to acting on your thoughts?"

"Todd's idiot best friend made a big deal out of announcing we each got a private dance in one of the bedrooms in the finished basement," Marcus said. "Can you believe this schmuck brought strippers into his home and offered up a bedroom for the *dances*?" Royce imagined Marcus using air quotes there, even though he would've been in a booth with no one to see him. "I'm sure his wife knew nothing about it. The nerve of—"

Father David softly hummed, ending Marcus's tirade. "We're not here to talk about Todd's behavior, or his best friend's, or anyone else who attended the party. I want to hear about *your* sins."

"You're right," Marcus said contritely. "I flat-out refused the private dance when they announced it was my turn. As I expected, the guys jeered and called me a pu—Um, names. It was humiliating. The dancers were laughing and chiding me too."

"Even the one who'd caught your eye?" Father David asked.

"Not her," Marcus said emphatically. "She looked sympathetic, but she was the one who eventually talked me into going into the private room."

"How?"

Yeah, how?

"She crossed the room to where I sat on the couch, leaned over, and pressed her lips to my ear, whispering, 'You can trust me. I promise to be a good girl and keep my hands to myself.' She straightened back up and looked at me curiously when I didn't immediately stand up and follow her. Then she saw my problem."

"You were aroused," Father David said, making Royce cringe.

"Very," Marcus admitted reluctantly. "I realized there was no way I was getting out of going into the room. There was no way in hell

I was the only one sporting wood, so I got up and followed her to the bedroom." He took a shaky breath and paused a few minutes before continuing. "She kept her word and didn't dance for me. We just talked. She told me her name was Crystal, she was new in town, and had recently started working at The Alley Cat. She did not attempt to touch me or seduce me. If I'm honest, she looked relieved that she didn't have to dance for me. I told her about my job and my kids. Then she nodded to the wedding ring on my hand and said my wife was a lucky woman. She'd found a rare man with honor, and it was no surprise he belonged to someone else." Marcus snorted derisively. "It didn't take Crystal long to realize I had no honor."

"How?" Father David asked.

"When our time was up, she smiled sweetly and moved to kiss my cheek. I don't know what made me do it, Father, but I turned my head, so her kiss landed on my mouth instead." Marcus groaned, and Royce imagined him running both hands through his hair as he'd been prone to do when he was frustrated. "A good man worthy of the praise she'd heaped on him would've at least stepped back and apologized, but I deepened the kiss when she parted her lips in surprise. My senses just went haywire, overloading and short-circuiting my brain. Candi and I have been working different shifts for a few years, which didn't allow much time for us to be intimate. We were on a particularly long dry spell at the time. Crystal wrapped her arms around me, pressed her body against my chest, and I was done for."

"Did you have sex with her?" Father David asked when Marcus was silent for too long.

"No, but only because Todd's buddy banged on the door and loudly announced our time was up. He said I could finish myself off in the powder room like the rest of them if I hadn't already jizzed in my pants. Vile jerk. The truth is, if he hadn't knocked when he did, I would've had sex with her. That's how strong the desire was. I borrowed the powder room as the asshole suggested instead."

Father David cleared his throat.

"Sorry, Father."

"Tell me how you went from almost breaking your vows to breaking them," Father David said calmly. The man's soothing voice was making Royce sleepy again, but he needed to finish the recording.

"Isn't it obvious, Father?"

"Not to me," the clergy replied.

"I knew where she worked, and I knew her name was Crystal. I convinced myself for a month or six weeks what I had experienced was nothing more than being horny after a long dry spell. I tried harder to be a better husband and father. Candi and I carved out more couple time for ourselves. No matter how hard we tried, I couldn't ignore how far we'd grown apart. I started to wonder if we married one another because it was what our families expected. We'd met in high school and dated through college, so marriage was the next logical step. Where does logic fit in with love?" Marcus asked.

"Perhaps a topic for another day?" Father David asked.

"Yeah," Marcus chuckled wryly. "It's sure easier to dissect other issues than face the one choking me."

"Very true," Father David agreed. "I take it you went to the club and sought out Crystal?"

Marcus's recorded sobs shredded Royce's heart. Sensing his distress, Bones looked up at him. Royce reached down and buried his fingers in the cat's thick, soft fur, petting him until the urge to howl and throw the recorder passed.

"Yes," Marcus finally said. "At first, we just talked. I paid hundreds of dollars just to have her undivided attention. She listened to me and expressed interest in my career, my kids, and me. She looked at me like I was someone important. Neither of us could deny our attraction or resist the temptation of being alone in the private dance rooms. I hate myself for it, Father. I'm weak and unworthy." Those weren't the words and sounds of an unrepentant man. They were the anguished cries of someone who'd broken vows that had meant the world to him at one time. In the process of shattering the trust Candi had placed in him, Marcus had broken his own heart and lost faith in himself.

"You know what you must do, son. You must tell your wife, ask her for forgiveness, and seek counseling to resolve the issues in your marriage. You must do it for your wife and your children."

"Yes," Marcus said. "I want to fix this. Things aren't right between Candi and me, but I want them to be. I want to love her like I used to and be the man she trusts me to be. I want to be the type of father Marc and Daniel deserve, and not the guy who cheats on their mother."

Royce was outraged Marcus hadn't mentioned Bailey until he realized she hadn't even been conceived at this time if Amber had been truthful about when their affair had begun. Father David hadn't dated Marcus's recordings, so he had to go with his gut, which told him Amber hadn't lied.

"The devil has tempted you away from your duties, but you can cast him out, son. When your body betrays your spirit and soul with sinful urges, you must pray harder. Let me guide you." Father David began to pray, but Royce's spinning brain tuned him out.

So, Marcus had been repentant in the beginning and had sought his priest's guidance. He'd said he was going to tell Candi so they could attend counseling. Had he told her three years ago when the affair had first begun? Had they attended counseling without him knowing it? It was possible. It hadn't been his business, after all.

There was an audible click where the tape had stopped. Thinking it was over, Royce glanced down and saw his player was still running, so the sound must've come from Father David's equipment when he made the recording. A second click occurred a few seconds later, followed by rustling clothes.

"Forgive me, Father, for I have sinned. It's been almost three years since my last confession."

Royce's stomach twisted from the desolation in his friend's voice. He'd never heard Marcus sound so lost.

"I haven't seen you in a long time, son," Father David said. "You don't sound well."

"I'm not well. You know why I stopped coming to church," Marcus said.

"I suspect, but I don't know. I thought our marriage counseling sessions were going well. They seemed to help you and Candice. She forgave you, and you were working through your problems. Then you suddenly stopped coming to them and quit attending mass altogether. Why aren't you well?"

Candi had known.

"Candi wanted to forgive me," Marcus said softly. "It's not the same thing as forgiving me. I can't blame her."

"It takes time, son," Father David said.

"I'm having thoughts about hurting myself," Marcus said. "I can't stop thinking that Candi and the kids are better off without me. I've failed myself and shamed my family. I've tried to be a good man. I've tried to resist the urges, but it's like I am a different man when I'm with Crystal."

"You're still seeing *that* woman," the priest said. There was a distinct chill in his voice that had been lacking when the confession began.

"I love Crystal, Father David. She isn't a villain. I pursued her."

"She's a harlot who sells her body to horny men like you, luring them away from their families and every value they hold dear. Is that the kind of example you want to set for your sons? That they can turn their back on their commitments to their wives and children whenever life gets hard. What about your daughter? Is a stripper the kind of woman you want her to associate with?" With each word, the priest's voice grew tighter and colder. "Forgive my boldness, son, but someone needs to shake some sense into you. Cut ties with that woman before it's too late. Candice will forgive you again. You'll feel better for doing the right thing. Pray hard. Try harder."

"Prayer isn't working," Marcus said, weeping full out now. "I still can't escape the voices, not even when I sleep. I prayed like you instructed me to, but it's not helping. I think I'm crazy. I feel like I'm on a runaway roller coaster with no end in sight. I keep thinking I need to see a doctor. Get some pills or something. I want to be here for my kids, Father. Candi deserves better. I'm going to do the right thing by her."

"You're not crazy. Those voices you hear are the devil whispering in your ear. Counseling will help, if you put forth the effort. Prayer will heal you," Father David said fervently. "You have to mean it, though. You can't just go through the motions, or else you'll fail."

"I agree," Marcus said.

"I'm so happy you've seen the light," said Father David, sounding like a smug bastard.

"I'm going to set Candi free and let her find a good man who treats her with respect and adores her. She should have someone like Royce. Maybe if I'm gone, they'll get together."

Me? Royce loved his Candi Apple, but desire had never been part of their connection. It was another sign of how disconnected Marcus had been when it came to his wife, and his best friend for that matter.

"Anyway," Marcus continued, "I know Candi suspects I'm still seeing Crystal, but she's too afraid to make a break, so I'll do it for her. I'm already the bad guy, right?"

"You're making a foolish mistake," Father David said.

"My mistake was not acting on my feelings sooner and not seeking medical attention."

"Pills," Father David scoffed. "You don't need pharmaceuticals to drive out the devil. Only prayer will fix this. Let me help you, my son."

Royce's blood boiled as he listened to the exchange. Marcus continued to talk about his growing despondency, not just his marriage or job frustrations, but with life.

"I feel like I am two different people. The family man and the fraud. These two lives eventually merge into one—a failure."

Rage turned to deep sorrow from the brokenness in his friend's voice. "No, Marcus," Royce whispered. "Human." A flawed human but one deserving of better advice than what the bastard priest was giving him.

"Living a double life is killing me little by little each day until death feels like the only place where I can find peace."

Royce could only shake his head as scalding hot tears poured down his face.

"I love Candi, but I haven't been in love with her for a long time, possibly our entire marriage," Marcus said. "Candi, the kids, hell, even the whole world, would be better off without me."

The conversation continued for what seemed like endless minutes with Father David's relentlessly insisting Marcus didn't need a doctor and only required more prayer. It was both reckless and dangerous. Marcus's responses were spoken barely above a whisper, and Royce couldn't tell if his best friend was looking for absolution or permission, but it was clear he'd made his decision about ending his life.

Royce almost stopped the tape right there, but he didn't. He needed to hear the rest, so he could understand where Marcus's head had been. He would do it for his best friend, no matter how much it hurt.

"Maybe you're right," Father David said after a long exchange.

Marcus sniffled. "About my decision to set Candi free?"

"No, Marcus," Father David replied. His voice was flat, robotically cold, and completely devoid of compassion or care. "Maybe this world would be better without you. May you burn in hell with the rest of the sinners." There was another click, signaling the recording was over. He waited for them to resume talking during another session, but there was nothing else.

Royce gasped, then whispered, "The world isn't better without you, Marcus."

His hand shook hard, and he dropped the player on Bones, who didn't appreciate the interruption to his nap. The cat dug his nails into Royce's legs as he launched himself to the floor.

"Son of a bitch, Bonesington," Royce hissed, looking down at the blood welling on his bare thighs just beneath his boxer shorts. "At least you didn't neuter me."

"We should probably put peroxide on those scratches," Sawyer said. *We.* Such a small, simple word, but one that eased some of the pain lancing Royce's soul. He wasn't alone. He had Sawyer.

Royce hadn't heard him come into the room and didn't know how much Sawyer had overheard. "Oh, hey. Did I wake you up?"

Sawyer crossed the room and sat beside him. He picked up the mini player from the floor where it landed after bouncing off Bones. "No," Sawyer said. "Bones nearly took me down in the hallway though." Sawyer carefully set the recorder on the coffee table, then looped his arm around Royce's neck, pulling him into his side.

"I listened to the tape, and now I know," Royce said.

Sawyer held him tighter, resting his chin on top of Royce's head. "You don't have to talk about it."

"I need to. Want to," Royce amended. Sawyer didn't say anything while Royce repeated what he heard on the tape. "Voices? Like a multiple personality disorder?" Royce asked, even though he didn't expect Sawyer to have an answer. "How could I not know any of this was going on? What kind of friend was I?"

"The kind who would've stuck by Marcus's side if you'd known. You and I both know there's a lot of stigma that comes with mental illness, and people are afraid to talk about it. Look what happened when Marcus turned to someone for help. Unfortunately, he confided in a person who was clearly prejudicial about mental illness treatment," Sawyer said.

"I'm so damn angry right now. I wish I could storm to the church and strangle Father David with my bare hands."

Sawyer pressed a kiss on the top of his head. "We'll dig up that bastard priest's remains and piss on them."

Royce chuckled despite the heartbreak. "I appreciate the thought, but I'm pretty sure it would be hard to discern Father David's ashes from the church rubble."

"Nonsense," Sawyer countered. "His bones would've been mostly intact. It's doubtful the fire burned hot enough to cremate him, and even so, some bone fragments would've remained. We'll piss on those."

Royce straightened and looked at his boyfriend. "You're fucking scary. Do you know that?"

Sawyer brushed the hair off Royce's forehead. "I never know when I'll need the knowledge."

Royce leaned in for a kiss. "You need to watch fewer documentaries."

"We need to go back to bed. There are killers to catch and cases to solve." Sawyer stood up and held out his hand to Royce. It wasn't a sign of pity or an actual offer to help Royce rise to his feet; it was a show of unity. *Us against the world.*

Royce slid his fingers between Sawyer's and stood up. Using their joined hands to pull him closer, Royce placed a kiss on Sawyer's lips. "Me and you, GB."

Sawyer nodded. "You and me, Ro."

CHAPTER 18

THE SHRILL ALARM PIERCED ROYCE'S TURBULENT SLEEP A FEW HOURS LATER. Sawyer reached over him and quickly shut it off before resting his head on Royce's chest.

"I feel like roadkill," Royce groused, trying to open his heavy eyelids.

Sawyer kissed his cheek, then rolled out of bed. "You look like it too."

Royce found enough energy to lift his right arm and flip Sawyer off, earning a chuckle. "My eyes feel gritty, as if someone buried my face in sand."

"It was Bones's litter box," Sawyer quipped. Someone was full of piss and vinegar this morning. "I think you should skip the workout and stay in bed longer." His voice grew softer as he walked away from the bed. Seconds later, water splashed into the sink basin in the master bathroom, and Royce figured Sawyer was brushing his teeth. Then his sainted boyfriend returned to their bedroom and draped a warm, damp rag over his closed eyes.

Royce sighed as the soothing heat had an immediate effect. "That feels good." Not as lovely as Sawyer's mouth working his dick or even the first sip of morning coffee, but it was what he needed most.

"Sleep, Ro. I'll wake you up in plenty of time to shower and wash the kitty litter out of your hair."

"Asshole," Royce groused before he drifted back to sleep.

The aroma of coffee woke him next. He lifted the now cool rag and found Sawyer sitting beside him on the bed, holding a cup. His skin glistened with sweat, and his hair was plastered to his head. Must've been one damn good workout. Royce was sorry as hell that he missed it. He'd started to think of the gym equipment as tools for foreplay. His body was in the best shape it had ever been in, *and* his dick was kept happy. Win-win.

"You're a saint," Royce said, scooting up into a sitting position. The sheet and comforter slid down his torso, and Sawyer's gaze followed their path. Royce loved how much Sawyer craved him and made a big show of stretching his arms over his head, putting more of his body on display. There was nothing saintly about the unabashed hunger in Sawyer's eyes. Royce's brain tried to return to the early morning hours and the things he heard on the tape, but he slammed on the brakes and steered it back to the man licking his bottom lip while contemplating the places he wanted to lick on Royce's body. "Why don't you set the cup down and get in bed with me?"

"I'm too sweaty," Sawyer replied.

Royce took the cup from his hands, set it on the nightstand, and threw back the covers. "The florist doesn't open until eight, and I see no reason why we need to head to the precinct first. I have a much better idea of how we can spend the extra forty minutes."

Sawyer grinned and stood up. "Yeah? How?"

Royce headed for the bathroom. "I'm better at showing."

After a quick stop to brush his teeth, Royce climbed beneath the spray of hot water with Sawyer, who immediately began washing Royce's body with soapy hands. The sorrow from hearing his best friend talk about his struggle with mental illness and Royce's guilt for not picking up the signs wouldn't wash down the drain with the suds. The pain was raw and real, but Sawyer's touch and whispered words against his lips provided a buffer, a balm of sorts, and reminded him he was alive in ways he never dreamed possible.

It wasn't about sexual gratification right then for Royce; it was about intimacy and connecting with a person who made him feel safe enough to cry and bold enough to love. Of course, his body reacted to the physical stimulation of Sawyer's slick hands moving over his flesh. It would take more than a heavy heart and a night of little sleep to crush his desire.

"Believe it or not," Royce said, kissing Sawyer's lips, "sex wasn't what I had in mind?"

"Hmmm." Sawyer firmly gripped Royce's hard-on and said, "Not."

Royce's laughter bounced off the tile walls. "I had planned to make breakfast for you and reveal another secret weapon in my arsenal in the process."

Sawyer tipped his head to the side as if he were thinking it over as he stroked his hand up and down Royce's shaft, rotating his wrist on the upstroke to rub his palm over the swollen head. "Is this secret as delicious as your double chocolate cake?"

Royce captured his mouth for a long kiss before pulling back. "Better. Crepes."

"Get out of here," Sawyer said. "You make crepes?"

Royce covered his heart. "You wound me with your doubt."

Sawyer snorted. "You bullshit me with your words."

"I guess you'd rather jerk me off than find out," Royce replied.

"Maybe I'm a greedy bastard and want it all," Sawyer said. "Cock, *then* crepes." He loosened his fist enough so his dick could join the party. "Good thing I excel at time management. Maximum production while expending minimum energy."

"Working harder, not smarter," Royce countered.

Sawyer's smile turned wicked, then he began jacking them off together while nipping and sucking Royce's neck. All he could do was hang on and whisper words of encouragement like faster and harder while Sawyer jetted them toward completion.

"See," Sawyer said when they clung to each other afterward. "I

224

bet we still have at least twenty-five minutes for crepes. Wow me, baby."

Challenge received and accepted.

A few minutes after eight, Royce pushed open the door to Sattler and Sons, triggering a doorbell-like sound to alert employees in the back that someone had entered the store.

A wholesome-looking guy in his early twenties stepped out of the walk-in cooler where he'd been placing vases of precut flowers. He wore khaki pants and a green polo shirt with the store's name and logo on it. "Good morning. Can I help you?"

"I sure hope so," Royce said, crossing the store. Sawyer remained near the door, surveying the area to make sure they weren't caught off guard. Whoever Rocky talked to on the phone the previous day was uneasy about discussing Bonita Brothers with him. Maybe they had lied about her no longer working there, or perhaps, they were afraid of the woman.

Like Bonita Brothers, this guy looked pretty generic from across the store with his brown hair, fair skin, and light eyes. But as he drew closer, Royce noticed the hints of red reflected in the fluorescent lighting, and the freckles smattered across his nose. The eyes he would've described as light were an unusual, mossy green.

"I'm Sergeant Locke," he said, gesturing to Sawyer. "This is my partner Detective Key."

Freckles blinked a few times, and Royce waited for the Locke and Key jokes, but they never came.

"I'm Mick Sattler," he said, extending his hand. The guy's handshake was firm, and Royce noted the numerous calluses, reminding him of his aunt Tipsy's hands. She'd spent countless hours working in her flower beds, saying it helped her relax and fed the nurturing side of her personality. People who hadn't known Darla Connors well might've laughed at the suggestion she'd even possessed maternal instincts, but Royce knew just how deeply her feelings were rooted. He'd worked in her flower beds enough to know that various species had different root systems—some shallow and simple and others deep and complicated. If Aunt Tipsy had been a flower, she'd have fallen into the latter category. Her exterior was beautiful and dainty and might lead a person to think she was fragile, but the woman could withstand a storm better than anyone Royce knew. She was the one person Eddie Locke backed down to, and that was no small feat. Royce couldn't look at flowers without thinking about her. She would've loved this store.

"Good to meet you, Mick," he said. "Are you *the* Sattler or one of the sons?" Not that it mattered. The kid looked anxious as hell, and Royce hoped to put him at ease.

"I'm the oldest son," he replied, offering a timid smile. "I hope you're here to buy flowers for a coworker, but it's doubtful you would've brought a partner who looks poised for trouble."

"I'm here to talk about Bonita Brothers," Royce said.

He swallowed hard. "Is she…hurt or in trouble?"

"Her family hasn't heard from her for a few days, and we're just trying to make sure she's okay," Sawyer said as he joined them.

Royce hoped the lie didn't backfire, but it was their best option. They didn't know who might still be in contact with Bonita, so they had to proceed with caution.

"Oh," Sattler said softly. "Bonnie must not have told her parents we broke up if they recommended you speak to me."

"Parents are often the last to know anything," Royce said smoothly. "We're looking for anyone who has talked to her in the last few days."

"That wouldn't be me," Mick said dryly. "She packed her things and moved out of our condo this weekend when I was on a golfing trip with my dad and brothers. I was so relieved it was over that I didn't follow up to see where Bonnie went. My mom fired her when she failed to show up for work again on Monday. She'd become so unreliable, but my parents hadn't fired her out of respect for me. Once Bonnie moved out, they weren't willing to overlook her blatant disrespect for their business."

"Fired her how?" Royce asked.

"Mom left her a voicemail message yesterday morning." Mick grimaced. "But only after the third unreturned phone call." The guy took a deep breath.

"You said she'd become unreliable lately. Did she exhibit other signs of drastic mood swings?" Sawyer asked.

Mick nodded. "She'd been spiraling out of control the last three or four weeks."

"About?" Sawyer asked.

"Anything and everything," Mick said. "I don't know what happened. Things were going great between us. We've dated off and on since we were thirteen and lived together for the last two years. The past six or seven months were hell. Bonnie had these vicious mood swings that seemed to come out of nowhere. One minute she was fine, and the next, she was screaming and pulling her hair." Mick took a shaky breath. "I begged her to see a doctor, but she wouldn't listen. I urged her parents to speak to her, but they thought I was overreacting. Bonnie started obsessing about true crime and injustice, researching cases all hours of the night. She didn't eat, she didn't sleep, and before long, I couldn't cover for her at work anymore. She started showing up late if she came in at all. She was making constant mistakes like messing up the orders and delivering flowers to the wrong locations."

"Does she have a history of mental illness or drug use that might explain her shift in behavior?" Royce asked.

"Not that I'm aware of, and I've known her since we were little kids," he replied. "I didn't break up with Bonnie or ask her to move out because I was concerned about her, even though she spent all her time humiliating me." Mick's face turned bright red, making those freckles stand out more.

"How?" Royce asked.

"It's embarrassing, and I doubt it's relevant to where she might be right now," Mick replied, averting his gaze to stare at the ground.

"Mick," Sawyer said gently, "it sounds like Bonnie is in a bad place emotionally. Right now, everything is relevant. We're not going to judge you, okay?"

Mick slowly lifted his head and made eye contact with Sawyer and nodded. "She had started asking me to do things to her."

"Things?" Royce asked. "Sexual things?" A chill snaked up his spine when Mick nodded. "What kind of things?"

Mick's face turned impossibly redder, and Royce worried the kid was about to implode.

"Relax, kid," Royce said. "This information goes nowhere."

"You mean it won't appear in an official report?" Mick asked.

"Do you want to press charges for something?" Sawyer asked.

"No. God, no," Mick said emphatically. "I just want this to all be over and live in peace." He blew out a frustrated breath, then covered his face with both hands. "Bonita wanted me to tie her up and pretend to assault her. And I... I couldn't get—"

Royce met Sawyer's gaze. They were drawing the obvious conclusions but needed the guy to say it.

Mick growled and lowered his hands. "I tried, okay? I couldn't get it up, and Bonnie mocked me. She told me I wasn't a real man. So, as you can understand, I was glad when I came home from my trip on Sunday and discovered she was gone." He looked up at them with pleading eyes and a trembling lip. "She's not hurt, is she?"

"That's what we're trying to find out," Royce replied.

"Have you talked to people at school? Any of her professors? She might've missed work and blown off dates with me, but she never missed school," Mick said.

"She hasn't shown up to any of her classes either," Royce said, hoping Rocky's intel was accurate.

"Oh, it's much worse than I realized," Mick said. "My dad used to tease us that we wouldn't have college tuition money for our kids because Bonnie would use it all on herself. She always countered how archaic it was for him to assume we would get married or have children." He shook his head sadly. "Bonnie already had two degrees and was studying for a third in psychology. I asked her what she wanted to do with it, but she couldn't give me a definitive answer. I just wanted her happy and going to college seemed to give her joy."

"Are there any particular professors we should talk to at the university? Any that she was especially close to or spoke about often?" Sawyer asked.

"The one she talked about most was Humphries. He was the case she couldn't stop obsessing over the past few months. She'd always liked the guy and had taken as many of his classes as she could, but nothing like the insanity she exhibited recently."

"What about any classmates we should talk to? Can you think of anyone she might be staying with?"

"Honestly? No. She'd said all her friends no longer understood her."

"Mick, would it be possible for you to provide a list of deliveries she made over the past six months?" Royce asked. "Maybe Detective Key and I can look for patterns that might give us some answers."

"I don't see why not," he asked. "It should be easy enough for me to access and compile the data into a spreadsheet."

Royce removed his card from his wallet. "Can you email it to me today?"

"Yeah, sure," Mick said. "I'll get started right away."

Royce and Sawyer shook his hand and thanked him for his help.

Once outside the shop, Sawyer said, "We're getting closer, Sarge. I can feel it."

CHAPTER 19

CHIEF MENDOZA LOOKED FROM SAWYER TO ROYCE AND BACK AGAIN. "Did you say Operation Venus Flytrap, Detective Key?"

"Yes, sir," Sawyer said, gesturing for Royce to explain the significance.

A few minutes later, Mendoza nodded and studied them closely. "Okay, this makes up for the gag gift. This is damn fine work, gentlemen."

"We had a lot of help," Royce said modestly.

"For the sake of plausible deniability, maybe you keep those details to yourselves."

"You got it, Chief," Sawyer said.

Mendoza's computer chimed, capturing his attention. "It's about damn time. I asked for this security camera footage twenty-four hours ago." A smirk spread across the chief's face as he quietly read the email. "It would seem the security at River's Crossing Estates isn't as tight as they've led their tenants to believe."

"What do you mean, Chief?" Royce asked.

"According to their website, they have security cameras strategically placed throughout the community to deter and prevent crimes before they occur." Mendoza snorted. "They have security cameras at the entrances and community buildings, but none at residential intersections or streets. So, we might be able to place Bonita Brothers at River's Crossing, but proving she was at Ms. Gross's residence is another thing." He glanced up. "You guys have done a great job at connecting dots, but we need definitive proof to say Bonita Brothers is Bonnie Parker and Beatrice Ryen." He moved the mouse, then clicked. "Hopefully, we'll find something on this footage, then we can recanvass the neighborhood for a witness who can place Bonita Brothers at Gross's house." He gestured for Sawyer and Royce to come around the desk and look at the footage with him.

"According to the motor vehicle records, Bonita Brothers has a 2013 light blue Dodge Dart registered in her name," Royce said.

"Should be easy enough to spot," Chief replied. At five thirty, a light blue Dodge Dart pulled into the community. Mendoza paused the video feed so they could match the license plate to the one they had on record for Bonita Brothers.

"It's an exact match," Royce said excitedly. Like Mendoza pointed out, they needed more to arrest Bonita and bring her in for questioning.

Chief played the tape on slow motion, pausing when the car moved directly in front of the cameras, giving them the best view through the windshield. Even though the driver wore a Sattler and Sons ball cap, they could see enough of her face to make a positive identification. A white florist's box sat on the passenger seat.

"That's Bonita Brothers," Sawyer said. "Let's hope one of the other cameras picked up something we can use as evidence."

They spent the next hour looking through footage from all the cameras, but she stayed off the feed until she was exiting the community nearly ninety minutes later. Just as the chief had the first time, he paused the video to confirm Bonita Brothers was driving. This time, the flower box was gone, and a briefcase sat on the passenger seat.

"I don't know what a Burberry briefcase looks like, but it's leather, and I think that deep purplish-red color is called burgundy," Royce said.

"I think it looks more mulberry," Mendoza remarked.

"It's a Burberry briefcase," Sawyer said. "It's impossible to make out in this frame, but it looks like a gold monogram on the front."

"I'll see if our tech people can enhance the photo for us," Mendoza said. "It's enough to bring her in for questioning, but I think we need to proceed with caution and continue to build a case quietly. The last thing we can afford is for Bonita to tip off Humphries that we're looking at her if they're in this together. He wouldn't trust her not to roll on him."

"I'm waiting for a list of places Bonita delivered flowers to, Chief," Royce said. "So far, we can't match anyone in our department to this woman, but we're not going to stop until we learn how she found out about the evidence and when it was moving."

"Excellent," Mendoza said. "In the meantime, send the rookies out to recanvass the neighborhood with pictures of Bonita Brothers and her car."

Royce nodded. "Will do, Chief."

"Any updates on the warrant for Gross's phone records?" Mendoza asked.

"No, sir," Sawyer replied. "Not yet."

"Will you follow up on that, Detective Key?"

"Absolutely, sir."

"I'd like to think we won't need them at this point, but we can't afford to get cocky and careless. Connecting Bonita Brothers to Gross's death and the missing evidence appears to be straightforward, but who else is involved?"

"Exactly," Royce said.

"I'll let you guys get to it. Keep me posted."

"Yes, sir," Sawyer and Royce both said.

The rookies were in the bullpen when they finished. Sawyer had briefly chatted with Carnegie on his first day back, but not at great length. Rather than send the rookies out by themselves, Sawyer and Royce went with them. It made more sense to be proactive than twiddle their thumbs and wait for the delivery report to come from Mick Sattler. *If* it came at all. Opie could've changed his mind as soon as they left if he'd been involved from the beginning. Opie? *Jesus.* He was starting to sound like Royce.

The four of them rode over to River's Crossing together, then broke into two teams. Sawyer wasn't a bit surprised when Royce chose Diego and knew damn well there was an ulterior motive. A few weeks ago, it would've been because he wanted to keep Diego away from Sawyer, but Royce was much more confident about his place in Sawyer's life. Nope. Royce wanted to talk to Diego about Levi. Sawyer didn't mind, because it gave him a chance to get to know Topher better, but he hoped Royce didn't make things worse for Levi instead of better.

Most of the neighbors surrounding Gross's residence weren't home, but they did talk to a lady who lived behind Vivian who stated the Dart was parked on her street for a while.

"How long is a while?" Topher asked. "An hour? Two?"

The woman scrunched up her face. "Longer than an hour but less than two," she said. "I noticed the car parked across from my house when I tossed some clothes in the dryer. It's an odd color of blue, so it catches your attention. Plus, I'd never seen it before, and I was being nosy." She waved her hand in the air. "I digress. I had set the timer for an hour and fifteen minutes. The car was still parked there when the buzzer went off. Some of the clothes were still damp, so I restarted the dryer for an additional twenty minutes. The car was gone when the buzzer went off the second time."

"Do you remember what time you started the dryer the first time?" Topher asked her.

"It would've been between five thirty and six. I'm sorry I can't be more specific."

"Thanks, ma'am. You've been very helpful."

She smiled and batted her lashes at Topher. "I can give you my phone number in case you need to ask me follow-up questions."

Topher blushed and wrote her number down in his notebook, where he'd made notes. "Did I handle the situation okay?" he nervously asked when they walked away. "I don't really plan to call her unless it's regarding the case."

"She is an eyewitness and could end up testifying," Sawyer said. "You didn't do anything wrong."

They met back up with Royce and Diego at their Charger when they finished. "How'd you guys do?" Royce asked.

Sawyer nodded for Topher to fill them in on what they learned.

"Lucky for you we didn't place a wager on which team got the best information or else we'd win," Royce said, gesturing to himself and Diego.

"Yeah?" Sawyer asked. "What do you have?"

Royce gestured for Diego to share their big reveal.

"The neighbor across the street placed Bonita's car parked in Gross's driveway at five thirty-five on Saturday evening."

"That's a very specific time," Sawyer said suspiciously.

"She said Bonita almost hit her. She recognized the car from the bi-monthly deliveries. Thinking she was ahead of schedule, she glanced at the clock and realized the flowers were later than usual."

"Plausible," Sawyer said.

Royce laughed. "Sore loser."

"I think we're all winners," Topher said judiciously. "You've proved Bonnie did indeed deliver flowers, while we proved she drove around the block, parked her car, and most likely returned to Gross's house on foot to kill her."

"I like this kid," Royce said. "Who's hungry?"

"I could eat," Sawyer said.

Diego and Topher both nodded.

"Great," Royce replied. "I know a place that serves excellent chicken salad sandwiches. My treat."

"Uh, yeah," Diego said, rubbing the back of his neck.

Sawyer narrowed his eyes at Royce over the top of the car once the rookies got in the back seat.

"What?" Royce mouthed.

Sawyer just shook his head and got in the car.

They arrived at Bytes and Brew between the late morning coffee rush and early lunch crowd, which meant Levi had plenty of time to make eyes at Diego, who seemed to eat it up. What the fuck was wrong with these two idiots? Royce gave him a smug look after placing his order, then stepped aside so Sawyer could do the same. Afterward, he tugged Royce off to the side.

"Stay out of it," Sawyer cautioned again.

"Come on, GB. Tell me you don't see the sparks between them," Royce countered.

"I do," Sawyer agreed. "I also see nothing but trouble if you go sticking your nose where it doesn't belong. They will find a way to work it out if they're meant to be in one another's lives."

"Boring," Royce said dramatically.

Sawyer started to reply, but his phone rang. "This conversation isn't finished," he warned Royce before punching the button to accept the call. "Detective Key."

"Hello, Sawyer. It's Dottie calling. I just wanted to let you know Judge Reinhardt signed off on your warrant. I've forwarded them to the phone companies for her landline and her cellular. Hopefully, we'll have them by the end of the day."

"You're a doll," Sawyer said.

"And you've been hanging around with Locke too long already," she teased. "I'll let you know when we have the records."

"Thank you." Sawyer hung up and smiled at Royce. "We got the warrant for the phone records."

"They might help provide a motive," Royce said.

Sawyer considered it. "You think someone killed her before she could turn over the evidence?"

"I think it's just as believable as Bonita killed her out of spite or jealousy," Royce countered.

Sawyer couldn't argue with his logic.

Diego lingered at the counter even after their food arrived at the table Royce had chosen in the corner of the café. From where Royce and Sawyer sat, they could keep an eye on everyone coming and going. When Diego finally joined them, Royce pointed at him. "What?" Diego asked.

"Don't fuck it up," Royce warned.

Diego rolled his eyes. "I'm not."

Sawyer knocked his knee against Royce's.

"Okay, then," Royce said, letting it drop.

Topher quickly changed the subject, and Sawyer enjoyed chatting about college football with him. He'd always preferred collegiate sports over professional but usually found himself in the minority there.

Midway through lunch, Royce's phone chimed. "Yes! Finally. We need to-go boxes so we can finish this back at the precinct."

"Did we get the list from Mick?" Sawyer asked.

"Yes, and it's a long one," Royce replied as he tapped out a message on his phone. "I'm pulling Blue and Ky in so we can divide the list and conduct interviews. I'll forward it to Holly too." Royce didn't mention why he was sending it to her since neither Diego nor Topher was aware of Operation Venus Flytrap.

Back at the precinct, Royce sent the rookies into the field with Ashcroft and Willoughby for training. Then he printed off a copy of Bonita's deliveries and multiple copies of her photo for identification purposes. Starting with the most recent dates, they worked their way backward several months, each of them circling deliveries to all the key locations where Bonita could've crossed paths with an individual who was in the position to know when the evidence was moving.

Royce sent Ky to Richmond Laboratories and asked Blue to interview the cops and crime technicians at the precinct because his jovial personality would raise fewer flags. Royce and Sawyer headed to the DA's office.

"Maybe you should do most of the talking," Royce told him when they arrived.

Sawyer raised a brow. "Suddenly feeling shy?"

"Nah, all you legal geeks speak the same bullshit. You're less likely to offend Babineaux."

Sawyer doubted they'd get a chance to speak to the DA, but he was wrong. Gillian Babineaux just happened to have a break between court appearances and meetings.

"You have ten minutes," Babineaux said when her assistant let them into her office. "Starting now."

"Are you holding a grudge?" Royce teased.

Gillian crossed her arms over her chest, pinning him with the fierce expression she usually reserved for interrogations and cross-examinations. "Tick tock."

Sawyer showed her Bonita's picture. "Do you recognize this woman?"

Babineaux studied the photo for a while before returning it to him. "Nope. Why?"

"You've never seen her in the building?" Sawyer asked.

Babineaux snorted. "I've never met this woman. Has she accused me of something?"

"No," Sawyer said quickly.

The DA narrowed her eyes. "Don't bullshit me and waste my time being coy. Who is the woman, and what are you trying to find out?" Babineaux asked. Leaning forward, she pointed at Royce first, then Sawyer. "It had better have something to do with nailing Franco Humphries's balls to the wall."

"I'm afraid it will take us longer than"—Royce looked at his watch—"seven minutes to bring you up to speed."

Babineaux silently studied them for a few seconds. "You're already high on my shit list, Locke. This had better be good." Then she picked up her phone and rang her assistant. "Hold my calls, Sylvia."

Babineaux's expression remained neutral and unimpressed while listening to them repeat everything that had happened, and how they thought it tied back to their missing evidence. "So, you're close to arresting a suspect in Gross's homicide?"

"We hope so, ma'am," Royce said.

"We also need to make sure we don't have a mole in either of our departments or at the lab," Sawyer said. Babineaux wasn't the kind of person you tried to manage.

"I haven't seen this woman, but I did receive the flowers on the printout. My mother sent them for my birthday. She adds a flower for each year. The bouquets are getting ridiculously big, but they brighten my day, and I look forward to them. I wasn't here when they were delivered, but Sylvia was. If she was at lunch, then one of the other assistants or attorneys might have accepted them. All I know is they were on my desk when I returned from lunch." She leaned forward. "And, yes, I lock down my files and confidential documents when I leave. Ask around but be cautious what you say just in case the leak is here."

"No problem," Royce said as they headed out of her office.

"Keep me posted," Babineaux called out.

"Will do," Sawyer replied.

Sylvia hadn't accepted the flower delivery, but it didn't take them long to find the person who had. Phil Trimble, a junior prosecutor, recalled seeing Bonita and placed the flowers in Babineaux's office. They questioned him about the woman's demeanor. "Did she act oddly or appear to be in distress?"

"No, not that I can recall," he said.

Then they walked him through the entire encounter from start to finish. Midway through, he recalled a comment she made about an upcoming trial. "I told her I couldn't comment or speculate."

"Do you recall which case?" Royce asked. Sawyer was impressed his partner's voice had remained calm.

"Of course," Trimble said. "The same one everyone was talking about and still is. Franco Humphries."

They continued to ask Trimble more questions but didn't learn anything else. A few other people in the building recognized her but couldn't recall specific conversations or any unusual behavior.

When they returned to the precinct, Ky was back from the lab, and Blue had wrapped up his interviews too. Mendoza pulled them all into his office for a progress report. Many people recognized her at the precinct, the DA's office, and the lab, but only Trimble recalled a specific encounter. It didn't mean she hadn't overheard what she wanted to know.

"How are we going to proceed with Humphries tomorrow, sir?" Sawyer asked the chief.

"We very carefully set a trap the arrogant son of a bitch can't resist stepping into," Mendoza replied.

CHAPTER 20

VIVIAN GROSS'S PHONE RECORDS WERE WAITING FOR THEM THE NEXT morning when they arrived at the precinct. Knowing they had time to kill before Humphries returned, Royce and Sawyer went through the staggering number of calls, then looked up the numbers to see who they belonged to. Royce's eyes began to cross, and the numbers blurred together after a while.

"Tiffany Humphries," Sawyer urgently said, snagging Royce's attention.

"What about her?" Royce asked.

Sawyer handed him the piece of paper and pointed to the highlighted number. "That's Tiffany's cell phone number. Vivian talked to her quite a bit the week before she died."

"She's Franco's attorney," Royce said, trying hard not to get his hopes up too high.

"Yes, and the phone calls between the two women while Humphries was incarcerated make sense," he said, pointing to older records. "Why would Tiffany call her after Franco was free? What the hell did they talk about at seven in the morning on the Friday before Vivian died?"

Royce's pulse sped up. "That's the same morning she called Vincenzo and told him about the new evidence she had on a client."

"Here's the outbound call to Vincenzo not long after she talked to Tiffany," Sawyer said, pointing to an entry an hour later. "There's no way in hell it's a coincidence. There are texts between Gross and Tiffany as well, including a quick exchange around eight thirty in the morning." They hadn't requested a script of the individual text messages because reading them would violate her clients' privilege. They could see the numbers she texted though, and Sawyer was right.

"You think Tiffany Humphries discovered something about her husband and went to Vivian instead of coming to the police?"

"Maybe Tiffany wasn't sure what she had, or maybe Vivian had convinced her the cops were crooked. Tiffany might've just wanted to tell someone and clear her conscience."

Royce nodded. "She could have stumbled across it accidentally and panicked. She wasn't sure what to do and called Vivian."

"It's as logical as anything else. The woman has no family around here, and she's surrounded by people who are convinced her husband is innocent," Sawyer pointed out.

"Let's tell the chief and see if he wants to alter our plans," Royce said.

"Stay the course," the chief said after reviewing the phone records. "I agree the timing of the text messages and phone calls is suspicious, but we need to see if Humphries leads us to Bonita Brothers." He glanced at his watch. "Their plane is due to land in a few hours."

Royce wanted to meet Humphries at the airport in person, but he had to hang back and see how things played out. He hated being sidelined, but the chief had made the right call. They spent the next few hours interviewing professors and staff at South University to see if they could offer insight as to where they might be able to find Bonita Brothers. Everything they'd learned aligned with Mick Sattler's statement the previous day.

They were headed to lunch at a bistro near the university when Royce's phone rang.

"We might have a problem," Mendoza said after Royce answered.

Royce stiffened when he heard the urgency in the chief's tone. "We're in the car. Let me put you on speaker so Sawyer can hear too." He tapped the button on his phone. "Go ahead, Chief."

"I just heard back from Humphries's detail. Their plane landed, but guess who wasn't on it?"

"Did Tiffany Humphries come home alone, or were neither of them on the plane?" Sawyer asked.

"Franco returned home alone."

Dread turned to outright fear. "Fuck," he said, slamming his fist against the steering wheel. "This isn't good."

"Damn. Do you think he killed her?" Sawyer asked.

"I think we're getting ahead of ourselves here, gentlemen," Mendoza said. "I agree it's very unusual that she didn't return home with him from their second honeymoon, but I need you to stick to the plan. Let's give Humphries the opportunity to lead us to Bonita Brothers. If not, you'll get your crack at him in a few hours."

"Yes, sir," Royce said. Every instinct told him to go straight to Humphries's house and confront the killer, but he knew the chief was right. He could not afford to act on impulse and emotion. They had a solid plan and needed to stick to it.

"I have contacts in Mexico I can call. Let me see what I can find out. We know what airport they flew into, which helps us narrow the search area a bit. You focus on Bonita and let me worry about Tiffany."

"Yes, Chief," Sawyer said.

No matter how difficult it was to concentrate, they continued searching for Bonita Brothers as discreetly as they could while waiting for their opportunity to speak to Humphries. They got it a few hours later when Mendoza called back to report Humphries hadn't left his house other than to retrieve his dogs from the neighbor.

"You're up, gentlemen," Mendoza said. "Don't lose your cool and blow it, Locke. He's going to do his best to provoke you. I'm going to issue the APB and BOLO for Bonita Brothers."

"I won't let you down, sir," Royce said vehemently. Or Tara, Christi, Abby, Harper, or their mothers.

They parked in front of Humphries's two-story house a few minutes later. It was a newer home built to look like a Victorian mansion but with cleaner lines and less ornate trim. The square footage seemed more than two people needed, but the man was all about his image. Colorful flower beds lined the porch, which extended along the front of the house and wrapped around to the right side.

Royce looked over at Sawyer, who studied him intently. "I won't fuck up, GB."

Sawyer winked. "I know you won't." Then he got out of the car, forcing Royce to shove down his rising anxiety and follow him.

Royce rapped his knuckles against the door and the dogs inside started barking like crazy.

"That's a lot of noise for two little dogs," Sawyer quipped.

Humphries wore his usual arrogant smile when he answered the door on the second knock. A bronze tan had replaced his prison pallor, making the bastard look well-rested and very pleased with himself. "Well, this is a surprise. I wasn't expecting a welcome-home committee. Forgive me if I don't want to share my vacation pictures with you, Locke." Humphries raked his gaze over Sawyer. "Sawyer Key. I've read quite a bit about you over the years." The crazy bastard tipped his head to the side and narrowed his eyes. "That church fire must've been scary. It's amazing it didn't damage your face...much."

Fury boiled inside Royce, but he kept his mouth shut and his hands relaxed by his side.

Sawyer didn't acknowledge Humphries's remark. "Can we come in, sir?" he asked. "We need to speak to you about an urgent situation."

Humphries sighed and rolled his eyes. "No, you can't come in, and I'm not speaking to you without my lawyer present."

"She's dead," Royce said on cue.

"I just heard the news today," Humphries said unemotionally.

"My wife and I were on our second honeymoon at the time, but you already know that, don't you?"

Had he picked up his tail?

"How would we have known that?" Sawyer asked.

Humphries's dark brow shot up. "Are we really going to act as if one of you didn't call Mrs. Meyers pretending to be from the university to pump her for information? There is no Sylvester Goodfellow on the staff or university's board."

"I don't know what you're talking about," Royce deadpanned. There was no way Mrs. Meyers could prove it was him since their numbers are blocked when they make outgoing calls.

"Right," Humphries said, rolling his eyes. "Go away. I have nothing to say to you. Call Bill Elderwood. He's taking over as my attorney."

Royce wanted to remark on his lack of emotion in regard to Gross's death, but he stuck to the plan instead. He waited until Humphries moved to shut the door in their faces, then said, "We think your life is in danger." That got his attention. Humphries opened the door again and pinned Royce with a disbelieving look. "And Mrs. Humphries too."

"Come again? Does this have something to do with Vivian's death?"

"It does," Sawyer said. "We're actively looking for a suspect who we believe is obsessed with you."

Humphries's brow furrowed. "Who?" He shook his head. "Scratch that. Let me call Bill and see when he can be available. One of us will be in touch." Sawyer started to offer him one of his cards, but Humphries shook his head. "Oh, I have his number," he said, nodding toward Royce. "Isn't that right?"

Royce knew he wasn't referring to his phone number either. *I've got yours too, mother fucker.* Mr. Psychology thought he had Royce all figured out, but they'd see which one of them won this game of cat and mouse. "I'll be waiting," Royce said.

Elderwood called Royce not more than five minutes later. The attorney chewed his ass for ten minutes about harassing his client before informing Royce that he and Humphries would be at the precinct at four o'clock.

"We'll see you then, Mr. Elderwood."

The attorney and his killer client showed up ten minutes early. Royce and Sawyer didn't want to keep them waiting since the ploy wouldn't gain them an advantage. Royce led them into a conference room and gestured for them to have a seat.

Humphries looked around the room, then smirked at Royce. "This is quite a different setup than last time, Sergeant."

The location for the meeting was also part of their plan. Talking to him in one of the interview rooms would only set Humphries on edge and make him less willing to talk. The video camera was mounted on the wall in plain sight but was less obvious than a two-way mirror.

"I want to make my irritation known for the record," Elderwood said. "I feel you've taken advantage of terrible circumstances to harass my client." The older man's face started turning red as his temper rose. "You had no business showing up at his home to question—"

Royce raised his hand to cut off his tirade. "Noted, sir. I also want to state for the record that Detective Key and I didn't go to your client's house to question him. We went there to warn him about a potential danger to him and his wife."

Elderwood briefly glanced at Humphries before narrowing his eyes at Royce. "What danger?" So, Humphries had left that part out, huh? Interesting. Royce was willing to bet the lawyer hadn't informed Humphries that his file was missing either. The guys weren't off to a good start.

"As we stated to Mr. Humphries," Sawyer said, "we think the person who killed Vivian Gross might be obsessed with him."

"You have a suspect in mind, then?" Elderwood asked.

"Yes, we do," Royce said, flipping open the file to remove the

245

enlarged photo of Bonita Brothers. He turned it around and set it in the center of the table. Both Elderwood and Humphries leaned forward and studied it. "Are you familiar with this woman?"

"She looks familiar," Humphries said. He looked up and met Royce's gaze head-on. There was no surprise or hint of recognition in the man's eyes, but Royce wasn't expecting a revealing reaction. "She also resembles every other white, fair, blonde girl that attends South University."

"Is this your suspect?" Elderwood asked.

Royce nodded. "Bonita Brothers."

"I'll take the bait," Humphries said in a bored voice. Royce expected him to yawn at any minute to let him know how unconcerned he was. "What makes you think she killed Vivian, and why on earth would she be a threat to me?"

They'd discussed at great lengths what they would need to reveal to Humphries and Elderwood to add legitimacy to the meeting. Royce and Sawyer cautiously took turns revealing enough pieces of the puzzle to form a clear picture of a dangerously unstable woman whose obsession might be driving her to harm the women closest to Humphries. They were careful to stay clear of anything tying Bonita Brothers to the missing bedsheet. They didn't share the image of Bonita taking Gross's briefcase that presumably contained Humphries's file and possibly the new evidence Gross had collected against him.

"I've taught thousands of students," Humphries said once they finished. "I can't even recall having a conversation with this one." He sounded a little rattled, but Royce wasn't buying his bullshit. Humphries was a master manipulator. "I would like to help you, but I don't know anything about the woman."

"Fair enough," Sawyer replied. "We mostly wanted to make you aware of the danger to yourself and your wife."

"Tiffany's only in risk of drinking too much, falling asleep on a Mexican beach, and getting a sunburn," Humphries said wryly.

"She didn't come home with you?" Royce asked.

"Her sister turned up unexpectedly and crashed our second honeymoon. I was angry at first but figured my wife had been put through hell and deserved a longer vacation," Humphries said, aiming a pointed look at Royce just in case it was unclear who he thought had put his wife through the wringer.

Bullshit. Tiffany Humphries had known her life was in danger and called her sister.

"Then you should stay alert until we've apprehended Ms. Brothers," Sawyer said.

"Thank you, Detective Key. I'm so glad you care about me."

Royce bristled at the dig, but Sawyer brushed his hand against his thigh beneath the table.

"If there's nothing else to discuss, we'll be going," Elderwood said, scooting back his chair.

Sawyer and Royce made no move to stop them from leaving. Humphries threw one last smug look over his shoulder before walking out and pulling the door closed behind him. Royce reached beneath the table and hit the button to kill the video feed, then made a tight fist. Seeing that bastard walking free made him want to hit someone or throw something, but neither of those things would make the situation better.

Royce rose to his feet and moved to the door, checking to make sure the two men weren't still standing on the other side before he closed it again and walked back to the table. Instead of returning to his chair, Royce sat on the edge of the table. Sawyer placed a comforting hand on his thigh.

"We didn't gain anything from this interview," Royce said.

"We didn't lose any ground either," Sawyer countered, smiling up at him. He glanced at his watch. "We have a ball game to get to."

Royce smiled for the first time since leaving their house that morning. He couldn't wait to introduce Sawyer to Candi and the kids. "We do."

Marc's game was ironically on the field named in Vic's honor. Royce recalled seeing Sawyer wearing a baseball jersey with the name Ruiz embroidered on the back of it as he tossed the ceremonial first pitch. So much had changed between the first visit to Victor Ruiz Jr field and this one. Sawyer was the love of his life, not just a virtual stranger Royce was wildly attracted to but determined to resist. Instead of hiding from his feelings, Royce embraced them.

"Hey, guys," Royce said cheerfully as they approached.

"Ro!" the boys cheered and ran over to him. He scooped them up even though Marc wearing his catcher's gear made it awkward. Little Miss Bailey started to squirm in excitement. Royce hugged the boys, then set them down.

"Hey, I remember you," Marc said, looking up at Sawyer. "You threw out the pitch on this field."

"I sure did," Sawyer said, extending his hand. "I'm Sawyer." Marc shook it like a little man.

"Are you Uncle Ro's boyfriend?" Daniel asked.

"I am," Sawyer said. "You must be Daniel."

"I am," Daniel mimicked, shaking his hand too.

Bailey let out a bloodcurdling scream, reaching her chubby hands for Royce. He quickly took her from Candi before she made their ears bleed.

"How's my princess?" Royce asked, kissing her cheek and making her giggle. Then he leaned down and kissed Candi's cheek too. "How's my Candi Cane?"

"Better," she said. "So much better." Royce felt a pang of guilt and second-guessed his decision to talk to her about Marcus's confession tape. "You look great." She did too. Candi had put some weight back on and no longer looked exhausted. For the first time in months, her smile reached her eyes. "Hello, Sawyer. It's good to see you again." She'd met him once at the precinct soon after he was hired, but this was the first time she was seeing Sawyer and Royce as a couple.

"You too," Sawyer said when Candi hugged him. "We wanted to

invite you and the kids over to grill out burgers and hot dogs after the game."

"Sounds good to me. What do you say, guys?" Candi asked the boys.

"Yeah!" they cheered.

Royce ruffled Daniel's hair. "Maybe Mommy can swing by your house to grab your swimming trunks because Sawyer has a pool."

"Cool!" the boys said.

Bailey responded to their excitement by squealing and kicking her Fred Flintstone feet.

The coach hollered for Marc to join the team, so the rest of them sat on the bleachers.

"Are you sure you want us there that late on a work night?" Candi asked.

"Positive," Royce said, hooking an arm around her.

Beside him, Sawyer started talking to Bailey, and it didn't take her long to ditch Royce so she could wrap another man around her pinky finger.

"Shameless flirt," Candi said, shaking her head.

The day had been a bizarre collision of the worst and best parts of Royce's life. He couldn't dwell about Humphries and obsess over what his next move would be, or he might not have noticed how right it felt when Sawyer slipped his arm around his lower back, or he could've missed seeing Marc tag out a runner at home plate. Royce had to accept the things that were out of his control and give his attention and time to the people he loved.

After the game, Candi swung by her house to get their swimming gear. By the time the crew arrived, Sawyer had a head start on the burgers and dogs.

"I'm starving," Marc said.

"Me too," Daniel chimed.

Royce went inside to pour glasses of lemonade but got caught up in watching Sawyer chat with the boys. Marc was gesturing wildly, and he could tell he was reliving his big play for Sawyer. Daniel mimicked and mocked his every move until Marc pushed him and Candi intervened. She made the boys have a time-out on patio chairs while she chatted with Sawyer. Whatever his guy said made her smile and laugh. Behind her back, the boys were making faces at each other, and Royce knew it wouldn't be long before another fight broke out.

Royce was still laughing at the boys' antics when Candi and Bailey came inside to see if he needed help.

"I love seeing that sappy smile on your face, Ro," Candi said.

"I love wearing it," he replied truthfully. "I love seeing a smile return to your face too."

"We're healing," she said. "Each day is a little easier than the one before." Candi reached inside her purse and pulled out an envelope. Crossing the room, she extended it to him.

Royce opened the envelope. There was a check inside for the amount he'd given her when the creditors were breathing down her neck. He pushed the envelope back at her. "I told you it wasn't a loan, Candi."

"I don't need it now that I'm receiving Marcus's benefits. I've decided to take your suggestion and sell the house to buy something smaller and more affordable. I wanted to hold on to the house for the wrong reasons, and it's time to let it go. Let the hurt go. You and I will find a different way to keep Marcus's memory alive for the kids."

Royce nodded because they would. Now came the hard part. "Candi, there's something I want to talk to you about, but I don't want to upset you."

She offered him a sad smile. "I can probably guess."

"Come with me a minute," he said, tipping his head to the opposite side of the house. "I don't want the boys to walk in and overhear us talking."

Royce led Candi to the study and asked her to make herself comfortable while he retrieved a few things from the bedroom. Her eyes immediately went to Marcus's tattered hat when he walked into the room.

"Oh my gosh!" she said, covering her mouth for a few seconds. "I didn't think I'd ever see that ratty hat again."

Royce took a deep breath and sat beside her. He set the hat and phone on the coffee table and showed her the tape player and cassette box with Marcus's name.

Candi closed her eyes and raised her hand to cover her trembling lips. Then she lowered her hand, blew out a shaky breath, and opened her eyes. Royce hated the pained expression on her face. "Is that what I think it is?" Candi asked weakly.

Royce had refused to watch news coverage for several days after the fire, but Rigby had told him the press had gotten wind of the recorded confessions. The identities of the victims never became public and Rigby destroyed all the tapes, except Marcus's, to keep it that way. Candi had never asked him if Father David recorded their sessions, but it had to be on her mind.

"Yeah," Royce said.

Candi tugged at the collar of her T-shirt. "I thought they were all destroyed." Sensing her mother's distress, Bailey began to fuss. "It's okay, baby girl," she said softly, but Royce wasn't sure if she was trying to convince herself or her daughter.

"All of them were destroyed except this one," Royce replied.

Candi nodded. "Did you listen to it?"

"Yes, I did. I needed answers. I needed to understand why—" His voice broke, and Royce cleared his throat.

"You know about the affair," she whispered brokenly.

"I found out when I started probing around to see if IA had a legitimate case against Marcus. I was stunned."

"I didn't ever want you to find out," she said. "I knew there was a chance you'd uncover something pretty awful if IA was investigating Marcus, but I knew you'd take the cheating news worse. You looked up to him, and I didn't want to take that away from you. It turns out I did anyway."

Royce covered her hand. "Don't blame yourself. None of what happened is your fault."

Candi rotated her wrist and laced their fingers together. "I wish that were true. Marcus wasn't the only one with secrets. I've kept something from you, too, because I didn't want you to hate me."

Royce shook his head. "It could never happen."

"I had asked Marcus for a divorce that weekend. I waited until I was out of town, then told him over the phone I was leaving him. I thought it was what he wanted, Royce. He'd been seeing Crystal off and on for three years." Royce was stunned at the casual way she'd said the other woman's name. "Marcus would break up with her every few months and recommit himself to our marriage, but it never lasted long. At first, I hated her. Then I started hating myself for putting up with Marcus's infidelity and for not being able to let him go. Why the hell would I want to cling to a man who thought so little of me? I would've given up more than Marcus though. I would've lost you and Holly in the divorce."

Royce shook his head emphatically. "No way."

Candi smiled sadly. "It's easy for you to say that now, but I've seen how this goes. Everyone chooses a side. You and Holly belonged to Marcus long before I came around."

Royce wanted to keep denying it, but he knew there was truth in her words. Instead, he released her hand so he could put his arm around her. "How did Marcus take it when you said you wanted to get a divorce?"

"Honestly, he sounded relieved. Maybe resigned is a better word. He didn't express excitement or rush me off the phone so he could hurry up and tell Crystal the good news. We had a calm conversation about the united front we would make for the kids. He said he loved me and I was the best thing to ever happen to him. I had this sudden thought that I was making a huge mistake, then realized he didn't mean he was *in* love with me. And you know what? It was okay because I wasn't in love with him either. Before we hung up, Marcus apologized for failing me, and he promised I would meet a more deserving man someday." Candi turned her head into Royce's shoulder and cried for a few moments before lifting a tear-streaked face up to look at him. "I was petty and didn't dispute what he said, but I swear to you, Ro. I had no idea he was going to hurt himself."

"Of course, you didn't," Royce said, holding her tighter. Then he told Candi about the conversation Marcus had with Father David about his struggles with mental health.

"How could I have missed the signs? I'm a trained professional," Candi said.

"With three kids, a busy career, and a husband who wasn't being honest with you about anything," Royce said. "What's my excuse?"

"Don't you dare blame yourself," she said fiercely.

"I will stop when you do," Royce teased. "We will make a commitment here and now to forgive ourselves and Marcus." It sounded so easy, but they both knew it wasn't.

"Deal," Candi said.

Royce kissed her forehead. Then he looked at the hat and phone sitting on the coffee table. Candi had assumed they were collected as evidence when the department investigated Marcus's death, but Royce had recovered them at Amber's apartment. He didn't want to lie to Candi, but he was limited on what he could say about Amber since she was an undercover FBI agent.

"I want you to have the stinky hat and phone," Candi said. Maybe she sensed his hesitation and mistook it as reluctance to part with them. There was some truth there as well. "I'm sure Marcus took thousands of photos during your fishing trips. God, the stories you two used to tell." She giggled for a second before sobering. "Burn that damn tape. Marcus deserves to rest in peace."

"Will do." Royce sure as hell had no plans to listen to it again.

"Mommy! Uncle Ro!" Marc yelled from the kitchen. "Dinner!"

"He's so suave," Candi said.

"Hurry! I'm dying!" Daniel added.

"He's so dramatic," Royce said.

Candi nodded. "Never a dull moment. Just you wait and see."

Royce laughed. "I just told Sawyer the story about the glitter slime incident and Marcus's certainty that I'd have kids of my own someday."

Royce and Candi shared a smile over the cherished memory of a flawed man they'd loved and lost. They were healing—day by day and step by step.

"Isn't this the part where you deny it until you're blue in the face?" Candi asked as they retraced their steps toward the kitchen.

They stopped when they reached the end of the hallway, taking in the adorable sight in front of them. The boys had put their differences aside to gang up on Sawyer, who was tempering his strength while he showed off his WWE wrestling skills in the living room.

"No, it's not."

Candi laughed joyfully until Daniel broke away and shimmied up onto the couch. He let out a war cry and bent his knees in preparation to jump onto Sawyer and Marc.

"I don't think so, young man," Candi said. "This isn't how we treat someone who is kind enough to invite us to their lovely home for dinner and swimming. I guess you don't want to try out Sawyer's pool that badly."

"Oh, come on, Mom," Daniel whined. He flopped onto the couch and crossed his arms over his small chest, then scrunched up his face and wailed. Royce didn't see any tears leaking from his eyes.

"Knock it off, Tom Cruise."

Daniel unscrewed his face and looked at Royce. "Who's that?"

"He's an actor like you. He does his own stunts too," Royce replied.

"Don't give him any ideas," Candi said to Royce before returning her attention to her sons. "All right, boys, let's wash our hands for dinner."

Sawyer directed her to the guest bathroom, then crossed the room, pulling Royce into his arms when he reached him. "How'd it go?" he asked.

"Better than I imagined, but that's been everything since you came into my life." Royce kissed Sawyer before he could return the sentiment.

Sawyer broke the kiss and smiled at him. "My mom called a few minutes ago. She invited us to dinner on Saturday, and I accepted."

"Great. Now we just need to avoid getting shot or set on fire between now and then."

Three days was a long time for them to find trouble.

CHAPTER 21

"**U**NCLE SAWYER IS HERE!" HIS NIECE CASSIDY YELLED AS SOON AS HE entered his parents' home. Uncle was one of his most cherished titles, and the kids barreling toward him were four of his most beloved humans.

Kennedy, at eight years old, and her brother Tyler, age six, did their best to keep up with the bigger kids: Cassidy, the oldest of the brood at twelve, and Tarron, her ten-year-old brother. He shouldn't have a favorite niece or nephew, and he would never speak the truth out loud, but he had a closer bond with Cassidy. She reminded Sawyer so much of himself at her age—book smart, not too keen on physical activity, and carrying extra weight that crippled a preteen's confidence. They often chatted about books and documentaries like two adult friends meeting up for coffee.

Cassidy reached him first, hitting Sawyer hard enough to knock him back a few steps. She wrapped her arms tightly around his waist and clung to him. "I've missed you so much. I hated that we weren't allowed to see you when you were recovering."

Sawyer hated hearing the tears in her voice and hated it more that he was the reason for her distress. "I missed you too, Cass," he said, hugging her tightly.

"That's the fastest I've seen you run in your entire life, Cass," Tarron teased when he arrived next. There was no censure or cruelty in his voice, he was just a kid making an observation, but Cass looked crestfallen.

"I can't run faster than your mouth though," Cass retorted.

Kennedy and Tyler arrived a few steps behind the other two, and Sawyer opened his arms to pull them all into a group hug.

"You don't look crispy," Tyler said, but with his slight lisp, it sounded like cwispy.

"Tyler," Cassidy admonished.

Sawyer laughed, knowing full well who'd told the kids he looked crispy. "Did your father call me a crispy critter, Ty?"

"No," Killian said, walking toward them, wearing a smug expression on his face. "I said you looked like a burnt marshmallow."

"I had bad dweams," Tyler said.

"Way to go, jack—" Sawyer remembered his audience at the last minute.

"Jackass isn't a bad word," Cassidy said. "It's an animal."

Tyler pulled back from the group hug, then looked at his father. "Jackass!" he yelled, then skipped deeper into the house where Sawyer presumed the rest of the family was.

"Jackass!" Tarron and Kennedy repeated as they followed behind Tyler.

Killian frowned at Cassidy. "Really, Cass?"

"Sorry, Uncle K. Technically, it's not a bad word, but I guess you don't want them screaming it at the grocery store."

Killian chuckled. "I'm more worried about school on Monday, but I wasn't referring to their new favorite word."

"What, then?" she asked earnestly.

Killian slipped an arm around her shoulder. "Maybe not make it so obvious Sawyer is your favorite uncle, okay? Throw me a bone once in a while."

Cassidy tipped her head to the side and thought about it for a second. "Nah." She gave Sawyer one more tight squeeze before following after her brother and cousins at a more leisurely pace.

"That's my girl," Sawyer told Killian. Then he pulled his brother into a headlock and rubbed his knuckles over his hair.

"Easy," Killian said, throwing elbows to break the hold. "Or, I'll return the favor." Killian stiffened and looked at him with mock horror. "Oh, wait. You don't have enough hair to mess up."

"I'm still way better looking than you," Sawyer countered.

They horsed around until they heard their mother clearing her throat. "Really? Which one of you taught the younger kids to yell jackass at the top of their lungs?" She looked good and pissed.

Killian and Sawyer looked at one another before facing their mother. "Cassidy," they said, knowing Evangeline's firstborn grandchild stood a better chance at forgiveness than they did.

Cassidy, who'd returned to the scene of her crime, gasped and covered her heart with both hands.

"Cowards," Evangeline said, rolling her eyes. "Where's Royce?"

"He should be here soon," Sawyer said. "We had to work our case today, following up on tips coming into the hotline." To no avail. Bonita Brothers was in the wind. "We split up so we could cover more ground."

They'd each taken a rookie with them. Sawyer chose Diego to give the guy a break from Royce's matchmaking attempts. He hadn't asked a single question about Diego and Levi's relationship, even if he was dying to know what the hell was going on. He got lucky because Diego had voluntarily disclosed he had plans with Levi this weekend. The only bright spot during the past few days was confirming that Tiffany Humphries was still alive and in Mexico with her sister as Franco had claimed.

"Candi had a plumbing emergency too, so Royce was going to see if it was something simple he could fix to save her the hassle and expense of calling a plumber," Sawyer added, following her through the house.

"He's a good man," Evangeline said warmly.

"Back off, cougar," Sawyer teased, adding a little growl to his voice.

Everyone was outside enjoying the mild temperatures. The back of his parents' home overlooked the Skidaway River. Each of the three stories had a porch extending the rear of the house. The first-floor porch was enclosed, allowing them to enjoy it all year. It opened to a vast expanse of lush, green grass leading to the river. To the left of the property was a boat dock where his brother-in-law sat fishing.

"I hope we're not relying on Nick to catch our dinner," Sawyer teased. He'd never met anyone with worse luck than Grace's husband.

"We'd starve," Grace said, seconding Sawyer's opinion. She looped her arms around his waist. "How's my favorite brother?" she asked.

"I'm standing right here," Killian said. "Why is Sawyer everyone's favorite?"

Evangeline snorted. "Let's get this out of our systems before my real favorite arrives."

"Royce," Sawyer, Grace, and Killian said at once.

"Where's Brianna and Dad?" Sawyer asked.

"I'm here," Brianna said, stepping through the door. She sounded weak and looked a little green around the gills.

"Are you okay, Bree?" Sawyer asked, hugging her gently.

"I'll be okay," she said, pulling back and smiling feebly at him.

"In about six more months," Killian said, reaching for his wife. "I'm sorry, baby. Want me to make you some ginger tea?"

"You're having another baby?" Sawyer asked excitedly.

"Uh-huh," Bree replied. Her tone was less than thrilled, but the brilliance of her smile kicked up about ten megawatts.

"Congratulations," Sawyer said, hugging them both.

"Dad is in his office. He's speaking to Senator Vincenzo about an upcoming fundraiser."

Sawyer nodded. "I'm going to head inside and wait for him to finish. There's something I want to discuss with him."

Evangeline searched his gaze. "Is everything okay?"

He nodded. "Yes." Or it would be. Sawyer kissed his mother on the cheek and retraced his steps through the house, turning left at the main hallway. His father's study, a place he loved as a child, sat at the very end. His father had left the double doors open, and Sawyer could hear his father's voice. Judging by his dad's jovial tone, the senator hadn't come clean with him yet.

Sawyer and Vincenzo hadn't fully worked out their differences, and although the tension had eased by the end of the second interview, Sawyer hadn't recanted his insistence that Jack stay clear of his parents. He didn't want them to get caught up in the aftermath of a scandal. It could damage his father's reputation with his clients. Now, Sawyer had to choose between warning his parents or honoring the senator's privacy until the story about his relationship with Vivian Gross got out, and he believed it would. These types of things never stayed buried. Sawyer had interviewed the senator's former fiancée over the phone, and Ms. Fairchild had emphatically stated she had no desire to leak the story to the press. He wasn't sure if it was to protect herself from being front-page fodder or because she hoped there was a chance for reconciliation after Vincenzo recovered from his heartbreak. Sawyer figured she'd be waiting a while if that were the case.

Sawyer could personally attest that the human heart could love more than once in a lifetime. He'd read a poem, or a passage in a book, or maybe it was song lyrics, that referred to the human lifespan in terms of seasons. The creator claimed there was a love for every season, starting with parents in the spring of a newborn's life. Each new love is part of a journey, propelling us toward the wintery end.

Sawyer paused in the hallway to look at the collage of family photos. His mother had chosen candid shots she'd taken over the years to adorn the walls instead of posed professional portraits. Each one told a different story and represented different seasons. There were snapshots of random holidays, ski trips in Vail, backyard campouts, birthday parties, and significant milestones such as getting their driver's license and graduating.

His gaze snagged on a photo taken of him and Vic sitting on the edge of the boat dock with their feet dangling in the water. They'd been drinking beer and watching the sun set over the river, which reflected the beautiful hues of pink and purple and burnt orange. Vic's arm was around his shoulders, pulling Sawyer tighter against his side. Sawyer could remember the conversation like it was yesterday.

"I'd hoped to beat this," Vic had said softly. "I wanted many more sunsets like this one with you. I wasn't ready to say goodbye. I'm still not."

"Then, don't," Sawyer had said. "I just read about—"

Vic shut him up by kissing his lips. "Please don't make this harder than it already is," Vic said after he pulled back. "I'm dying, Sawyer. No experimental test will change that, and I don't want to waste the time I have left traveling and feeling sicker than I already do. I just want to enjoy every last sunset with the man I love."

Though it broke his heart, Sawyer had agreed. It would've been cruel and selfish to insist otherwise. They drove to his parents' house every night to watch the sunset and enjoy a beer. It was during one of those evenings that Vic found the courage to discuss life after he was gone.

"What are you thinking about?" Sawyer had asked.

"That you're going to share these majestic sunsets with another man someday. I hope he'll know how lucky he is."

"Never," Sawyer had said vehemently.

Vic had chuckled and held him tighter. "Just you wait and see." It took nearly two years before Sawyer could admit Vic had been right.

Sawyer continued his trip down memory lane, his eyes landing on another photo of him on the boat dock. It was hard looking at the thirteen-year-old version of himself. The obese, awkward kid with the bad acne was a part of him, and a reason why he'd become a tad vain about his looks.

The summer after the photo was taken, Sawyer had hit a growth spurt, which helped him shed extra pounds, and he took weightlifting as an extracurricular class in middle school. He'd thought it would be better than taking a gym class where he'd be forced to participate in group sports with kids who'd bullied him for years. He'd had enough of being chosen last in elementary gym classes to last him a life-time. He'd made the right call. The high school football coach taught weightlifting, and Sawyer learned more about himself and his body during those two semesters than any other time in his life, except for his freshman year of college. He'd started seeing a dermatologist for his skin and learned to treat food as fuel. Royce teased him about his strict skincare regimen and diet, but he'd understand when he saw these photos. And he would see them.

"Sawyer," his father said, pulling his attention away from the pho-tos. "Were you coming to see me?"

"Yes, I wanted to talk to you privately about Senator Vincenzo."

"Ah. Jack said you might, but perhaps we should save it for later since others might get nosy and interrupt us."

"Who? Like me?" Evangeline asked as she walked toward them.

"I'm glad you're here, Mom. I want to include you in the conver-sation also," Sawyer said.

Evangeline patted his cheek. "Rest assured, dear. Jack has already told us everything, and unless you think he killed Vivian Gross, the rest isn't our business. People are entitled to their privacy, even state senators."

"No, the senator isn't involved in her death," Sawyer said. "I just didn't want you to get caught up in the aftershocks when the scandal explodes in the media."

"Jack feels the same way, which is why he called to warn me that he's releasing an official statement after Vivian's burial late next week. He's wrapping up the final arrangements. If he announces it now, Vivian's funeral will become a media circus."

"You can say that again," Sawyer said. He debated asking his dad if the senator had decided to continue his campaign or resign but con-cluded it wasn't relevant. It was apparent Jack still had his parents' support either way. And besides, they were adults who could make decisions for themselves. He heard Royce's voice in his head, teasing him. *Control freak.*

Sawyer's phone buzzed with an incoming text. Removing it from his pocket, he saw it was from Royce.

Things got wetter than I anticipated. I'm going to swing by my place and grab a quick shower and change. Be there soon.

You better! Sawyer replied.

"I can tell by your sappy expression it's a text from Royce," his mother said. "He better not be shot or on fire."

Sawyer laughed. "Nope. Drenched. He'll be here soon." Sawyer couldn't wait to share his first sunset on the dock with Royce.

CHAPTER 22

ROYCE WAS GRATEFUL FOR TWO THINGS: QUICK REFLEXES AND A PATIENT boyfriend. Without the first, Candi's second-story bathroom floor might've sustained a lot more damage. The valve to the toilet had snapped off when Royce attempted to fix it, and he had wrenched the water off before too much gushed out. If not for Sawyer's patience, he'd be in the doghouse big-time.

He'd harassed Sawyer enough times about withholding his mom's dinner invitation and was now running late when the universe finally aligned for them to attend. Then again, maybe Sawyer was mad. Perhaps the humor Royce detected in Sawyer's response was wishful thinking.

Damn, Royce. Stop being a putz and get a move on. Royce pocketed his phone and found his house key on the ring. It had been weeks since he used it. Glancing at Aunt Tipsy's overgrown flower beds, he sent up a silent plea for her not to hate him.

Royce needed to decide what he was going to do with the place. Maybe it was presumptuous, but he suspected filling out a change-of-address card was in his near future. Selling the house felt wrong, but he didn't want to be someone's landlord either, unless… An idea occurred to him. Jace was probably tired of living in his apartment over the body shop where he worked, and Holly had always loved the house. From what he remembered, Aunt Tipsy showed her a lot about planting and pruning flower beds. Holly had sucked up the attention and the knowledge like a sponge since her homelife hadn't been much better than theirs, which was why she'd understood Royce's struggle with intimacy over the years. It probably was why she'd tolerated Jace's bullshit longer than she should have too.

Holly and Jace were different now, and Royce was confident they would make it. He hardly recognized the man his brother was becoming, but he figured Jace would say the same about him. As far as Royce was concerned, Jace *was* his family. His younger brother, sister, and father ceased to exist in his new world. Now when a bar owner called him looking for restitution because Eddie Locke had busted up his establishment, Royce responded with "Eddie who?" His heart felt lighter with the hard stance and his bank balance got heavier.

Royce unlocked the door and pushed it open, moving a mountain of mail that had gathered beneath the mail slot. His only debts were his credit card, home and auto insurance, utilities, and his car payment. He received e-statements for all of them. Some he had automatically deducted and others he paid on apps or online. Royce had no earthly idea how he'd collected so much junk mail, but he stepped over it on his way to the bedroom. He could sort the bullshit out another time when Sawyer and his family weren't waiting on him.

Don't be nervous. Don't be nervous. It was easier said than done after he'd made such a big deal about it to Sawyer. Royce had no reason to be worried. Evangeline adored him and Baron and Sawyer's siblings liked him. He hadn't met the nieces and nephews, but kids loved him. They recognized one of their own. By the time he peeled himself out of his soaked clothes, he had calmed the fuck down. Royce rushed through his shower and dressed in clean, dry clothes. He'd had enough hair product left there to style his hair, so he wouldn't look like a complete bum. Sawyer loved his hair messier, and he'd happily let him run his fingers through it later.

An idea struck him when he passed his closet on the way to the bedroom door. He'd told the truth when he said he couldn't fit into his dress blues, but the white hat would sure as hell still fit. Royce could easily find a pair of aviator glasses at a drugstore. He just needed some super skimpy underwear. *Aha!* Candi had purchased him a red, white, and blue Speedo as a gag birthday gift one year. He'd buried it in the bottom of his underwear drawer instead of throwing it out. Royce retrieved the swimming briefs from his dresser and held them up in the air. He'd need to do some trimming and maintenance down below before jamming his junk in the tiny scrap of fabric. Sawyer would love it.

Royce fisted the trunks, tucked the hat beneath his left arm, then turned off the bedroom light and exited his room. He'd had every intention of stepping over the mail on the way to collecting his keys from the small table by the front door, but his eyes snagged on a large envelope with his name handwritten on the front of it. Royce's breath caught in his throat when he saw the name of the sender was V. Gross, and the return address written below was the same as the crime scene he had visited six days ago.

Holy fuck.

Vivian Gross had sent the new evidence she'd obtained on Humphries to him.

"I've got you now, you fucker," Royce said.

He set the Speedo and hat on the table and picked up the envelope with shaking hands. He started to peel back the tape sealing it when he remembered his training. Gloves. He needed gloves. He kept a spare box in his kitchen drawer, where others kept things like plastic wrap and aluminum foil. Before meeting Sawyer, most of his dinners arrived in takeout cartons, so he didn't have much use for those things. He never knew when he was going to be called out to a crime scene and would need gloves.

With a pounding heart, he carried the envelope into the kitchen. Royce opened the drawer, slid on a pair of nitrile gloves, then tore into the envelope. Even though his kitchen counters looked clean, they wouldn't be sterile enough to avoid contaminating evidence, so he decided to study one piece at a time. The first thing he pulled out was a letter from Vivian Gross.

Detective Locke,

I know you and I have had our share of differences lately, and I've said some harsh things about you in the press, but I didn't know where else to turn. New evidence regarding Franco Humphries dropped into my lap, and I had to make a tough choice: do what was best for a client, or do what I knew was ethically required of me, even if it meant losing my license to practice law. Betraying a client and my oath isn't in my best interest professionally, but I have to look in the mirror and like who I see. I can live without being an attorney, but I cannot live with knowing I helped a serial rapist and murderer go free to continue terrorizing women.

While Franco was incarcerated, Tiffany found a safe-deposit box key hidden in a secret compartment in her husband's desk. They had a joint box at the same bank, and this key had a different number. She talked herself out of opening it, choosing to believe what Franco told her. She said his demeanor drastically changed once he came home from the county jail, and she began fearing for her life. Tiffany hoped the safe-deposit box was the key to her freedom. The bank teller was too busy asking prying questions to recognize the key was for a second box Franco had opened without her.

What Tiffany found inside was very disturbing and quite damning for Franco. She wasn't sure who she should turn to, because I'd done a great job of convincing her you couldn't be trusted. I understand the irony of me turning to you now. Enclosed are photographs of the contents of the safe-deposit box. Tiffany has moved the items to a secured location Franco isn't privy to, or me either for that matter. The photos of the evidence were enough to make me act.

Best regards,

Vivian Gross

Royce slipped the letter back inside, then pulled out the eight-by-ten photographs Tiffany Humphries had most likely snapped with her phone and later printed. There were dozens of charcoal sketches of women restrained to beds in various states of dress and stages of consciousness, including the four coeds, and a Ziploc bag with personal items most likely belonging to the victims. Most serial killers kept souvenirs. Humphries wasn't as unique as the prick thought he was. As damning as all of it was, the photos that interested him the most were ones taken of monthly planner entries showing the dates and times of Humphries's guest lectures at other universities. Next to the entry pages, Tiffany had placed newspaper articles about sex workers killed during the same time frame and snapped a picture. There were more than two dozen entries and corresponding articles.

"Fuck. This is way worse than I thought." No wonder Tiffany phoned her sister.

Royce's pulse soared as adrenaline rushed through his body. His hands shook as he slid the final piece of evidence back in the envelope. He started to feel lightheaded and realized he'd been holding his breath.

Breathe, dumbass.

He practiced Sawyer's yoga shit until he felt steadier on his feet. Sawyer! He had to let him know what he discovered. Royce tucked the envelope under his arm, then grabbed his keys and headed out to the car where he'd left his cell phone. He'd turned so sharply into his driveway that the phone had slid off the passenger seat and onto the floorboard, landing by the passenger door. He'd been too miserable in his wet clothes to care and had left it in his locked vehicle.

Royce punched the button to unlock the Camaro, then walked around to the passenger door. He picked up the phone and called Sawyer. He heard a click and thought it was Sawyer picking up, but the line rang again. The hair stood up on the back of his neck when he realized the noise came from behind him. *Humphries.*

He started to turn to meet his nemesis, but an electrical current shot through his body, starting at the back of his neck and speeding its way to his legs, which had suddenly lost their ability to hold his weight.

Sawyer answered his call. "You better be calling to say you're on the way."

"Asshole," Royce slurred.

A second, longer zap caused his body to jerk and fall forward, smacking his head hard against the doorframe.

Royce's vision started to dim, and the world began to spin as the ground rushed up to meet him. He tried calling out for Sawyer, but Royce couldn't get his mouth to form words. Then there was nothing but blackness.

CHAPTER 23

SAWYER HEARD A SOLID THUMP FOLLOWED BY A BARELY AUDIBLE GROAN before the connection ended. "Royce!" he shouted, even though he knew it was futile. "Oh, fuck. Oh, fuck." Fear screamed through his nervous system, threatening to short-circuit Sawyer's brain and sweep his legs out from under him. *Pull it together, Key.* The last time he reacted without thinking, he nearly died and could've taken Royce out with him. A calm head had to prevail, and Sawyer needed to rely on his training, not emotion.

"Sawyer, what's wrong?" Evangeline asked, gripping his arm.

He just shook his head as he dialed for help. "Officer down," Sawyer firmly said when the dispatcher answered. He knew he wasn't overreacting. Royce had slurred like he was incapacitated, and the loud thump could've been his body falling to the ground. God no. Sawyer choked back his fear, then rattled off his badge number and Royce's home address, which he believed was his last known location. "I repeat. Officer down. Send units immediately." Sawyer disconnected the call and turned to face his parents. "I have to go. Something is wrong."

Tears streaked his mother's face, but she nodded.

"Keep us posted," his father said.

"I will," Sawyer called over his shoulder as he raced down the hallway and out of the house. *Please let them be in time. Please let them be in time.*

His phone rang as soon as he started backing down his parents' driveway. Sawyer saw it was the chief calling and hit the button on his steering wheel to answer. "Chief, I was just about to call you."

"What's going on?" Mendoza asked. The chief's voice was firm but calm, which was just what Sawyer needed to pull himself together the rest of the way.

He told the chief what happened, not leaving any detail out. He didn't care if the chief thought it was odd Royce was having dinner with him and his family. Keeping their relationship secret was the last thing on Sawyer's mind.

"Units are on their way to his house, and I'm heading there myself," Mendoza said. "I'm only a few minutes away."

"I'm on my way," Sawyer said, breathing through his rising panic.

"Just stay on the phone with me," Mendoza said.

"Yes, sir."

Mendoza kept Sawyer talking by making him account for Royce's day, which prevented his mind from imagining every worst-case scenario. It was a miracle he didn't get pulled over as he broke every speed limit and traffic law on his way to Royce's house.

"I'm here," Mendoza said. "Two patrol cars are here but Locke's car isn't." That did not make Sawyer feel better.

"I'm two blocks away," Sawyer said. He disconnected the call once Royce's house came into view.

He screeched to a halt, threw the car in park, and killed the engine. Mendoza met him halfway up the driveway. "We have shattered pieces of black plastic and glass in the driveway."

"His cell phone," Sawyer said. "Humphries probably smashed it so we couldn't track it."

"Don't get ahead of yourself," Mendoza cautioned. "Maybe Royce hadn't arrived here yet. Officer Dwyer is checking to see if he was involved in a car accident. Maybe you heard the tail end of it when the airbag went off or something. It could've knocked him uncon-scious. I've sent Steinman and Riggins to canvass the neighborhood."

Sawyer knew his life had turned to pure chaos when he found himself hoping his boyfriend was knocked out by an airbag instead of abducted by a serial killer. "There's one quick way to find out," he said, holding up the Duke key on his chain. It was the first opportuni-ty he'd had to use it since Royce gave it to him.

Mendoza said nothing as he followed Sawyer up the driveway. He unlocked the door and pushed it open. The first thing Sawyer noticed was the white Marine Corp hat sitting next to a colorful piece of fab-ric on the table next to the door. What the fuck was that doing there? Then he took in the massive pile of mail.

"Locke doesn't spend a lot of time here, huh?" Mendoza said when he noticed it.

Instead of answering him, Sawyer said, "There was no weight against the door or sounds of paper scraping against the floor, so he's been here already."

"We don't know for sure it was this evening," Mendoza coun-tered. Sawyer understood what the chief was trying to do, but it made him want to hurl things.

"I know another way," Sawyer said, then headed toward the mas-ter bedroom. Mendoza didn't remark about Sawyer knowing where it was, but it was impossible he hadn't noticed. The man didn't reach the rank of chief without being damned observant.

The tiled walls in the shower were wet, and the scent of Royce's body wash was strong in the air. He pointed to the soaked clothes hanging over the shower curtain rod. "He's been here."

Suddenly the white dress hat by the front door made sense. Royce had grabbed it to surprise Sawyer. Why had he set it down by the door, then? To pick up the mail? Leaving it there was uncharacteristic of Royce. His brief time in the Marine Corp had a lasting impact on his tidiness. Sure, he was in a hurry and might've been nervous about the family dinner, but something had made him pause and set the hat down. Had he planned to pick up all the mail or had a specific item caught his eye?

Sawyer darted out of the room and headed into the kitchen. There on the countertop was a piece of clear tape with remnants of a manilla envelope stuck to it. The picture was becoming clearer in Sawyer's mind, but it didn't bring him comfort.

Gesturing to the tape, Sawyer said, "I think Vivian Gross mailed the evidence she had on Humphries to Royce's house. It would've been easy enough for her to find his home address, and she would've had no idea he hasn't lived here in months."

Mendoza's brow furrowed, but he listened without interruption as Sawyer explained his theory. "You think Humphries was following Royce and struck when he got the chance?"

"I think someone knew the evidence existed and silenced Vivian. We had assumed the killer stole it along with Vivian's briefcase and Humphries's file. What if Vivian mailed it off before Bonita Brothers got to her?"

"That's a big assumption, Detective," Mendoza said calmly, but Sawyer saw the spark in the man's dark eyes. "If your theory is right, Bonita, Humphries, or both, have been trying to track down this information."

"No one would've predicted Vivian turning to Royce for help after her scathing remarks to the media," Sawyer added. "They were getting desperate." His blood chilled at the thought. If he was right, Humphries had the evidence and Royce.

"Chief," Officer Steinman said, rushing through the front door. "A patrol car responding as backup spotted Bonita Brothers's car abandoned three blocks away."

"She was lying in wait," Sawyer said. "She knocked him out, then drove him off in his car." He couldn't move. Couldn't breathe. It wasn't smoke restricting his airway this time; it was fear.

Mendoza nudged Sawyer toward the front door, breaking the hold that panic had on him. "Steinman, you stay here and keep the premises secured. Let's go see if Bonita's car can give us clues to where she's been hiding."

"We'll need a warrant to search it," Sawyer said.

"Not to look through the windows," Mendoza countered.

Sawyer followed the chief to his SUV. Other than the police radio chatter, they rode in silence for three blocks to where Bonita's car was parked beneath a carport. The tall weeds and detritus littering the property indicated the house was vacant. Sawyer strode over to the car, hoping it would give clues. It was too much to expect a map with an X marking the spot on the front seat, but Sawyer knew the amount of mud caked in the wheel wells and splattered on her paint was significant. It looked like she'd taken the small car off-road.

Mendoza dialed his cell phone, placing the call on speakerphone. "Valentino, where's Humphries?" he asked when a man answered the phone.

"As far as I can tell, he's still at home, Chief," the man said. "From my vantage point down the street, I can see both cars are parked in his driveway. The little old lady who lives next to Humphries was starting to get suspicious, so we've had to pull back a bit. It's difficult to tail suspects in residential neighborhoods like this one."

"When was the last time you saw Humphries?" Mendoza asked.

"Last night when he answered the door to accept his pizza delivery," Valentino replied. "It was around seven."

"Any unusual activity today?" Sawyer asked.

"He's been lying low a lot since returning home from vacation, only leaving the house to walk the dogs or get food." Because Humphries knew they were watching him, and he was establishing new habits to lure his detail into a false sense of normalcy.

"Did he walk the dogs today?" Chief asked.

"Not since I arrived, but I just took over for Johansen about an hour ago, Chief," Valentino replied. "Want me to call him and find out?"

"No, I want you to go knock on his door and make sure he's

home." When there was no immediate reply, Mendoza added, "Right fucking now, Valentino. Sergeant Locke could be in grave danger."

Grave danger. Don't you dare freak out now, asshole. Sawyer could hear Royce's voice so clearly in his head, and it helped him remain calm.

They heard Valentino's car door opening and his footfalls rapidly smacking against concrete as he ran toward Humphries's house. "What do you want me to say if he answers, Chief?"

"Tell him you're selling magazines. For fuck's sake, Val," Mendoza groused. "Worry about that if the bastard answers." *If.* Sawyer and Mendoza exchanged a grim glance. They both knew Humphries wasn't going to answer the door.

They said nothing, only listening to Valentino's breathing as he sprinted down the street until he reached Humphries's house. Then came the sounds of Valentino pounding on a door. *Bang. Bang. Bang.* "Savannah Police Department!" Valentino yelled as he continued slamming his fists against wood. "Open up, Mr. Humphries."

"No dogs," Sawyer whispered.

"What?" Mendoza asked.

"His dogs aren't barking, which means they're not inside and neither is he," Sawyer replied.

The pounding stopped suddenly, and Sawyer hoped to hear Humphries's voice, but instead, Valentino said, "This is official police business, ma'am. Please go back inside your house."

"Kiss my ass," an elderly lady said. "You people should be ashamed of yourselves for harassing a good man like Franco." It was Lucretia Meyers—dog sitter and Franco defender.

"Ma'am—" Chief disconnected the call before they could hear the rest of his response.

"Son of a bitch," Mendoza snarled.

Humphries was missing and so was Royce.

"Based on the mud on her car, she's been hiding someplace rural. I'll see if her family owns property," Sawyer said, pulling up the public records on the Chatham County auditor's site. After a quick search, he came up empty. "Both her parents and grandparents have moved out of Georgia, but I'd hoped maybe her grandfather still owned property like a fishing or hunting cabin or something." *Fishing.* He dialed Rocky's number.

"Catch a break in the case?" Rocky asked when he picked up.

"Maybe, but it's not the kind we want," Sawyer said grimly. "When Clyde Brothers talked your ear off, did he happen to specifically mention where they went for their hunting and fishing adventures?"

"He mentioned Bryan County. He'd said Reggie's family had an old homestead there with a run-down cabin on it. The place wasn't much, but it was a nice break from work and family stress. He said Reggie talked about demolishing it and selling the land when property values went up a few years back."

"Anything else you think could be helpful?"

"Nothing comes to mind. What's going—"

Sawyer disconnected the call without saying goodbye or thanking the PI. He'd ask Rocky to forgive him after he got his man back. And he *would* get him back. Sawyer switched to the auditor's site for Bryan County and typed Dozer in the search field. Sure enough, Reggie hadn't sold the lake property in the northern part of the county, and according to the auditor, there was still a small structure on it.

"I know where Royce is, Chief."

CHAPTER 24

I HAVE A LITTLE SURPRISE FOR YOU, BABY.

Surprise? Baby? The voice penetrating Royce's sleep wasn't one he recognized. He was too tired to care, so he let the comforting darkness reclaim him. Sawyer would surely be waiting for him there with eager hands and mouth. Royce's heart started pounding just thinking about his boyfriend. The thumping grew louder, pulsing through him. Sawyer was really rocking his world, even if Royce couldn't see him. A shrill whistle ripped through his fantasy. *Train? Tornado?* Alarm spiked through him, and he tried to claw his way out of the brain fog but couldn't muster the energy. Sawyer's embrace beckoned for him.

Bam!

Royce's body lurched hard to the right, and his head smacked against something cold and unyielding, jarring him awake. His jeans were soaked, and for a moment, he thought he'd slipped on Candi's bathroom floor and knocked himself out. Then he got a whiff of urine and realized he'd pissed himself. Humiliation flooded his body until he remembered getting zapped with a stun gun. Twice. He tried touching the painful knot on his head, and that's when he discovered his wrists were bound together in front of him with zip ties. Not good. Unfortunately for Royce, understanding how dire the situation was didn't come until after he let his assailant know he was awake. He'd just given up a significant advantage.

"One false move, and I'll zap you in the testicles," Bonita Brothers said calmly.

Royce turned his head and studied her. She didn't resemble the fresh-faced woman they'd seen in photos from her pre-Franco days. Her hair looked greasy and hung limply over her shoulders, her clothes were filthy, and she reeked of body odor. How Royce hadn't smelled her coming was beyond him. Then his eyes landed on the scabbed scratch marks on her forearms. Vivian Gross had fought hard for her life, collecting her killer's DNA in the process. There was no doubt in his mind Fawkes would match it to Bonita Brothers.

"Those wounds look infected," Royce said. "I hope you stopped at the drugstore for some peroxide."

"Are you always a smartass?" Bonita asked.

"Absolutely. It's amazing what people will reveal when you get a rise out of them."

She hadn't blindfolded Royce, so he could see they were in his car, and she was driving him out to a very isolated location, which didn't bode well for him. Bonita didn't plan to leave him alive to talk. Her driving his beloved car over an uneven, overgrown path between dense trees was what had roused him. Wherever they were, the grass hadn't been cut in months, maybe even years, and underbrush and low-hanging branches scraped his paint job.

"Take it easy on my ride," Royce said, bracing his bound hands on the dashboard.

"Why? You'll never get to drive it again. The fish at the bottom of Boggy Pond won't care about the scratches." Boggy Pond was a lake in Bryan County near Pembroke. He and Marcus had visited plenty of times, but they'd never traveled terrain this rough.

Amateur. With little effort, Royce got Bonita to confirm she planned on killing him and how she planned to dispose of his car. "Because you're going to kill me like you killed Reggie and Vivian? Is Reggie's body in Boggy Pond?"

Bonita twitched in her seat but didn't answer him. She'd either realized her mistake or was playing tough girl. Royce knew, with the right prodding, he could get her talking. What did he want to know more? How she planned to kill him, or whether Humphries helped her orchestrate the murders.

"How did Humphries communicate with you from prison?"

"He didn't," she said flatly.

"Oh, come on," Royce said. "You expect me to believe you planned and executed the evidence heist all on your own?" He forced himself to laugh and hoped like hell his plan didn't backfire. His gun was in the glove box, and she would've seen it when she got the zip ties out.

"I didn't need a man to help me figure anything out. People are stupid, lazy, and love to gossip. I easily gained the information I needed to know, then formed a plan and *executed* it."

"Impressive," Royce said. Recalling what Holly said about Bonita's online alias, he decided to poke the bear again. "I might buy that with Reggie but not Vivian. She was smarter than the average person."

"She was a traitorous slut," Bonita hissed.

"Because she fucked Humphries?"

"Shut up! Shut up!" the deranged woman yelled, pounding the steering wheel with her fist. "He wouldn't touch that disgusting piece of trash. You're just saying that to get me to talk."

"Gotta pass the time somehow," Royce said. "How is Vivian a traitor, then?"

"She conspired against Franco with Tiffany. I saw them meeting at a café when I followed—" She shut up as if realizing she said too much. It didn't matter. Royce could see it so clearly. Bonita had stalked one of them, witnessed the envelope exchange, and alerted Humphries.

"Are you in the camp who believes I planted the evidence or the one who says Humphries didn't kill those women?" Royce asked.

Bonita didn't reply. She gripped the steering wheel tighter and her body practically vibrated with rage. Royce worried he'd gone too far and decided to focus more on escape than gathering evidence. He considered his options. Royce outweighed her by a good eighty pounds, and even with bound wrists, he'd have an opportunity to knock her off balance and get away. The harsh terrain meant she wasn't driving very fast, and he briefly debated opening the door and rolling out of the car. Bonita had gone through the trouble of fastening his seat belt, but if he timed it right, maybe he could unbuckle his seat belt, open the door, and roll out of the car. It worked in the movies. By the time she stopped, he'd be on his feet and running into the woods. The plan didn't have a high rate of success, but it beat rolling over and playing dead while she and Humphries tortured him. Royce had no doubt the sick fucker was involved too.

"He's going to kill you once you're no longer useful, Bonnie," Royce said.

"Shut up."

"You do know his plans to kill Tiffany fell through, right? Oh, wait. Did he tell you he killed his wife while in Mexico?" Royce started laughing, even though there was nothing funny about the situation. A sane person would've recognized how forced it sounded, but Bonnie glanced over at him long enough for Royce to see she was fucking out of it. There was a madness in her gaze that froze his insides.

"You're a liar," she spat.

"I'm not lying, Bonnie. Tiffany Humphries outplayed her husband. You killed Vivian for nothing."

"No," she said, shaking her head. "Tiffany is shark food at the bottom of the Pacific. Franco chartered a boat the night before he returned home, slit her throat, and pushed her body overboard. It's better than the traitorous whore deserves for turning her back on Franco. I would've made her suffer more."

"She's hanging out with her sister on the beach," Royce said. While they hadn't spoken with her, Mendoza's contact sent photographic evidence she was alive and sunning herself on the beach. He was going to keep an eye on the women on the off chance Franco had hired a hitman to kill them.

Bonita laughed. "You bought that bullshit story he fed you? I thought you were supposed to be brilliant."

"No, my partner is the smart one." *Sawyer.* Royce couldn't allow himself to worry about what Sawyer was thinking or doing, or he could miss an opportunity to gain the upper hand. "I talked to Tiffany on the phone," Royce lied.

She glanced at him again with narrowed eyes. "You're lying."

"You're guessing. We'll clear this up when Franco arrives," he said smugly.

The car crested over a small incline, and at the bottom of the hill, Savage Creek flooded the valley from recent heavy rains. Royce couldn't tell how deep the water was, but he could see muddy tracks going up the other side. Neither hill was steep, but his Camaro had rear-wheel drive and wasn't equipped for off-road mudding. He couldn't believe her little Dart had made the trip in and out, but at least she had front-wheel drive. With a fast head start, she'd probably pulled it off easily enough. As if Bonita read his mind, she hit the gas hard as she approached the bottom of the hill, slamming into the water with a jolting thud and sickening crunch. *There goes the front spoiler.* The evil bitch cackled like it was the best amusement ride she'd ever been on, before whooping and gunning the gas.

Royce gripped the door handle with both hands for stability as she fishtailed up the hill until gaining purchase on dryer ground midway up.

"If it hadn't been for you, they'd still be alive, and Franco and I would be living on a beach someplace."

This woman was delusional, but Royce wanted to keep her talking, especially when they crested the hill and a dilapidated cabin came into view. The rotten roof hadn't caved in yet, but it was only a stiff breeze away from collapse. No fucking way he was voluntarily submitting to whatever they had planned for him.

"My arresting Franco ruined your plans?" he asked to keep Bonita talking.

"Yes," she hissed. "We'd started dating before you manufactured fake evidence and arrested Franco. He was going to leave his wife for me. We were going to start over."

"That's what he probably told Tara, Abby, Christi, and Harper before he killed them. You were going to be victim number five."

"He did not kill those whores. I saw them flirting shamelessly with him. They'd go out of their way to entice him. They must've latched on to someone else who killed them. Those sluts had it coming." There was deranged, then there was this girl—a whole new classification of insanity. If he didn't already know better, Royce would've thought Bonita killed the four coeds.

"How did they entice Franco?" Royce asked.

"Abby made a fool of herself by lingering in the library on the nights he researched classes, Christi saved a piece of his favorite pie for him every day, Harper made sure his request to speak with the dean got put ahead of everyone else's, but Tara was the worst. She often showed up early to clean his office, knowing he was working late. Once, I saw her enter the men's restroom when he was inside. I could tell by the smirk on her face she planned it on purpose. Nasty whore."

I saw her enter. How long had she been stalking Humphries?

Bonita was the kind of person who just blended in and skipped people's notice. Healthy people's attention, anyway. Franco Psycho Humphries would have observed her lurking around, and he would've used her adoration and mental instability to turn her into a perfect weapon no one saw or suspected. Royce wanted to ask her how she finally gained favor with Humphries but realized he was running out of time as she slowed near the cabin.

This is it. Now or never.

"It's not too late," Royce said. "Put this car in reverse and drive us out of here. I will speak on your behalf at your trial. You're sick and need help. You're not evil. I can help you if you save my life."

"Fuck you."

Royce's body tensed as he prepared to spring into action, but then the shadows shifted on the darkened, rotten porch on the front of the cabin, and Franco Humphries stepped forward. The mottled sunlight penetrating the canopy of tree leaves overhead glinted on the pistol pointed toward the car.

"This should be fun," Bonita chirped as she put the car in park and killed the engine. For good measure, she zapped Royce once more in his side. He jerked and his teeth rattled, which only made her laugh. "So much fun."

Humphries gestured with the gun, indicating he should get out of the car. Bonita unbuckled his seat belt and waved the stun gun again. "Get out, or your nuts are next."

"What's with you and my nuts?" he asked, opening the door.

It was awkward getting out of the car with his hands bound, but he managed. His legs felt clumsy and weak at first, but the more he moved, the quicker he regained his strength. Royce was grateful he didn't have any symptoms of a concussion. He kept his hands in front of his chest as he squared off against the serial rapist and killer. His heart pounded, but he refused to show any signs of weakness. Instead, he smirked at the man holding the gun steady on him. "Let me guess. This is all just a big misunderstanding."

"No," Humphries said. "I'm going to kill you."

Yet, he remained a safe distance away, aiming the gun at Royce instead of killing him on the spot, which meant he planned to toy with Royce first. Fuck that noise. Royce wiggled his fingers as discreetly as he could to keep the blood flowing. If his fingers went to sleep from lack of circulation, what limited use he'd have of them would be significantly compromised.

"What took so long, love?" Humphries asked.

Bonita giggled. He knew she'd be twirling her hair if he looked over at her. She'd climbed out of the car but hadn't walked around to Royce's side of the vehicle. "We got stuck behind a train for twenty minutes near Pembroke." That explained the shrill whistle, the heavy thumping, and vibrations. "I wanted to tie him up with a bow, but it would've drawn too much attention. I made him piss himself, so surely that counts for something." Her eagerness for Humphries's praise was revolting.

"You did well, love," Humphries said without taking his eyes off Royce. "I couldn't have done any of this without you."

"You'll have plenty of time to show your appreciation once we get rid of him," Bonita replied.

"I have a name," Royce groused.

The sick smile Humphries aimed at Royce only drove home how much this woman was in danger. One moment, Humphries had the gun pointed at Royce, and the next, Humphries turned it on Bonita.

"No, Fran—" *Pop!*

Royce didn't look to see if Humphries's aim was true and Bonita Brothers was dead. He needed cover and bolted for the woods—awkward at first but gaining speed as the adrenaline pumping through his veins helped to clear the *oh fuck* from his system.

Pop!

The ground exploded two feet in front of him on the right, so he cut to the left. Running in a straight line would've been faster, but it would also make it easier for Humphries to shoot him. Royce sharply zagged to the right again.

Pop!

Tree bark to his left exploded, burying splinters in his face. Royce kept his knees pumping, hauling ass as best he could with his arms bound awkwardly together. Once inside the woods, his foot snagged on a vine in the undergrowth. He stumbled and almost went down but somehow stayed upright.

Whomp. Whomp. Whomp. Whomp. Whomp.

At first, Royce thought the noise was his heart pounding, but then the sound got louder. A helicopter. It was flying pretty low too. Probably looking for marijuana crops. He needed to get out of the copse of trees and see if he could flag them down. As farfetched as it sounded, the pilots might be his only hope of surviving.

"You can't outrun this gun," Humphries called from behind him.

Oh, yeah? He'd already fired three times. Unless Humphries brought a second magazine, he would eventually run out of bullets.

"I'm going to kill everyone you love," Humphries yelled triumphantly.

"By talking them to death?" Royce shouted. "You can't shoot for shit." It was brash and stupid, but he would not die cowering from this man or begging for his life. "I cannot wait to expose you as a monster to the world. I win. You lose."

Royce's heart raced, and his lungs labored as he headed up an incline. He didn't know what was on the other side, but he didn't have time to talk himself out of going over the edge.

Pop!

Dirt and leaves exploded by his feet when he crested the top of the hill and leaped, flinging himself into midair. He'd never wanted to be a bird and he hated flying. Royce's stomach started to drop seconds before gravity yanked him by the ankles, pulling him down toward the earth again. The fall wasn't as bad as it could've been, and he landed on a plateau that jutted out from the side of the hill. Knowing Franco would be right behind him, Royce scrambled over the edge and began looking for cover, because he'd be too easy to pick off as he tried to climb out of the gulley on the other side.

Fallen trees of various length and girth lay scattered on the ground. Maybe they'd been cut down by loggers and left behind for some reason. Royce was grateful that several were big enough to provide shelter. It would be impossible for Franco to know which one he was hiding behind without investigating each log.

Royce had just ducked out of sight when he heard leaves rustling above him followed by loose rocks scattering down the incline.

"Come out, come out wherever you are, you pussy," Humphries said.

Hiding from this fucker rankled him, so he forced himself to view it as strategizing. Topping the list: don't be stupid and give away your hiding spot and find something to disarm him. Royce saw a thick stick that was at least two and a half feet long. With his hands bound in front of him, he could easily grip the stick with both hands. Adrenaline still surged through his body, making it hard to remain still while Franco started making his way down the hill.

"I think I'll start by killing Marcus's widow, but not until I have a lot of fun with her."

Royce closed his eyes and breathed as quietly as he could. Something small like a woodland creature scurried in the underbrush two logs over from the one he crouched behind.

Pop!

Still not dead, asshole.

"Then I'll laugh as I watch the life drain from your lover's pretty brown eyes. I never took you for queer. Just goes to show how little we really know about people."

Royce stayed completely still as Humphries's voice grew louder as he drew nearer. He heard sticks and branches snapping beneath the killer's feet because he wasn't bothering to hide his approach. Humphries was convinced he had the upper hand, and it was up to Royce to disavow him of the notion. Tightening his grip around the stick, Royce sent up a prayer that he would time his attack perfectly and catch Humphries off guard because the cards were stacked against him. *Challenge received and accepted, mother fucker.*

Snap.

The sound came from just on the other side of his hiding spot. Royce surged upward, swinging the stick in an arc. Franco had been looking beyond his hiding spot, so he was late turning the gun in Royce's direction, allowing Royce to bring the stick down over the arm holding the gun. Royce heard the bones in Humphries's wrist break seconds before the man started screaming in agony as the gun fell from his slack hand. Taking full advantage of the situation, Royce bull rushed the man, pitching them forward in a somersault down the slope of the gulley. His body found every sharp rock embedded in the ground, cutting his face, jabbing him in the knees and shoulders as he barreled faster and faster until he crash-landed into the stank runoff at the bottom. He heard more bones breaking and waited for pain to flood his body, but it didn't. The impact briefly knocked the wind out of him, and he lay there gasping for air like a fish out of water as he gathered his wits.

Whomp. Whomp. Whomp. Whomp. Whomp.

The helicopter was closer, sounding like it was just about on top of them. Something warm trickled down the left side of Royce's face, reducing his vision to only his right eye. He knew without looking it was blood because he could smell the tangy metallic scent. Royce's head throbbed from where a rock gouged a cut above his left eye. Beside him, Humphries moaned in severe pain and it didn't take Royce long to figure out why. The man had multiple compound fractures in his leg.

"Help me," he whispered.

Royce saw red and it had nothing to do with the blood running down his face. "Like you helped those women when they begged for their lives?" Even if they'd been drugged or gagged, Abby, Tara, Harper, and Christi would've been aware at some point that they were in grave danger. They might not have been able to verbalize their plea, but it would've been in their eyes, and this sick son of a bitch killed them without remorse.

Royce rolled to his knees and crawled the few feet that separated them. He was banged to hell, but with a broken wrist and broken leg, Franco wasn't in any condition to fight him off. Royce easily rolled Humphries over on his stomach, gripped his hair, and shoved his face into the water gathered in the gulch. It was shallower here than the area Bonita drove his precious car through, but it didn't take much water to drown a person.

It turned out that a man who didn't value the lives of others really prized his own. Humphries started thrashing. Royce realized he might not be as different from his father as he believed, because he brought his knee up and pressed it between the struggling man's shoulder blades, using his weight to hold Franco down. Victory surged through Royce as he realized he was seconds away from getting vengeance for the ladies.

Sawyer's face appeared in his mind followed by images of the future he so badly wanted with him. If he killed Franco Humphries, he'd ruin any chance of having that life. Even if Royce skirted formal charges, *he'd* know he was a cold-blooded killer and no different than the man he hated with a passion. He wouldn't be worthy of Sawyer's love, and there was nothing he wanted more.

The women and their mothers deserved justice and it wouldn't be served if Humphries died right now. Stripping away his polished veneer so the world could see the monster beneath is what he'd earned. A life in a small cell without all the luxuries he was accustomed to was where he belonged. Existing as someone's prison bitch instead of thriving on his students' and fellow professors' adoration was the fate he'd merited.

Royce roared, but lifted his knee off Humphries, then dragged him out of the water by his hair. Rolling Humphries over onto his back. Royce smiled down at the man who gasped and wheezed for air. "Fuck you, Humphries. I win."

The helicopter circled above again, urging Royce to get going. Humphries was in no condition to drag his ass back up the hill to fetch his gun, and even if he did, Royce would be long gone.

Sawyer's face reappeared in his mind, prodding him to climb the hill, even though there wasn't a place on his body unaffected by the tumble. Sawyer would kiss his bruises though. Luckily, the hill on the opposite side of the ravine wasn't as steep, so it was easier to scale. His knees gave out when he was within a few feet of the top.

Almost there. Keep moving.

Royce crawled the remaining few feet until he reached the top of the hill and pulled himself up and over to safety.

CHAPTER 25

CHIEF MENDOZA HAD STARTED THE RESCUE MISSION BY PHONING Commissioner Rigby, and between the two of them, they called in some favors owed to them. Mendoza's friendship with Bryan County Sheriff Abe Beecham went back to their police academy days. Beecham was more than ready to assist them. By the time they made the thirty-five-minute drive, Beecham had already had his Specialized Response Team assembled, which was the equivalent of SPD's SWAT division Mendoza had led before being promoted to chief.

Rigby wasn't about to be outdone by the boys and flexed her muscles, getting them eyes in the sky. Georgia Department of Natural Resources had an aviation unit in the area looking for illegal marijuana crops.

All of these arrangements were set in motion while they were on the road, so by the time their SUVs reached the rendezvous point at an old logging road off of Route 119, the guys in SRT had already unloaded their ATVs and had even brought two extras. The chopper had already started buzzing over the forest.

Mendoza and Beecham hugged quickly after Sawyer and the chief exited their SUV. They were opposites in nearly every way. Abe Beecham with his blond hair, green eyes, and golden skin was built like an Abrams tank, while Mendoza was whipcord lean with a swarthy complexion, dark eyes, and black hair.

"Thanks for your help, Abe," Mendoza said affectionately.

"Good to see you too, Lio. It's been too long," Beecham said. "Let's get your guy back, then we can catch up over a few beers." He gestured for them to follow him to the SRT's bearcat where they had an enlarged aerial map spread out.

The area was mostly forest, but there were a few clearings in the vegetation, and in one of them sat a small structure Sheriff Beecham or someone in the unit had circled. "This is the property where we think your suspect is holding Detective Locke hostage." *Hostage.* Then he showed them the best route up to the cabin. "DNR's helicopter gives us eyes above, and it also helps cover the noise from the ATVs approaching the cabin." Beecham went through the rescue mission and circled places on the map where he wanted officers on the perimeter providing cover and making sure the suspects didn't escape. They would ride the ATVs only so far before closing in on foot. "Mendoza and Key are with me, Baxter, Miller, and Moses," Beecham said.

Nearly every member of their major crimes unit made the trip, and they paired off with Bryan County Sheriff's deputies to move into position on the perimeter Beecham had designated on the map.

"We heard a few shots fired when we first pulled up but nothing since then," Beecham said. Sawyer's steps faltered and Mendoza fisted his tactical vest to steady him. Beecham continued, "As you saw from the map, it's a very rural area, so those gunshots could belong to someone out hunting or target practicing. Stay alert."

"Can I trust you to keep your head, Key?" Mendoza asked firmly.

"Yes, sir," Sawyer said, forcing his fear aside to focus on the mission.

Dressed in full tactical gear since the ATVs wouldn't exactly sneak up on anyone, Sawyer and Mendoza climbed onto their four-wheelers and followed the four men from SRT into the woods.

"This is DNR Officer Reynolds," said a husky voice over the

comms in Sawyer's helmet. "We're flying over the old homestead again. It looks like there's a downed person near the abandoned cabin." Fuck. Oh fuck. Were they too late? No way. "The infrared camera didn't detect heat signals inside the structure. We're passing over the surrounding property now. The dense trees hamper visibility, but our thermal equipment will still find them."

Sawyer leaned forward as they raced up the logging trail. Royce couldn't be dead. He refused to believe it.

"We've got two heat signals in the woods," Reynolds said excitedly. "The first one appears to be down in Adam's Gulch, which is on the west side of the property. The second signal is on the other side and isn't too far from a clearing."

"Can you hover around the area and be our eyes?" Beecham asked.

"Ten-four, Sheriff."

Beecham, who was driving the lead ATV, made a sharp cut to the right and accelerated hard, so everyone in the group did the same.

Hang in there, dickhead. We're coming.

They drove parallel to a valley, which must've been Adam's Gulch. The thumping from the helicopter rotors grew louder, and Sawyer knew they were almost there.

"Got eyes on one of the runners," Reynolds said. "Looks like he's covered in mud and banged up pretty bad. There's no way for us to know if he's friendly, so we'll have to treat him like a hostile until you approach." To the runner, Reynolds said, "Put your hands up and get down on your knees." After a brief pause, Reynolds repeated his order. If Humphries or Bonita was pursuing Royce with a gun, stopping and getting on his knees was a death sentence.

"Do not shoot unless fired upon," Beecham ordered the DNR officer.

Beecham cut right again, heading toward the sound of the hovering helicopter. When they burst out of the woods into the clearing, Sawyer spotted Royce running toward the aircraft.

"That's Detective Locke," Mendoza said into the comms. "Do not shoot."

Humphries wasn't in the clearing. Had the helicopter scared him off? As much as Sawyer wanted to check on Royce, he needed to make sure Humphries didn't evade capture and become the case that haunted Royce for the rest of his life.

"Where's his pursuer?" Sawyer asked.

"Appears to still be in the gulch," Reynolds said.

Then he guided Beecham, Mendoza, and Sawyer close to the signal. They parked their ATVs and crept toward the edge of the valley with their rifles trained in front of them. Peering over the side made them a target for the shooter, which none of them wanted.

"This is Sheriff Beecham," the stern man said. "We have you surrounded, and there is no escape. Put your weapon down and climb out of the gulch."

"I'm not armed," said a whiny voice. "I lost it when I fell down the hill. I broke my leg when I landed. Send help."

"Could be a trick," Sawyer whispered.

"This isn't my first rodeo, Detective," Beecham groused. "We go on three." He pulled a flash-bang grenade from his tactical vest and lobbed it over the hill. *Bam!* The explosion reverberated through the gulley. Humphries didn't return fire, so Beecham counted them down, and they charged over the hill and into the ravine.

Once the smoke cleared, Sawyer saw that Humphries had suffered two nasty compound fractures in his right leg and had lost a lot of blood. He had wisely kept his hands where they could see them, and there was no weapon near him. Mendoza started scouring the hillside looking for the lost weapon while Beecham patted the prone man down to look for more, and Sawyer tied a tourniquet around his leg to stop the bleeding. No one would blame Sawyer too much if he took joy in watching the man wince and cry out in pain. At least he didn't grab the bone fragments protruding from his leg and viciously twist them like he wanted to.

Sawyer raced up the hill as fast as he could, seeking out Royce and finding him surrounded by a cluster of deputies. One of them had cleaned Royce's face as best he could and applied butterfly bandages over a gash above Royce's left eye. He'd need stitches, but the temporary fix would do for now. Royce glanced up when he heard Sawyer approach.

"It's about fucking time," his boyfriend said, stumbling toward him.

Sawyer replied by hugging him. He was seconds away from crying or kissing Royce in front of everyone, so he distracted himself with humor. "You will do anything to get out of dinner at my parents' house."

"Asshole," Royce said, gripping him tighter.

The DNR aviation unit landed the chopper and used the equipment on board to haul Humphries out of the gorge. Mendoza had already stated he wasn't letting the serial killer out of his sight. He made a quick detour over to make sure Royce was okay and to thank the Bryan County team for their assistance.

"I'll have to take a rain check on the beer, Abe," he said over his shoulder on the way to the chopper. "I'll even throw in dinner."

"I'll take you up on that, Lio. Juicy steaks sound good to me."

"You're on. Name the date and time," Mendoza said. "I want a full report on my desk tomorrow, Locke."

"Yes, sir," Royce said. Then he brought Beecham up to speed, starting with Humphries shooting Bonita Brothers outside the cabin. As he spoke, Royce kept rubbing his bloody wrists. Sawyer regretted not kicking Humphries in the balls when he'd had the chance.

"We'll secure the scene and take it from here. Can you find your way back to the SUVs?" Beecham asked Sawyer.

"Yes, sir. Thank you so much." Sawyer turned to Royce. "You've lost quite a bit of blood. You good to drive Mendoza's ATV, or do you want to ride with me?"

"With you," Royce said.

"We'll get the extra ATV back," Beecham said. "You want me to radio for an ambulance to meet you?"

"Nah," Royce said. "Asshole can drive me. Thanks again, Sheriff."

Beecham nodded. "Any time. Take care, fellas."

Royce didn't say much when he followed Sawyer to the ATV. Royce climbed up behind Sawyer, slipping his arms around his waist to hold on. "So, hey. Is it just me, or did you pick up on some interesting vibes between Mendoza and Beecham?"

"Don't start," Sawyer said, shaking his head. He started the ATV, then said, "Hold on tight."

"Planned on it," Royce yelled over the engine.

Sawyer drove them carefully out of the woods. Mendoza had already radioed their team, and everyone was there to greet them when they drove out to the original rendezvous point at the logging road.

Royce exchanged hugs and assured everyone he was fine. He insisted they all go home, but Blue, Ky, and Holly went with them to the nearest hospital so Royce could get treatment.

"I don't suppose we can keep this a secret from Jace," Royce asked Holly.

"No fucking way," she replied.

"My gun and shoulder holster should be in the glove box of my car back at the cabin," Royce said.

"Beecham will make sure you get them back," Sawyer assured him. "Your car too."

"You won't believe what that crazy woman did to my best girl," Royce groused.

Sawyer reached over and linked their hands. "I'm more worried about what she did to my best guy."

"I'm fine." Then Royce told them about the envelope of evidence Vivian Gross had sent to his house. "I assume it's in the car, unless Bonita threw it out a window."

"Let's just get you taken care of right now," Blue said, patting Royce's shoulder.

The hospital got Royce back into a triage room relatively quickly and assessed his injuries. Since none of them were life threatening, the mood relaxed and the nurses allowed Blue, Ky, Holly, and now Jace to join Sawyer and Royce back in the tiny room. Sawyer loved them dearly, but he wanted five minutes alone with his guy. He sent his mom a quick message letting her know Royce was okay. She'd wanted to jump in the car and head straight over, but he talked her out of it.

"Hey," Royce said softly, scooting over farther, making more room for Sawyer. "You know what I could really use right now?" Everyone in the room snorted. "Not that, or at least not with all of you in here," he said, shaking his head. "Evangeline's cooking."

"I promise you my mom will fuss, fawn, and feed you," Sawyer said.

"I think it's time you guys consider looking for other jobs," Jace said abruptly.

"This is who we are, and this is what we do," Royce answered.

Jace looked like he had a lot more to say, but his nurse returned and started putting Humpty Dumpty back together again.

It was well past dinner by the time the staff cleaned and closed Royce's head wound, pulled the splinters out of his face, and treated the abrasions on his wrist and various cuts all over his body. Sawyer called his mom to let her know they were heading home.

"Be here tomorrow by four thirty for dinner. Do not try to hog him all to yourself, Sawyer."

"Cougar," Sawyer groused after she hung up on him.

As much as Sawyer wished he could have a lazy Sunday at home with Royce, he knew they'd spend most of it at the station writing reports and wrapping up the case as best they could for Babineaux.

Holly rode home with Jace, so after dropping Ky and Blue off at the precinct, they climbed in Sawyer's car and headed home.

"I had a chance to kill him." By Royce's scathing tone, Sawyer knew he was referring to Humphries.

"But you didn't," Sawyer countered.

Royce breathed deeply. "I wanted to."

Sawyer reached over and laced their fingers together. "But you didn't."

Chuckling, Royce whispered, "I almost did."

Sawyer squeezed his fingers. "But you didn't."

"I deserve a reward for my restraint," Royce said.

"Yes, you do."

Royce yawned big enough that his jaws popped. "My poor car."

"Insurance will repair the damage," Sawyer said.

"Yeah, but I think I'm going to sell the Camaro or trade her in."

"What? Why?" Sawyer asked. It was the first time Royce had ever mentioned wanting to get rid of the car.

"She's not a good fit for the next phase in my life," Royce said. "I'm going to need something...bigger."

Sawyer smiled. He was pretty sure he knew what Royce meant, but his boyfriend could barely hold his head up, so it wasn't the right time to have the discussion. A man could hope though, right?

Sensing Royce was injured, Bones was affectionate even though they were late getting home.

"Are you hungry?" Sawyer asked.

"I could eat," Royce said. "I don't feel nauseous or anything." By some miracle, he didn't have a concussion after suffering multiple blows to the head. "I want to shower first."

"Then I'll start dinner unless you need help in the shower."

"Need help? I can manage, but I always want your company."

"You go ahead and start the shower. I'll preheat the oven for pizza and meet you in there."

Sawyer smiled when Bones followed behind Royce like a little mother hen, which meant he'd plant his furry ass on the bathroom counter and observe them in the shower like the little perv he was. Sawyer turned on the oven and headed to the shower.

When he reached their bedroom, Royce was stretched across

their bed still wearing the scrubs they'd given him at the hospital. Bones was lying on his chest, giving Sawyer his *don't fuck with me* look.

Meow.

Sawyer threw up his hands in surrender. "You win this round, Bones."

CHAPTER 26

"**P**APERWORK, PAPERWORK, AND MORE FUCKING PAPERWORK," ROYCE grumbled as he hit enter to send the final report to Mendoza.

"I think that's the first chapter in the book titled *The Things They Don't Tell You at the Academy*," Sawyer quipped. He was kicked back in his chair with his boots propped on his desk. The asshole had finished his report an hour ago. He'd encouraged Sawyer to go home or find something fun to do while he finished up, but he'd chosen to stay. Royce understood why, and if the situation were reversed, he wouldn't want Sawyer out of his sight either.

Recalling what his brother had said when he'd shown up at the ER last night, Royce said, "Do you think Jace is right?"

"About what?" Sawyer asked. "He's said a lot of things in the short time I've known him."

"Maybe we should find a different line of work. I mean, we've been shot, set on fire, and abducted by a psychopath in the past few months. It does seem excessive, even to Hollywood action-movie standards."

"Please," Sawyer scoffed. "I saw all of those things during the first act in a cop movie once. We're doing just fine. For the record," he said, lowering his boots to the ground and straightening in his chair, "I've only been set on fire. The other two mishaps are all yours."

Sawyer studied his expression for a second. "Why? Are you giving it serious consideration?"

When he'd woken up disoriented in the middle of the night feeling like he was still running from a madman through the woods, Royce had briefly considered Jace's comments. "Maybe we should become private investigators and put Rocky Jacobs out of business. I insist we use the word dicks in our agency name."

Sawyer tipped his head to the side and pursed his lips as if he were really considering it. They both knew he wasn't, just as they knew the suggestion wasn't sincere. "Hmmm. There'd be many long stakeouts to catch cheating spouses."

"Hand jobs to help the time pass faster," Royce countered, waggling his brows. The bullpen was empty since it was Sunday, and Mendoza had shut his office door.

"Are you serious, Ro?"

"Your hand jobs make everything better," Royce replied. Then he laughed at Sawyer's scowl. "I don't want to be a PI. I can't see myself doing anything other than police work."

Mendoza poked his head out of his office. "Can I see you guys for a minute?"

Dread settled in Royce's gut. He had a feeling Mendoza figured out they were more than partners and was going to split them up. He could tell by Sawyer's wrinkled brow he was worried too. Neither man said anything on their way to the chief's office.

"Shut the door behind you, Locke," Mendoza said. "I'm not expecting anyone else to report to work today, but it pays to be cautious."

"Yes, sir," Royce said, shutting the door and taking a seat next to Sawyer.

"First things first," the chief said, reaching into his desk and extracting Royce's shoulder holster, gun, and badge. "Check to make sure the magazine is full. Missing bullets will need to be accounted for, either by you or someone with Bryan County Sheriff's Department."

Royce emptied the magazine on Mendoza's desk to show no one had tampered with his firearm. Then he reloaded the clip and shoved it back in his gun.

"Your car is still evidence. It should be ready for release in a few days."

Royce and Sawyer had seen pictures of the damage to the front spoiler, grill, and undercarriage. He hadn't been joking with Sawyer about getting a different set of wheels. Not only was his Camaro tainted, he did have plans that would require a larger vehicle. Royce recalled the tricked-out Tahoe they'd borrowed from the motor pool and thought a similar ride would make an excellent replacement for the future he wanted to have with Sawyer.

"No problem, Chief," he replied.

"I just got off the phone with Tiffany Humphries. To say she's relieved her husband is in police custody is a gross understatement. Mrs. Humphries told me she secured the original evidence from Humphries's safe-deposit box in her gym locker. She will be home Tuesday morning and will deliver the evidence to DA Babineaux directly."

"That's great news, Chief," Sawyer said.

Royce nodded.

"The stolen bedsheet from the Riker case was discovered in the trunk of Bonita Brothers's car along with Vivian Gross's brief-case, which included the Humphries file." The chief exhaled deeply. "While searching the abandoned cabin and surrounding property for additional evidence against Bonita, they uncovered a shallow grave."

"Oh, man," Royce said. "Reggie Dozer?"

"Yeah. Mr. Dozer's body was too badly decomposed to deter-mine the cause of death on site, but it doesn't matter unless we can prove Bonita Brothers acted on Humphries's behalf."

"If we can believe her, Bonita acted alone there," Royce said. He'd put their conversation in his ten-thousand-page report, but unless the chief was a speed reader, not enough time had passed for him to have reviewed the entire thing. "They did plan Vivian's and Tiffany's murders together though."

"I skimmed over your report before I called you in here," Mendoza said. "We'll go over it in more detail later, but I wanted to touch base on a few important things so you can get on with your afternoon." The chief studied them intently for a few minutes before he cleared his throat. "Look, I'm the last guy on earth who wants to broach personal relationships and issues that happen off the clock, but there are times when it's unavoidable. I'm going to pretend not to know the two of you are in a relationship as long as it doesn't interfere with the job."

"Yes, sir," they both said.

"That's settled, so moving on," Mendoza said. "Humphries's crime spree in multiple states makes working with the FBI inescapable."

"With your permission, sir, I'd like to make that call myself."

Mendoza looked suspicious but nodded. "Get out of here, fellas. See you on Wednesday."

"Yes, sir, Chief," they said, rising quickly and heading out before he could recant the days off.

"You're going to dangle the Humphries evidence over the FBI's heads until you find out what you want to know about Amber's undercover case, aren't you?" Sawyer asked.

"Hell, yeah," Royce said, dialing a number. Knowing what had brought Amber to Savannah was the final piece of the puzzle surrounding Marcus. After a minute or so, Royce left a voicemail message for Agent Duffy to call him about a case that could make his career. "The least douchey of the douchebags," he quipped, smiling at Sawyer after he disconnected the call.

"I know just what I want to do on our days off," Royce told Sawyer on their way out of the precinct a few minutes later.

Thumbing the fob to unlock his Audi, Sawyer said, "I have some ideas too."

"Get your mind out of the gutter, GB. I was referring to car shopping."

Sawyer laughed as he climbed behind the wheel. "I was thinking we should check out some real estate listings."

"What? Why?"

"I thought we could find a place that's just ours," Sawyer replied. "We haven't talked about making it official, but it's the next logical step."

"I've been giving our living situation some thought too," Royce admitted. He told Sawyer what he'd decided to do with Aunt Tipsy's house. "Home is wherever you are, so there's no need for us to drastically uproot our lives. Your house has always felt right to me."

"You sure you're not just saying that to make me feel better?" Sawyer asked.

"Have I ever said anything just to appease you?" Royce countered.

Sawyer laughed and shook his head. "No."

"Then I won't start now, asshole." Glancing at the clock, Royce said, "We better head to your parents' before life blows up in our faces again."

"Oh, yes," Sawyer said dryly. "We don't want to keep my mother waiting. I'm sure she's ready to fawn all over you."

Chuckling, Royce said, "I'm fawn-worthy."

"That and so much more." Sawyer's dark gaze promised more than his words ever could.

Royce's phone rang on the drive out to the Keys' house on Isle of Hope. He laughed when he saw who was calling. "That sure didn't take him long," Royce said to Sawyer before answering. "Agent Duffy, my best buddy, best pal."

"What can you possibly know that will make my career at the Bureau?" the man asked dryly.

Royce gave him the Cliff's Notes edition.

"Why do you sound so smug?" Duffy asked. "You can't avoid turning that evidence over for too long."

"Who says I want to hold on to it?" Royce asked. "I want to make sure it gets in the right hands. This is the kind of case that has documentaries made about it every few years. It's also the kind that paves the way for lucrative careers."

"And whose hands would that be?" Duffy asked.

Royce smiled at Sawyer. "Whoever will tell me why Amber Neilson was working undercover in Savannah."

Duffy heaved a frustrated sigh. "Who else knows about the evidence?"

"No one outside my department. You're the first fed I called. So, what do you say?"

"Ever heard of Ed Menske?" Duffy asked.

The name had come up when discussing clients who might want Vivian Gross dead, so Royce was familiar with the name. "Yeah, you guys wanted to send him to prison for racketeering, human trafficking, and money laundering but had to settle for a tax evasion conviction instead."

"We wouldn't have nailed him on that much if not for Neilson," Duffy said. "She'd worked the McGraw connection for two years and stuck with it for another year after we sent Menske to prison since her cover wasn't blown. She was preparing to leave her assignment for good when she was killed."

"Oh man," Royce said. "Did she find what she was looking for?"

Duffy didn't answer right away, and Royce figured he would roll out the tried and true need-to-know dialogue. Instead, Duffy sighed and said, "Yes. That's all I am going to say. You can read about it in the paper someday like everyone else."

"Fair enough. Expect an email from me soon, Duffy," Royce said. "You might want to get camera-ready by investing in a nicer suit, a new haircut, and whiter teeth." Royce disconnected the call. "I'd hoped to feel better once I knew why she was in town."

"Do you?" Sawyer asked, reaching for his hand.

"No. It's still just fucking sad." Maybe there is an afterlife and she's with Marcus again.

Royce didn't have much time to dwell on it because they arrived at the Keys' house. Evangeline fawned and fussed over him just as Sawyer predicted, but she was joined by Bree and Grace, while Baron, Killian, and Nick took good-natured jabs at him. Sawyer gave him a tour of the stunning home, and Royce nearly told Sawyer he'd changed his mind and wanted a place just like his parents. Royce loved the wall of photographs and seeing Sawyer grow up before his very eyes from an adorable baby to an awkward teen, to the beautiful man he loved. He paused at the image of Vic and Sawyer sitting on the dock and listened as Sawyer shared the significance of the spot. He felt a pang in his heart but not from jealousy or even heartache. It was gratitude because Vic had adored Sawyer so wholly and selflessly that Sawyer was willing to love again.

The kids warmed up to him just as Royce expected, and he placed a wager with Sawyer that he'd become the favorite uncle within six months. Evangeline prepared all the same dishes she'd made when he was recovering from the gunshot wound. Royce ate until there wasn't even room for the beer he and Sawyer carried out to the boat dock an hour before sunset.

They sat in Sawyer's favorite spot on the dock, and Royce understood why he loved it so much. Just as the sun kissed the earth, Sawyer looked up at the sky, and said, "You were right, Vic."

CHAPTER 27

"**T**HIS IS NOT HOW I WANTED TO SPEND MY DAY OFF," ROYCE WHINED. Sawyer ignored him and kept pushing the grocery cart. "Stop whining, and I'll buy you a can of the horrible squirty cheese."

"Fine," Royse groused. "What time are the murder club members coming over?"

The lady walking toward them stiffened, then whipped her cart around and headed in the opposite direction.

Sawyer chuckled. "Look what you did. That woman thinks we want to commit murders instead of solving them."

"Spending my day off at the grocery store when I could be in bed with you makes me homicidal," Royce countered.

"Didn't I spend the morning with you at three different car lots looking for the perfect SUV?" Sawyer asked. He hadn't minded it, especially when Royce found the one he wanted because the back was plenty big enough for camping, fishing, and sporting equipment. *Just how many kids was he planning to adopt?*

"Yes," Royce admitted. "Are you going to pretend like you can't wait to hear your audiobooks on the kickass stereo system?"

"No," Sawyer said.

"So, let's grab some frozen pizzas, wings, and chips and get home so we can spend the rest of the day naked."

"Could you say that any louder?" Sawyer asked, looking around.

"Yeah, I could say it a lot louder," Royce replied. "I could include hand gestures to avoid confusion."

"This is our last Operation Venus Flytrap meeting, and we have special guests coming tonight. I will not feed them crappy frozen pizza and junk food," Sawyer said, changing the subject before Royce backed up his threats with action.

Royce's grumpy expression softened. "Emma, Dinah, Jennifer, and Sarah are looking forward to meeting everyone who helped get justice for their girls."

"So quit your bitching and let me do this right. Go look at magazines or something while I finish shopping."

Royce narrowed his eyes suspiciously. "Are you going to put my junk food back?"

"No."

"Are you going to pay for the groceries and leave without me?"

"Possibly," Sawyer said dryly.

"I'll find you if you do, GB." Royce winked before heading to the book and magazine aisle, which enabled Sawyer to choose the rest of the ingredients for his menu in half the time it would've taken with Royce. Now he understood why his mother had always made him and his siblings stay at home with their dad when she went grocery shopping.

When Sawyer reached the magazine and book aisle, he was surprised to see Royce deep in conversation with Lynette Goodwin. Royce was holding a book in his hands, and she was thumbing through the pages, stopping to point out some things. Royce wasn't the former mayor's biggest fan. Her black shirt with pink polka dots showed off a small baby bump. She glanced up when Sawyer approached. Her gaze was wary at first but relaxed when she realized who it was.

"There were some Nosy Nedras giving Mayor Goodwin a hard time when I came down the aisle," he said, which explained a lot. Royce hated hypocrites more than anything, and the probability that the women casting stones at the mayor were without sin was very low.

"Just call me Lynette." The woman smiled shyly. "Thank you again for your assistance. I should be used to it by now, I guess."

"No," Royce said emphatically. "No one should ever get used to that kind of taunting. You made a mistake, you apologized, and now you're trying to live your life. I think you should have the chance."

Wow. Those women must've been exceptionally cruel. Or Royce believed she was sorry for the hurt she caused her family and decided she'd had enough criticism and didn't need his too. It was how Sawyer felt about Jack Vincenzo, who had decided to suspend his re-election bid after Vivian's funeral.

Lynette sniffled, and her lips trembled. Sawyer sensed the tears were coming next. Instead, the mayor straightened her shoulders and lifted her chin. "Thanks again. Take care now."

"You too," Sawyer said, watching her walk away.

"She and Ryan are having a rough time," Royce said, recapturing Sawyer's attention. Royce tossed a hardback book on gardening in the cart and started walking down the aisle. "Her girls are pissed, Ryan's family has all but turned their backs on him, and Skip filed for divorce and moved in with his boyfriend in New York."

"And here I thought I finished shopping fast," Sawyer remarked.

"You did," Royce said. "After I ran off the Nosy Nedras for cornering a pregnant woman and making her cry, the information kind of burst out of her." Royce shrugged. "Oh, they're having a boy. I remembered Ryan was so convinced they were having a girl. She said he'd painted the nursery ten different shades of blue already. Then she noticed the book I was looking through and asked if I'd decided to take up gardening."

Sawyer stopped and stared at his boyfriend. Was the real Royce Locke snatched up by aliens while Sawyer was picking out the best loaves of French bread?

"I explained how I wanted to move some of Aunt Tipsy's flowers to our house. She told me it was called transplanting and said fall was usually a good time to do it. She recommended I do some research first before I attempt it or call an arborist." Royce stopped too and faced him. "Layers, asshole. Remember?"

"That wasn't what I was thinking, dickhead." It was precisely what Sawyer had been thinking.

Royce stared at him over the length of the grocery cart, and it reminded Sawyer of the time they squared off on the first day they'd met. "Then what were you thinking?"

"Are you going to tell me what Aunty Tipsy's real name is?"

Royce threw his head back and laughed. "That information is on a need-to-know basis."

They both knew Sawyer could easily find the information in the county records by looking at the property transfer or even ask Jace or Holly. Where was the fun in that?

"I have my methods of getting perps to confess."

Royce smiled wickedly. "Challenge received and accepted, baby."

Sawyer wanted to shove him up against the bookshelves and ravage his smug mouth. *Breathe in. Hold. Release.* His yoga breathing only encouraged Royce to taunt him more, but he pushed the cart around him and headed to the checkout.

Once they paid for the groceries and wheeled the cart outside, Royce leaned into him.

"If we hurry, there's still time to fool around before dinner prep. We can swing by and pick up my white hat and buy a pair of aviator glasses from the drugstore," Royce said, then started walking faster. He didn't look over his shoulder to see if Sawyer sped up too, because it was a given.

"Don't forget that star-spangled Speedo."

As they neared Sawyer's car, he passed two elderly gentlemen chatting in the parking lot.

"Can you believe how hot and humid it is for October?" one asked.

"Makes a person want to commit murder," his friend replied.

Heat, Humidity, and Homicide would no longer be the title of Sawyer's autobiography. Not because those things didn't exist or had ceased to matter to him. Thanks to Royce, those things were part of his life, but they didn't *define* who he was. These days, he was all about happily ever after. Sawyer had a new working title for his life's story.

The Grand Adventures of Dickhead and Asshole.

The End!

Please turn the page to learn more about my plans for Royce, Sawyer, and the gang.

Want to be the first to know about my book releases and have access to extra content? You can sign up for my newsletter here: http://eepurl.com/dlhPYj

My favorite place to hang out and chat with my readers is my Facebook group. Would you like to be a member of Aimee's Dye Hards? We'd love to have you! Click here: www.facebook.com/groups/AimeesDyeHards/

Dear readers,

Thank you, thank you, thank you for taking this journey with me. These guys mean more to me than I can ever put into words. Now, I will answer my most frequently asked question.

What's next for Royce and Sawyer?

Lots! The Zero Hour story arc is complete for them, but we haven't heard the last of the guys.

First, we're going to let them bask in their love for a little bit. They've earned some privacy. Later, they will be back to solve mysteries that take place during BIG moments in their lives. I don't know when or how many books or novellas will go into the next story arc. I will let you know more once the guys have shared it with me. I expect them to drop by my blog and newsletter service to say hello occasionally too. They will appear in the spinoff series I've already started to write.

What's this spinoff series about, you ask? Well, when I wrote Zero Hour, many characters chatted with me about writing their stories, but three were the most vocal, so I've decided to start with a trilogy for them.

Jonah, Felix, and Rocky will start a new venture using their skills as a GBI agent, an investigative reporter, and a private investigator to right some wrongs. I quickly learned, that as great as their chemistry is, they're not meant for each other romantically. Book one in the new series belongs to Jonah, book two belongs to Felix, and Rocky will end the series with a big bang, I'm sure. These are storylines I've wanted to write for a few years now but didn't have the right characters to star in the roles. Everything in my universe has aligned to make this possible, and I cannot wait to share these men and their love stories with you. I anticipate the first book will release in May.

From the bottom of my heart, I want to thank you for supporting my dreams and taking these wild rides with me. I am eternally grateful.

xoxoxo
Aimee

OTHER BOOKS BY
AIMEE NICOLE WALKER

Only You

The Fated Hearts Series
Chasing Mr. Wright, Book 1
Rhythm of Us, Book 2
Surrender Your Heart, Book 3
Perfect Fit, Book 4
Return to Me, Book 5
Always You, Book 6
Any Means Necessary, Book 7

Curl Up and Dye Mysteries
Dyeing to be Loved
Something to Dye For
Dyed and Gone to Heaven
I Do, or Dye Trying
A Dye Hard Holiday
Ride or Dye

Road to Blissville Series
Unscripted Love
Someone to Call My Own
Nobody's Prince Charming
This Time Around
Smoke in the Mirror
Inside Out
Prescription for Love

ACKNOWLEDGMENTS

First, I need to thank my husband and children for their constant support and encouragement. It's not easy living with a writer who often disappears into a fictional world for long periods of time. They do so many things to help me out so that I can realize my dream. I love you guys more than words can ever express.

To my creative dream team, thanks seem hardly enough for all that you do. Miranda Turner of V8 Editing and Proofreading, thank you for your tireless work, feedback, and many laughs while editing. Jay Aheer of Simply Defined art is an incredible artist, and I love how she brings my words to life. Stacey Blake of Champagne Formats is also an amazing artist who does incredible interior formatting, illustrating, and designing for e-books and paperbacks. It truly takes a village to whip me into shape. Judy Zweifel of Judy's' Proofreading, Jill Wexler, and Michael Beckett did a great job of proofreading and polishing so my manuscripts shine.

To my lovely PA, Michelle Slagan. I'm not sure how I ever did this without you. I love you to the moon and back!

I want to thank the Brittany for being a wonderful critique partner and Racheal and Melinda for being amazing alpha readers. And to my betas, Kim, Dana, Jodie, Michael, and Laurel, I appreciate your honest feedback. I love working with you all.

ABOUT AIMEE NICOLE WALKER

Ever since she was a little girl, Aimee Nicole Walker entertained herself with stories that popped into her head. Now she gets paid to tell those stories to other people. She wears many titles—wife, mom, and animal lover are just a few of them. Her absolute favorite title is champion of the happily ever after. Love inspires everything she does, music keeps her sane, and coffee is the magic elixir that fuels her day.

I'd love to hear from you.
Want to connect with me? All my links are in one nifty location.
Click here:
https://linktr.ee/AimeeNicoleWalker

CPSIA information can be obtained
at www.ICGtesting.com
Printed in the USA
JSHW040143050420
4997JS00003B/1187